Book One of The King of Ireland series

WARRIOR

SPIRIT

the romance of Irish love …. the miracle of redemption

JEAN CARROLL

Grá Amháin Publishing

COPYRIGHT

ACKNOWLEDGEMENTS

Editor – Anita Reedy

Cover and logo design and photography – Michael Rubright

Typing and critique – Elizabeth Benkovic

Typing – Diane Lewis

Critique – Harford Writers Group, Vivian Dumas, Sharon Saracino, Brenda Thomas, Magda Alexander and the MRWMem Self-pub Group, Ken Rubright, Michael Rubright, Shelly Chamness and Katie McGuire.

DEDICATION

I dedicate this book to Kenny, Michael, and Elizabeth
without whose love and encouragement,
this book would not have been finished.

For Katie, my best friend, who passed away this year and
who loved unconditionally.
I will always miss you.
"Love ya, kid!"

Forgiveness says you are given another chance
to make a new beginning.
Desmond Tutu

No matter how far wrong you've gone
you can always turn around.
Unknown

PROLOGUE

Today is spring-like for March at Cheltenham racecourse in England. It's Gold Cup Day, the culmination of Festival Week at the track. Blackie stands outside the Jockey's Room, tight-lipped and rolling his eyes, listening to Keary, his brother-in-law and his cousin, Sean, lecture him on his responsibilities.

Blackie likes to ride the race in his head while changing into silks and they're screwing with his pre-race ritual. They're pushing it. Blackie's seesawing on the edge of belligerence, held back by the knowledge that his sister, Jill is in the stands, keen to see him race.

Red faced, Keary says, "After you ride this race, you need to get your arse home and take some interest in your future."

"My future's waiting for me at the finish line today."

"Maybe someday you might accept who you are," Keary yelled, throwing his arms up in frustration.

"I know exactly who I am. I'm the guy sleeping off a drunk in bed with a hooker."

"Don't say things like that, man. That's ridiculous! You're better than that." Sean piped up.

"Oh, right, Sean. You were on the road with me. How many times did you find me hung-over or coming down from a high, laid up with some bimbo?"

"Okay, but I've found you at the roulette wheel in Monte Carlo with a gorgeous woman on your arm, as well." Sean retorted.

"It amounts to the same thing no matter what my bloodlines are. That's who I am, Keary. I know it and you need to believe it. I am *not* king material. You know how much I despise the idea."

"But you have the blood of a thousand Irish warriors and kings in your veins," Keary exclaimed.

"They must have been a damn sorry lot then." Blackie sighed, tired of this same old argument.

"I don't care what you say; you have it in you to be a great leader." Keary said.

"Bullshit! You're deluding yourselves, all of you. So lay off. I've got to get ready." Blackie entered the building, slamming the door behind him.

"I'm sick of his crap about this," Keary huffed. "Come on, Sean. Let's find Jill and watch the race."

*　　*　　*

Mickey Reegan, Blackie's unscrupulous ex-agent was also at the track. Blackie fired him several months ago after finding out Mickey used him to make some more dirty money. Mickey was good at that.

The grandstand was packed. Mickey could smell the greed of the crowd; their all-consuming hope was almost palpable. He knew from experience how excited they were but he was grim and nervous. There was no room in his heart for joy today, only revenge. He clutched his tote ticket with a sweaty hand. He had placed a huge wager but not on the favorite.

All his pals were giving him the 'bum's rush' since Blackie sacked him because they all held Blackie in such high esteem.

Okay, so he has connections in high places, sure. All the stupid blokes think he's their prince. What bullshit!

Mickey chuckled over his neat little scheme to fleece those well-heeled broads.

The kid was a popular guest on those weekends in the Hamptons. He got his jollies, didn't he, the bastard. I made a nice spot of cash for meself just making sure he showed up. So what? His royal bloodlines didn't keep his ass out of the gutter with the rest of the snobs.

The start of the three-mile, two and a half furlong, Gold Cup steeplechase was imminent. The horses and riders lined up, ready to go. Mickey pushed through the crowd at the rail, knocking a little kid to the ground, so he could have a good view of the finish.

Stupid brats!

"They're off!" yelled the announcer. A deafening roar went up from the grandstand. The horses thundered past the crowd and onto the course. They were a blur of motion as they raced, bunched in a cluster at first. They braced themselves to jump the first hurdle and they were over. Mickey always loved racing. The beauty of the race transfixed him; the jockeys' silks, a kaleidoscope of colors, the horses, every muscle straining to be in front, their flanks shining with sweat, their nostrils flaring to suck in as much air as possible.

The sound of it excited him; the pounding of the horses hooves on the turf, like freight trains hurtling to their stations, the horses' labored breathing and the jockeys screaming curses at each other and their mounts.

The race was a test, both beautiful and violent; a test of the riders' bravery and the spirit of these beautiful creatures, who were born to run, to win until their hearts burst.

Mickey hated watching now, now that he was out of a job, now that one of the worlds' most successful jockeys had sacked him, now that he was hoping to exact retribution.

Halfway through the race, as Mickey watched through binoculars, a lone horse pulled in front. Its jockey rode with the abandon of a madman. At each hurdle, his horse rose gallantly, as though lifted higher by the sheer will of the rider. The horse pulled ahead by a larger gap, leaving the rest trailing behind. The horse and rider sailed, victorious, over the last fence as Mickey held his breath, waiting.

Then, in a split second, tragedy struck! The horse fell and spilled the young rider in the path of the oncoming horde.

* * *

The next morning, Mickey ripped open the paper eagerly as he hunched over coffee in his hotel room and found what he was looking for. The headline read:

Champion International Jockey, Blackie O'Brien, in Near Fatal Accident at Cheltenham.

Mickey smiled then. A smug, cold smile.

·ONE·

Two years later near Middleburg, Virginia, USA

As Meg Conners got closer to her destination, she saw more and more horse farms. She was hauling her two beloved horses, in a rented van, to their new home on a farm outside of Middleburg, Virginia.

With a letter of recommendation from her former trainer and stable manager, she finally got two stalls at the world famous steeplechase stable, Killarney Farms.

As she drove, she daydreamed of taking her riding to a higher level, if not professional, maybe Olympic.

God, it would be so awesome if I could get there. It's going to be hard work but with the right help, I can do it.

She smiled at the thought of actually achieving her goal.

Meg spotted the large, wooden sign for Killarney Farms and slowed down to turn into the long driveway. She stopped the van and sat for a few minutes to calm her queasy stomach where the waffles she had for breakfast felt like a lead weight. Her palms were sweaty just thinking about meeting people whose abilities far out-shown her limited expertise.

Looking at the farm took her breath away. It stretched out for miles on either side of the driveway. It was spectacular. Well maintained with horses grazing in small paddocks. The sight of the many barns, track and numerous cottages on the property piqued her curiosity. The main house sat on a slight hill surrounded by ancient oaks. The stone house was huge. Every inch of the neatly manicured farm reeked of money.

Meg drove farther down the drive and stopped near the first barn she came to and cut the engine. She opened the front door of the van so the horses could get more air and take in their new surroundings. There wasn't anyone around so she entered the barn and walked down the long, spotless center aisle breathing in the clean, fragrant smell of fresh hay and the scent of horses. She'd never been in such a beautiful stable. The stalls were large and solid, open windows streamed in warm sunlight. Several curious, well-groomed heads stared at her over the doors.

A group of men stood around the door at the far end, intently watching a horse and rider work on the track. No one noticed her, so she cleared her throat. All of them turned around and stared at her. Sweat trickled down between her breasts.

"Excuse me, I'm Meg Conners and I talked to Sean O'Brien about bringing my horses in today. Could one of you come and help me unload them and get their stalls ready?" Meg asked, bravely.

One of the men said "Sure, Miss."

She let out the breath she held and walked back out to the van.

*   *   *

Blackie was stunned when he saw her. Tiny and slim, she was delicately gorgeous with a sweet face. Mesmerized by the seductive sway of her hips as she turned and walked away, a bolt of desire shot through his loins like electricity.

A man could get lost in those big green eyes. I'd like to run my fingers through that long, shiny brown hair. I bet it feels like silk and…whoa, where the hell did that come from?

Blackie knew only too well where it came from. He heaved a big sigh.

His young protégé, Casey, made a move to follow her.

I'll be damned, Blackie thought, and grabbed Casey's collar with an iron grip that stopped the kid in his tracks. Blackie loosened his hold when he realized Casey was choking.

"I've got this," he growled as he strode after her.

"Bollocks! What the divil's got him?" Casey exclaimed as the other men smiled.

*   *   *

Meg stood by the trailer unlocking the tailgate when she was aware of a man walking toward her. The first thing she noticed was the way he moved, smooth like a cat, confident as a young lion. He wore scuffed boots, tight jeans, so faded they were almost white, revealing long, muscular legs and a baggy, old Cornell sweatshirt. His overall silhouette was trim. Broad shoulders and boyishly slim hips.

She tore her eyes away from the jeans, moved up to his face and couldn't stop staring. He had to be the most incredible-looking man she'd ever seen. He was gorgeous with a rugged, slightly dangerous appearance from the stubble shadowing his jaw. He had coal black hair in need of a cut; he was tan, from being outdoors a lot and definitely looked about her age.

He was dark which made his eyes even more startling. They were the most unusual, intense shade of sky blue. His gaze focused on her eyes, flickering only once to the van. She felt uneasy and a bit threatened until he got closer and smiled. Her mouth dropped open.

The killer smile and amazingly white teeth made him look even better, if that were possible. Meg had to mentally pinch herself so she'd close her mouth and stop staring like an idiot. She wondered, fleetingly, if she had drool on her chin. He was beautiful.

"Well good day to you then, miss, I'm Blackie," he said in a soft baritone with an Irish lilt to his voice.

"I'll be glad to help you with your horses. Can they stay in the van for a few minutes while I bed down their boxes?"

"Hello," she stammered, "that will be fine."

"Okay, then, I'll be right back." He turned and as he jogged back into the barn, she noticed he looked just as good going away. There was something odd about his gait though, a limp maybe?

In about fifteen minutes he came back, unloaded the horses and put them in their respective stalls. She noticed that he talked quietly to the horses as he led them, her mare, nuzzling his arm gently. He showed her where to put her equipment in the tack room.

"Tell me about your horses. Are you after fox hunting, then?" He stood near her with his hands stuffed in the pockets of his jeans.

"The mare, Cloudy Day, is my baby, I've had her for five years and she's a great hunter and pleasure horse. She's very sweet tempered and gentle. She's a Cobb, Thoroughbred mix. The gelding is new to me, I've only had him six months and he's temperamental. He's a Swedish warm-blood and I hoped to try eventing with him but I think he's a little too much horse for me. I'm not very experienced at it, so I'm thinking I might just try dressage with him. His name is Sandman."

Blackie just listened while he looked at the horses over the stall doors.

"They're both beautiful horses, but I'd have to see them in action and maybe try the gelding myself before I could give you any advice. The mare needs some conditioning. Then you might be able to do more with her."

Meg wondered about his ability to advise her.

Do the grooms here ride the boarders' horses? I guess they usually ride the racehorses. He might be helpful.

He talked to her with his hands still stuffed in his pockets. She loved his accent and was having trouble concentrating on what he was saying, though because he was so good looking.

"Listen, I have some other work to do, so will you be back tomorrow?"

"Yes, I planned on it. I wanted to check out the facilities and work them in a ring or wherever, if that's okay?"

"All the facilities are at your disposal."

"Thanks, Blackie."

"Sure and you're welcome. I'll meet you here in the morning, give you a tour and then we'll take a look at your horses."

He flashed another lethal smile and walked away.

Blackie walked away from Meg as quickly as he could without seeming rude. He felt a nervous knot in his gut.

Man, she's hot! What the hell! Why am I nervous? I've been with a ton of beautiful women before. She loves horse so she's going to be around here for a while and seems like a nice girl. It would be a big mistake for an asshole like me to hook up with her. Bet I could get her in the sack in a couple days and... NO! Wait, I don't want that sort of relationship anymore. I could use a good shagging though but that would be the end of it. Mmm, that tight little butt of hers...oh, God help me, I'm in big trouble here.

Meg couldn't take her eyes off him.

Get a grip! Don't get this excited over a stable hand you just met. Good Lord, what am I thinking? I want to focus on training the horses and my riding without any distractions, especially from a man.

Meg had sworn off men since her relationship with Jim Mechlan in college had gone sour. She'd had a crush on him and thought he loved her until the romance ended with her first and only, disastrous sexual experience in the backseat of his car.

She got in the van and backed it up in the driveway to leave, almost hitting a new, silver Porsche®.

Yikes! That was close. She wondered who owned it.

*   *   *

The next morning Meg got to the stable about seven-thirty and parked her trusty old Honda next to the Porsche. She got her grooming gear from the tack room and walked to her stalls. She looked in, was surprised to find both horses were in immaculate stalls and beautifully groomed, even their manes and tails were trimmed and shaped perfectly for braiding. She assumed Blackie had done the grooming but didn't expect him to do all that. It seemed a little extreme even considering the high fees.

Is this guy being pushy? I'm not getting involved no matter how hot he is.

"Come on, Cloudy girl; let's see what this place has to offer." She tacked the mare up and led her outside. She walked her over to the ring, entered and mounted up. The ring was a dream. It was so much more professional than at any other stable where she'd boarded. It was huge, beautifully leveled and maintained with lots of expensively made, creative jumps. Meg smiled at the happy little tingle in her belly.

Two

Every day when Meg got to the stable, the stalls were cleaned and Blackie was grooming her horses.

"You don't have to do all this. I can do it," she told him. Not that she minded seeing him every day. His beautiful face and those big, blue eyes mesmerized her

He's soooo hot! If testosterone had a name, it would be 'Blackie'!

"Sure, and it's my job. It's a service for the boarders here. I don't have any other horses to take care of right now, so this is fun for me."

"Well, okay, I certainly appreciate it."

"You're welcome, then. Whatever I can do for you, just let me know," he said while he brushed Sandman.

"Could I see the rest of the farm sometime?"

"Sure. Were you after riding this morning?"

"Yes, I wanted to."

"Okay. After that I'll give you the tour."

"That would be great. Tell me about all the people who work here."

Meg loved sitting there and watching him as he moved around working on the horses. He had to have the sexiest butt she'd ever seen on a man and the muscles in those long legs bulged when he moved. Every time he raised his arms to brush Sandman's back, his tee shirt rode up so she got a peek at a hard, flat belly and amazing abs. His strong hands that caressed the horses every time he touched them fascinated her. She wondered how it would feel to have his hands caressing her.

Good Lord! Think about something else, you idiot.

He knew his way around a horse that's for sure, doing an expert job of grooming and doing it efficiently. He didn't take any grief from her antsy gelding that tried to get away with bad behavior. Sandy tried to nip him and Blackie said, "Stad," to him in a low, gruff voice that she didn't catch. The horse snorted and showed the whites of his eyes but seemed to think better of misbehaving. Here was somebody Sandy couldn't bully.

"What did you say to him and what language was that?"

"I told him to stop. That was Irish or Gaelic as it's also called." He pronounced it *guy-lick.*

"That's cool. Is that your first language?"

"Well, no, English is, but I grew up speaking both languages at home, so I sort of mix the two."

"Where's home?"

"I'm from Ireland, near Killarney. My parents still live there."

"How come you came over here?"

"The story's pretty much the same for everyone else here." He said, deftly steering the conversation away from himself. "Keary Connelly's the manager and Jilleen, his wife, does the books and takes care of all of us. Sean O'Brien trains the racing string, Casey O'Hara's the jockey, Ned Moran is assistant trainer and the rest of us pick up the slack." He turned around and caught her checking him out.

"This beast is done. Do you want me to tack him up, then?"

"No, I think I'll ride Cloudy first," she said, red-faced that he'd caught her looking.

"Sure," he said with a slight smile and put Sandman back in his stall. He led Cloudy out and was saddling her when a young man came running in and said something to Blackie in Gaelic and Blackie answered him in the same language.

"What's going on?" Meg asked.

"That was Casey. He needs me to help load horses going to the track. I'll be back soon."

He handed her Cloudy's reins and took off at a trot. She noticed that limp was more pronounced today.

As Meg led Cloudy outside and swung into the saddle, she noticed two huge semis parked at another barn and a lot of activity going on. Blackie, Casey and a bunch of other men were loading horses, tack and equipment.

She concentrated on working Cloudy, warmed her up, worked the mare through gaits and basic exercises then started her over some fences. After about an hour, she slowed down the workout so the horse could cool off. Walking Cloudy around on a loose rein, she saw Blackie was leaning on the fence watching. She waved. He smiled and waved back. He met her at the gate, followed her into the stable and rubbed Cloudy down while she put her tack away and got Sandman's stuff. While she tacked up the gelding, he finished with Cloudy.

"Why don't you take him into the indoor hall so he won't get distracted and he'll be easier to handle? I'll be there in a minute."

Meg led Sandman over to another barn, which contained an impressive indoor riding hall. It was a huge rectangle with lettered signs at intervals around the walls and neatly raked crushed stone underfoot. It was dim until Blackie entered, flipped a bunch of switches, turning on lights that lit up the hall. She mounted and started the gelding through several gaits to warm him up and then worked him through basic moves. He was hard to handle and she wasn't able to control him the way she wanted.

She cooled the horse down and walked over to where Blackie was standing. He smiled and her heart did a flip-flop. That smile really got to her.

"You're doing well with him, but I think he needs a stronger hand. I don't mean you can't ride him, I just mean he'll be fine if he learns to behave. Sometime I'll try him and see what I can do. That's if you don't mind me riding him?"

"Sure, I can use all the help I can get."

Hmm, I wonder how good he is?

She rode Sandman back to his barn and Blackie walked beside them.

"You're not saying much today." Meg said.

"I'm just thinking about things I need to do. Hey, let's put him away and get lunch up at the house, then I'll give you the grand tour."

"Actually, I can't today, I forgot, I have errands to run before I go to work."

"Shit. I want the others to get to know her. Maybe tomorrow.

"Okay, I'll see you tomorrow, then." He smiled but didn't look happy. He walked out of the barn and Meg finished up, got in her car and drove off. I wish I could stay, she thought as she turned out of the driveway, but I have too much to do.

That's stupid. I can't get too close to him. Having lunch with him. I need to keep things professional with this guy.

THREE

After a few weeks, Meg and Blackie settled into a routine. He'd clean the stalls and have both horses cross-tied in the aisle when she got there. He'd work on Sandman and Meg would groom Cloudy. She got a calm, relaxed feeling working so close with him, enjoying the smell of the horses, the feel of their sleek coats, and the physical effort doing work they loved.

It's cool being with a man who enjoys doing grunt work. I guess he wouldn't be a groom if he didn't.

She loved being near Blackie. He not only looked great, he smelled wonderful. Like soap, Old Spice and something else, very masculine, maybe leather. He didn't let her get too near him though. If she did, he stepped back and somewhat nervously stood there staring at her.

Oh boy, the owners must not like the help getting too friendly with the clients. On the other hand, maybe he's just shy. But that's good. I won't have to worry about him making a move on me.

Occasionally, Meg would bump into him on purpose, just to see what he'd do. He still moved away and gave her a look. Blackie, not exactly shy, was getting annoyed.

Crap, is she clumsy or just a tease? If she bumps into me one more time, I'm going to jump her right here in the aisle.

*   *   *

He started telling her Irish jokes while they worked. They were funny and mostly stupid. He delivered them in this thick Irish accent, so sometimes she could barely understand him.

Q: Why can't you borrow money from a leprechaun?

A: Cos they're always a little short.

He said the punch line then grinned, if she laughed, then he laughed. He had a great laugh. It bubbled up from deep inside him and lit up his face even more than when he smiled. That smile. His smile was charming, sly and knowingly sexual but his laugh was pure, unadulterated, childish glee.

*   *   *

The next day she got there a little later than usual and Blackie had already finished the stalls and grooming. As she tacked up Cloudy, she heard a lot of shouting from the racing barn. She ran outside, looked in the direction of the noise and saw Blackie up on a horse, a tall, handsome, red-haired man in jeans holding the bridle and they were arguing.

Suddenly he yanked Blackie off the horse. Blackie pulled away and swung a punch at him but was off balance and the blow didn't connect. The redhead let go of the horse and punched Blackie. Blackie responded with a solid hit that knocked the redhead to the ground. As Meg got closer, she realized they were shouting at each other in Gaelic. Two of the other men grabbed Blackie as the red-haired guy slowly got up. Casey stood there wide-eyed.

"What happened?" She asked, shocked and just as frightened as Casey looked. He glanced at her and hesitated, "Blackie's not supposed to be riding and Sean tried talking him off, but he wouldn't listen."

Meg raised her eyebrows.

Oh, so that's Sean O'Brien. He's almost as cute as Blackie who has more nerve than brains because he's going to be in crap up to his neck for punching his boss!

Blackie got loose, punched both of the guys who were holding him and they dropped like stones. Then he went after Sean again and hit him hard, knocking him to his knees. Blood started gushing out of his nose. Meg grimaced at the sight. They were still screaming at each other. Finally, Blackie turned, took his helmet off and threw it at Sean.

Sean yelled, "I got my orders from Keary, so take it up with him."

"Fuck you and fuck Keary!" Blackie yelled and stomped off past Meg without seeing her. He stalked out of the barn and up toward the house.

"Isn't he afraid of getting fired for doing that?" She asked Casey.

"Sack Blackie?" Casey said, staring at her as if she had two heads. "I don't think that's going to happen."

This episode of violence scared Meg witless. What if this kind of thing happened a lot here? After all, it was only men at the farm, except the manager's wife and Meg hadn't met her yet. She wondered if Blackie had instigated the fight.

Maybe it's just a guy thing and doesn't happen often, I hope. I better go see if he's hurt.

*   *   *

Blackie ran up to the pond so he could be alone. His gut twisted with rage. His face flushed and his eyes filled with tears.

Shit! Damnit! Why can't they leave me alone? Don't they understand how much I miss racing? All I've ever wanted to do since I was a kid was race. God, I loved the way I felt when I raced. The speed, the lust I felt in my gut to win. Jesus, the adrenaline rush alone was like a drug. Driving a horse over the last fence to the finish line was so physical it was amazing. It's a damn obsession and it's gone. What the fuck is left and there's nothing to replace it?

He picked up a stone and hurled it into the pond, blinking back tears. He whirled around when he heard a noise, his faced hardened with anger. It was Meg.

"Hey." She said softly. When he saw her, his relaxed a little.

"Hey," he said gruffly.

She moved closer and asked, "Are you okay?"

He turned back to the pond and said, "Sure." He threw a few more stones in and then sat under a nearby tree. He glanced over and patted the ground next to him. "Come here."

She hesitated then sat next to him. His mouth was bloody from Sean's right cross. Her heart rate increased considerably. She got an overwhelming desire to kiss the hurt away.

What on earth am I thinking?

"What was that all about?"

"A difference of opinion." He replied with a frown and a weary sigh.

"Casey said it was because you aren't supposed to ride."

"Casey has a big mouth," he snapped.

"He didn't say anything. I asked him. Why won't Sean let you ride?"

He remained quiet for a moment and then said, "It's complicated."

"You won't get fired will you?"

He laughed and said, "You ask a lot of questions."

"I'm sorry, I didn't mean to pry. I just didn't want you to lose your job."

"Thanks," he smiled at her. "Sean and I have been fighting like that since we were kids."

"Oh."

That doesn't make any sense. Have they worked together since they were little? That's very strange. Maybe Blackie's family worked for the O'Brien's back in Ireland. I'm confused.

"Listen," he said. "I need to get cleaned up, so I'll see you tomorrow."

"I'm planning on being here. I hope you feel better."

He got up, ruffling her hair and slowly walked to the barn with his hands stuffed in his jeans.

This whole incident completely unsettled her. She'd been relaxed around him and felt safe. But now that she'd seen this violent side to him, she was unsure about being alone with him at the barn. She didn't like how she felt and decided to go home without riding.

She had a suspicion that there was a lot more to it than was obvious and he wasn't talking.

*   *   *

The next day when Meg arrived, Blackie had both horses cross-tied in the aisle and was grooming Sandman.

"Top of the morning to you, Miss Connors" he said, cheerfully. "How are you this fine day?"

"I'm terrific," she said, glad he was in a better mood. She relaxed instantly and forgot her worries from yesterday. He had a whopper of a black eye but when he flashed that smile, she spotted an extra glint in those big, blue eyes.

He was bending over Sandman's hoof when she asked him what he'd like her to do. He dropped the hoof; stood up, his eyes stopped briefly at her chest and then flickered up to her face.

He smiled and said, "We'll find something for you to do, Miss Connors, in the meantime you could groom Cloudy."

"Yes, sir." She said and saluted him. "And stop calling me Miss Conners-it's Meg."

"Aye, I'll do that, then."

They were both busy grooming and working around the horses. She was cleaning Cloudy's feet, bent over with her back to Blackie. When she stood up and turned, he was leaning one arm on Sandman's back and had a currycomb in the other hand. He gave her a slow smile, his lids slightly lowered over smoldering eyes.

Uh-oh.

"I was just admiring you're uh … hoof-cleaning technique."

"Oh, really? I've been admiring yours for weeks."

He raised his eyebrows, chuckled and said "Touché."

She smiled a little flirty smile back at him,

"Let's tack up Sandman first." Christ, what am I doing, he thought. She's young and innocent. She sure as hell doesn't need a player like me.

So, Meg put Cloudy in her stall. They worked together, saddling and bridling and adjusting the leathers and he brushed up against her as often as he possibly could. Every time he did, she got a rush that surprised her. He led the gelding to the indoor arena. When she took the reins and went to mount, he was very close behind her, with his mouth next to her ear and said, "Can I give you a leg up?"

She stuck her leg out and he flipped her effortlessly into the saddle. She rode Sandman and he watched for almost an hour when his cell phone rang. He talked a minute and looked at his watch. He hung up and said, "I have to go. Meet me up at the house for lunch at one o'clock."

Meg nodded and he was gone. She wasn't sure what all the increased flirting was about but she liked it. She could still feel him near her.

FOUR

It took Meg a while to cool Sandman down and scrub the dried sweat off him. When she turned him out in the paddock, he was like a kid getting out of school. He kicked a happy hoof in the air and raced off to claim his freedom.

"Have fun, Sandy, you earned it."

Meg paused to savor the sun's reflection on his glistening coat and inhale the grass's perfume.

Okay, time to go find that hunky groom.

Hustling up to the house, she knocked and a beautiful, auburn-haired woman answered.

"Hello," she said with the same lilt to her voice as Blackie.

"Hi, I'm Meg Connors. Blackie said to meet him up here for lunch."

"Oh yes, you have the new horses here. Come in. I'm Jill Connelly. It's nice to finally meet you. He's in the back room watching TV." She led Meg through the welcoming kitchen and intimate dining room to a hallway.

"Just walk back there and it's the last room you come to. Lunch will be served in about ten minutes."

"Thank you, I'll tell him."

The house was incredible, elegant but decorated in warm tones and well-loved antiques. Her steps muffled by luxurious Persian carpets, her head swiveled to take in all the oil paintings of hunt and racing scenes. She followed the sound of a TV back to a large but cozy family room with an enticing u-shaped couch in front of a wall-sized TV. Blackie was lying there sound asleep.

He was breathing softly and totally relaxed, his boots off; dumped on the floor. He was more than enticing in those revealing jeans and hiked up tee shirt, exposing impressive abs. Meg had to squelch the impulse to touch him.

Get a grip. What's the matter with you?

She did touch his arm lightly and said, "Blackie."

He stirred, mumbling something and stretched lazily like a cat. He hypnotized her as his muscles rippled when he flexed each part of himself from head to toe.

She dared to touch him again and said, "Blackie, lunch is ready."

He didn't open his eyes and said softly, "Okay, thanks Jill."

"It's not Jill, it's Meg."

His eyes flew open and he sprang up running his hands through his hair in an unsuccessful effort to tidy it.

He looks yummy all tousled and did he just blush?

"Uh ... well ... hello, then. I didn't realize how tired I was. Where's Jill?"

"She was in the kitchen and sent me back to get you. She said lunch would be ready in about ten minutes. Are you sure it's okay for me to be here? I mean did she know I was coming? I don't want to make extra work for her."

He laughed, "Jill doesn't fix it anyway, the cook does and she always puts out way too much food. Come on, I'm hungry," He grabbed her hand and led her back to the dining room, that now had a sideboard groaning with great smelling food and a bunch of men at it filling their plates.

"Grab a plate, then," he said and got in line. Casey was in front of him and then Sean, who had a bandage over his nose. Blackie said hello to Casey, but he and Sean just nodded stiffly to one another without speaking.

Jill got in line behind Meg and smiled. "I see you found him."

"Yes, he was sound asleep."

"That's usual. He gets up early and works hard. He still gets tired faster than he used to, so as soon as he sits down, he falls asleep. I see those two are still at odds," she said, nodding toward Sean and Blackie. "Sometimes the testosterone gets a little thick around here. It'll be nice to have another woman to talk to." She touched Meg's shoulder in a friendly gesture that gave Meg a little shiver of pleasure.

"Sean has a girlfriend but she doesn't ride, so we don't see her that often."

"Does Blackie have a girlfriend?" Meg asked.

"No, he doesn't," Jill said with a knowing little smile. Meg flushed with embarrassment.

Oh, boy. That certainly was subtle.

There was a ton of food put out: fried chicken, salad, boiled potatoes and cabbage, ham, green beans, fresh fruit and scones.

Meg helped herself to a little of everything and sat next to Blackie. He had enough food on his plate to feed a lumberjack and sipped orange juice. She wondered where he put all that food since he had no visible evidence of body fat.

Crap, it must be nice. I even look at that much food and it goes right to my butt.

Keary, the farm manager, came in a few minutes late and said hello to everyone. Blackie introduced Meg, and Keary said it was nice to finally meet her. There was obviously a lot of tension in the room with no one saying much, making Meg feel ill at ease.

Blackie started talking to her quietly about the horse show season that would begin in the next few weeks. He thought she should enter and he'd take her in the farm's van. The idea of spending all day on Saturday or Sunday with him was more than exciting.

After lunch Keary said, "Blackie, we need to talk."

"About what?" Blackie said with an instant attitude.

"Uh … we can talk later."

"Why not now?"

"Fine," Keary said with a weary sigh. "There's no excuse for the fight you and Sean had. You broke his nose, again."

"Yes, there is, when he yanks me off a horse like a child," Blackie said indignantly.

"When are you going to learn to control your temper? He was only doing what I asked him to do."

"Then the fight needs to be with you, doesn't it?"

"Blackie, honey," Jill said softly, "They're only doing this for your own good."

"My own good! Don't you guys understand how much I miss my life? So don't do me any favors," Blackie snarled and stomped out.

"Shit!" Keary said and ran his hands through his hair. "You just can't reason with him. What horse was he on?"

"It was JZ. He didn't like how he was jumping for Casey, so he made him get off, jumped on and was ready to take him out on the track when I stopped him. I mean that horse is nuts. I worry about Casey up on him so I wasn't going to let Blackie ride him. I asked him nicely to get down but he instantly got mad and said I was treating him like a baby. So I grabbed his arm and yanked him off and of course that started the fight." Sean answered.

"Well, eejit, you might have known that was going to happen." Keary said.

"I know but I was afraid he was going to get hurt. I hate it when he's mad at me like this." Sean said with a sad sigh.

"Doesn't he ride very well?" Meg asked.

They all laughed.

"He can ride pretty well, we're just doing this for his safety," Jill explained then she glanced at Keary and hesitated.

"He got hurt two years ago and he still hasn't fully recovered, so we're trying to keep him from getting injured again."

"Is that why you said he gets tired faster than he used to?"

"Yes. He's still not one hundred percent. He doesn't have as much stamina as he once had."

"That must have been bad to take this long to recover," Meg said.

Keary said softly, "It was, yes."

"We should let him tell you about it when he's ready. It's his personal business and it's better if he tells you," Jill said.

Just then, Blackie came stomping into the kitchen and yelled, "Meg!"

"Uh-oh!" Meg said and ran out after him.

He sounds pissed. I hope he's not angry with me.

"What was that about?" Keary asked with raised eyebrows. "He sounded a bit possessive to me."

"There's something going on between them, but I'm not sure what just yet," Jill said.

"What do you mean? Is he sleeping with her?" Keary asked.

"Oh, no, not yet, anyway. It's funny though. I've been down at the barn when they're together working on her horses. They're in their own little world and don't even notice me. He's nervous around her."

"Blackie! Nervous around a woman? That's rich." Sean piped up.

FIVE

Meg ran after Blackie and found him back at the barn. He had a hard set to his jaw and was slamming the grooming utensils into a trunk.

"Would you like to go for a ride?" He asked. "I know a lot of great trails around the farm. Uh ... I can ride Sandman while you ride Cloudy."

"Sure, I'd love to see the trails."

Meg wasn't sure if this was a good idea after hearing what was said at lunch, but wasn't about to interfere.

They tacked the horses up and led them outside. He gave her a leg up and then vaulted into his saddle like a gymnast. She had yet to see him ride and at first glance, he looked like he was born on a horse. He took off at a trot and she followed. They moved down a dirt road that ran beside the barns and into the woods. The woods were beautiful with the sun dappled through the trees and whisper quiet. She loved the mossy, damp smell. He kept at a trot for about twenty minutes and then went back to a walk. He reined back so he could ride next to her.

"How do you like the trail, then?"

"It's beautiful. Riding through the woods is my favorite."

"Yes, me too. I love it most in the fall when the leaves are on the ground. Do you want to go to a show this weekend?"

"That would be great. Do you have time?" She got a knot of excitement in her stomach at the thought.

"Sure, I love shows and I want to take you. It's a hunter show, so do you want to take both of them? And yes, I have plenty of time. Does this guy jump?"

"Yes, but as usual I have a hard time controlling him, so he's inconsistent," Meg said.

"Do you want to do some jumping? There are jumps on one trail and they're only about four feet."

"Okay, let's go," she said with enthusiasm.

So, Blackie moved off at a canter and led her to a new trail where she could see jumps coming up. Sandman flicked his ears back and hesitated but Blackie pushed him so he sailed over the jump. Blackie let out a happy whoop and grinned ear to ear when he glanced back at her. Meg could feel his enthusiasm as she and Cloudy galloped after him.

They raced through the woods, savoring every minute and took all the jumps. She could tell Blackie was an unbelievably talented rider. He had natural balance, very soft hands and it was obvious that he loved it from the gleam in his eyes. They came thundering out of the woods and. He slowed to a trot and they rode along a ridge between two fields that over looked a little valley. The view was spectacular. The valley stretched for miles of rolling hills and a small river meandered down the middle, glistening in the sun. Blackie slowed to a walk and let Sandman have his head. Meg moved up beside him and he was breathing hard, his eyes electric with happiness.

"Man that was fantastic! This guy is great. I like him a lot. How did you and Cloudy like that?"

"Great trail and this view is awesome."

"This is my favorite spot on the farm," he said as he looked down the valley.

" Thank you for this, I haven't had this much fun in a long time."

"I'm glad. I think everything's better when it's shared," he said.

"You ride so well, how come you don't do more with it?" She asked hesitantly.

He looked at her without saying anything for a minute and then looked away with a little frown and sighed. "I got seriously hurt a couple of years ago and it kinda put a damper on things."

"I'm sorry, I didn't mean to pry," Meg said.

"That's okay. I'll tell you about it at some point. That's why Keary and the others don't want me riding. They'll probably have a shit-fit when they find out about this little excursion."

"I can keep a secret," she said.

He smiled, "Okay, it's a deal."

"But you seem like you're in great shape and you ride so well, I don't see why there's a problem."

"Well, looks are deceptive," he said ruefully.

He doesn't want to talk about it. It must have been bad and I don't think I should push him. I'm not sure I want to know but I'm curious.

He took off at a trot again and swung through another small wood and came out on the other side of the barns. They dismounted, rubbed the horses down and put them in their stalls.

"I'm going to clean my tack, since it's only three o'clock," she told him.

"Okay. Are you after staying for dinner or do you have to work tonight?" He asked.

"I have off tonight and I'd love to stay, if it's okay."

"Of course it's fine," he smiled. "I'm going to go up and watch TV until dinner."

"I'll be up soon." She told him with a secret happy feeling inside.

*   *   *

Two hours later, Meg walked up to the house and knocked. Jill came to the door and said, "You don't have to knock, just come in, then."

"Is Blackie here?"

"Oh yes, he went to watch TV, but I'll bet he's asleep. He said he was really tired when he came in."

They walked back to the TV room and there he was sound asleep on the couch again. He looked scrumptious laying there all rumpled.

"He looks cozy and cuddly," Meg said.

"He's always after cuddling, he always has."

"What do you mean?"

"Well he's a very physical person and loves to cuddle. Maybe because our Mom held him so much when he was a kid."

"Our Mom?" Meg said, surprised.

"Yes, he's my little brother. Didn't you know that?"

"No, wow."

After that fight with Sean, I guess that explains why he didn't get fired. That's very interesting.

"Anyway, Mom had a little boy when I was three who only lived for a month. His name was Patrick. Then she had Blackie and held him a lot. Even when he was five or six, she held him until he went to sleep."

"I like the idea of cuddling," Meg said.

"Why don't you crawl in there with him and take a nap. He'll love it."

"I don't know, I mean, we're not dating or anything. He might think I'm putting the moves on him and he's not interested."

"I don't think it'll be a problem and I'm thinking he likes you. He won't do anything. untoward, at least not here in the TV room," Jill laughed.

"Don't worry he's really a sweetheart of a guy."

"I'm beginning to realize that."

"Okay. I have to see about dinner, so enjoy your nap." Jill said and left.

Meg stood there considering. It was tempting to snuggle in with him but she hesitated.

He looks so yummy. This is going to start something that I'm not sure I want started. I don't think I want to get involved. Oh, boy would I like to get next to him and ...

Just then, Blackie stirred and opened his eyes.

"Hi." She said.

"Hi, yourself," Blackie murmured and stretched.

Meg stared at him, wide-eyed not knowing what to say next.

"What's up, Meg? Is dinner ready?" He asked as he swung his legs to the floor and grimaced. "Ouch, crap!" He grabbed his back and bent over, obviously in pain.

"What's wrong?" Meg squeaked in alarmed.

"Shhh," he said, "don't let Jill hear us."

"What?" She mouthed.

"My hip is killing me. I guess from our ride."

He stood to walk around, limped badly and winced.

Oh my God! I am so in deep do-do here. They're going to be pissed at me for letting him get hurt. What happened? He didn't fall. Oh, no!

"Shit" he said. He arched his back, stretched and winced again. He did a series of different stretches and walking around.

"It's loosening up."

"Am I going to be in trouble because I let you ride?"

"No, that's my responsibility. Don't worry about it. Besides it's our secret, remember."

"Yeah, but I don't want you to get hurt either."

"It's okay. I'm just not used to it yet. It'll get better. I won't get hurt riding Sandman."

"If you say so."

"Let's go see what's happening with dinner."

SIX

Sean, Casey and Keary were already filling their plates. Blackie guided Meg into line with a hand on the small of her back. She was trembled, acutely aware of him touching her. The heat from his hand felt like warm toast on her skin.

They got in line with Jill. The food again was way too much. Roast beef, lake trout, mashed potatoes, broccoli, carrots, salad and rolls. The sight and aroma of the food made her mouth water. As usual, Blackie had a lot of food on his plate. She couldn't believe he could eat that much.

"Are you really going to eat all that?" Meg said as he tucked into his food.

"Yes, luv, I have to keep me strength up," he said in a thick Irish accent and they laughed.

Then Sean said to Blackie in Gaelic, "Buille faoi thuairim mé shagging léi, a dhéanann tú de dhíth ort neart." *I guess shagging her you do need your strength.*

Blackie instantly threw his fork down and started to go after Sean.

"Son of a bitch" he said and then to Sean in Gaelic, "Níl aon cheann de sin ag dul ar do chuid faisnéise." *There's none of that going on for your information.*

"Sean, what's wrong with you?" Keary yelled.

Then Sean again said to Blackie, "Tá sé seo ar cheann do na leabhair taifead sin." *This is one for the record book then.*

"Shut the fuck up, Sean," Blackie yelled at him.

Sean yelled back, "Tá mé ag rá ach riamh go raibh tú cairde le bean i do shaol. Gach raibh tú go raibh leaba riamh iad agus ansin Dumpáil iad." *I'm just saying you were never friends with a woman in your life. All you ever did was bed them and then dump them.*

"Sean, stop!"Keary pleaded.

Blackie was standing now and in Sean's face, "Fuck you!"

Then he sat down abruptly and covered his face with his hands. When he raised his head, he looked devastated.

"Is that what you think of me, that I'm incapable of a real relationship?"

Sean was shocked at this statement.

"No, I'm sorry, that's not what I think. I was actually trying to tease you but it didn't come out right," Sean said, his eyes wide and tearful.

"No shit, Sean, I don't believe you," Keary yelled.

Blackie stood up and said, "I'm outta here, I'm not hungry anymore." And stomped out.

Nobody said anything after that.

"I guess I'll be going home now," Meg said. "Thank you for dinner."

"You're welcome," Jill said and smiled at her.

*   *   *

After she left, a heated discussion took place.

Jill said to Sean, "I can't believe you said something so crude to him and with Meg sitting right there. What were you thinking?"

"I don't know. He's always looking at her as if he's going to jump her, so I thought they were sleeping together. I mean look at his track record with women."

"I know but he was talking to me earlier about her. He likes her but he said he's never liked a woman he wanted to have sex with before. This is new and he likes the feeling and wants to have a real loving relationship with her and then you go and say something like that."

"We're on shaky ground here with him emotionally, don't you realize that?" Keary said to Sean.

"Yes, but he was always so tough before and took everything that came at him in stride. He was always so confident in himself."

"Well that's all changed, Sean. It changed when he almost died on that race-track and you need to get that through your head. He's not the same anymore. Emotionally he's very fragile," Jill said, sadly.

"I want the old Blackie back," Sean said close to tears.

"Well I think when he gets it figured out; he's going to be even better. A really great man," Keary said with tears glistening in his eyes.

SEVEN

The next morning Meg walked into the stable but didn't see Blackie. The horses were in dirty stalls and not groomed. She decided to go up to the house to see if he was there. Jill answered the door and said she hadn't seen him. "I think he's still asleep in his apartment. He's miserable so he didn't come up for breakfast."

"Where's his apartment?"

"It's over the barn where your horses are." Jill said.

"Over top the barn? He lives in the barn?" Meg asked, in shock.

"Yes." Jill laughed. "He likes to be near the horses. He designed it himself. You'll love it. As you go in the barn, on the left is a keypad to the elevator. Just hit the 'Up' button and it will open."

"Wait a minute. He has an elevator that goes to his apartment?"

"Yes, Meg. Go on, he'll probably be glad to see you. Just knock on the door when the elevator gets to the top." Jill said, still smiling.

"Okay, thanks."

Oh, boy. Is this guy quirky or what? Who the hell lives in a barn? Hmm, I bet he's hungry.

She decided to drive to Middleburg and buy a bunch of burgers and fries at the local McDonalds. When she got back to the farm, she took the elevator and knocked on his door with a sweaty hand and knot in her belly.

Am I stupid for doing this? I'm an idiot for getting involved in this at all. He got away with that fight because he's the manager's brother-in-law but what was the argument about last night? Oh God ...

Blackie yanked the door open with a vengeance, ready to jump on whoever was there. His face softened when he saw her. He smiled but the smile didn't reach his eyes. All he had on was a pair of old sweat pants.

Mmm, he looks good enough to eat.

She was startled to see he had a green, somewhat square tattoo that looked sort of like a maze on his left pec.

Okay, so what's that about? I'm not about to ask, either.

"Hi," he murmured.

"Hi. What'd you have for breakfast?"

"Uh ... coffee and a Poptart."

"You must be hungry," Meg said and handed him the bag of food.

"Wow, junk food!" he said happily. "Come in."

He put the food on the coffee table and padded into the kitchen. "Want a soda?"

"Yes, that sounds great," she replied and sat down on the couch.

She took in the apartment and was impressed. It filled up the whole top of that huge barn, beautifully decorated and masculine. The foyer opened onto a spacious living room, dining room, kitchen combination. The appliances were all stainless steel and the latest technology. Oak cabinets hung over a black and tan granite counter with a rustic farm table centered in the kitchen.

A burgundy couch dominated the living room accented with huge, tan overstuffed chairs with burgundy and black pillows. There was even a fireplace under a wall-size flat screen. Light streamed in through the three skylights. Beyond that, Meg could see a gigantic bed, some kind of workout bench, dressers and an alcove that had to go back to a bathroom.

The temperature was perfect and she couldn't hear or smell the barn. The whole place was spotless and neat except for stacks of books everywhere.

This is amazing. How could he afford to do this? Maybe his parents paid for it. Who is he?

He brought both of them a Coke and sat down on the couch next to her. He dug into the bag of food happily. "This is great, I'm starved. You brought a lot of food! Half of this is for you isn't it?"

"Just one of each for me, the rest is yours."

"Yum, I haven't had any of this stuff for years." He took a big bite out of a burger and groaned. "God, that's good." He had a ballgame on and they ate and watched TV. He ate all of his and then inspected the fries left on her plate.

"Are you going to eat those?"

She handed them to him and he smiled. He finished the fries and leaned back in the couch next to her and sighed, decidedly content.

"Man that was good. Thank you." He looked at her and smiled. "Are you after taking care of me?"

"I guess a little, do you mind?"

"No, I like it."

"Why didn't you go up and have breakfast and lunch with the others?"

"I'm sulking," he said, "I know that sounds childish, but that's what I do when they bug me."

"I didn't mean to intrude, I'm sorry," she said.

"No, that's okay." He snuggled closer to her and settled into watch the game. She got a huge rush being next to his body and suddenly felt uneasy.

Maybe it's not such a good idea to be alone with him right now. He's way too tempting.

"Hey, why don't you get your butt dressed and let's go for a ride."

EIGHT

She continued to watch TV while Blackie walked in to take a shower.

"Want to wash my back?" he said from the bathroom.

"Cute!" She said.

"My front?" He asked, laughing.

"In your dreams, hurry up."

She noticed when he walked away from her that he had another strange, ornate tattoo down the center of his back. At the top of it was what looked like a large "less than" symbol.

Holy crap! That's an unusual tat. It's beautiful. I'm definitely not asking about that one.

Twenty minutes later, he returned, showered, shaved and looked terrific. His mood had brightened considerably. He had on a black t-shirt, riding boots and her favorite low, tight-ass jeans.

"Hey, you look like you've cheered up." She said enjoying the view of him walk toward her.

"Why not? I'm going for a ride with a beautiful woman."

As they left his apartment, she commented, "I've never known anyone who lived in a barn before."

"It's a little different." He laughed. "When I was a kid, I was always sneaking out of the house at night to be near the horses. Most of the time, they'd find me asleep in one of the stalls. I had this built when we moved here for privacy and to be near the horses."

"It's fantastic! Did you build it yourself?"

"I designed it and helped to build it. The parts I could do anyway. The rest, I hired contractors to do. I love it. It suits my purpose and is very comfortable. I can get away from the rest of them when I want to."

"And you have your own private elevator."

"Uh … it used to just have that ladder and then when I was hurt, we put the elevator in." He said and blushed.

"It's nice the owners let you do all this."

"Yes, well, they're very nice people."

They took the elevator down, got the horses ready, and led them out of the barn. She was getting ready to mount Cloudy when Blackie walked up behind her, leaned into her and whispered with his mouth against her ear, "Would you like a leg up?"

Her heart flipped and she knew she was blushing from the huge rush she got. Meg wanted to just turn around in his arms and kiss him but she stuck her leg out and he flipped her into the saddle

"Let's take a different trail today."

"Okay, lead the way."

He took off at a trot and she followed. They rode along the edge of a field next to the woods. Meg loved watching him ride he was so good.

Turning into the woods, Blackie slowed to a walk. The peace of the woods surrounded them like a bower; the breeze gently waving the branches; the birds singing their love songs.

He reined Sandman back to ride next to her. Quiet for a few minutes, he stopped, Meg halted Cloudy and Blackie stared at her. He moved Sandman over close, leaned in and kissed her gently on the mouth.

His lips were soft as he brushed them like a whisper over hers. The jolt and rush she got wasn't exactly soft. She instantly wanted more but he had already kicked Sandy into a dead run.

*　　　*　　　*

Christ, what am I doing?

He jerked the horse away and put him into a gallop to cover up his surprise and embarrassment. Embarrassed! He'd never felt that way before, kissing a woman, even when he was a kid. The instant arousal caught him off guard, another reason to get out of there before she noticed. He knew her mouth would be that sweet. As he galloped off, he licked his lips to savor the taste of her.

*　　　*　　　*

She was startled. He'd caught her off guard. It took her a beat to react and then she took off after him.

Oh my God. He just kissed me.

She'd been wondering what it would be like to kiss him, but hadn't expected it to be that gentle or potent. The kiss had plucked her like a harp string all the way to her toes.

*　　　*　　　*

They galloped through the woods and it was glorious. It made her feel wild, free and happy.

They burst out of the woods, Sandman bucked as usual, jumped sideways and tripped. He went down hard and rolled onto his side. It flashed in her mind that Blackie was under him, but he'd jumped off and landed on his feet. Sandman stood up, wild-eyed and ready to run. Blackie whistled softly and grabbed the reins. He rubbed the horse's head briefly and ran his hand down Sandy's legs, then walked over to Meg. Blackie was limping slightly.

Oh crap, she thought, he's hurt.

"He's okay. I don't feel any problems and he's not limping. I think he's just scared." "*He's* not limping, but you are," she said. "Are you okay?"

"I think so, yes. I hit the ground a little hard. Don't worry, let's get back. I'm just going to move him at a slow trot. You watch and tell me if you see any stiffness."

He moved off, Sandman seemed fine from her point of view, and Blackie was looking down at the gelding's legs. A few minutes and he seemed satisfied, moving into a canter. They went along the edge of another field, crossed a dirt road and back to the barns. They dismounted and led the horses inside. Blackie was limping worse.

"Come on, you really did something," she fussed.

"It's okay. I'll sit in the Jacuzzi tonight and it'll be good."

Meg stood in front of him, put her hand on his chest and made him stop.

"I feel awful! I'd hate it if something happened to you riding my dumb horse. I'd hate it if you got hurt at all." She was almost in tears.

He put his arm around her, kissed her temple very gently and whispered, "I'm okay."

He turned and said, "Hey, tomorrow's the horse show! I'll have everything ready when you get here. I'm excited. This is going to be fun."

NINE

The next morning, when Meg got there, Sandman grazed, un-groomed, in the paddock. The van was loaded with tack, Cloudy groomed and braided. She searched around for Blackie and found him sitting on a hay bale, his head leaning on the barn wall, his eyes closed. She touched his arm lightly and he opened his eyes.

"It's bad isn't it?" She asked.

"It's not great. I just took a pain pill. Can we just take Cloudy; I'm not up to taking both of them?"

"If you're hurting, we don't have to go at all."

"No, I want to go. This pill should kick in soon and I'll feel better."

"Do you think we should go and get you x-rayed? I'm worried."

"No, I just jammed it when I jumped off. I'll get Tim to work on it and then do the Jacuzzi again tonight. Let's get going. Cloudy's ready to go and so is your equipment."

"Listen, I think we shouldn't go. You should rest," she said.

"No, you listen," he said in a nasty tone, "we're going to the damn show and that's the end of the discussion. I told you I'd be fine, now get in the van."

"You can't order me around, damnit. You're stubborn as hell. I'm not going anywhere," she said, crossing her arms over her chest and sticking her chin out.

"Oh, yeah!" he grabbed her arm, marched her out with one hand, grabbed Cloudy's lead rope with the other, opened the door and shoved Meg in the van.

He slammed the door, loaded Cloudy, got in and pulled away. They rode in silence until they got to the show. He parked the van, cut the engine and turned to her.

"Look, Meg, I'm sorry, I just didn't feel up to arguing with you."

"So, let me get this straight, if you don't feel like discussing something, then you just get your way."

He stared at her for a long minute then got out of the van and unloaded Cloudy. Meg saddled her and trotted over to sign up for classes without further comment.

During the show, she watched him when he wasn't looking. He went over to the concession booth and got a couple hot dogs and a beer. He sat in the stands and watched her classes. She was excited that she won four of the six classes she'd entered. She wanted to share her pleasure in winning with him, but she figured he was still mad.

She'd seen him during her last class, but when she got back to the van, he wasn't around. She loaded Cloudy and the tack and walked around a bit more, searching for him. Meg decided maybe he hitched a ride home with someone else. She opened the van to get her cell phone and he was lying on the seat and looked pale. He tried to get up when she opened the door and winced. Meg felt awful for getting mad at him.

"Hey, you did great, I'm proud of you," he smiled at her wanly. "Maybe you should drive. This medicine makes me groggy and the beer didn't help."

He slid over to the passenger side, obviously still hurting.

He looked at her and said, "Meg, I'm sorry, I shouldn't have talked to you like that."

She slid over close to him. "I'm sorry too and I'm doubly sorry you're hurt." She leaned over and kissed him quickly on the cheek. He pulled her close and hugged her.

"Please forgive me," he whispered.

"Nothing to forgive, you didn't do anything wrong. I guess we just had our first fight." She said trying to lighten the mood.

"Does this mean I get make-up sex?" he asked with a tired little grin.

"Very cute!" She said and turned the engine over.

He slept all the way home and Meg put Cloudy in her stall and left the equipment for later.

"What are you going to do?"

"I'm going to crash and call Tim in the morning to see what he can do."

"Will you be okay by yourself?"

"I will, yes. You should go home; it's been a long day."

He limped into the elevator and she drove home. She figured she'd call him in the morning.

Meg didn't quite know how to deal with this. They weren't dating and she didn't know that much about him. He learned to ride in some other life and because of an injury was now working as a stable hand and fighting with his employers who let him get away with everything except riding. She couldn't stop thinking about him and didn't even know his real name. Everyone indulges him like a child.

What's that about?

*   *   *

Meg called Blackie's cell in the morning and he answered right away.

"Yes," he said.

"Hi, it's me. How are you? What's going on?" she asked.

"Hi, I'm doing okay. Tim's here and he's been working on me for a while. He thinks I just pulled a muscle. I think he's using the horse liniment on me but it feels better. Then I get to sit in the Jacuzzi and you'll be able to stick a fork in me because I'll be done. What are you doing?"

"I wanted to see how you were and you sound like you're in good hands. I'm going to come out to the farm to ride, so do you want me to stop in to see you?" She asked, hopefully.

"I do, yes. I miss you. I have to take it easy so we'll watch TV and have dinner."

"Great! I'll see you later."

Ten

Meg went to his apartment and knocked. He opened the door barefoot and in jeans and a T-shirt. She thought he looked irresistible as usual.

"Hi", he said and flashed her that incredible smile, "I'm glad to see you. I missed you. Come on in."

"Yeah, I've missed you too. How's your hip?" She asked. As she walked past him, he ran his hand down her back and left it there to guide her into the room. His hand was making her skin tingle and it felt good to be near him. She realized just how much she did miss him and it shocked her a little.

"It's doing great. Tim worked his magic on me. You want to watch TV awhile? I'd rather go riding but Tim said to cool it for a few days, so I'd better listen. If Keary sees me limping around, it's just going to prove his point about me riding." He walked in behind her and started toward the kitchen.

"Do you want a soda? I ordered pizza."

"Perfect." She said and sat down, "TV's good, I'm tired myself." He came over with the drinks and sat down next to her, close to her, his body touching hers, their legs touching. It made her crazy! She could hardly focus on what he was saying.

"I'm starving and I love junk food," he said as he tucked into the pizza. She loved watching him eat, he enjoyed it so much.

"You really love to eat, that's healthy."

"I know. I'm always hungry. I'm actually just getting my appetite back. I didn't feel like eating for a long time after the accident. I lost about ten pounds. I weigh about one-seventy now, thanks to Tim. At one hundred thirty pounds, I was sick and looked it. Doing the workout program, that Tim set up has done wonders. My muscle tone and volume have really increased."

I can tell and a big 'Thank You', Tim.

"Why didn't you want to eat?"

He hesitated for a few minutes before he answered.

"I went in and out of depression after the accident and a lot of it was from recuperating from so many surgeries. The morphine made me sick and I'm still addicted to it."

He looked at her and didn't say anything as if he was considering what to say next.

"Does it scare you that I get depressed?"

"I don't think so, but I'd hate that you felt bad. That would make me sad."

He seemed relieved then said, "It's actually been awhile since I had an episode. They're getting farther apart so I don't think about it too much anymore. I just wanted you to know."

"Thank you for telling me. By the way, what's that tattoo on your back mean?"

She realized she was prying again when he paled at her question.

Oh, great. I asked him the wrong thing again.

"Uh … just some old Irish stuff I got once when I was drunk. One of those really stupid things guys do, you know."

"Oh, it's cool. I wondered what …

"Are we going to the show this weekend?" He asked, deftly changing the subject again.

"Yes, I'd love to go if you want to. If you feel up to it."

"Let's plan on it then. The weekend after there's one up near McLean that you might like. It's got a basic dressage class that would be good for Cloudy," he suggested.

"That sounds like fun. Do you think I'm up to it?"

"We can go over the basic test routine until then. It shouldn't be hard for you. You want another soda?" he asked.

"No thanks."

"I want to ask you a favor."

"Okay, sure, what?"

"Can I start riding Sandman seriously and do some dressage? I know he's your horse and I won't mind if you say no. I just like the way he moves and he's feisty. What do you think?"

"That's fine with me; you can handle him better than I can."

I hope I'm not going to regret this. If he gets hurt again, Keary will kill me. I suppose I'm liable if he's injured using my horse. Oh, boy. I want to help him start riding again, but I'm getting a bad feeling.

"Okay, thanks, Meg. We can have fun with him. Hey, let's watch TV. You have a choice- *Live Free or Die Hard* or *Shoot'em Up?*"

"How about *The Wedding Date?*"

"Sorry, no chick flicks today!" he said laughing.

"I guess the *Die Hard* one, if we must," she huffed.

"Good choice, lady." He put the movie on, leaned back on the sofa and scrunched closer to her. It felt so delicious to be that close to him and she wanted to get closer. They talked a little bit about the movie, but she could see he was getting sleepy. His eyes were half closed.

"Are you planning on taking a nap? Maybe I should leave."

"I was, yes. A nap would be grand. Would you care to join me?" he said with a sly smile.

"Uh, I don't think that would be such a good idea. It's a little soon, I mean we're not ...

"Oh, no, no! I just meant do you want to actually take a nap with me, here on the sofa, I wasn't being lecherous."

Yeah, right. But the idea of being near him and sleeping turned her on.

"Well, I am kind of tired."

"Good," he scooted closer and settled in to watch TV.

It wasn't long, he was asleep and she wasn't far behind him. They must have slept for a couple hours. When she woke up, Blackie had his head on her shoulder and an arm thrown over her waist. He was nice and warm and she got a rush being up against his body. She reached out and stroked his hair which just intensified the feeling.

This guy's going to make me absolutely crazy.

He stirred and she moved her hand away quickly as he opened his eyes. He looked up at her, smiled and the full impact of those incredible eyes, took her breath away.

"Hi," he said, softly, "what time is it?"

"It's about six o'clock," she said.

"Mmm, it's almost dinner time, I'm hungry," he said as he stretched languidly.

"You can't possibly be hungry already." The man had to have warp speed metabolism.

"Hey it's been a couple of hours, let's go." He scooped her up and they walked up to the house.

"How was your nap?" he asked her.

"Good, I feel incredibly refreshed."

"See, I knew you'd like it and it's always more fun with someone else." He smiled and she wondered if he just liked sleeping next to someone or he was putting a move on her. Hmm?

They had a nice dinner. No one said much except Blackie who was chattering away about going to a horse show on the weekend.

Keary said, "Where've you been Blackie? We haven't seen you since last Thursday or Friday."

"Oh I wasn't feeling so good so I just stayed in and rested," Blackie said evasively.

"Didn't you eat?" Jill asked him.

"I did, yes. Meg brought me some food."

Blackie stood up and stretched, "I'm going to crash. I'll see you in the morning, Meg."

"All right. Good night."

Blackie left to go down to his apartment and Meg stayed to talk.

ELEVEN

It was Sunday and by the time Meg got to the barn, Blackie was up, had braided the horses' manes and loaded the tack. He was walking out of the barn with Sandman when he looked up and saw her. She got a smile and could tell he was in a great mood.

"Good morning, then, Meg, great day for a show. The weather's going to be perfect. If you want to get Cloudy out, I'll load her for you."

"Good morning to you too," she said and gave him a little flirty smile in return. He did a double take and his smile widened.

When she was in the stall giving Cloudy her morning carrot, she heard a car crunch on the driveway gravel. As she led the mare out of the stall, she saw Blackie approaching some man. When she got closer, she recognized, Bob James, an old friend of hers from college.

"Can I help you?" Blackie said.

"Yeah, I'm looking for a friend of mine, Meg Connors?" Bob flicked his eyes to her and said, "Oh, there you are!"

"Bob, what a nice surprise! I haven't seen you in ages." Meg gave him a hug which Bob return affectionately. Blackie scowled at her, looked at Bob and said with a slight edge to his voice, "And you would be?"

Bob looked at Meg hesitantly and then back to Blackie.

"I'm sorry, Bob James, an old friend of Meg's. I heard she had her horses here and I thought I'd drive by to see if she was going to the show. If you're going, Meg, how about I drive your van and help with the horses."

"I always take her to the shows, if that's okay with you," Blackie said with a sharper edge to his voice and stiffened body language.

"And just who are you?" Bob now seemed a little confrontational himself. Meg wondered what the hell was going on and why Blackie was getting his back up.

"I'm Blackie O'Brien and this is my farm."

"What on earth did you just say?" She exclaimed. Bob scanned back and forth between Blackie and Meg, hesitated, raised his eyebrows and said, "You're *the* Blackie O'Brien?"

"I don't know, how many are there?" Blackie said defiantly as Meg stood there with her mouth open.

"I've followed your career for years. You have to be the most brilliant race rider in the world!"

"Thanks, I guess."

"What are you talking about? This is *your* farm?" She sputtered as she grabbed Blackie's arm but he shook her off. Blackie and Bob stared daggers at each other.

"Maybe I better just go and, hopefully, I'll see you at the show, Meg," he said.

"Good idea," Blackie said standing there with his hands relaxed at his sides but with an attitude like a snake ready to strike.

Bob turned and started walking back to his car when Meg exploded at Blackie.

"What do you mean? Since when are *you* the boss around here? And your name is *O'Brien?*" Meg said, throwing her arms in the air.

"Since I was born," Blackie yelled back.

"I thought Sean was the boss! I signed a contract with S.B.L.O'Brien. Who the hell is that?"

"Oh, excuse the shit out of me! I'm sorry I didn't inform you, but *I'm* S.B.L.O'Brien and I sign all the contracts." He said getting louder. "Blackie's a nickname and Sean's my cousin."

"I thought Sean owned the farm and Keary is manager. All this time you led me to believe you're a stable hand. What's that about?" She demanded.

"I didn't lead you anywhere! You didn't need to know my fucking last name for me to help you with your horse! You don't seem to care who I am when I'm mucking out your stalls! What the fuck difference does it make who I am?" Blackie was livid now. "And another thing, forget who I am, who the hell is that guy?"

"A friend."

"How close a friend? That was a cozy little hug you gave him."

"None of your damn business. It's deceitful as hell not to tell me. All this time you've been acting like a stable hand, cleaning stalls and grooming," by this time she was screaming at him.

"I always do that stuff. You think I walk around here like some big shot and never get my hands dirty?" He was now in her face with his fists clenched.

"You lied to me," she shrieked and punched him in the chest.

"No I didn't, damnit, I just wanted you to like me for me and not because I was the boss. No one treats me like the boss around here anyway. Sean and Keary run things and I've always done the race riding!"

"You mean *you're* their jockey? Why didn't you tell me? I can't stand liars!" She yelled and threw another punch but he caught her fist before it connected. He slammed her up against the tack room wall, pinned both her hands up with his and pressed his body against her. He kissed her violently, ravishing her mouth with his tongue and she got a rush that went all the way down to where it counts. He pulled away from her and stared, wide-eyed.

Meg was just as shocked as he was but it only took her a couple of seconds to recover. She jumped on him and he caught her. She wrapped her legs around him and kissed him as passionately as she could. He moaned and staggered backward into the tack room, sitting down hard on one of the trunks with her on his lap.

He wrapped his arms around her and kissed her again, harder and deeper, his breathing getting ragged. He moved his head back and looked at her with lowered lids, his eyes electric with desire.

She kissed him again and he put his hands on her butt and pressed her down into him as he moved his hips up to meet her. She could feel that he was rock hard under her and it felt fantastic. They kissed again, franticly and he groaned, or maybe that was Meg.

Oh, God. This is moving too fast. I can't control him. I can't control me! Ohhhh, I want his mouth on me. I want more ... Ahhhh.

It drifted into her lust fogged brain that things were getting out of hand fast. She didn't want to stop, but someone had to control this. She pushed away from him and got up.

"What the hell just happened?" She said, panting.

"I'm not sure," he said breathing hard, "but I liked it."

"We're going to be really late for the show if we keep this up."

"Or we could not make it at all," he said with a wicked smile.

"Get over yourself, we have to get moving, I'm in the third class!"

They left the tack room, put Cloudy in the van and took off for the show. They rode in silence for a while.

"Why were you so hostile to Bob?"

"I'm not sure. When he said he was taking you to the show, I got this flash of anger. Then another emotion popped up ... jealousy."

"Jealousy! Really?"

"Yeah," he said gruffly.

"You don't have any reason to be jealous of Bob. He's just an old friend from school and besides he's gay."

"That's good to know, but I don't have any right to be jealous of you and some other guy. I guess I'm assuming more than I should be at this point. I haven't sorted out what my feelings are yet and today surprised and confused me a little. I do have feelings for you, you know."

I can't believe he just said that. I'm overwhelmed and I wasn't planning on any distractions. Boy, was I wrong

There was a long silence. Then she said, quietly, "Well I guess I have feelings for you too."

He smiled.

"What just happened in the barn caught me off balance and we need to talk about it. I like you a lot but I wanted our relationship to progress farther before it got complicated with the sex thing. That's one reason why I didn't tell you who I am. My whole life has been filled with women who were attracted to me, because of who I am, my celebrity, the money, the connections."

Is he kidding? He thinks that's why women were attracted to him.

"Are you really that famous?" She asked.

"Well, apparently not, you never heard of me. I'm mostly well-known in European and UK racing circles. I did win Aintree four times."

"Aintree, like Grand National, Aintree?"

"Yes."

"Wow, now I am impressed."

"Well that's all ancient history now."

"Why do you say that?"

"Let's don't talk about my old crap. I'd rather talk about us."

"Good idea. So who owns the silver Porsche?"

"Me."

"And you own the whole farm?"

"I do, yes, but we all share in the profits from the racing stable. Well, Sean and Keary do and the lads all make around sixty thousand a year. I live on the money I made racing. I don't actually spend much. I live there and the racing stable is incorporated so it pays for all the farm supplies and any living expenses. I buy my own clothes and cars."

"What do you want to do now?" She said hesitantly, "You know, about us?"

"I think we should start dating like any normal couple. This deal of the princess and the stable hand is getting old."

She laughed nervously. "You think we're a couple?"

"Well, I guess I want that."

"I agree about dating but how are we going to decide when the sex thing won't complicate our relationship?"

"Let's just go out and have fun and see what happens. I haven't had any normal dating experience. I'm certainly not going to force you to do anything you're not ready for."

"I think I was ready back there at the barn."

"I know, I could tell and so was I."

"Okay, show time," Blackie said as they pulled into the show grounds.

They unloaded the horses, saddled Cloudy and left Sandman tethered to the van. Blacki gave her a leg up and she trotted to the ring and got in line for her first class-Novice Hunters. During the class as she was moving around the ring, she saw Blackie leaning against the railing sipping a beer. After a few minutes, she saw Bob approach Blackie.

Great, another pissing contest.

Bob said to Blackie, "Sorry if I interfered with anything going on between you and Meg."

"Don't worry, you didn't. I was being possessive when I don't have the right to be. Not yet anyway."

"She's a great girl and I don't want to see her get hurt."

"I don't ever intend to hurt her."

"I don't know if I trust that coming from someone like you." Bob replied.

"And why is that?"

"Well, you've got quite a reputation; as a world class steeplechase rider, but also as a real womanizer, someone who's heavy into alcohol and drugs, and also as a man who can be very dangerous."

"Gee thanks, but most of that is over. I haven't ridden since the accident or done much of anything except recuperate. However, I can still be dangerous if the need arises."

"I'll remember that." Bob said as he walked away.

After her last class, they loaded the horses and the equipment and got in the cab of the van. Blackie didn't start the engine and they just sat there.

"You did well with the classes today. You had some nice wins."

"Thanks."

He turned and looked at her. "We have to talk."

"I know."

"I think it's obvious that we have the *hots* for each other. What I need from you are some ground rules to control the situation until we're ready to move our relationship to a different level."

"I thought we had decided to date and see where it goes."

"Well, I guess I'm asking if I can kiss you whenever I want, you know that sort of stuff," he asked.

She smiled and said, "I'd be disappointed if you didn't."

"Great!" Scooting across the seat, he pulled her close and kissed her.

He can move fast. Oh, boy.

At first, his mouth was very soft and gentle. Then he kissed her deeper and more insistently. She was suddenly on fire as he moved his mouth down her neck and kept going until he got to lace. She couldn't breathe so she pushed him away.

Oh, my God, he's got to be the world's greatest kisser.

"I won't be able to control _myself_ if you keep kissing me like that. Look, Blackie, I don't exactly have a lot of experience in the ... ah ... sex department. So if you're expecting ..."

"I'll keep that in mind and I'm not expecting anything, Meg. I promise I'll ratchet it down a notch from now on."

"That's good." She said, closing the front of her shirt. Right then she wanted him to ratchet it up two or three notches.

"I guess now I have a ..." he stopped and looked at her, hesitating.

"What?"

"A ... *girlfriend?*" He just sat there staring at her for, she guessed, confirmation.

"Is that what I am?" She smiled.

"I think so. I hope so." He smiled big and said. "I've never had a girlfriend before."

"You're not serious?" She said in shocked disbelief.

"Seriously, never." he said. "That makes me feel great."

"Uh, me too." Meg couldn't believe he thought of her like that already. She also wondered what on earth was wrong with the rest of the women in the universe, that this guy had never had a girlfriend.

"You want to go out to dinner and maybe a movie tonight? I actually clean up pretty good."

"Sounds like a deal to me. Pick me up around seven o'clock."

"Perfect." he said and gave her one of those sexy smiles that lit up those big, blue eyes.

Dear Lord, what have I gotten myself into? He's incredible.

TWELVE

Meg drove home to get ready for her first date with Blackie. She was so excited. She took a long, hot shower and went through her closet, trying to decide what to wear.

She chose a periwinkle blue, wrap dress that showed a little cleavage. Leaving her hair hang long and loose, she used a touch of make-up. When she heard his car pull up, she flew downstairs to open the door.

"Wow, you look fantastic. A lot nicer than in your riding gear." He gave her one of those smiles and walked in. He looked scrumptious in khakis, a white shirt, navy, sport coat and a navy and red striped tie.

"You do clean up great. You don't look like a stable hand now."

He gave her a little bow and said, "Thank you, my lady." They got in the car and he asked, "Do you like Italian?"

"Yes, I love it."

"Good. I made reservations at this little place in Alexandria called Poro Ristarante. The food is good there."

They parked and he opened the car door and helped her out. He walked behind her but sort of guided her along with his hand lightly on her back.

She loved the restaurant, very upscale with nice linens and lots of atmosphere. He ordered dinner for them both along with some vintage year of red wine. Everything was delicious. He certainly was more sophisticated than she would have thought and started to relax with him.

"So, you're a famous jockey? You don't look like a jockey. You're pretty tall." She said.

"I'm five-ten, but remember I was a steeplechase jockey and they're usually normal size people, not small like flat racing jockeys."

"Why is that?"

"The steeplechase horses tend to be older, stronger and bigger. They can carry more weight. My racing weight was around one forty."

"You can't race at all anymore?" She asked.

"No, the accident put a stop to the racing."

"Was it a car wreck?"

"No, it was on the race track."

"What happened?"

"Actually, I don't remember the accident at all. I just remember waking up in the hospital in a morphine-induced haze. You'll have to ask Sean or Keary what happened."

Yeah, why the hell didn't I die in the stupid accident? How did I survive being trampled by all those horses?

"Were you hurt badly?"

"I was, yes. My right hip was ... Let's talk about you. Tell me about your work at the gallery?"

Okay, he doesn't want to talk about that.

"I love being around all the art and working with the artists. It's a very creative job."

"Can I come and see it sometime and maybe we could have lunch?"

"I'd love to show it to you. That would be fun. Do you miss your parents and Ireland a lot?"

"I do, yes. I love my parents but we don't see eye to eye on a couple of things."

"So Sean's your cousin and Jill's your sister. It's very much a family business then."

"Yes. Sean and I were raised together. His Dad and mine were brothers. My folks adopted him when his parents were killed in a car wreck when he was two.

He's six months older than me and we've always been close. You'd never know it the way we fight," he said and laughed.

"That's so sad, but it's neat that you guys are all together.

"I don't know what I would have done after the accident if it wasn't for them."

While they were talking, Blackie stopped and stared at her.

"What?" She said.

"You're really beautiful, you know," he said, seriously.

She was instantly flustered. She didn't know what to say. "Blackie, thank you, I'm embarrassed. No one ever told me that before."

"You're kidding, right? So you only dated men who were blind, then."

"No, it's just, well thank you, I'm very flattered," She said trying to gain some composure.

"I'm not trying to flatter you, it's what I see."

He sat there, pensive, for some time, deep in thought. She thought maybe he didn't want to talk anymore.

"Meg, do you believe in God?"

"Yes, I do."

"I mean do you really believe in that power?"

"Yes, completely. Why?"

"Why would God save someone from certain death?"

"I guess because God loved that person," she said, not sure where he was going with this.

"Suppose this person was wicked?"

"I'd think God loved this person in spite of it. It's all through the Bible how God loves and forgives people who have committed great sins."

"I mean why the Hell would he save this person? Should the person now do something to redeem himself? And what? Why would God give him a second chance?"

"Boy you're into some deep stuff here," she said hoping to lighten him up a bit.

"These are questions I've asked myself for a long time," he said frowning.

"You mean since your accident?"

"Yes."

"Maybe God has a new, more important plan for your life and he saved you to do that."

"You believe God has a plan for us all?" he asked.

"Yes I do and we, most of the time, don't even realize it's being played out. Do you believe you were that bad of a person?"

"There's no doubt in my mind. I did a lot of terrible things and enjoyed every minute of it. I know damn well, if the accident hadn't killed me, my lifestyle would have" he said with a grim set to his mouth.

"Maybe God caused your accident to make you take a closer look at your life and the things you were doing."

Blackie stared at her for a long time with a strange shocked look on his face. *This is a little spooky. What is he thinking?*

"Are you okay?" She asked softly.

"If that's true, then God took away the thing I loved most in the world. Is that my punishment?"

"I don't know if its punishment. I think more of a wakeup call to change your life."

"To do what? Change it how?"

"What did you do that was so awful?" She asked, sticking both feet in her mouth. She couldn't believe she had actually said that out loud.

He let out a big sigh, "I'd be too ashamed to tell you, Meg. I guess I need to tell you soon so you know what you're getting yourself into. I have a lot of emotional baggage, Meg, and some of it is serious. Not tonight, it's too soon in our relationship to dump all of it on you."

"I'm a big girl and I have some baggage of my own. What, are you going to wait until I'm hopelessly in love with you before you tell me? At that point, I won't be able to get out."

He looked at her again for a long time. "You're right; you should know all the shit up front."

"I care about the person you are *now* Blackie; the past is just that, past. What I've seen is a caring, hard-working man who has been through a lot and I want to know more."

"I'm afraid if you know more, you won't want me at all," he said with his head bowed.

"You have to trust that it won't come to that," she said reaching over and touching his hand.

"Okay, promise me you'll let me know straight, if you want out, if it's too much for you."

"I will, I promise. Hey, could we lighten this up a little? We're supposed to be having fun on our first date," she said, trying to be upbeat when she had a sick feeling in her gut.

"You're right, that was all kind of heavy. Let's hit a movie; you can pick a chic flick. That should be upbeat."

"Okay, let's go."

They saw 'Fools Gold', a cute and funny movie. Blackie reached over during the movie and took her hand. His skin was warm and rough, but his grasp gentle. She had a hard time concentrating on the movie with him touching her. It was delicious! They laughed a lot during the movie and his mood had definitely improved.

"Do you want to get coffee and dessert? I'm still hungry," he asked, with a shy smile.

"Let's walk. I'm stuffed but I could use coffee. I wouldn't want to deprive you of more to eat, either."

"I'm not that hungry, I just don't want the evening to end yet. I'm having a good time, Meg."

"Me too, I haven't dated in quite some time and it feels good to be out."

"It's nice to be *sober* and be with a woman," he said and stopped dead and stared at her.

"That probably wasn't a smart thing for me to say on the first date," he blushed and blew out a big sigh.

"You mean you have a drinking problem?"

"Not anymore. It's just there was always a lot of partying going on after the races and that's where I usually met women."

He stopped again and his shoulders slumped, "Can we change the subject?" He said with a frown.

"Sure, I'm sorry I said that."

"That's okay, but you're right," he said and didn't say anything for a while. They finally got to the Cheesecake Factory and went in. They talked more over coffee and dessert; mostly about the horses.

"Tomorrow why don't you come and have breakfast and visit with Jill while I work. I have to help Sean load horses and he's going to the track with them so he won't be around. I can't actually believe we're finally doing this. I've been thinking about asking you out for some time but wasn't sure if you'd want to go," he said.

"Why wouldn't I? You should have asked. See, we've been wasting all this time."

"Keary's going to be in D.C. in the morning, so we'll have the place almost to ourselves.

We can play with Sandman all day in the arena. How does that sound?"

"That's a good idea. I want you to ride him and not worry about getting caught."

"They don't scare me. I'm tough;" he laughed. "Anyway, I don't feel like getting in another fight right now, but I'm not backing down."

"Hey, by the way, how'd you get the name 'Blackie'?"

"Well, when I was born, I had all this black hair. My dad started calling me 'his little Blackie' and I guess it stuck." He laughed.

"Awww ... that's so cute! But what's your real name? What does 'SBL' stand for?"

He stopped laughing and blushed again.

Uh-oh. Maybe I shouldn't have asked. Why am I always saying the wrong thing to him?

I need to think about all this when I'm alone.

"It's just this old-fashioned Irish name. It's long and sounds dumb. Do you have a middle name?"

"Yes, it's Elizabeth." She told him, realizing that he'd just changed the subject again away from himself.

"Megan Elizabeth, very pretty."

They drove to her condo slowly. She didn't want the date to end either.

"Okay, this is Sunday; do you want to go out Wednesday night?"

"I'd love to."

He pulled up in front of her place and turned the car off. He just sat there for a few minutes. "I really had a good time, Meg."

"Me too, this was wonderful."

Is he going to kiss me or what?

He looked at her for a few minutes, then sighed and got out of the car. When they got to her door he turned her around and kissed her. Sparks went off in her head. He had a very sweet, gentle mouth. Then he put his arms around her, drew her against him and kissed her again. This kiss was hot! His mouth was not as gentle as he slipped his tongue in her mouth and groaned. She almost passed out. That kiss was incredible! His mouth said he wanted more but he pulled away from her.

"Do you want to come in?" She breathed.

"No, I better not. I don't want to come in until I can stay all night," he said firmly.

"Okay, that's a pretty good idea. I'll see you tomorrow. Good night."

He leaned over and kissed her quickly. "Sweet dreams," he said and smiled. He jogged down the steps and roared off in the Porsche.

"Sweet dreams." She said out loud and sighed. "That's putting it mildly."

THIRTEEN

The next morning Meg drove to the farm with her head in the clouds. She had to pinch herself to realize she wasn't dreaming. Jill was in the kitchen with a cup of tea when Meg entered.

"Good morning." Jill smiled at her.

"Good morning to you. Has Blackie been in yet?" Meg asked hopefully.

"He has, yes. You missed him by ten minutes. He'll be back before too long."

Meg guessed that she must have looked crestfallen because Jill started to laugh.

"What?" Meg said.

"You two are going to be sooo cute together."

"What do you mean?"

"You and Blackie. He's been in here all morning chattering away about your date last night. He never shut up. Keary didn't know what to do. He just watched him go on and on and listened with this little smile on his face."

"Oh God, what did he say? Did he have a good time?" Meg asked breathlessly.

"Yes, Meg, I think he had a wonderful time. He's very happy this morning."

"Oh, I almost forgot. I didn't see you after the show. Did he tell you about the fight we had yesterday?"

"A fight! No, he didn't say anything. What happened?"

"I found out who he is and I was so pissed at him for lying to me."

"Meg, what are you talking about? What do you mean, who he is?"

"Oh, just the fact that he's a famous jockey, his name is O'Brien and he owns this farm, that's all. All this time I assumed he was a stable hand. I feel so stupid."

"I thought you knew. You mean he didn't even tell you his name. That's ridiculous. Why would he do that?"

"He said because he wanted me to like him without knowing who he was."

"I guess that made sense to him. What happened after the fight?"

"Well, we sort of made up in the tack room." Meg said with a sly smile. "Then we went to the show and he asked me to go out after for dinner."

"Now I know why he was whistling this morning." Jill said with a chuckle.

"He said we should start dating like normal people."

"That's a great idea and he did have fun last night."

"Oh, God, that's fantastic." She hugged Jill.

"He was worried that he messed up. Apparently he said something that he thought was going to put you off," Jill said quizzically.

"Oh, I'm sorry he's worried about it. He didn't mess anything up. I was a little concerned when he said it."

"What did he say?" Jill asked, frowning.

"We were talking about finally dating. I said I hadn't dated in awhile. Then he said it was good to be sober and be with a woman. He instantly got upset about saying that."

"Oh, God, poor guy," Jill said, "He wants to change all that so much."

"What happened to him? Does he have a drinking problem?" Meg asked hesitantly.

"Oh gosh, Meg. I don't know where to start. No, he doesn't have an alcohol problem now, but he did. Let me go back a bit," Jill said with a sigh.

"No one's ever had much control over Blackie, even our parents. They had a little bit when he was younger, but once he turned eighteen, that was that. He pretty much ran wild and then he fell under the influence of this agent named Mickey Reegan. Mickey made a lot of money off Blackie's talent and managed to get Blackie in a lot of trouble. He was one of the major "movers and shakers" of the jet set type among the racing crowd. He introduced Blackie to all the wild partying including alcohol, women and drugs."

"Drugs!" Meg exclaimed.

"Yes, unfortunately, he was addicted to cocaine. He's trying very hard to get past all that. A lot of bad things happened to him because of Mickey's influence. Blackie won't talk about most of it. I hope you'll give him a chance to prove that he's changed. He really is a good guy."

"I know he is, Jill, and, of course, I'll give him a chance. Who am I not to?" she asked.

I'm not so sure about this. Drugs, for God's sake! How am I going to deal with that? This is just the kind of thing I didn't want to distract me, damnit. I like him so much, though.

"Meg, I don't quite know how to put this, but Blackie has always been a sort of wild and free spirit. My Dad loves it. He says it goes back to his ancestors who were Irish warriors and kings. Dad has always encouraged it; however, it makes it hard on the rest of us. Dad says he has this *warrior spirit* inside him and that's what drives him. It's been subdued since the accident, but I see it starting to surface again as he gets better. If you had seen him ride in a race, you'd know what I mean. He could ride any horse and get them over jumps just by the strength of his will. He was unbelievable to watch." Jill suddenly looked sad. "I'll never see him ride like that again. He's so different now, unsure of himself. Sean gets so upset because of the way Blackie is now. He's the youngest of all of us, but Blackie was always the leader, always fearless."

"You know Jill, he might surprise you," Meg said with a secret little smile. Jill looked at her quizzically but didn't ask.

"Is he really descended from warriors?"

"Meg, he *is* descended from fierce warrior kings who took Ireland by force from other kings and invaders, like the Vikings. He's the direct, male descendent of Brian Boru, the last High King of Ireland."

"You're kidding, right?" she said, completely dumbfounded.

"No, I'm not kidding. Our dad is the current king or would be if Ireland had one but he's content to breed horses and sit in Parliament. So Blackie is next in line."

"This is unbelievable. I have to have time for all this to sink in. What am *I* supposed to do with him? I can't handle some *wild spirit*," Meg said, completely blown away by all this information. "And another thing, what's with that crazy tattoo down his back?"

"Uh … Meg, uh … " Jill paled, then changed the subject. "Calm down, sweetie, you already have more control over him than any of us ever did."

Just then, Blackie came breezing in the door. "Hello, ladies," he said cheerfully. He walked over and kissed Meg softly on the mouth, "And how are you this morning?" he said with his head back just a few inches so she got the full impact of those gorgeous eyes.

"I'm fantastic, how about you," she said, mesmerized by him.

"Never better" and he kissed her again lightly and smiled. He prowled around the kitchen looking for something to eat. He came up with a handful of leftover bacon and a biscuit.

"I'm still hungry," he said pouring a cup of coffee and sitting down with his snack.

Jill looked at Meg with wide eyes and raised eyebrows, trying, not too successfully, to hide a smile.

"Okay, are you ready to go and play with the horses," he asked Meg.

"Definitely, I can't wait," she said, jumping up. He drained his cup and gave Jill a hug.

"We'll see you later."

*   *   *

They went to the barn; he saddled Sandman and led him to the indoor arena. Blackie vaulted into the saddle and adjusted the stirrups. Gathering the reins, he moved off with Sandy dancing a little, but settled down right away.

He started Sandman at a loose rein, extended walk and the horse relaxed. Blackie took up the reins and used his legs to get the horse into a collected walk, with Sandy's forehand very light and his weight back on his hindquarters. He moved him into a collected trot and did some beautiful circles then into the center, reversing the direction he was going and back out to the rail to circle again at the opposite end.

On the other side of the arena, Blackie made him do a half-pass to the right. A half-pass is where the horse moves forward and diagonally at the same time by crossing its legs in front of each other. At the center X, he moved smoothly into a half-pass to the left and back to the arena wall. Meg was in awe. She didn't have a clue that Sandman could do any of this and Blackie hadn't as much as moved an eyelid. He still remained in perfect balance and position.

He put the horse into a collected canter and did a circle at the end of the arena, then crossed diagonally through the center X changing leads and then did another circle at the other end. He tracked to the left and put Sandman into an extended trot, which was breathtaking. He just floated along the ground.

Blackie brought him back to a medium then a collected trot and moved half-way around the arena then slowed to a walk and finally let him have his head on a loose rein. He stopped in front of her and she could tell Blackie was excited.

"He moves well and responds instantly to my aids. He's great! I love riding him."

"That was fantastic, you're unbelievable. I didn't know he was trained to do that."

Blackie actually blushed from the praise. "I'm kinda out of practice."

He dismounted and patted Sandman. "Good boy, great job. It won't take much work to get him doing upper level tests."

"Really!" She said, excited. "So you think he can do it?"

"I do, yes. Let's cool him off."

After they wiped the sweat off Sandman and brushed him down, they turned him out in one of the paddocks. Blackie carried the tack and she stowed the grooming equipment in the tack room.

He came up behind her and touched her hair. She turned around and he was very close. He put his hand on her cheek and gently ran his thumb over her mouth, looking at it hungrily and then moved his eyes up to hers. She saw desire in his eyes and something else, longing.

He moved his hand to the back of her neck, drew her face to his and kissed her. He kissed her mouth, then her cheek and then soft little kisses all around her mouth. It made her tremble. She let herself drift into his aura of desire.

He put his leg in between hers, pulled her into him and engulfed her with a long, deep kiss. She was suddenly on fire. She leaned back against a saddle rack and opened her legs for him. He pushed his leg farther in between hers, ran his hands under her shirt and up her back. She suddenly couldn't breathe.

He started kissing her shoulder and ran his tongue all the way up her neck and into her mouth again. She was starting to feel out of control. He was making muffled groaning sounds and breathing harder.

"Blackie," she breathed into his ear.

"What?" he said softly.

"I thought we were going to control this and wait," she said reluctantly. He didn't say anything. He sighed and hugged her tighter with his face in her hair. He held her until his breathing slowed and he moved back and looked at her.

"You're right. I said I would control it and not let it get out of hand. I'm not doing too good a job am I?" He sort of laughed.

"That's okay, I'm not helping much either," she said and ran her fingers through his hair. He put his head down on her shoulder and blew out another big sigh.

"Wow," he said as he moved slightly away from her. "This is not going to be easy."

"Thank you." She said kissing him lightly. "Most guys wouldn't have stopped."

"Well, I respect you and our decision and I believe in keeping my word, no matter how hard it is." He looked at her and laughed. "That wasn't a good choice of words, was it?"

"Oh yeah, I guess not," she chuckled too.

"Let's go up to the house and have lunch. Are you hungry?" he asked her.

"Yes, actually I'm famished."

*   *   *

As they walked up to the house, he put his arm around her neck, pulled her head ove and gave her a 'Dutch rub' on top of her head with his knuckles. She grabbed for him but he swiveled out of reach and backpedalled in front of her, laughing. She ran after him and he turned around and scooted in the kitchen door, laughing harder. Keary and Jill looked up as they burst into the dining room still laughing.

"Hello, you two. Sounds like you had a good morning," Keary said smiling.

"We did, yes." Blackie answered and jumped in line for food. Meg looked at them and they were both smiling with raised eyebrows and a questioning look.

FOURTEEN

"Hey, Jill, can Meg ride Black Jack after lunch?" Blackie asked her suddenly. Meg looked at him in astonishment.

"Sure, I don't see why not. What are you guys doing?" she asked.

"I want to show Meg some dressage movements and how to execute them. Cloudy isn't responsive enough and Sandy's too much for her, so I'd like to use Black Jack. I'll put them on the lunge line first. Is that okay with you?"

"Yes, can I come and watch? I might learn something," Jill asked.

"Yes, of course, and I doubt if I can teach you anything you don't already know," Blackie said as he got up. "I'm going to take a short nap in the TV room. Don't let me sleep too long," he said to Meg.

He did look tired and as she watched him walk down the hall toward the family room, she thought he might be limping slightly. Uh, oh! She hoped Jill hadn't noticed.

*   *   *

Meg stomach was so jittery so thought so might throw up. Just the thought of riding Jill's warm-blood stallion and learning from Blackie was almost overwhelming. She hoped she could do what he wanted. She knew how good he was as a rider; now what kind of teacher was he? Blackie went in Black Jack's stall and led him out. He was unbelievably beautiful! Blackie cross-tied him and started grooming him.

"Are you sure he's not too much for me," she asked.

"You'll do fine. He's very gentle and a lot easier to handle than Sandman."

"Okay, if you say so, but I've never ridden a stallion and the idea is a little scary."

"It just makes him more sensitive. You'll see. Hey, all of us studs are more sensitive." "Oh, gag me, very funny."

"I'm going to put you on the lunge line first until you get used to him."

He saddled the horse, using Jill's dressage tack and led him out of the barn. He had a special halter on Black Jack over the bridle with the line attached. They went into the arena and Blackie gave her a leg up. He started adjusting the stirrups and studying her sitting there.

"A dressage seat is a lot deeper than a jumping seat, so your legs need to be longer. You have to have a lot of flank contact." He put her foot in the stirrup after adjusting it, stood back and looked. He lowered it another notch and studied her again. He seemed satisfied.

Just then, Jill came into the arena and waved.

"Hi guys, hi Black Jack.' The horse pricked his ears and nickered at her voice.

"Awww, that's so sweet, Black Jack said "Hi", too," Meg said and waved to Jill.

"Okay, you two, cut out the girlie stuff," he said, still focused on what he was doing.

Meg made a face at him and Jill laughed.

"Okay, move your legs back, they're too far forward and put your heels down. Your seat has to be really deep."

"It feels awkward and unstable," she said.

"I know, it will at first, but once you get into it, you'll be surprised how much better you ride," he said. He stepped back and studied her again.

"Legs back a little bit more. Okay, now pick up the reins. Just use the snaffle and leave the curb loose for now. Hands lower and back over the pommel." He looked at her again.

"Okay," he moved away from her and whistled softly, "Black Jack, siuil (Gaelic for walk)," and the horse started walking in a circle around Blackie as he gradually let the line out so the circle got bigger.

"Okay, get some contact with his mouth and flex your calf muscles."

Black Jack became collected and pricked his ears. He was now alert and ready to do what she asked him.

"Okay, now squeeze your calf muscles quickly and relax and he should trot. I don't want you to post, just sit to it."

She did what he told her and Black Jack went into a slow, smooth trot. She couldn't believe how sensitive he was. She felt insecure, however.

"Keep your legs still; they're all over the place." Blackie said softly to her.

"Now when I tell you, squeeze your right hand and at the same time, move your right leg back an inch. Do it now."

Black Jack moved into a slow, rocking canter on the correct lead. Meg was amazed! This horse was so responsive!

"Keep your legs still," Blackie said again, more firmly. She tried to concentrate on sitting deeper, using her balance and relaxing her legs.

"That's it, good girl," Blackie said

She kept going around and was kind of getting the hang of it. She stole a look at Blackie and he was smiling.

"Okay, now when I tell you, bend your hands in and get deep in the saddle. Flex your butt muscles slightly, okay now!" She did what he said but Black Jack did not slow down.

"Relax, Meg," Blackie said evenly. She concentrated on relaxing and sitting deeper and the horse slowed to a walk. Wow! This was so cool. She loved it! Blackie said something else to the horse and he turned in and stopped in front of Blackie.

"That was good, Meg. If you work on the lunge without stirrups, your seat will feel more secure."

"That was wonderful, Meg," Jill applauded and ran into the center with them. She patted the horse's neck and scratched his face.

"You guys should use him for Meg. I only get time to ride him maybe two to three times a week and that isn't enough exercise for him," Jill offered.

"Are you sure, Jill, because that would be great? Cloudy is just not up to this." Blackie said.

"Jill, I can't ask you to do that, this horse is too good," Meg said.

"I'm serious, he needs the exercise. Blackie, are you going to show her some more exercises?" Jill asked him.

"I wasn't today, no. I wanted to show her some aids and work on her seat. Why, do you want to ride him?"

"No, I wanted to watch *you* ride him," Jill said looking at him seriously.

"What?" He looked at her with wide eyes. "But I haven't."

"Oh yes you have, you don't fool me," she said, smiling at him. He glanced at Meg and then back at Jill.

"I, uh ... but what about Keary?"

"If I thought you'd get hurt doing this, I'd tell him, but I don't think you will."

He looked at Meg again and she nodded. He waited until she dismounted and then vaulted into the saddle. He sat there and looked at Jill again.

"It's okay, honey, go ahead," Jill said.

He sighed, adjusted the stirrups for his legs. He worked the horse around the arena, doing just general moves and was perfect. Then he started doing incredible stuff. He was doing half-pass, shoulder-in, flying changes, passage. Meg was mesmerized! She looked at Jill who had tears in her eyes.

"He's so brilliant. I love watching him ride," Jill said. "What a miracle he is. We never thought he'd walk again and look at him."

"I know." Meg said, savoring the look of joy on his face

At that point, he rode over to them and dismounted. "What'd you think?" he asked Jill.

"You're awesome," she said and hugged him. "How have you been practicing? Does it hurt your hip?

"First, are you telling Keary?" he asked her.

"No, not if you don't want me to."

"Not yet. I've been riding Sandman and he's good. At first my hip was sore but now I'm used to it."

"Good. What are you planning to do with this?" Jill asked

"We thought we'd enter some low-level competitions soon and see how he goes. Other than that, I'm not sure where we're going with it."

"Actually there are a lot of competitions going on now. They're usually Training Level classes up to Gran Prix and you're good enough to enter third or fourth level. Meg should start with the Training classes," Jill told him.

"You think so? Jill, that sounds good, I think we'll do that. Thanks, Jill," Blackie told her as they walked back to the barn. Blackie groomed Black Jack and turned him out. Jill went up to the house and Meg stayed to keep him company finishing up.

"Hey, I'm really tired. I think I'll crash and see you in the morning. I had a great day and you did a fantastic job on Black Jack," Blackie said as he put his arms around her.

"I had a wonderful day and thank you for showing me the dressage."

"You're welcome," he said as he kissed her. "You know I really miss you when you go home. I can hardly wait until morning," he said as he kissed her again, deeper and then said, "Good night, Meg."

"Good night, Blackie.

*　　　*　　　*

Meg got to the stable late the next morning and Blackie was already hard at work.

"Hey," he said and kissed her lightly on the mouth. "I put the horses in the paddock and I'm almost done the stalls."

"You don't always have to clean my stalls; it's my responsibility," she hugged him, "but thank you anyway."

"I don't mind, I need to do things around here anyway. Actually I want to work Sandman again and get him really moving on the dressage program."

"Well let's finish up these stalls."

They finished putting down some sawdust and then put clean straw on top. Blackie stood there and sniffed the bedding.

"I love the way fresh straw smells."

"So do I," she said and pushed him down on top of it, jumped on him and started tickling him. He was rolling around laughing, trying to get away from her. He pulled her down in the straw and they were rolling around laughing like kids. Suddenly he stopped and looked at her with that hungry look, kissed her hard and pulled her on top of him. He ripped her shirt open, grabbed her breasts roughly and then put his hands between her legs. She felt a frenzied urgency to be against him, kissed him deeply and held him down with her knee. She kissed him again and pulled his shirt over his head. His eyes were fierce with desire. He suddenly rolled over on top of her and she could feel how hard he was. He was gasping for breath as he pushed her legs apart and pressed himself against her. He moved his hips back and forth and she came in a burst of exquisite sensation and cried out in a prolonged gasp.

He rolled off and was still breathing as if he had been running. She lay there completely spent.

"Oh God!" She sobbed, "I'm so embarrassed!"

"No, no don't be, it was completely my fault."

"I shouldn't have started playing around and teasing you."

"No, I'm a grown man, not a teenager. I should be able to control myself."

She sat up and he pulled her over, drying her tears with his fingers.

"Come on, sweetie, don't cry. It's not that bad. I promised you I wouldn't do this and I'm sorry."

He leaned back and unzipped his jeans and she said, "What the hell are you doing now?"

He laughed, "These jeans are too damn tight for this stuff. It hurts."

"Cute!" She said and got to her feet.

"I'll be with you in a few minutes after I calm down."

She glared at him as she grabbed her top and left him in the stall. She ran into the tack room to put her clothes back in some kind of order. Her hands were shaking. She always had such an intense reaction every time he touched her.

I've got to get a grip on myself. He's not going to control this so I need to, somehow.

She was buttoning her shirt when he walked into the tack room. He turned her around and she made an exasperated sound and gesture. He took his hands off her quickly and held them up defensively.

"Meg, I'm sorry! Are you angry with me?"

"Yes, I am! Oh no, not really." She told him. "Oh, I don't know what I am. This is getting ridiculous. Either sleep with me or stop getting me so hot and bothered!"

He stood there looking contrite. He reached out and started buttoning her blouse.

"You're right, Meg." he said. "It's just whenever I'm near you, I can't control it. You have to admit that today you started it. I was just innocently standing there sniffing the straw and you jumped me. You can't really blame me if I got in the spirit of the whole thing."

He smiled as he finished buttoning her shirt. She couldn't help herself. She had to smile at him being defensive.

"Okay, you. You do have a point," she said playfully, punching him in the gut. He faked bending double in pain. She pulled him up by his hair and he was smiling.

"You *know* I'm right!" She said

"I know, I agree. I'll try to keep it light, I promise," he said and took her in his arms and kissed her very sweetly.

"You know, I forgot, I have to go to DC with Keary to see the accountants. I have to go get changed. I'll see you later then," he kissed her again and left the barn.

FIFTEEN

The next day when Meg got to the barn, Blackie had Sandman already saddled. He looked up when she walked in.

"Good morning, Meg, how are you this morning?" he said cheerily.

"I'm great; it's good to see you. I missed you last night," she walked over and kissed him. He pulled her close and kissed her back.

"I missed you too," he said huskily.

"Down cowboy, weren't you doing something?"

"Hey, you came over and kissed *me*," he said angrily and stuffed his hands in his pockets. "You always blame me for letting things get out of hand, but you sure as hell spread your legs when I want you to and don't call me *cowboy,* damnit."

His words were like a slap in the face. She was shocked and had to fight back the tears.

"That just shows you that I'm as frustrated as you are. I want you so bad I can't stand it but we have to wait until *you* figure out how you feel about me. What crap!"

She turned and stomped out of the barn. He ran after her and grabbed her arm, swinging her around to face him.

"Meg, we can't fight over this. Both of us are too stressed out over it. Please forgive me for saying that. Your comment just hit me the wrong way. I'm really sorry."

She saw remorse and pleading in his eyes. She moved into his arms and hugged him.

"I'm sorry too. I know it's not all your fault. It's plenty mine too. I don't want to fight either. I'm sorry I made you angry. I didn't mean to." She put her face up to him and he kissed her.

"Okay, can we start this morning over again?" He asked her.

"You bet. Let's get to the arena."

Blackie led Sandman and put his other arm around her shoulder.

"I'll get my head straight about this soon, I promise, honey."

"I'll wait as long as it takes," she said.

"Okay, thanks."

God, I can't stand not having her. If I don't sleep with her soon, I'm going to go raving, fucking insane. It terrifies me though. What if I sleep with her and then I hate her and don't want her again just like all the hookers and party girls I've been with. I know I love her. I can't ruin this.

*   *   *

They went into the arena and Blackie led Sandman to the center. He vaulted into the saddle and started the horse through gaits and movements. She watched and as usual was in awe of his talent. He worked for almost an hour and then was cooling Sandman down when Meg heard the door open. Sean came in and stood next to her.

"What the hell is he doing? He knows he's not supposed to be riding. Son of a bitch! He always does exactly what he wants to do." Sean started to get loud; Blackie heard him and turned toward them.

"This is entirely your fault! Why are you letting him ride your horse? You're encouraging him to go against his family!" Sean yelled at her.

Blackie jumped off Sandman and got in Sean's face.

"Don't ever yell at her again! This was my idea, not hers!" he yelled at Sean with his fists clenched.

"Then what the fuck is wrong with you? Hasn't this family gone through enough? Are you trying to *finally* kill yourself?" Sean yelled back.

"What about what *I've* been through? I can't give up riding no matter what you all say and I won't! I'm not backing down!" Blackie yelled.

"You selfish bastard! We didn't think you'd live much less walk again and look at you. But you're not satisfied with merely walking you have to ride too. You can't have everything you want. Now she's encouraging you *against us!*"

At that, Blackie slugged him hard and Sean hit the ground, out cold. Blood running out of his nose.

"Shit," Blackie yelled and hit the wall with his fist.

"Fuck," he paced back and forth a couple times and then took out his cell.

"Keary, get over to the arena and bring some ice. Sean's probably got another broken nose," he paused and blew out a big sigh. "I hit him," he said and hung up.

He put the phone in his pocket and knelt down beside Sean.

"Sean, come on buddy, wake up." Sean groaned and stirred slightly when Blackie patted his shoulder.

"Be prepared for another fight when Keary gets here," Blackie warned her. "Could you get hold of Sandman while I watch Sean?"

"Sure." She ran into the arena, calling the horse who looked scared.

Keary and Jill came in with a couple packs of ice. They knelt down over Sean and put the ice on his head and nose. He moaned and rolled over onto his back. Jill had a towel and dabbed at his nose. Keary jumped up and went after Blackie.

"What the hell is wrong with you?" Keary yelled in his face but Blackie held his ground. "What was *this* about?"

"I was riding Sandman and Sean came in and started yelling at Meg, saying it was her fault."

"Just grand, the same old shit! Was it worth hurting Sean again? What is wrong with you? When are you going to control yourself? I'm sure he wasn't picking on Meg on purpose. Why can't you keep your little, million-dollar ass off a horse? Do you have a death wish?" Keary yelled at him.

Meg saw Jill start to say something and Blackie shook his head at her and she kept quiet.

"No. I don't have a death wish. I know if I can handle a horse or not. He needs to leave Meg out of this fight. It was my idea and I asked her if I could ride her horse. She's had misgivings about it from the beginning. Why can't you all see that I'm not doing anything dangerous! I'm sorry Keary, but I can't give up riding. It's too much a part of who I am!"

"If you'd actually *accept* who you are, maybe you'd be more careful. We've tried to protect you so the line can continue, but all you've ever done is be reckless. You don't give a shit for the feelings of those who love you."

"Oh, Christ, don't bring that bullshit up again," Blackie said.

"Oh, yes, thousands of years of Irish kings is bullshit! I'm really tired of that attitude!" Keary yelled.

"Blackie, what is he talking about?" Meg asked, confused about this continuing fight.

"Meg, I already told you!" Jill exclaimed.

"I didn't think you were serious. I guess it didn't sink in."

"I'm the fucking prince of Ireland, that's who I am and I don't want any part of it. Nobody recognizes the nobility in Ireland. It's archaic, elitist, sexist, and stupid. I don't want to hurt you guys, but this is *my* body and *my* life and I'm going to live it *my* way! Come on Meg," he grabbed her hand and pulled her and Sandman behind him as he walked out of the arena.

"Don't go far, you two. I want to talk to you both after lunch," Keary yelled after them.

*   *   *

Blackie walked fast and she could hardly keep up with him. He kicked stones out of the way as they walked. She didn't want to say much of anything until he cooled down. He unsaddled Sandman and started brushing him down so hard the horse was quivering in fright.

"Here, let me do that," she said and he handed her the brush and stuffed his hands in his pockets. He started pacing and kicked whatever was handy- a bucket, the wall. Sandman was skittish and jumpy.

"Blackie, go outside and kick stuff, you're scaring the horse," she said, finally.

"Shit!" he said and sat on a hay bale.

She finished grooming, put Sandman in the stall and sat next to Blackie. She took his hand in hers and he squeezed it. She could feel how tense he was.

"What are we going to do?"

"I'm going to keep riding and I don't give a shit if they don't like it. What's he going to do, fire me, throw me off the farm? I wish they'd just leave me alone."

"Jill was going to tell him she knew and take up for you. Why didn't you let her?"

"I don't want to start trouble between her and Keary. I don't want her to have to take -sides. He's her husband and I'm her brother. She should stand with him. It's not your fight either. It's between me and Keary. I won't stand for anyone putting any blame for this on you. It's totally my decision to ride. You tell me if Sean bullies you again."

"Honey, Sean didn't do anything to me; he was just upset." she said trying to placate him. She didn't want him fighting with them over her.

"No, I won't tolerate him yelling at you like that. I won't have it," he said, raising his voice.

"Okay, calm down." He took her hand in both of his and rubbed it. She could see how unhappy he was over this situation. His family loved him dearly and he loved them the same, but this was tearing them apart. She put her arm around him and he leaned his head on her shoulder and sighed.

"I don't know what I'm going to do about this. It's too much stress. I don't want to have to hide what I'm doing. It makes me feel creepy." He put both arms around her and they sat there like that for a long time. She could feel him start to relax a little. He raised his head and kissed her very gently.

"Do you think I'm being selfish and stubborn, Meg?"

"No, I understand how you feel about riding. I also understand that they're terrified that something will happen and you'll be crippled or worse. I worry about that myself when I know you're going to ride. Jill's just happy that you're alive and can walk. I don't think any of them are able to get past that. Not yet, anyway."

"I don't want to worry or hurt them, but I have *some* confidence in my ability to ride again. I didn't have that confidence back six months ago. Now that I've been riding, it's starting to come back. Before the accident, I knew I could do anything. I was fearless, nothing stopped me. I want that feeling again, but everyone's fears are undermining that."

"You'll get it back; it will just take awhile longer. Hey, what did Keary mean about your million-dollar butt?"

"Oh, that. It cost a little over a million bucks to fix my hip."

"A million dollars! Why'd it cost so much?"

"They got this doctor, a reconstruction, orthopaedic specialist from Zurich. I guess he was kind of pricey. He had to replace a lot of bone, like my hip joint; it's stainless steel and titanium."

"He did an amazing job. Your hip looks good and works incredibly well from the way you ride."

"Thanks, Meg. I'm glad you like the result."

"Yes, I do. Does it feel funny?" she asked him.

""No, I can't tell the difference from the other hip. My right side is heavier and I've had to learn to compensate."

"Why is it heavier?"

"There's a lot of metal besides the joint, holding it all together. I don't notice it unless I'm diving, then I have to compensate to keep my body straight."

"Diving? You mean like in a pool?"

"Yes. I used to dive for Cornell when I was up there."

"That's cool. You're amazing and ...

"Fuck it! Let's go get lunch and stay for the lecture afterwards," he said kissing her again.

"Oh great, that sounds like fun," she said as they walked up to the house.

SIXTEEN

Keary and Jill were eating lunch when they got to the dining room.

"Where's Sean?" Blackie asked them.

"He's lying down with ice on his face as usual," Keary said, scowling at him.

"Keary, you know I don't want to hurt him, he just knows how to push my buttons." Blackie said defensively.

"Oh really, how the hell would I know that, you've broken his nose like four times. Pretty soon he won't be able to breathe."

Jill looked at Meg and rolled her eyes. Blackie stared at Keary a minute as if he was going to argue. Then he turned and went up the stairs.

Keary threw his napkin down and said, "Jill, Meg, you guys better talk to him and see if you can get him under control. The next time he hits Sean, I'm going to call the police and charge him with assault!"

"Keary, you wouldn't! You know how much trouble he'll get in," Jill pleaded.

"Why would he get into a lot of trouble," Meg asked, her stomach clenching.

"Because he's a martial arts instructor and he'd be charged with 'assault with a Deadly weapon'," Keary said wearily.

"I knew I didn't want to hear that answer. What else don't I know about him?" She exclaimed.

"That's another thing! When is he going to come clean with this girl who he supposedly loves?"

"He told you he loves me?"

"Jesus Christ, you mean he hasn't told *you* yet?" Keary said, shaking his head.

"Keary, calm down, please! Hasn't today been bad enough?" Jill said, giving Meg a tired, little smile.

"I don't know what to do with him. He says he's not backing down on the riding thing," Meg told them.

"Okay, you two are going to hear all about that God-awful accident and then maybe he'll appreciate how *we* feel. I even have a video of the thing."

"Oh, good God, Keary! You wouldn't show them that?" Jill said, alarmed. "I can't watch it," she said, visibly shaken.

"I know, honey, I won't show them, but it might get through that thick skull of his."

Just then, Sean and Blackie came downstairs. Blackie had his arm around Sean's shoulder and they were laughing. Sean had a purple eye and a swollen nose.

"I see you two made up, good. So, Blackie, you're determined that you're going to ride, no matter how we feel?" Keary said bluntly.

"Keary, I understand how much I put you all through with the accident, but …

"Blackie you have no idea the nightmare that this family went through with that accident.

I know you don't remember any of it and I'm thankful to God that you don't. However, I'm going to tell you and Meg exactly what happened so you know where we're coming from. It's not that we want to take riding away from you; we know how much you love it. We're just terrified that something will happen to you." Keary said, his voice wavering.

"I won't give it up. I'm not going to get hurt, damnit."

"Shut up, Blackie and listen."

"It was two years ago and Blackie was winning the Cheltenham Gold Cup in England. He was in front by a length and a half and in his favorite position, second from the rail. They took the last fence, his horse tripped, went down and

Blackie landed on his back. He quickly rolled to his side and his helmet popped off. We were watching this through binoculars.

It was the most terrifying thing to see and then it got worse! It looked like the horse behind him landed right on him and then kicked him in the head." Keary told them haltingly. He had to stop to get himself under control.

Jill jumped up. "I can't listen to this," she said and went upstairs.

Blackie was frowning.

"Then the next horse hit you. Then the rest of the field went past and we couldn't see you anymore. We ran to the ambulance but it had already left so the guards took us out to the track."

"When we got there, it was the worst thing we'd ever seen. Your sister fainted as soon as she saw you. Sean and I went out on the track after you with the paramedics."

Keary choked up and Sean had tears in his eyes.

"Blackie, when we got to you it was like a war zone. There was blood everywhere. Your head and face were covered in blood, your silks were red; the fucking grass was red. Sean threw up and I thought I was going to pass out. We thought for sure you were dead." Keary took a deep breath.

"The medics said they got a pulse. They put a collar on your neck and carefully put you on a back board. As soon as they turned you over, you started having trouble breathing, so they intubated you. That helped a little but not much. They started all kind of IV's. I rode in the ambulance with you and those guys were doing everything they could to keep you alive."

Blackie was staring wide-eyed at Keary.

"They took you into the ER and let me stay for a few minutes. They cut your silks off. You were pale as a ghost, but your body was red and purple where the horses trampled you. You stopped breathing again and they said your lung had collapsed because your chest was crushed." Keary put his face in his hands and just sobbed. Sean got up and left. Keary got himself under control in a minute.

"So they cut a hole in your chest and stuck a tube in and all this blood came gushing out. They made me leave because they were rushing you to x-ray and then to surgery. We waited for ten hours before we could see you. They let us go into ICU and you had tubes and wires going in and out of you everywhere. The doc talked to us and told us you had a fractured skull. You were on a respirator because you couldn't breathe on your own and would need more surgery when you were stable. They said the whole right side of your pelvis was crushed and they weren't sure if they could repair it. They thought they might ... have to amputate your right leg."

Blackie gasped. "Jesus, Keary!"

"You went through six more surgeries and it was three weeks before you came to." Keary had to stop and take a deep breath and wipe his eyes. Blackie had his head in his hands.

"Every minute of those three weeks we were terrified to answer the phone because they didn't give you much chance of pulling through. The orthopaedic surgeons told us you'd never walk again. There are bone grafts from your legs plus cadaver bone in there. All those bone fragments tore the hell out of your insides, so they had to remove half your bladder. Then there was the horror of watching you go through all the pain you suffered. And believe me you really suffered. And then we had to watch you struggle to learn how to walk all over again. I couldn't take that again, buddy, I love you too much."

"I'm sorry! I'm sorry!" Blackie said, wiping his face. "Listen, I'm going for a drive. I need to be alone. Meg, can you stay here in the house tonight? I need to talk to you. I'll talk to you in the morning, Keary. Call that shrink you're always bugging me to see first thing tomorrow and make an appointment for me. Thanks." He turned, went out and they heard the Porsche start up and roar away.

Meg panicked. She felt like she had caused this by letting him ride Sandman. "I'm really sorry; I didn't mean to cause trouble. I feel so awful that I upset all of you and now Blackie is miserable. I think I should leave."

"No!" Keary said, "Please don't do that; he'll need to talk to you."

Jill came back down with Sean.

"Did Blackie leave? He was upset wasn't he?" She asked. "Did you tell them all the horrors?"

"Yes." Keary said sadly. "He went for a drive. He wants Meg to stay here tonight. He asked me to call Dr.Walhman and make an appointment for him."

"Oh God!" Jill said, biting her lip. "Did he really? Well maybe it's the best thing. He needs help with all of it."

"Is it okay if I stay? I did bring clothes with me today, but they're in his apartment."

"Of course, it's fine. Let's run down and get them before he gets back. Meg, don't worry. He actually needs to work through the feelings he has about the accident and guilt about his past. The impact of the accident and the trauma it caused him physically and emotionally is still in his head. So I think it's better to get it out now and let him work on it."

"I guess. I just feel so awful that I made him feel this bad and I wouldn't have let him ride my horse if I had known."

"That's another thing we can talk more about. You can't get anything settled with him when he's angry or upset. Maybe if we get his doctors' okay, he'll be able to do some dressage. You can see how traumatic this whole thing has been for all of us." Keary said.

"Meg, he's going to be fine. It'll be good if he goes to see this doctor. Maybe he can help him sort it out." Jill said.

"Oh, what happened to the horse?" Meg asked.

Keary frowned and looked at Sean. "Do you know, Sean? I didn't even think about it."

"Me neither. It was so chaotic getting him to the hospital, I didn't notice or care that much. I'm sure the owner took care of it."

SEVENTEEN

Meg woke up the next morning in a strange bedroom and had no idea where she was. Then it came to her that she was in Blackie's family's house and realized that he hadn't come home and talked to her last night. She jumped out of bed, pulled on some clothes, brushed her teeth and bounded downstairs to find Jill and Keary drinking coffee.

"What happened to Blackie?" She demanded. "He was supposed to come back and talk."

"He's in his apartment." Jill said. "His car was there this morning but I have no idea what time he got in. Usually his car wakes me up."

"I think he'll come up when he's ready. He said he'd talk to us today. I made an appointment for him at eleven, so he'll need to get up soon," Keary said.

Meg grabbed some coffee and a donut and sat down. She could hardly sit still, jumping up and pouring more coffee.

"Meg, calm down, he's going to be good," Jill said.

"I hope so." Meg said.

In a few minutes, Blackie walked into the kitchen. He looked good but tired. He was freshly showered, shaved and dressed to go out.

"Good morning." He said seriously.

He came over, kissed Meg gently and sighed. He turned and got some coffee and sat down. She didn't like the look in his eyes. It scared her.

"How are you this morning?" Keary asked.

"I don't know yet. Did you make an appointment for me?"

"Yes, it's at eleven. Did you get any sleep?"

"No." Blackie said and looked at his watch. "Where's Sean? I need to talk to all of you."

"He's still asleep, I think, I'll go get him," Keary said.

"Okay." Blackie said. He stared into his coffee cup and didn't say anything. Meg had a sinking feeling in her belly. She reached over, hesitantly, and took his hand. He put hers to his lips and kissed it. Just then, Sean and Keary came down the steps. Sean came over and ruffled Blackie's hair and said, "Hey, buddy."

Blackie smiled up at Sean and said, "You look like shit."

"I do, yes." Sean laughed.

Sean's face was pretty much black and blue. He got coffee and a donut and sat down.

Blackie said, nervously. "I thought about this all night and what I wanted to say. First of all I want to apologize for any pain or worry that I've caused you." Jill started to protest, but he stopped her.

"No, Jill let me say what I have to say. I'm not sure what I'm finally going to do. For right now though, I promise I will not ride, at all." Meg touched his arm in sympathy and he shook his head.

"Meg, it's okay. Let me finish. I have to figure out what I'm going to do with the rest of my life, but for right now, I won't ride. I want a normal life. I want a life with a good woman and I realized I don't want her to end up with a man in a wheelchair. I don't want to be crippled either. I want kids and I might not be able to if I'm crippled. I don't know, maybe I'll go back to school." He rubbed his hands over his face and looked at Meg who had tears in her eyes.

"Hey, don't cry, Meg, this is the best thing to do for everyone."

"Blackie, I know how hard this will be for you," Keary said.

"Keary, you have no idea how difficult this is going to be," Blackie said, annoyed.

"You're right, yes. I never had the passion for riding that you have. I'm very happy that you decided to do this. It's unselfish of you. We'll help you as much as we can. I'm sorry I've been so hard on you about it. You know it's because I love you." Keary said.

"I know. I love you guys too. Just be patient with me because I probably won't be in a cheerful mood all the time. I have a lot more to say. Keary said something yesterday about coming clean with Meg. I have a lot to tell her but there's a lot that you guys don't even know." He looked at his watch again.

"I have to leave in forty-five minutes if I'm going to be on time." He sat back, looked at Meg and blew out a sigh. "Meg, I know I should have told you up front, but I was afraid if I did, it would be the end for me."

"Oh, Blackie, don't say that."

"Let me get this out." He hesitated for a minute and then said, "First, I'm an alcoholic and a drug addict."

"But I've never seen you drunk," she protested.

"I'm a binge drinker, which is bad. If something sets me off, I'll drink until I can't stand up. Alcohol poisoning is very dangerous and I've gotten pretty close to killing myself a few times."

Jill gasped at this statement and started crying softly.

"Jill, you're not helping me." Blackie said, giving her a sympathetic look. Keary put his arm around her.

"I'm addicted to marijuana, morphine, cocaine, prescription pain meds and I've tried heroin. I've been in rehab three or four times. You all know some about the women but there's more." He glanced at Meg.

"Meg, I hate to tell you this. I'm so ashamed of it all. I can't believe some of the things I've done." He took a deep breath and shook his head. He went on again in a few minutes.

"I started meeting women at the Jockey Club parties or parties that Mickey got together. They were showgirls or party girls that were sort of groupies. Then later, they were all hookers." He stopped, looked at Meg again and there was so much pain and remorse in his eyes.

"Then I started getting invited by these rich society women to their estates in the Hamptons. I went for the whole weekend. Of course most of the time, I was either drunk or high. I got to be a very popular houseguest. It was basically nothing but weekends of sex, drugs, gambling and drinking. Of course, the accident put an end to all of it.

That's part of the reason I was so sick after it. I was also going through withdrawal from various substances. Once, I broke into Mickey's office, looking for drugs because he always had a stash in there."

"Christ, if I could find that bastard, I'd kill him!" Keary said.

"What I found was a ledger that he kept of fees that were paid to him. He kept all the drug deals in there. What I found was that, for the weekends I was in the Hamptons, Mickey got paid $20,000 a pop. So, I became a high-paid hooker myself. That's when I fired him." He said with a frown.

"Blackie, that wasn't your fault, you were taken advantage of by Mickey because of your drug problems." Jill retorted, her face flushed with anger.

"No, I was an adult and knew exactly what I was doing. I've done some bad shit, you guys. If I wasn't a bad person, then how could Mickey corrupt me?" He looked like a whipped puppy.

"Blackie, why didn't you tell me?" Meg asked, saddened by his misery.

"Meg, I couldn't. Why do you think I question the fact that I'm alive?"

"What do you mean, you question that you're alive?' Keary asked.

"Because I don't understand why I didn't die on that racetrack. All the bad things I've done, why would God save me? Why would he give me, of all people, a second chance?" he said with tears in his eyes.

"Oh my God, honey, you're not a bad person. You have to believe that!" Jill said, sobbing.

"Christ, I'm so fucked up! All this shit is in my head, all the time and it makes me crazy. I can't race anymore, so what do I do the rest of my life?" Blackie said, putting his head in his hands. "Meg, I think you're making a serious mistake being with me. I'm really messed up. I don't know if this doctor can help me. I better go. I'll see you when I get home."

*   *   *

About three hours later, Blackie pulled up by the barn and sat in the Porsche. Jill stood at the dining room window and watched him.

"He's still just sitting in that car. I hope everything went well with Dr. Wahlman. I'm so worried about him and you too, Meg. I want you guys to be happy and I don't want all this crap to ruin things for you."

"I'm going to do my best not to let it, Jill. There's only so much I can do. Blackie has to come to terms with his past."

"He's coming up here," Jill said as she quickly sat down.

Blackie walked in the door looking very tired with red, puffy eyes.

"Hi, guys." He said, walked over to Meg, pulled her into his arms and buried his face in her hair.

"Can you ever forgive me for this awful mess?"

"Blackie, first you have to forgive yourself," she said, holding him tight. He backed up and looked at her.

"That's what Dr. Wahlman said."

He let her go and walked out to the kitchen coming back with coffee. He sat next to Meg and took her hand.

"How did it go?" Keary asked.

"Okay, I guess. He asked me a lot of questions. We got into the whole accident thing and that took a lot of time. We talked about all the shit that happened with Mickey. He thinks there's a lot of subconscious crap that I've buried. There's so much I can't remember thanks to the drugs and alcohol. He says he wants to hypnotize me to get some of it to surface. Do you guys think I should do that? He said he needs my permission."

"I think you should do whatever he thinks will help, Blackie." Keary said.

"I'm tired. I didn't sleep last night and then talking to him wore me out. I think I'll eat something and then crash in the TV room."

Blackie got up and went to the kitchen to scrounge something to eat. Jill motioned to Meg to go help him.

"Can I fix you something?" She asked him and leaned against him.

"I don't know what I want," he said, standing there with the fridge door open.

"There's chicken, I can nuke some for you."

"You don't have to wait on me. I can do it!" he said, a little annoyed and slammed the fridge door.

"I know you can. Maybe I just came out here to be with you."

"I'm sorry; I'm too tired to be around." He leaned into her and gave her a soft kiss.

"Do you think you can handle all this? Do you think you can handle me and all my shit?" he said seriously.

"I don't know, but I'm willing to try." She said, not confident that she could.

"That's just what I needed to hear from you. I can't do this without you, Meg. Hopefully, if I get myself straight, I'll be a decent person to live with." He kissed her urgently this time and she kissed him back just as passionately. God, she wanted him so bad she was losing control.

"Forget the food, let's go take that nap," he said as he took her hand and pulled her toward the TV room.

She figured this was going to turn into another *no sex* session of hot passion like it usually did. At this point, she didn't care. A little passion would be preferable to the last couple of days of fighting, hearing about the accident, and revelations from the past. Meg needed some real comforting and figured Blackie did too. They were both emotionally spent. He pulled his boots off and flopped on the sofa, turning on the TV. He patted the sofa next to him. As soon as she sat down, he put his arm around her shoulder and hugged tight.

"I don't know about you, but I'm exhausted. All this has drained me," he said wearily.

She could hear the stress in his voice and feel the tension in his body. "I know. Me too."

"I'm sorry to put you through all this. I'm going to try very hard to get my head straight."

"I know you will. Let's lie down and get some sleep. I'm too tired to talk rationally about anything."

"You're right," he said scooting them into a prone position, folding her against his body.

* * *

Sometime later, Meg felt someone touching her arm and opened her eyes. Jill was next to her kneeling on the floor.

"Shhh. Do you guys want to eat? I'll let you wake him up," Jill whispered. Meg nodded and Jill left the room. Blackie was out. He was breathing a little heavy and she could tell he was in a deep sleep. She slowly wiggled out from under his arm. He mumbled something and turned over onto his back, still sound asleep. She had to smile because he had half an erection going on. She wondered what he was doing in his sleep. God, he was beautiful!

She tore herself away, went into the dining room and realized she was famished.

"Hey, where's the man?" Keary asked.

"He's out like a light. He's so tired I thought I'd let him sleep and he can eat when he wakes up. I know *I'm* hungry," she said digging into the usual huge buffet.

"How's he doing?" Jill asked.

"I'm not sure. I got the impression that he was feeling hopeful that Dr. Wahlman can help him."

"That's good. I hope so too," Jill said.

Keary, Jill and Meg finished eating and were talking for about an hour when Blackie padded down the hall. He looked like he was still half-asleep. He sat down next to Meg, put his head on her shoulder and closed his eyes.

"Are you awake, sweetie?" Jill asked him.

"No, but I'm starving to death," he said, sleepily.

"Can you get your own food?" Meg asked him.

"Yes, as soon as I'm awake enough to hold a plate," he said, rubbing the side of his head against her. He sat up and opened his eyes. He looked at her and smiled. He was adorable; all sleepy and tousled.

"Hey, Keary, what's up?"

"Not much. Did I tell you what the accountants had to say?"

"No, how bad is it?" Blackie asked him.

"Hey it's good! Profits are up this year. Of course, we're not back to where we were when you were riding." Keary said, and then was sorry he'd said it.

"Oh, yeah," Blackie said, sadly.

"Sorry I brought it up, buddy." Keary said.

"That's okay, Keary. I have to get used to it being over. I can't get it back, so I have to move on." Blackie said. "I think I'll get some food. I'm so hungry, I feel sick." He got up, heaped a plateful, went to the kitchen and got juice. Meg watched him eat and then she yawned.

"Okay you, I'm going home. I'm still tired. Good night, you two." She said to Jill and Keary.

"Good night, Meg." they said. Blackie got up, took her hand and walked her to her car.

"Thanks for being there for me today, Meg. I can't wait until our date. Call me when you get in bed. I want to say good night when we're both in bed," he said.

"That's a little kinky, but okay, I will."

"You think that's kinky, huh?" He pulled her against him and kissed her hungrily. He leaned her up against her car and put his hands under her top. He had his leg between hers and pushed it tight up against her.

"Oh, God, Blackie!" He kissed her again, almost brutally, exploring her mouth with his tongue. He then kissed her neck, her shoulder, the swell of her breast. He went down on his knees, kissed her belly and moved lower. She thought she might go crazy with desire. He got up again and she could tell he was fully aroused. He pushed his body in between her legs and she opened them more so he could get to her. Biting her neck lightly, he pushed against her harder and harder. She was getting dizzy and couldn't breathe.

"Let's go up to your apartment, please. I can't take this any longer," she begged him.

"No, wait." His breathing sounded like a freight train. He rolled his hips around in a circle and pushed harder. She cried out when she came and he followed, hugging her tight until his breathing slowed.

"God, Meg! I can't control myself at all." he said, still breathless.

"Well, I wanted to go up to your apartment. Why didn't we?" She asked, totally provoked with him.

"Because when you said that, I was almost there and so were you."

"So we wind up doing *this* in the driveway!"

"Nobody's around. We're out in the country," he said, defensively.

"That's not the point! Are we ever going to make love, in a bed, naked?" She asked, getting more annoyed with him.

"Of course we are. I'm sorry." He pulled her close and kissed her again.

"Crap!" She said, punching him on the arm, "What's a woman got to do to get laid around here?"

He burst out laughing. "Honey, that's really funny. We'll get there, I promise," he said and hugged her.

"Okay, I'm outta here."

EIGHTEEN

One afternoon when they were finished working with the horses; Blackie suggested they go out on the weekend with Keary, Jill, Sean and his girlfriend, Katie. Meg thought it was a good idea but surprised because they always went out alone.

"Okay, that sounds like fun. I'll call Jen at the gallery and ask her to go."

"Good, I'll mention it to Sean and Keary. Where should we go? You want to try a club where they have dancing or just a bar?" Blackie asked.

"Hmm, dancing would be good. Do you like to dance?"

"It depends on how much I've had to drink."

"I thought you weren't drinking anymore," she said a little sharper than she intended.

"I'm not. I'm talking about the past and it was a joke, so don't look so worried," he said, "I'm not going to get drunk, okay."

"Okay," she said and he pulled her over and kissed her. "I'm working hard on that old crap with Dr. Wahlman. I want to be better for you." he kissed her again, lingering over the kiss this time. His kisses always took her breath away.

"But I do worry about you, a lot," she said and meant it.

"Well, stop it because I'm good. Hey, ask Jill if she knows a cool place we can go."

*   *   *

Meg went up to the house to talk to Jill about this new idea of his and found her in the kitchen going over some recipes.

"Hi, Jill."

"Hey," Jill smiled when she looked up. "How are you today? What's my bad little brother up to?"

"I'm good and he wants to go to a night club with all of us together and I thought I'd ask Jen from the gallery. Blackie met her when he visited me at work once. Just out of the blue, he said we should go."

"That's unusual. I thought he wanted you all to himself? I don't know, maybe he just wants to do more social stuff with you."

"Is there a nice place in Richmond?"

"I've been hearing about this place called *Rocks* that's supposed to be exciting. I'll Google it. You call Jen and I'll ask Keary and Sean. What about this Saturday night? Is that good? We could get Jeremy to drive us all in the limo."

"Limo? Who's Jeremy?"

"You've seen Jeremy around here, big guy, about six-six and muscular. He hangs out at the gym mostly. He's Blackie's bodyguard and we keep the limo in one of the garages for when we all go somewhere together."

"Wait. Black has a bodyguard?" Meg said, wide-eyed.

"He does, yes. Our parents insisted on it when Blackie turned eighteen. He was in trouble all the time and half the time, we couldn't find him. Jeremy's supposed to be his valet and Blackie hates the idea of personal servants, so Jeremy kind of stays in the background. Since the accident, it hasn't been a problem. Jeremy's very nice and he and Blackie kind of became friends and hang out once in awhile. He won't let Jeremy do anything for him, though. So Jeremy helps Tim and does odd jobs around here."

"That's just weird. I've seen him around, he looks like the Incredible Hulk. Going out in a limo, that'll be soooo cool. What are you wearing?"

"I guess some kind of slinky pants outfit. You want to go shopping?"

"Oh, yes. Blackie's not going to wear jeans is he?"

"I doubt it. He has some cool clubby sort of clothes. He usually looks pretty hot when he goes out."

Jill and Meg had a ball shopping. Meg bought a pair of silky, black, skintight pants and a backless, halter top with sequins in gold and black. Jill bought the same pants in dark green and a silvery beaded top.

On Saturday night, Jill said they would pick her up, so went home early to get dressed.

She saw this huge stretch limo pull up out front, Blackie got out and came up to her door. When she opened it, his mouth dropped open and she smiled.

That's exactly the reaction I was going for.

"Wow, you look incredible! Turn around. God, Meg, I love it! Mmm, that top is sexy." He hugged her and ran his hands down her bare back. He looked yummy himself. He had on black, tight pants, white silk shirt, an unstructured grey jacket and black boots.

"You look pretty hot yourself. I don't think I've ever seen you this duded up," she said whistling at him.

"Don't get used to it, I'd rather have on jeans," he said, smiling. "Let's go."

They got in the limo and made introductions to Ted, Jen's husband, and Katie, Sean's girlfriend. She was very cute, blond and sweet looking.

When they got to the club, it was enormous with a shiny dance floor you could see yourself in and an outside patio where couples were sitting with drinks. They got a table in between the bar and the dance floor, then ordered appetizers and drinks.

Blackie was in a great mood. He kept lightly trailing his fingers up and down Meg's bare back making her crazy. He asked her to dance on a slow song and she realized she had no idea if he could dance. His body felt hard and hot against hers and he had some smooth moves. The next dance was a sexy slow one and suddenly he had changed the way he was dancing. Now he was doing the *dirty dancing* thing with his leg between hers and a lot of slow pelvic rolls with both arms wrapped around her tight. Her knees went weak and she felt the heat right where he intended it to go. He dropped his hands to her butt and she had to bite her lip to keep from moaning. The song ended, he slid his hand down her arm, taking her hand led her back to the table. He went up to the bar to get them more drinks and Jill leaned over and whispered.

"How'd you like that last dance?"

"Omigod, I thought I was going to spontaneously combust. Where did he learn that?" Meg panted.

"I don't know, but that was hot," Jill said, fanning herself.

"What kind of dance was that?" Keary asked laughing. "His hip seemed just fine doing that."

Blackie came back with drinks.

"Hi, sweetie." he said softly, his mouth against her ear. "How'd you like the dance?"

"I loved it, but if you do more of it, I can't take responsibility for what I might do to you on the dance floor." Meg said, teasing him.

"Hmm, sounds like fun to me," he said nuzzling her hair.

Sean, Katie, Ted and Jen were dancing. Jill was sitting with Blackie and Meg as Keary went and got more drinks. Meg looked at the crowded bar and saw an old girlfriend of hers from college. She told Blackie she was going to say hello to a girl she knew and would be right back.

He whispered, "Hurry back," and kissed her.

She was talking to her friend when she felt someone up against her butt and turned. There next to her, too close to her, was Doug Hall, an old boyfriend. Doug was generally a jerk and she had only dated him a couple of months. He said how glad he was to see her but was sort of hanging on her. She shrugged him off but he kept getting close.

Blackie was at the table when Sean and the others came back from dancing, talking excitedly with flushed faces.

Keary noticed that Blackie was frowning and asked him, "What's up?"

"What's a jealous rage feel like, Keary?"

Keary followed Blackie's gaze and saw that he was watching Doug and Meg.

"It feels like you'd like to kill the guy messing with Meg at the bar," Keary said and laughed.

Blackie jumped up and walked toward the bar.

Keary snapped his fingers at Sean, "Sean, watch it! Blackie's going after the creep bothering Meg at the bar."

Sean swiveled his head toward Blackie and said, "Oh, shit, this is trouble!"

*　　*　　*

"Excuse me, but do you mind keeping your leg off my girlfriend's ass?" Blackie said, with a low growl.

"Whoa, buddy, she and I are old friends. We used to date, didn't we, Meggins." Doug said, slurring his words.

"Well she's with *me* now and I don't want you touching her!" Blackie said through clenched teeth.

"Blackie, it's okay, I've got this under control. I told him to get away from me." Meg said, hoping to defuse the situation.

"No, you don't have it under control, *Meggins.* He keeps touching you and now he's going to stop." He said, turning to Doug. "Do you understand what I'm telling you? You are *not* going to touch her again."

"Blackie, don't make a scene. Let's go back to the table and forget it," she said trying to placate him.

"I'm not going to forget it and don't tell me what to do, Meg. You're with me and no jerk is going to put his hands on you, do you understand?"

"Hey, you don't own me. I wasn't doing anything wrong. I can take care of myself and I was until you butt in!" She shoved him and he grabbed her arm, pulling her away from the bar.

"Let's take this outside, Meg." He went to move her past Doug and Doug stopped him and said, "Hey, Buddy, maybe she doesn't want to go anywhere with you." Blackie punched Doug in the gut with his left hand. Doug doubled over, gasped for air and started to vomit on his shoes.

Blackie sat him on a bar stool and said to the bartender, "Give this guy some coffee he's had too much to drink."

Blackie then dragged her outside and let go of her arm in the middle of the parking lot.

"What the hell are you doing?" She yelled at him, feeling like she was going to erupt with anger.

"I was trying to protect you and you start giving *me* a hard time," he yelled back.

"Protect me! Is that what you were doing? It seemed like you were pissed because some guy touched me and threatened your manhood, not that you were protecting me from some jerk. I told you I had it under control."

"No, you didn't. I was watching you. You'd tell him to stop it, push him away and in two minutes he had his leg up against you again. Do you want him touching you?" He asked, scowling at her.

"Blackie you know better than that; of course not," she said trying to control *her* temper.

"Did you sleep with him when you were dating?" He demanded.

"No, I didn't and besides that's none of your damn business! You've got a lot of nerve asking me about *my* past."

He stared at her, startled. "You're right. Who am I to ask you any questions? It's just when I saw him touching you, I went insane. I wanted to kill him. I've never felt jealousy over a woman before, but I know one thing." He got in her face, his eyes piercing hers and said, "If I ever see another man touch you again, I *will* *kill* him! I'm a very possessive male."

"What's wrong with you? Why are you so jealous and upset over me?"

"Because I ... because." He turned and pounded his fist on the top of the nearest car.

"You can't say it, can you? You're afraid to say it. Guess what, you can't have me until you say it." She yelled at him, her lips trembling.

"Hey, I haven't heard you say it, so I don't want you until I hear it from *you*." He yelled back.

"I love you! I love you, damn it. You idiot! I don't want anyone else but you. You have no reason to be jealous," she screamed at him.

He stuffed his hands in his pockets and backed up against the car. They stood there glaring at each other.

*　　*　　*

Keary, Jill and the others had been watching the incident at the bar. When Blackie hit Doug, Sean sucked his breath in, "Ouch! He's punched me in the gut before. It feels like a horse kicked you."

Ted said, "Is he always this violent?"

"No, he's just a little on edge right now about Meg." Jill said.

"I thought things were good between them," Jen said, "Meg's been so happy."

"He's just unsure of where he stands with her and he's not used to being jealous," Jill said.

"I don't think he has anything to worry about. Meg's mad about him. He's all she talks about," Jen offered.

"Jill," Keary said, "Sean and I are going outside to keep an eye on things. I'm going to call Jeremy to get ready to leave, just in case. You all better be ready to go if there's a problem."

*　　*　　*

After a few minutes, Blackie reached over, grabbed her arm and pulled Meg close to him. He wrapped his arms around her and kissed the top of her head.

"Meg, I'm scared. I've never felt anything like this for a woman before. I'm afraid I'm going to do something stupid and mess things up with you. I'm at a loss how to handle our relationship, but I'm trying hard. I know I screwed up tonight but I couldn't control it. I'm sorry."

"I know you're trying and this is new for you but you need to trust me. I don't want anyone but you, Blackie. What do you care if he touches me? He's pathetic. He's a loser who can't get his own woman, so he's hitting on someone else's."

"Are you my woman?"

"I hope so," she said looking into his eyes. He kissed her hard and deep and she could feel his frustration.

Just then Doug staggered out of the club and made his way to his car.

"Hey, buddy, she'll go down on you, cause she gives good head," Doug yelled.

Blackie tensed and made a move to go after Doug. She could see the rage building in his eyes and she went pale with fear.

She held his arms and told him, "Forget it, he's trying to get in your head and mess with you. He's lying."

Doug yelled again, "Hey, does she do 'doggie style' for you because she loves 'doggie style'."

That was it. Blackie broke away from her, fast and went after Doug. Doug saw him and made a run for his car but Blackie caught him before he reached it. The first punch flattened Doug. Blackie picked him up; hit him in the belly and then an uppercut to the face. She heard the crunch of bone. She started back to get help and ran straight into Sean and Keary.

"Go get in the limo, fast, we'll get Blackie," Keary yelled. She ran and jumped in the limo, followed by Jill, Ted, Katie and Jen.

"What's happening?" Ted asked.

"There're going to grab Blackie and then we're out of here," Jill said.

Suddenly the door opened and Blackie landed on the floor of the limo with Sean on top of him. Keary jumped in last and yelled to Jeremy to take off. The limo sped away with Sean and Blackie still in a heap on the floor and trying to get untangled.

"Get the fuck off me, Sean!" Blackie yelled, pushing at him.

"I will when you calm down!" Sean yelled back.

"Get off now!" Blackie pushed Sean and they both struggled into seats. Blackie was breathing hard, his hands were bleeding and he looked wild and scary. He glared at Sean, then slumped back in his seat and stared out the window. No one said anything.

After about ten minutes, Blackie said quietly "I need to apologize to all of you for ruining the evening. I'm not good at controlling my temper and I don't have the whole 'boyfriend thing' down yet."

Everyone except Meg mumbled, "That's okay, we understand."

"No, it's not okay." Blackie said.

After a few minutes, Ted quietly asked Keary why they had to leave so fast.

Keary glanced at Blackie, hesitated, then said, "Well, chances are that guy's going to call the police and would have charged Blackie with assault."

"Hell, that's no big deal, I've been in bar fights before and when the judge knows everyone was drinking, charges are dropped and you pay court costs," Ted said.

"Unfortunately, Blackie is a martial arts instructor and it's recorded on his driver's license," Keary explained.

"Oh shit," Ted said and gave Blackie an uneasy look.

Blackie just kept staring out the window. Jill picked up one of his bloody hands but he gently pulled it away.

Ted asked Sean, "Was the guy hurt badly?"

"I couldn't tell much but he didn't look too good," Sean answered.

Meg's stomach was in knots. What the hell was she going to do with him? She loved him but she didn't know how to deal with this violent side of him. They had to talk about this more.

Blackie looked at her and said, "Meg, I love you. I love you so much I can't stand it. Our not sleeping together isn't working. I'm going insane. I know it was my rule but we have to change it."

She couldn't stand it. He looked so pathetic sitting there being miserable. She knew how frustrated he was because she was too. God, I love him, she thought.

She quickly moved, sat on his lap and kissed him. He wrapped his arms around her and buried his face in her neck.

They left Jen and Ted off and then Meg. She told him not to get out.

"I love you. I'll talk to you tomorrow. Everything's good between us so don't worry." He nodded but still looked like a beaten dog. She let herself into her condo, pulled her clothes off, fell into bed and passed out.

NINETEEN

As they were riding back to the farm, Keary glanced at Blackie and asked him, "Are you okay?"

"No, I'm fucked," he said.

"If there's trouble over the fight, our lawyers can probably get you off," Jill said.

"I don't care about that, I mean with Meg. No woman in their right mind would want a man that acts like that."

"She said you two were good," Jill said.

"Yeah, wait till she thinks about it all night. Let's go back to the club and see if that guy's okay. I hit him pretty hard. Meg will love it if I've maimed the bastard," he said.

"Are you sure you want to do that? If the police are there, they'll arrest you," Keary said.

"I don't care, let's go."

They went back to the club, but Doug had gone home in his own car. The bartender said he thought Doug had a broken nose, but wasn't sure.

Blackie and the others went back to the farm. Jill offered to put antiseptic on his hands but he refused and said he was going to bed.

*   *   *

Meg had quickly fallen to sleep last night from exhaustion after the fight. She didn't sleep well though and kept waking up, thinking about the whole scene at the club. Her gut was in knots just thinking about how violent Blackie could be. She thought he was feeling better since he started seeing Dr. Wahlman. The scene last night blew her positive feelings to bits.

She wondered how badly he had hurt Doug and if the police would arrest Blackie. He hadn't even been drinking. God knows what would have happened if alcohol had been involved. Of course Doug had been drunk enough for the both of them.

In the morning, she woke up early and lay there with this terrible feeling of unease in the pit of her stomach. How was Blackie? Should she go to the farm and confront him? Should she call him or call Jill and see what was up?

Meg didn't know how to handle this situation with him. Would an ultimatum about the violence be too much for him? Or should she just be understanding and not make an issue of it?

She decided to call Jill and see what the situation was. She dialed the number at the farm and Jill answered.

"Jill, its Meg." Her voice shaking.

"Good morning, sweetie, how are you?"

"I'm okay, just shaken up by last night. Has he been up there yet this morning?"

"No, I haven't seen him. His car is gone. I don't know what time he left. He might be headed your way. Last night he was pretty much convinced that you were going to break up with him. He was miserable. He made us go back to the club to check on that Doug guy, but he'd already left under his own steam."

"Oh, wait; he just pulled up, Meg. He has a bag with him so he probably went to get food so he won't have to come up here. Do you want me to call you if I find out what he's doing?"

"I guess so. Do you think I should come over, see him and talk about it? I don't want him to think it's over because it's not. I know he's a mess but I love him too much to give up on him."

"I'm glad to hear you say that. I was worried last night that you might call it quits. He needs to know that you're still there for him. I'll poke around a little and see what his mood is today. Maybe I'll get Keary to talk to him. I'll call you back and you should probably get ready to come over. I think it's best if you guys talk no matter what. Bye." Jill said and hung up.

*   *   *

Jill and Keary talked about the situation for a couple hours when the phone rang and it was Blackie.

"Jill, can I talk to Keary?" he asked.

"Sure, honey, how are you this morning?" He didn't answer her so she said, "Hold on. I'll go get him." She put the phone down and got Keary.

"Keary, it's Blackie on the phone and he wants you. He sounds funny."

Keary frowned, getting up to get the phone. "Hey Blackie, what's up?"

"Can you come down here, Keary?"

"Sure, I'll be right down."

Keary hung up and turned to Jill. "He wants me to go down there. This doesn't sound good to me. I'll call you if there's a problem."

*   *   *

Keary knocked on the apartment door and Blackie answered. He looked so serious it set alarms off in Keary's head. He walked in and turned around. Blackie had his hands stuffed in his pockets and leaned against the wall. Keary stared at him.

"What's up, buddy?" Blackie just stared back for a long time and Keary was starting to sweat.

"I've been looking at that for a couple of hours." He nodded his head in the direction of the kitchen counter. Keary turned and followed his gaze. Sitting there were two quarts of Jameson, one opened and a glassful already poured.

"Good Christ, Blackie, how much have you had?" Keary exclaimed.

"None yet." Blackie said, glaring at the liquor.

"What do you want me to do?"

"Talk to me." Blackie said, sort of in a daze.

"You do like the dear stuff, then."

"If you're going to get bolloxed, you should do it right."

"Are you going to drink it and what can I say to talk you out of it?" Keary asked.

"Keary, I thought I had this under control. After the accident, I pretty much dried out completely and haven't had a problem. This is scaring me because I really want to drink that, all of it. I thought I was doing really well and Dr. Wahlman was helping me. I don't believe what I did last night. Now today all I want to do is drink." Blackie said, his shoulders and mouth slumped.

"Last night wasn't that bad. The guy didn't press charges. He was drunk anyway. Why has it made you this miserable?" Keary asked.

"Because I'm an idiot! I've screwed everything up with Meg and I can't handle it."

"You haven't screwed up with her. She's already called after your dumb ass this morning. The girl loves you, man. When are you going to quit pissing around and get to it?"

"I don't know. I'm an asshole. Did she really call?"

"Yes. She wants you, dummy. What do you think would happen if she came here and found you hammered?"

"It'd be all over," Blackie said shaking his head.

"Well don't let it happen. Do you want her more than you want this shit?"

"You bet I do. I want her more than anything in the world," Blackie said.

"What can I do to help you?" Keary asked.

"Pour it down the drain."

"You come here and do it."

"I can't, I want it too bad."

"Yes you can. Come here, I'll help you." Keary pleaded. Blackie stood there for a long time, looking at the bottles. Then he looked at Keary and Keary almost cried at the pain in his eyes.

"Come here," Keary said, holding out his hand.

"I can't believe it still has this much power over me." Blackie said, taking a step toward Keary.

"I love you, buddy. Come here and we'll do it together." Blackie walked slowly over to Keary and he put his arm around Blackie.

"Come on show me that you want Meg and a wonderful life with her and you don't need this crap."

Blackie picked up the glass and Keary broke out in a cold sweat. After a few minutes, he poured it down the drain. Then he picked up the bottles, one in each hand and poured them away, too. Keary hugged him and Blackie let out a sob.

"Keary, I can't let this happen again. I have to find some other way to cope when something happens."

"You will, just stick with Dr. Wahlman. He's an expert on addictions among other things. I think he can help you and we're all here for you, including Meg. Come up to the house and get something to eat. Talk to your sister. She's worried about you. Hey, you should be proud of yourself. You just did a big thing, pouring that out. *I'm* proud of you!" Keary said, hugging him again.

"I love you, Keary."

*   *   *

They both walked up to the house. Jill was in the kitchen and looked at Keary with raised eyebrows. He just rolled his eyes and shook his head.

"Hi, you two. Are you hungry, honey?" she said to Blackie. She could see that he was miserable. She hugged him and said, "Are you okay?"

"I am now. Is Meg coming over? I miss her. Is she pissed at me?

"No, she's worried about you. Call her and tell her you want to see her. She's waiting for a call." Jill told him.

"Okay and yes I am hungry," he told Jill as he released her and went to the phone. He sat there for a few minutes, fidgeting with his hands.

"Are you sure she wants me to call her?"

"Absolutely."

*　　*　　*

Meg was moping around when the phone rang. She answered it, thinking it was Jill.

"Hello," she said but no one answered.

"Hello," she snapped.

"Meg." Blackie said quietly.

"Hi, I'm glad you called. I was worried about you."

"I'm okay. Do you want to come over today?" He asked clearing his throat.

"Of course. I'll be there soon. I miss you."

"I miss you too. I'll see you," and he hung up.

She thought he sounded a little funny but was happy he called. She was eager to see him and knew they had to talk about last night. He was human and she didn't want him to think every time he messed up, she was going to bail. She jumped in her car and sped out to the farm.

*　　*　　*

When Blackie hung up, he said to Jill and Keary, "She's coming out. I guess I better tell her what just happened. I need to be brutally honest with her at this point."

"I'd say so, yes. She needs to know," Keary said.

"Know what?" Jill asked.

"You want to tell her or should I?" Keary said.

"Why don't I tell her when I tell Meg? I don't want to talk about it twice. Anyway, I'm starving," he said. He went into the dining room to get breakfast. Jill grabbed Keary and whispered.

"What happened?"

"Shhh, he's okay now. Let him tell you. Things were dicey with him earlier, but he did great," Keary whispered back. They went into the dining room, got food and sat down with Blackie to eat. He picked at his food and didn't say anything.

"I thought you were hungry?" Jill said.

"I guess I'm not. I don't feel all that good. My stomach's in knots. I'll just drink some juice," he said. He got juice but still just picked at the food.

*   *   *

When Meg got to the farm, she parked next to the Porsche and went up to the house. Jill, Keary and Blackie were all in the dining room

"Good morning, you guys." She said and went over and kissed Blackie.

"Hey, good morning," he said with a shrug.

"Are you okay?" She asked him and he turned his head away.

"I don't know. I haven't decided yet," he told her.

"Oh. Are you still upset about last night? I mean we're good but we've got to talk about it." She said and got something to eat.

"We do need to talk and there's more to talk about today," he said looking at the floor. She turned around and stared at him.

"Oh, really?" She said and he nodded.

"Why don't you eat first and then we'll talk." She saw Keary and Jill exchange worried looks.

Great! What now? Wasn't last night enough?

She sat down next to him and he paled. She touched his arm and said softly, "Blackie, whatever it is, it's okay. Come on, don't look so nervous.

I love you," she said and kissed him. He kissed her back and his eyes welled up.

"Honey, what is it?" She put her arm around him and hugged him.

"I bought two bottles of Irish this morning and was going to drink both of them because I figured last night blew it with you," he blurted out. She sat there with her mouth open, shocked at this revelation.

"Did you drink any?" She asked him and looked at Jill and Keary who were wide-eyed.

"I didn't, no, but I wanted to. I called Keary and he talked me out of it. I thought I could handle things better than this. I thought I had the drinking under control, but I guess I don't." He said, hanging his head.

"Blackie, I don't know what to say."

"You don't have to say anything, I get it." He said and started to get up.

"Wait, where are you going? Sit down and let's get through this. You can't run away from this. You have to face it. You can't run away from me either. I'm here to be with you through this. You have to trust me, Blackie."

"Are you serious? You still want to be with me after this?" he said, staring at her.

"Yes, that's what I just said. What don't you understand about *I love you*? This stuff scares the hell out of me, but what if *I* had a problem that was difficult and scary; would you break up with *me*?"

"Of course not."

"Well, I won't either," she told him. "What did you do with the liquor?"

"I poured it down the drain," he said.

"That's great! You didn't drink it. That's wonderful."

"Yes but Keary had to help me. If I hadn't called him, I'd be wasted by now."

"But you did ask for help. That's what people who love you are here for; to help you when it gets tough."

"I don't deserve you, Meg. Is briá liom tú."*I love you.*

"What did you say?"

"I said, *I love you,* in Irish."

"Awww, I love you too, Blackie."

He pulled her onto his lap and kissed her. "Where do we go from here?'

"What do you mean?"

"Are we still dating? Do you trust me enough to be with me?" he asked.

"Of course! I've always trusted you. I know you wouldn't hurt me, ever." She said, looking into his eyes. "I think you have to start trusting yourself."

"Thank you," he said, stroking her hair. "Can I see you Friday night? I have tickets to a concert."

"Yes, that would be great. We need to get back on track."

"Guess what?" he said with a little smile.

"What?"

"I'm really hungry." They all laughed.

TWENTY

Blackie and Meg were speeding along I-95 after taking in a Dave Matthews concert at the Kennedy Center in DC. They had a wonderful time, Blackie holding her hand all evening. He was relaxed and his eyes shone with some emotion she couldn't put her finger on.

On the way back to Georgetown, they talked a little about the concert and made plans for the horses' training. Mostly he was quiet.

She knew she loved him and wanted to be with him. So far he hadn't made any moves in that direction. She wanted to be able to touch him so much. Just the thought of being able to touch him anywhere she wanted, anytime, was taking over her brain. Three weeks ago, she had bought a box of condoms. Wishful thinking!

He slid the Porsche to a stop in front of her condo and walked her to the door. He stared at her for a few minutes.

"What's wrong?"

"Nothing, I just like looking at you in the lamplight." He bent and kissed her gently, then pulled her close and kissed her deeper. She made a little sighing, moaning sound.

"Are you okay?" he asked.

"Yes, I'm very okay."

He smiled and said he would see her tomorrow, got in his car and pulled away.

She unlocked her door, not bothering with the lights. Throwing her keys on the foyer table, she went upstairs and took a long, hot shower. She put on boxers and a tank top and crawled into bed.

Crap! It's only eleven. Great.

*   *   *

Jill and Keary were in their bedroom. Keary was asleep and she was reading. She heard the Porsche pull up by the barn and jumped up to look out her window.

"Damnit! Blackie's home."

Keary woke up and asked her what was wrong. "Oh, Blackie just drove up."

"What's wrong with that, he always drives up to the barn?"

"That's the point, I was hoping he would finally stay overnight with Meg."

"So, let me understand this. We're up and awake, hoping Blackie's going to get laid?"

"Exactly. Hey wait, he's turning around and leaving! Yes, he's going back!" she said with a fist pump.

"You're that excited?"

"Mother of God, Keary, where have you been?"

"Well, honey, come back to bed and I'll show you how excited *I* am that Blackie's going to get laid."

*   *   *

Meg had fallen asleep when a noise outside woke her. She went to her window and Blackie's car was out front idling.

Oh, God, something must have happened. Maybe he was in an accident.

She ran downstairs, opened the door and he was just standing there looking down at his shoes.

He raised his eyes to her and she said, "What's wrong?"

"Nothing." He said staring at her. "Can I stay until morning?"

She couldn't say anything. She was in shock.

"Please don't say no." He said biting his bottom lip.

She opened the door wide and said, "I thought you'd never ask."

He walked in and stood there looking at her. He took her hand, kissed her palm and then pulled her to him and kissed her. They both put their arms around each other and he kissed her harder. Their tongues met and sparks went off in her head. They broke apart and he handed her a package he had in his pocket. "I stopped at the drugstore and bought condoms. Wishful thinking, I guess."

He smiled and so did she. He pulled her into him again and they kissed deeper and more urgently.

"Let's go upstairs," he said his voice husky.

He took her hand, pulled her up the steps and she led him to her bedroom. He put his hands under her top and gently caressed her.

She gasped with pleasure, pulled his shirt off and said, "Can I touch you?"

"Of course, you never need to ask me."

"I want to be able to touch you everywhere and as much as I want." He raised his arms in a sort of "be my guest" gesture. She went behind him and ran her hands over his back. The warmth of his skin made her fingers burn. She put her hands on his shoulders and slowly moved down his arms, feeling the ripple of muscles. She circled in front of him and slowly caressed his chest. All the time she was touching him, his eyes had such intensity they burned into her heart.

By now his breathing was getting ragged. She slid her hands down to his belly and he trembled.

When she unzipped his jeans, he gasped and sucked air in. He was fully aroused and big.

Really big!

Uh ... what on earth am I going to do with this much man?

Suddenly, she got a rush of 'cold feet' but didn't have time to think about it because he scooped her up and flopped here on the bed. He pulled his jeans off and got in bed next to her.

"Jesus, sweetheart, I can only stand so much!"

He kissed her gently at first making her shiver with anticipation. Then harder and more urgently as he probed her mouth with his tongue. He moved his mouth down her throat, kissing and licking her with soft little bites. It suddenly got so hot she couldn't breathe. He reached down, pulled her boxers off and took the tank top over her head.

"God, Meg, you're so beautiful."

He gently kissed her breasts, circling her nipples with his tongue. Those hands that she had watched caress the horses, now caressed her. Those gentle fingers trailed over her body like a whisper, slipping inside her. Her soft whimpers drove his desire even higher. He craved relief from the frustration of the past months. Relief that only she could give him.

Rockets were going off in her head. She arched against his hand, wanting more.

"Oh, Blackie, I want you so much. Love me now," She gasped. He pushed her legs apart with his knees and moved lower, kissing her belly and gently biting her.

"I want to taste you," he whispered. "I want to possess you."

He moved lower and did something incredible with his tongue that drove her wild. She was almost there when he stopped and kissed the inside of her thighs.

"Don't stop," she begged.

"Don't worry I'm not going to stop." He continued, using his teeth and tongue and she exploded in waves of pleasure that flowed up from deep inside her. She wanted him so badly, she thought she would scream. He moved up next to her and slowly caressed and kissed her.

"Please now!" She pleaded.

When he climbed on her and gently eased inside, she moaned and opened herself for him. Inside her, he found softness, warmth and welcome like a nest that was home. When she shuddered helplessly and closed around him, he was a goner.

"Oh, Meg!" he gasped and stopped. He was still for a minute, his forehead on her chest, trying to regain control. He started to move again, slowly and she climaxed again with a violent release. Crying his name, she arching her back to get closer to him. He started moving faster, deeper and breathing hard. His body was tense and trembling with urgency. He thrust into her one last time, deep and hard, then groaned. He was still and she could feel him pulsing inside her.

She wrapped her arms and legs around him and held him tight. She caressed his head and shoulders, overcome with emotion that this man, that she loved and had wanted for so long, was finally there with her, now, in her bed, in her embrace, his body inside hers. He filled her physically and emotionally, binding her to him forever.

He's mine, she thought. God, I love him! His love-making was even more spectacular than she had imagined it would be and suddenly, she wanted him again.

He relaxed slightly and kissed her gently on the forehead, then her neck and then very softly and sweetly on her mouth. He was still for a long time, then rolled over on his back and pulled her on top of him.

"Blackie, that was wonderful. I never thought it could be like that," she said, snuggled against him.

"That wasn't exactly my best effort. I couldn't hold off any longer. I've wanted you for so long, I can't believe we're finally together."

"I was thinking the same thing."

He put his hand under her chin and tilted her head back so he could look into her eyes and said, "My dad told me something a few years ago, I guess to get me back on track. He told me that sex was so incredibly wonderful when you have it with someone you love. And now I know he was right.

TWENTY-ONE

They made love again and again during the night. Several times they showered together and she was embarrassed by that at first. She had never even been in a bathroom with a man, much less a naked one. She relaxed about it quickly because Blackie was very playful and funny with the whole thing.

Sometime during the night he said he was exhausted and lay there spent. He watched her, amused, as she happily explored his body. He complained that his knees felt like rubber so she massaged his legs.

"I love it when you touch me, Meg. Your hands are so soft and gentle."

She noticed a small tattoo on his left hip bone.

"What's that?"

"An old tattoo," he said.

"What is it?" she said, looking closer.

"Uh … it's a lion's head and it doesn't mean anything," he snapped and rolled onto his side.

Well, I guess he doesn't want to talk about that.

She was saddened by all the scars he had. His hands were scarred, across the knuckles. There was a thin scar on his forehead up near the hairline and another just under his left eye. He had a long one on his right collarbone. She traced her fingers over the scars on the side of his chest. He said they were from the accident.

She was appalled by the horrible scars that extended from the small of his back; over his hip and butt, to the top of his right thigh. She kissed them gently and he was so touched by the gesture, he hugged her and said, "Meg, I feel like I'm dreaming. I can't believe you love me. I'm afraid I'll wake up."

"I feel the same way; but, Blackie, this is real. It's real for us, here and now. Isn't it wonderful?"

"It is, yes." He said, gruffly, pulling her on top of him and they made love again.

*　　*　　*

Meg woke early and was cuddled up against Blackie. He was nice and warm and she didn't want to move but she had to use the bathroom. It was only six-thirty. She crept out of bed, quietly and he rolled over and sighed.

When she got up she could hardly walk; everything was sore. She did her thing, brushed her teeth and jumped back in bed, waking Blackie. He did the same bathroom routine and slid back under the covers.

"Hey, good morning." he said softly, scooping her into his arms. She couldn't believe that he had any energy left, but she apparently was wrong, because he made love to her just as vigorously as the first time. The next time she woke up it was ten o'clock and Blackie was sleeping face down, looking comatose.

"Blackie, it's ten o'clock."

"Mmm."

"I have a bridal shower to go to at two this afternoon."

"Am I invited?"

"No."

"Then I don't have any reason to move, do I?"

"Come on I have to get ready. I'll call you later and we'll do something tonight."

"You almost killed me last night. I think I'm numb."

"Don't be a baby, get up and go home."

He rolled out of bed and winced when he got up. "Jesus, my back!"

He pulled his clothes on, came over and took her in his arms, kissed her long and deep and said, "I love you," and limped downstairs. She almost called him back but she was exhausted. She heard his car pull away and realized she had a smile on her face and a happy little tingle in her belly."

*   *   *

Jill, Keary and Sean were in the dining room talking after breakfast. Keary was at the sideboard getting more eggs when he saw Blackie pull up.

"Guess who is home?"

"Really?" Jill jumped up and looked out the window. Sean joined them.

"What's going on?" Sean asked.

"Blackie spent the night at Meg's."

"Well it's about damn time."

Blackie got out of the car and put his hands on his back and arched it, grimacing. He slowly limped into the barn.

"Oh man, he looks like he's been through the wringer and he's limping," Sean commented.

"Good, I'm glad to see he looks like he didn't get much sleep." Jill chuckled.

"You women. Always glad to see a man's downfall." Keary laughed.

"Oh, right! He's tired but he looks pretty damn happy."

"He'll crash for the rest of the day." Sean said. "I'll go down and check on him later."

*   *   *

Around six o'clock, Sean ambled down to the barn and entered the apartment from the ladder, disabling the alarm system and quietly walking in. Blackie was still in the same clothes, on the bed, on his back, breathing softly. Sean sat on the bed next to him and nudged him gently.

"Blackie, come on, it's six o'clock."

He stirred and groaned, "Six o'clock! Meg said she'd call me when she got home from her girlfriend's thing. I need to get cleaned up."

"Didn't you shower at Meg's?

"No. I had plans to sleep all day and spend more time with her. She roused me out early cause she had a thing to go to with her girlfriends."

"And you got up and left? That doesn't sound like you," Sean said.

"I did, yes, and I figured something out this morning."

"What's that?" Sean asked.

Blackie looked up at him and said, "For the first time in my entire life, Sean, I'm madly in love. I had no clue how different it would be to be inside a woman that I'm in love with. It's like being inside her soul. I'll never get enough of her."

"Holy shit, dude, you're whipped."

"I am, yes, and happily so."

"Well, congratulations. I'm glad you finally figured it out. All I have to say is, the bigger the stud, the harder his fall," Sean chuckled.

"I have to admit you're right."

"I never thought I'd hear that from you, but I'm happy for you." Sean said, punching him on the arm.

"Thanks, Sean. I'm happy too." His cell rang.

"Yeah? Hi, baby, I miss you. How are you feeling? I'm pretty worn out myself." He listened silently for a minute and suddenly sat up. "What's the matter, Meg? Are you okay? Did I hurt you? God, Meg, I'm sorry. Listen, we're both tired, so I'll come and pick you up and bring you back here. We can have dinner, watch a movie and relax. Bring some stuff so you can stay the night. I'll see you soon."

*　　*　　*

The bridal shower was lots of fun but she kept day-dreaming through the whole thing about last night with Blackie.

Her girlfriend Molly took one look at her and said, "Oh, boy, you did the deed with the jockey last night, didn't you?"

"How can you tell?"

"You just have that glow and the dreamy smile hasn't left your face. Details, details."

"All I'm going to say is that he's incredible and I can't wait to see him again."

"I thought you were walking a little bowlegged," said Michelle.

"Jeez, you guys."

They all had a good laugh. She called Blackie when she got home and he was teasing her about how much of a wreck she'd made out of him, so she told him she wasn't in such good shape herself.

She jumped in the shower and was still sore. She hoped it would go away on its own. She knew she didn't want to have sex tonight, well maybe she did, but it probably wasn't a good idea.

She got clothes, pj's and toiletries together, threw them in a gym bag and ran out when she heard Blackie pull up. Still sore, she gingerly got in the car and he pulled her over and kissed her.

"God, I missed you, I couldn't wait to get here. Are you okay?"

"Yeah, I'm still hurting a little."

"I'm sorry I hurt you, Meg, how am I going to keep from hurting you again?"

She touched his face with the palm of her hand. "Don't worry, we'll work it out." He smiled and kissed her.

As they drove back to the farm, she thought how good it was to be with him. She knew it had just been this morning when he had made love to her one more marvelous time, but she had missed him all day. She kept looking at him, not believing that they were now together, when it wasn't too long ago that he was reluctant to get close to her. He was so wonderful and he loved her.

He was talking about something but she didn't hear him, she was so in her own dream world.

"Meg, are you listening to me?" he asked bringing her back to earth.

"I'm sorry, what?"

"What were you thinking about, you were smiling?" He laughed.

"You, and how wonderful it is that we're together," she told him.

"I've been thinking about that myself. You know I was worried that after we made love, my feelings for you would change, but I love you more than ever. You don't know how happy that makes me. It's like a big weight has been lifted off me." He said, reaching over and taking her hand.

"So what do you want to do with the horses?" he asked her. "Do you want to keep riding Black Jack and learning dressage? I guess I'll just work around the stable for now. Maybe I'll go back to school. To study what? I don't know. Do you think I could get into vet school? That might be fun."

"That's a great idea. I thought about it once but I didn't have the grades to get in. What's your degree in?"

"Actually I have three degrees. A BS in Animal Husbandry, a MS in Kinesiology and a MS in Equine Nutrition."

"Are you kidding me? What's Kinesi ...?"

"It's the study of human movement and it's really interesting. I try to keep in shape so my body will move when I want it to and do what I want it to."

"Well, it certainly does what *I* want it to."

"Mmm, thanks, sweetie." He smiled back at her. They pulled up to the barn and slowly got out.

"Grab your stuff. I'm starved," he said as he took her hand. They were walking up the path to the house when he pulled her over. He leaned his back on a tree and hugged her against him. She put her arms around him and laid her head on his chest. He kissed the top of her head and stroked her hair.

"I love you, Blackie," she said, her face buried in his shirt to breathe in his scent.

"I love you too, Meg," he said. "I'm a lucky guy."

*   *   *

Sean was getting seconds of dinner and saw them pull up. "Hey, the love birds are home."

"Sean, do *not* make any suggestive remarks or tease him," Jill said adamantly as she looked out the window. "I don't want any fights tonight. Ahhh, look, they're soooo cute together."

"Jesus, gag me. Okay, okay! I'll keep my mouth shut."

"Good, thank you," Jill told him, with a glare.

Blackie and Meg came in and said hello to everyone as they dug into the buffet.

"What's going on?" Blackie asked Keary.

"Not much. A couple horses are going to the track tomorrow and four are coming back from Fair Hill. I think the blacksmiths are coming soon. What's happening with you two?" Keary asked.

"We're just working with Meg's horses. I'm teaching her dressage. Other than that, I guess I'll just do whatever needs to be done around here," Blackie said without much enthusiasm. "Meg's spending the night."

"Of course, I'll make up one of the guest rooms for her," Jill said.

Blackie looked stunned. "No, she's staying with me in the apartment!"

"Did you ask her if she was comfortable with that arrangement?" Jill asked, trying to be serious.

He looked at Meg sheepishly. "Well no, but it'll be a lot more fun to stay with me, if you want?"

Everyone burst out laughing except Blackie. He looked surprised and then realized he was being teased.

"Okay you guys, very funny," he said and actually blushed.

After they finished eating, Blackie asked her if she was ready to turn in.

"Yes, I am kind of tired."

"Okay, let's go. We can watch a movie if you want," he said.

She was tired and definitely wasn't up to anymore love-making after last night and again this morning. She was still uncomfortable and hoped he would be able to control himself better now. She decided to make her feelings plain as soon as they were alone. They walked down to the barn, Blackie taking her hand again.

"Blackie." She said and turned to him. He pulled her close.

"Listen, young lady. I think we better lay off fooling around for a while until you feel better. That is if you can control yourself," he said with a big smile.

"Me! You're the one that's constantly horny!"

"You have to be kidding! You're always grabbing me and starting trouble," he said, dancing away from her as she swung at him.

"I'll get you," she said and chased after him, both of them laughing.

He grabbed her as they turned into the barn and kissed her very deeply.

"Keep that up and you *are* in trouble," she said kissing him back.

"I love you and I want you bad tonight, but I don't want to hurt you, so this is as far as it goes. I can't promise what will happen tomorrow." He laughed. "You know I'll be satisfied just having you in my bed tonight."

They went up to his apartment and started getting ready for bed.

"Do you want to watch a movie?" He asked.

"You know I'm awfully tired. I thought I'd just turn in."

"Me too," he said puttering around the apartment, not doing anything in particular.

Even though they had just been as intimate as two people can be; she felt self-conscious getting undressed in front of him. So she was messing around with her stuff, trying not to take her clothes off yet. He looked at her, smiled and went into the bathroom. She heard the shower running, so she changed her things. She put on a silk, short chemise and wondered now if it was too sexy since they wanted to cool it tonight.

This is complicated already.

She jumped into bed wondering what side he slept on, deciding to choose the center and covered up.

In about ten minutes, Blackie came out of the bathroom, toweling his hair dry.

"Mmm, you look all cuddly in there. I'll be with you in a sec." He went over by the door and set the alarm, threw his towel in the hamper and jumped in next to her. He turned her on her side and snuggled up behind her. He ran his hands over her nightie, turning her on big time.

"This feels good, just like you, soft and silky. I love you sweetie. Good night," he said softly and hugged her into him.

"Good night, I love you too."

*   *   *

This whole scenario was pretty much the same for the next four days. Blackie was very attentive and affectionate, but that's as far as it went. She was beginning to think something was wrong, maybe she did something to turn him off. The fifth morning, she couldn't stand it any longer. She had to ask him what was up. So, while they were grooming the horses, she stopped and stared at him, hands on hips. She got his attention in about a minute.

"What?" He said and stopped grooming, "Did I do something wrong?"

"No, you're not doing anything *wrong;* you're just not doing *anything*, that's the problem."

"Give me a clue what we're talking about here?"

"Are you ever going to make love to me again?"

"I thought you'd let me know when you're ready," he said frowning.

"Well, I'm ready!"

A slow smile started forming on his face. He threw the brush down.

"Let's go." He said, unhooking Sandman and putting him in the stall.

"Now!"

"I can't wait any longer," he said.

She quickly did the same with Cloudy. Blackie grabbed her hand, pulled her into the elevator and pushed the button.

As soon as the doors closed, he mashed her up against the wall and kissed her so hard her jaw hurt. He picked her up and held her against the wall with his hands under her butt. He was already totally aroused and pushed hard between her legs. Meg always thought those love scenes where couples were tearing each other's clothes off, were bogus. No one was in that much of a hurry. Well, guess what? She ripped his t-shirt off and was pulling at the front of his jeans. He had her sweater and bra off. She was frantic. She wanted him bad. He had almost her whole breast in his mouth. He put her down long enough to yank her jeans down and they both pulled them and her panties from her feet. She unzipped his jeans; he picked her up again and in one quick move was in her. She gasped, crying out in ecstasy. He pushed a couple of times, groaned and was still. They were both gasping for breath.

"I hope like hell nobody wants to use this elevator," he said, with his mouth on her neck. He put her down and they both gathered their clothes. He pushed the up button and they went into his apartment. He closed the door. They stood there looking at each other.

"Whoa, what was that? I thought I was the one going buggy here. You surprised me. What do you want to do now?" he asked her.

"Well, *you* better take a nap, because I'm not done," she told him, surprised by the intensity of her still present desire. He stared at here, wide-eyed.

"You mean I've met a woman who has the same kind of libido that I have," he laughed.

"Apparently!" She snapped, defensively. "I never would have believed it of myself until now, but in the elevator, I couldn't wait to get your clothes off. And I still want more. I never felt this way before and I can't control it." He crossed the room and hugged her.

"Are you okay? This time, I was going to be careful and gentle so I didn't hurt you." he asked, concern in his voice.

"I'm fine. I'm a little light headed from that. I think I'll sit down." She went over and sat on the sofa, Blackie went in the kitchen, got two sodas and sat down next to her. He just looked at her with a wide grin on his face.

"Cut it out. You look like a kid in a candy store You men. I can't believe you're this happy over what I just told you. I'm confused by it. I never had a lot of sexual feelings before."

"I guess I just bring out the best in you," he said, smugly.

"I think you should probably say that you *put* the best *in* me." They both laughed and hugged each other.

"Hey, how about that nap now?" he said.

"Sounds good to me." He scooped her up, plopped her on the bed and got in. They cuddled up and fell sound asleep.

TWENTY-TWO

Meg was in the kitchen talking to Jill when Keary came in. He had a suit on and had been to D.C. on business. He put his briefcase down and kissed Jill. He looked exhausted.

"How was your trip?" Jill asked.

"Okay," Keary said, letting out a big sigh, "I went over everything with the accountants and things are good. Profits are up from last year. Seems we're bouncing back from Blackie not riding anymore. Casey and Patrick, the new apprentice, are starting to win a higher percentage of races but the two of them together still aren't winning like Blackie did. Where are he and Sean?"

"The blacksmiths are here and there are sixteen horses, so they're both helping," Jill said and Keary nodded.

Just then the phone rang and Keary picked it up.

"Yes." Keary said, "What! Holy shit! We'll be right down." Keary slammed the phone down. "Fuck! One of the horses kicked Blackie in the back, let's go."

"Should I call 911?" Jill exclaimed.

"No, not yet, Sean didn't sound hysterical."

*   *   *

They ran down to the racing barn. Blackie was lying on the ground on his right side, obviously in pain.

Keary knelt down to talk to him. "How bad is it? Can you move your legs?"

"Yes and I'm not having any trouble breathing, so I think it's not bad, it just hurts like hell."

"Do you think you can get up?"

"Yes, give me a hand," Blackie held out his hand. Keary braced his feet and pulled Blackie all the way to standing. Keary sat him on a hay bale and let him catch his breath.

"Let's get your shirt off, I want to take a look." Keary gingerly helped him. When he raised his left arm, he grunted. Keary stared at his back along with everyone else.

"Jesus! That looks bad, Blackie, is your breathing still okay? Take a deep breath." Blackie did and grunted again.

"I can take air in so I don't think my lung is punctured, it just hurts. What's it look like?"

"You don't want to know."

There was a large, hoof-shaped contusion on the left side of his back that was blood-red, purple and had lumps in several spots.

"Fuck!" Blackie said, "Just let me sit here a few minutes till it stops throbbing and I'll be good."

"How the hell did this happen?" Keary asked, hands on his hips.

"Sean and I were holding the horses for the blacksmiths. I got bored just standing there, so I started pulling the old shoes off the next horse in line, to make things go faster. Anyway when I pulled off Sunny's hind shoe, he jerked his leg, I stumbled a few steps behind him and he let go with a kick that just connected perfectly."

"For chrissake, Blackie, why couldn't you just be bored for once? Why are you always getting into something and getting hurt?"

"Sorry! I just thought it would help speed things up and I'm not always getting hurt, damnit!" Blackie said, scowling at Keary.

"You messing around doesn't speed things up, it just costs us more time, money and down time because you're hurt."

"Keary," Jill gasped at what he said.

"I'm fucking sorry I'm such a drain on the economy around here!" Blackie glared at Keary, red-faced. "Now that I'm not winning races, I'm a fucking liability, is that it? Shit happens all the time, it's not my fault. These fucking, stupid animals are dangerous, you know that. You ought to be glad it was me instead of one of the farriers. They might sue you. I won't; then again maybe I will."

"I didn't mean it that way, Blackie."

"Oh, right. How do you think it feels to not have anything to do around here anymore? I try to put in a day's work so I don't feel like a goddamn liability, but I guess I am. Shit, okay, I'll start paying rent and for the food I eat. How's that? Will that help?"

Blackie coughed hard and spat blood out on the ground. "Shit! Go back up to the house, we still have ten horses to do."

"Come on, you're not in any shape to do anymore today," Keary pleaded.

"Fuck you, Keary, don't tell me what to do. Just get out of my sight so we can finish."

"Fine!" Keary turned to go back to the house and Jill followed grabbing Meg by the arm to go with them.

"I want to stay and make sure he's okay," she said.

"It's best to just leave him alone right now; Sean will watch him," Jill said and started in on Keary.

"Keary, what the hell is the matter with you, saying that to him? You know how sensitive he is about not having much to do anymore. You really hurt him!" Jill said.

"I know. I'm dog tired and I can't stand him getting hurt. He's always getting into stuff and then something happens. I know he's probably going crazy not being able to ride. I know it's not his fault. It came out wrong. You know I wouldn't hurt him for anything. I just can't take it anymore, Jill."

"I know, but you can't say mean things like that!" Jill said.

"I'm going to go take a shower," Keary said.

Jill and Meg sat in the TV room. They watched TV for awhile and then Keary came down and joined them.

"What's for dinner? Has Blackie come up yet?"

"No, haven't seen him or Sean and I don't know what Annie fixed. Let's go see."

They trooped into the dining room and got something to eat. About a half hour later Sean and Blackie came in, both of them dirty, dusty and sweaty. They stopped in the kitchen and washed up, then came in to fix their plates.

Sean said hello but Blackie was quiet. He was moving very slowly. He sat down gingerly and grimaced. He leaned over and kissed Meg's cheek.

"Hi." He said softly.

"Are you okay?" She whispered. He shook his head, slightly. He looked terrible. The front of his t-shirt had diluted blood all over it. He just sat there for a few minutes before taking a long pull on his drink and one small forkful of food. Sean looked at Keary and sort of rolled his eyes and shook his head.

"How'd it go, Sean?" Keary asked.

"All the horses are done and bedded down for the night. The blacksmiths are paid and they just left."

"Who paid them?" Keary asked. Sean just sort of nodded toward Blackie.

Blackie took another drink and coughed. He wiped his mouth with the napkin and Meg saw it was red. She touched his arm and he shook his head. "It's okay," he whispered. He nibbled some more on his food.

"How's your back, Blackie?" Keary asked him.

"Fuck you," he answered belligerently.

"Alright, calm down, Blackie, I know I hurt your feelings. What I meant to say came out wrong. You know I don't feel that way." Keary said, his shoulders slumped.

"I don't know anything. People tend to say what they mean. You don't have to worry about it because tomorrow I'm going to look for a job. I'll find something to do. If I put the word out at all the big stables, maybe I'll get a job walking hots. Maybe I could do *that*. Then I'm going to move out."

"Blackie, don't do that! We can figure something out. You know how much Keary loves you; he didn't mean it that way." Jill said.

"Love has nothing to do with it. If I'm useless, I'm fucking useless. I've been wrestling with this whole issue since the accident and you all know it. The only thing I've ever wanted to do my whole life was taken away from me in a split second. I haven't been able to figure out what to do with the result and the result is that I'm now useless to a big time racing stable. It's not enough for me to help load the horses going to the track or the shoeing or helping Meg with her horses. I enjoy all that, but it's not racing, it's not a career, it's not *anything*. So I have to figure this out all by myself."

"Blackie, can't I help you, somehow," Meg asked.

"You can help by just being with me. As long as I know you're there, I can work this out. Don't worry, whatever I do, you're going with me, Meg. Anyway, I need to go take a pain pill and lay down," he said and got up to leave.

"Blackie, I think you need to see a doctor," Keary said.

"Just leave me, Keary!" Blackie said as he kissed Jill on the top of her head.

*   *   *

As soon as they were out the door, Jill lit into Keary. "Have you lost your stupid mind? We can't have him out there working for some other stable doing God knows what. He won't be walking hots, that's for sure. They'll have him riding, if only to exercise the horses. They might even let him race. You have to fix this, Keary. You have to fix it now! Mom and Dad are going to freak!" Jill yelled at him, a vein popping out on her forehead.

"I know, I know! He's not going to listen to me now. What all happened down at the barn after we left, Sean?"

"He was in a lot of pain, but he was so angry, he just went and got another horse and held it for the guys. He kept coughing up blood. He must have punctured his lung. I don't know, he said he could breathe okay. He asked me to go and get his checkbook and he wrote them a check and they left. I haven't seen him this pissed in a long time. God, Keary, it was his riding that put us on the map for chrissake." Sean said red-faced.

"Don't you think I know that? I don't want him going to work anywhere else. He has to work this out himself, though." Keary said.

"Keary, listen, Blackie told me not to tell you, but I saw him riding weeks ago. He was showing Meg some dressage moves on Black Jack and I asked him to ride. I did because I knew he'd been practicing dressage with Meg's gelding. Meg says he can do amazing stuff with the horse and he's untrained. He was going to enter him in some local dressage competitions to see what he could do. I don't know what he's thinking now since he promised not to ride"

"The day you guys had the fight in the arena, was when I was watching him. I was going to tell you then, but he stopped me. But Keary, you should have seen what he did with Black Jack. He was brilliant! He could turn dressage into something to do. You know Blackie's good enough to take the right horse to the Olympic level." Jill told him.

"Why didn't you tell me then?" Keary asked her.

"You guys were too angry and he told me to forget it."

"I wonder. If he could make a name for himself in dressage, he could start his own training facility. I guess he couldn't get hurt doing dressage. I'll talk to him tomorrow and let him know we would support him in this, maybe he'll stay. He can use the farm to get started." Keary said.

"That's a great idea," Sean piped up, "I've seen him do some and he's fantastic. Let's get him to do it."

"He needs to cool down first," Keary said. "I hope he's not hurt too bad. I hope Meg can handle it. At some point she'll need to get used to this stuff happening if they stay together."

*   *   *

Blackie and Meg went back to his apartment. He looked bad and she knew he was hurting.

"I'm filthy but my back's hurting too bad. I don't think I can stand in the shower long enough to get cleaned up."

"Can you get in the Jacuzzi? That might help. We could put some Epsom salts in it. You just sit in it and I'll wash you."

"Make it hot but not too."

"Okay." She turned the water on, got the salts and poured some in the water. It was good and hot and as soon as it was filled, she started the jets. She went to get him and he was sitting there almost asleep. She took his boots and socks off and he got up and shuffled into the bathroom. He found some codeine in the cabinet and took one. She got him to sit on the toilet lid and helped him take his clothes off.

"Let me brush my teeth. I can't stand the taste of blood in my mouth any longer." He stood and slowly brushed his teeth.

"If I'm going to help you, I'll need to get in with you, so I guess I need to get naked, too."

"I'm sorry I'm in too much pain to enjoy it."

She helped him get in the tub and got in behind him. She noticed the awful scars on his right hip again and felt a stab of sadness. What a terrible thing to happen to him.

His back was worse; very angry looking. He sat in the hot water and closed his eyes and just let the warmth penetrate awhile. She got a cloth, soaped it up and washed his face, neck, shoulders and arms. She didn't want to make him get up, so she just used the now soapy water to wash the rest of him. She shampooed his hair and rinsed it. He had his eyes closed the whole time.

"Meg, you're so good to me. I love you so much. Ours is the relationship I've dreamed of for a long time."

They just looked into each other's eyes and he smiled. "I'm turning into a prune, maybe I should get out."

"Okay," she laughed.

He put on pj bottoms and eased into bed. She put a towel under his head in case he coughed up more blood. He was instantly asleep and she crawled in next to him and passed out.

She woke up around seven and he hadn't moved. There was still a fair amount of blood on the towel. She slowly caressed his face and he looked up at her.

"Hi, what time is it?" he said softly

"Seven. Do you want to try and get up? You're still coughing up blood.

He looked at the towel, "Oh, shit. I guess I better get x-rayed."

He started to get up, yelped in pain and lay back down.

"Great. It feels worse than last night." He slowly got up and walked into the bathroom. She sprayed deodorant for him and then helped him with underwear, jeans, socks and shoes.

"Go in the closet and get me a zip front sweatshirt. I know I can't raise my left arm." He called his doctor who said to come right over. So they got in her car and took off for D.C.

*   *   *

Jill was looking out the window and saw them leave.

"Meg just bundled Blackie into her car and they took off. I'd imagine for the doctor's or the hospital."

"Okay. They can handle whatever they need to do," Keary said.

"Don't you even care if he's hurt?"

"You know better than to ask me that, Jill. You know how much I worry about him. They're together and she doesn't need his sister and brother-in-law always taking over. They're adults."

"I know, but I'm so used to it being us who takes care of him and who he turns to," Jill said frowning.

"You have to let go, Jill and so do I."

"At least call the doctor and find out what's going on," she pleaded.

"You know, I bet Meg calls and tells us how he is and what's happening."

*   *   *

When Blackie and Meg got home, Jill poked her head out the door and beckoned them to come up to the house. Blackie groaned.

"*Now* what did I do? You go up and see what she wants. I want to lie down and take a pill."

"Okay, I'll be back soon. Do you want me to get you something to eat?"

"No, I'm not hungry. Don't stay long" and he went into the barn.

When Meg got to the house, Jill asked where Blackie was.

"He said he wanted to rest." Meg said.

"What did the doctor say? Is he alright?" Jill asked, wringing her hands.

"He doesn't have any cracked ribs and no lung punctures, but he does have a lot of blood from broken capillaries. That's why he's been coughing up blood since it happened.

"Oh, God. I can't stand it when he's hurt. What is the doctor doing about it?"

"He just wants him to rest and get another x-ray in three days."

"Is he eating?"

"He says he's not hungry." Meg answered.

"Oh, dear. Anyway, Keary wants to talk to him. Why don't you come in and sit down a minute. I'll fix something you can take down and heat up when he feels like eating."

Meg went into the dining room and Keary got up.

"Hi, Meg, is he alright?" Keary asked, with a frown, his face flushed.

"He's okay; he has to go back in three days. No fractures."

"I need to talk to him, Meg. We can't have him leaving here." Keary said. "Is he coming up?"

"No."

"I've been thinking. I want to talk to him about using the farm's facilities for his own business." Keary said.

"Like what?" She asked.

"Well, like a dressage training center. If he got a name for himself by winning competitions, I think he could make something out of it. I understand he likes your horse."

"Yes, he does, he thinks he has a lot of potential."

"Blackie would know. Let me talk to him and we'll see. You think he's cooled down enough to talk to me now?" Keary asked.

"I think he's cooled down some, but he's still in pain."

"I'll let him sleep awhile and then I'll come down. If I call first he'll say he doesn't want to see me. Okay?"

"I guess. Jill's giving me some food to heat up later. How about I give you a buzz when he's awake and has eaten, he might be in a better mood."

"Thanks, Meg," Keary said smiling.

"Between all of us maybe we'll be able to take care of him," Jill said.

"Yeah, maybe," Meg said and shrugged.

Meg took the food and walked down to the apartment. Blackie was cuddled up on the sofa with a comforter over him, sound asleep. She sat down near him and got a book to read. Of course, she fell asleep right away.

A few hours later she woke up and Blackie was standing over her touching her hair.

"Hi, honey," he said and kissed her forehead. She reached up and touched his face.

"How are you, are you still hurting a lot?"

"I'm okay; I feel a little better, no coughing. I gotta pee," he said and went into the bathroom. When he came out he sat down next to her and said, "Man, I'm hungry."

"I have just the thing. Jill sent a bunch of food down. Just let me nuke it. You want a Coke?"

"Yes, please," he said smiling. He shifted around and still grimaced when he moved a certain way.

She fixed the food, got the drink and sat down next to him.

"I'm glad to see that you're hungry, that's a good sign."

He leaned over and kissed her softly on the mouth and then he started in on the food with a little gusto. She turned on the TV and then went to the bathroom to call Keary on her cell.

"Give it about twenty minutes." She said quickly.

When she came out, Blackie was watching a movie and finishing up the food.

"I feel better. I needed food. Now I need you. Come here." He pulled her close and kissed her with a little more interest.

"Hmm, you taste good. I'm sorry I've been such a mess," he looked at her with smoldering eyes.

Oh, goodie. He's getting romantic and Keary will be here any minute.

Blackie kissed her again and this time it was deep and urgent. He was breathing hard when a knock came at the door. He jumped back from her and yelped in pain, "Shit, who the hell is that?"

"I'll see." She got up and answered the door. Keary came in.

"Great timing, Keary," Blackie said, pissed.

"I'm sorry," Keary said, flushing. "Did I interrupt something?"

Meg smiled at him and he rolled his eyes.

"Duh, yes." Blackie said and got up and got another soda. "You want a beer?" He said to Keary.

"I could use one." Keary sat down in a chair across from Blackie.

"So, what's happening?" Blackie asked casually.

Keary took a deep breath, "I've been thinking a lot about what happened yesterday. I need to apologize to you for the things I said. You don't deserve to be talked to like that. You've always been a vital and central person in this operation. I hope you know how much I've always respected your abilities. You still can be a vital part; we all just need to find out what it is. I know you've been trying to do that. None of us want to see you leave here. It would kill us."

Blackie just listened with his head down.

"Anyway, here's what I want to propose. I understand you have an interest in trying dressage."

Blackie looked at her, "Meg, what the hell?"

"Don't jump on her. I think it's a fantastic idea and so do Jill and Sean. I think you should work with Sandman and the farm can afford to buy you more horses if you want them. Once you've made a name in dressage circles, I was thinking you could use the farm's facilities for your own training center. Your own business. We could even renovate the place to your specifications. What do you think?"

Blackie looked up and stared at Keary, considering the offer.

"Are you serious?"

"Absolutely."

Blackie got up, walked over to Keary and held out his hand

"You've got a deal," he said and smiled.

Keary shook his hand and got up and hugged Blackie. He stood back and looked at him.

"You know I love you."

"Yeah, yeah, I love you too."

"Were you planning on working with Sandman tomorrow or is your back too painful yet?" Keary asked.

"It is better, not great, but I said I wasn't going to ride anymore. Why?"

"I want to watch you ride him."

"You want me to ride and you're going to watch?"

"Yes."

"Okay," Blackie said with a shrug.

"Good, just let me know when you're ready. Goodnight you two." And Keary left.

Black turned and looked at her for a long, thoughtful minute or two.

"What?" She asked.

"What do you think of his idea?"

"I think it's great. I mean you already have big time name recognition in racing circles; all you need is to be recognized as a dressage expert instead of a steeplechase jockey."

"You think I can do it?" he asked.

"I think you can do anything you set your mind to."

"But I do have physical limitations. Suppose I get to a real competitive level and my hip craps out on me?"

"You've never let anything stop you before."

"But the accident did stop me, dead in my tracks, as a race rider."

"Okay. See how it holds up when you start working Sandy every day and hard. Don't make any decisions until then. You could talk to your surgeon again."

He smiled at her. "I think this could be great!"

"Me, too."

TWENTY-THREE

Blackie, Sean and Meg were standing at the rail of the track watching Casey work a new horse over the hurdles. Several weeks passed since Blackie rode for Keary who was blown away by Blackie's ability to do dressage. Everyone enthusiastically agreed that Blackie should proceed with showing and work toward a training business. Meg and Blackie were successful at a few local shows with Blackie winning several 2nd Level classes. Sean and Keary were making a concerted effort to include Blackie in training decisions for the chasers.

Sean and Blackie were talking about the way the horse was working.

"Sure and he moves well enough but I'm not crazy about the way he takes off at the fences. He's taking off way too soon and he's going to end up hurting Casey," Blackie said.

"I don't see it," Sean said. "He looks okay to me. It's Casey's fault if he isn't taking off right."

"Not necessarily. Casey's trying to correct it but it's not working. I'll ask Casey what's what. Signal him to bring the horse in."

Blackie leaned against Meg and bent down to kiss her neck. They had been sleeping together for some time now and never got enough of each other. Everyone was used to Blackie being openly affectionate with her. Actually, they were living together. She spent all her time except for working at the gallery, at the farm. Blackie had a fit if she stayed in her condo over night.

Just then Keary walked up and said, "Hello, you three. How's the new gelding?"

"Pretty good," Sean said. "Blackie has a problem with him."

"What?"

"I don't know; I don't like where he takes off."

"You're the expert on how and where they should jump," Sean said.

"Yes, that's me, the expert," Blackie said sarcastically.

"Come on now, we talked about this. That's one of your new roles around here, the racing expert, and you certainly are that," Keary said.

Blackie just had his head down and nodded. Keary put his arm around his shoulders and hugged him.

"Anyway, I need you to go to Ireland to buy some horses." Blackie glanced up with his mouth open.

"Why don't you take Meg with you? I'm sure she'd enjoy seeing Ireland."

Blackie smiled and looked at her. "How many do we need?"

"Maybe four or five. You can go to Goff's and see what they have. Take Meg to the National Stud while you're there."

"Ohmigod, I've always wanted to see that!" She was so excited she couldn't stand still. Her excitement made Blackie grin.

"Sean, why don't you and Katie go too?"

Sean's mouth dropped open and he stared at Keary a minute in surprise then said, "Great, but don't you need me here for the racing?" Sean said.

"I do, yes, but I think we can manage without you two screw-ups for a couple weeks. Actually, after Ireland you could fly down and see what's going on at New Market."

"What's New Market?" Meg asked.

"A race track, barns, bloodstock sales in England?" Blackie explained. Blackie and Sean high-fived each other.

"Are you serious? You're taking me to England too!" She shrieked.

Blackie laughed and put his arm around her neck and said, "I am, yes. We're going to have a blast."

"We'll go over the details before you guys leave. Blackie, you make the reservations, since you know the best places to stay or you could stay with your parents while you're there."

Blackie instantly got pissed. "Oh, is that it, then? Getting me to go see them. Shit!"

"Blackie, calm down, you don't have to go see them, but it would be nice to have them meet Meg. They'll have to eventually."

"I guess you're right."

"I was thinking maybe, since you're at the sales, see if they have any warmbloods or whatever that you could use for dressage," Keary said quietly.

Blackie just looked at him a minute. "Yes, a good idea. You're serious about this?"

"I am, yes."

"Thanks, Keary," Blackie said.

Keary grabbed him, ruffled his hair and walked away.

"I'll call the airline and hotels and make reservations. Can you two go to Tattersalls?"

"Okay, now what's that?" Meg asked.

"Only the biggest bloodstock sales in Europe."

"Oh, this is so exciting." Meg said, bouncing on her toes.

"I'll ask her. We can do London too. This is so cool." Sean did a little jig and walked away smiling.

Blackie turned to her, "This is going to be fun. You know it's been over three years since I've been home." He hugged her again. Those big, blue eyes of his were lit up with excitement.

TWENTY-FOUR

Meg couldn't believe she was going to Ireland with Blackie to buy racehorses. The first place they were going was Goff's Bloodstock Sales in Kill, County Kildare. Blackie booked them rooms at the Killashee House hotel in Naas near the sales. Sean and Katie were going along. After the sale, they'd visit Blackie's parents. Meg was fairly nervous about that. Blackie didn't get along with his parents and Meg hoped they liked her. Blackie said he didn't care if they like her or not, but she did.

After that they were going to a place outside of London called Tattersall's in New Market to look at more horses. It seemed like it was going to be a hugely expensive trip, but she didn't ask about finances. Whenever she got upset about the cost of something, Blackie always told her not to worry, it wasn't a problem.

She was busy trying to pack but wasn't sure what to take. Blackie said he'd take care of his stuff but she hadn't seen any evidence of it yet. She thought she'd ask Jill and walked up to the house while he was working at the racing barns.

"Meg, honey, I was hoping to see you. How's the packing going?" Jill asked.

"Hi, Jill, that's why I'm here. I haven't a clue what to pack. Give me some ideas. Blackie hasn't packed a thing."

"Oh, don't pay any attention to him; he always waits till the last minute. Don't let it stress you though, he's traveled so much, he knows what he's doing. Of course, you'll want to take lots of stable clothes; those are what he'll wear almost the whole time. I would take quite a few outfits for fancy restaurants. He has expensive taste in places to eat. He travels in casual but nice clothes, so I'd take about five pretty, pants outfits. They might have one fancy dinner at my parents', but all the rest of the time he'll be in jeans. How long are you guys going to be gone?"

"Three weeks, I think, I'm not sure. I better ask him.

Just then, Sean walked in and washed up.

"Meg, hi, are you getting ready for the trip? Katie's going nuts figuring out what to take. I kind of know because I've traveled with him before but I wasn't sure what to tell her."

"I'll call her, Jill just filled me in on what I'd need," she said.

Blackie came in the door and washed up. Then he walked into the dining room.

"Hi, guys, hi, sweetheart," he said kissing her. "What's up?"

"I can't believe we're actually going to Ireland," she said.

"I know, I can't wait, we're going to have a ball," he said, standing behind her and circling her in his arms.

"The plane's ready and hotels are reserved. I hope you guys like this place. It's fairly close to Goff's."

"Katie's upset about the sleeping arrangements at Mom and Dad's," Sean told him

"Why?" Blackie asked.

"She doesn't want to shock Mom by us sleeping together. I've taken girls there before and Mom automatically put us in separate rooms," Sean said.

"I've got news for my mother. Meg and I are sleeping in the same room or I'm not staying," Blackie said firmly.

"Honey, I don't want to upset your mother either," Meg said.

"Jesus H. Christ, you too. We're adults, that's ridiculous!" Blackie said. "I'm not changing the way I live because my mother's not happy with it; then again she's never been happy with my lifestyle. I've never taken a woman there before. She should be happy I've found a decent girl that I love. Fuck it!" and he stomped out.

"Oh great. Is this going to be a real problem?" Meg asked. "I don't want to go against your parents' rules, but you see how he's going to be."

"Actually, I don't think it's going to be a problem. Mom knows about you and how happy he is. She also knows that you're living together and she hasn't said anything," Jill said.

"I guess we are living together. I hadn't thought about it before. I haven't seen my condo in months. I better go calm him down. See you guys later," she said and went after Blackie.

*   *   *

Meg found him in the barn, grooming Sandman. He didn't look quite as angry. He turned and stopped what he was doing.

"Are you ashamed or embarrassed by the fact that we're living together?" he asked.

"No, of course not," she answered. He stared at her for a few minutes.

"I mean we're not married, doesn't that bother you?"

"No, I love you too much and I couldn't wait any longer to be with you."

"I know, I couldn't wait any longer, either. I'll have to do something about this situation." He said firmly.

"Like what?

"Never mind, this is the end of this conversation and we're sleeping together at my parents' house," he said decisively.

"Great." She said and turned to go.

"Meg, come here, honey," he said softly. She went to him and he folded her in his arms and kissed her tenderly.

"Don't worry; I love you more than anyone in the world. My Mom will know it and approve. I'm also going to make it right."

"I just don't want to start trouble between you and your parents."

"Don't worry, you won't."

Twenty-Five

Jeremy drove them to Dulles in the limo. They were all immensely excited to be going to Ireland. The girls never shut up, chattering continuously about the trip. Meg was almost hyperventilating from the non-stop talking and the jittery, tingling in her stomach. Katie bounced in her seat as she prattled on and waved her hands in the air.

Sean felt the excitement in his gut but was having too much fun watching the girls. Blackie was quiet. It was three years since he set foot on Irish soil. He ached to get there. He wouldn't admit it, but his heart warmed at the thought of his parents' welcoming embrace. His parents, horses and Ireland were all woven together deep in his heart.

They pulled into the General Aviation terminal and glided to a stop next to a gleaming white Lear jet with a green stripe.

"We're here ladies," Blackie announced.

"Ohmigod, is that yours?" Meg gasped.

"It belongs to the farm."

Katie and Meg squealed and hugged each other. The guys just laughed as they pulled the girls from the car.

Meg couldn't believe her eyes. The plane was beautiful. Blackie led her up the carpeted stairs into the cabin that was just as beautiful as the outside. Decorated in soft beige and green, Meg settled into one of the pillow-soft seats. She inhaled the "new car" smell and was amazed at how quiet it was when the pilot closed the door.

They dug into the pizza and drinks Blackie ordered and didn't even notice the rocking chair smooth take-off. The four of them played cards, talked about the trip and Sean and Blackie shared Irish facts and folklore with Meg and Katie.

Finally winding down, the two couples retreated to opposite ends of the cabin, Sean dimmed the lights and they were asleep.

Meg woke up when they were approaching Dublin Airport and shook Blackie awake.

"Come on, honey, we're getting ready to land." She couldn't wait to put her feet in Ireland. Blackie sat up and looked out the window.

"I always love coming home," he said, his eyes shining. "Good morning sweetheart, how are you? Did you sleep well?"

"Yes, I had a wonderful night. I'm always comfortable cuddled up against you."

"Good, let's get ready to de-plane."

They loaded their bags in the SUV Blackie rented and drove toward Naas. The countryside was beautiful, rolling and a lush green color she'd never seen before. They registered at the hotel and piled into their elegant adjoining rooms. Meg and Katie were so excited, they kept chattering about how lovely everything was. The guys just rolled their eyes.

It was late and the sale pavilion was closed so they changed and went to the hotel dining room for dinner. The meal was wonderful but expensive and Blackie, of course, picked up the check. They were tired from the trip and turned in early.

The next morning she awoke to Blackie kissing her neck. She turned and looked at him. He had a frisky glint in his eyes, so she kissed him hard.

Mmm, good morning to you too," he said huskily. He kissed her again, taking the kiss deeper while caressing her lovingly. It wasn't long and she was just as ready as he was. They slowly made love to each other and took their time about it.

"I love being away together like this." He murmured afterwards.

He ordered breakfast in their room while she took a shower and dressed in jeans, boots and a sweater. She put her hair up in a ponytail and came out just as breakfast was arriving.

"You look cute," Blackie said. "Are you hungry?"

"Not after what you just did to me."

"Oh really, you're going to lose weight on this trip then. I think you better eat," he laughed.

The food was delicious; a full Irish breakfast. After they ate, he took a shower and dressed in his usual attire.

Sean and Katie were ready, they jumped in the car and roared off for Goff's, Blackie driving. They parked and found the office where Blackie had to register as a buyer and a representative of Killarney Farms. He signed a draft drawn on an account at the Bank of Ireland for €80, 000. He also gave them his credit card.

"I might want to buy some horses personally and I'll use that."

"Yes sir, Mr. O'Brien. Here's your buyer registration and number," the broker said.

"Okay, let's go back to the stable area. Sean, do you want to ride any of the chasers we find to check them out? You know what, I should call Dad and see if he needs any horses while we're here," Blackie said.

"I guess I'll ride. You're better at gauging how good they are, but if you have an accident, I'll be killed by Keary and Jill," Sean said.

"Well, we'll see what we find. We could both check them out. It's not like I'm going to race or anything. I'll call Dad," Blackie said and made the call on his cell.

"Dad, hi, it's Blackie. Sean and I are over at Goff's for a few days. I was wondering if you need any horses. Anything we buy, I'll have them delivered to you and then we can ship ours from there."

He listened for a few minutes.

"Yes, we're going to your house after we're done here. Oh, we have our girl-friends with us, if that's okay? Sure. Meg and Katie. Yes, Dad. Okay, tell Mom hi and we'll see you in a few days. We'll call before we leave here. Killashee House in Naas. Okay, I love you too Dad, bye."

Blackie disconnected and said gruffly, "He wants two chasers," and moved on to the stable area. Sean rolled his eyes at Meg and caught up with Blackie. As usual, when he was doing anything with horses, Blackie was extremely focused. Katie and Meg could have caught on fire and he wouldn't have noticed. Every once in awhile, he'd stop at a stall and consult his catalog. Sean didn't say anything, but deferred to Blackie as always. He stopped in front of a big chestnut gelding's stall and looked for a long time. Then he consulted his catalog.

"What do you think, Sean?"

"Yeah, he's promising," Sean agreed.

"Okay, that's #421, let's put him down for a try-out."

They both moved on. The girls followed at a distance because they wanted to talk. At one point, they were chattering away and Blackie turned and gave them a look. Another eye roll from Sean. This was business, no goofing around. So, Katie and Meg pulled back. All of the horses were beautiful; shiny and sleek. She didn't see how he picked out one from another. Next he stopped at a bay colt's stall. Not quite as big as the chestnut, but heavier in build. He came over and nuzzled Blackie and he scratched the colt's nose.

"Okay, put this one down, #380. I like his breeding."

"Didn't we have a brother of his at one time?"

"Yes, I won a lot of races with him, too. It was Rock Hill. He looks a lot like him."

This routine went on for some time. Katie and Meg decided they needed a break when they saw a drink kiosk and ladies room.

"Blackie, we're going to get a drink. Do you guys want something?"

"I'll take a large coffee," he said, still all business.

"Get me a Coke," Sean said. Blackie gave her an €20 note.

"We'll be over on that side, so you can find us," Blackie said and motioned to the right.

"Okay, we'll catch up to you," she said and they took off. Their first stop was the ladies room and then they found a little table and sat. They got tea and scones and were happy for a break. Meg knew Blackie could keep up this pace for hours without a break. She bet Sean would have liked to come with them.

"It feels good to sit down," Katie said with a sigh. "Is Blackie always this serious?"

"Only when he's focused on horses. Usually he's pretty playful, but this is business, so he won't relax."

"You two are good together; he seems very nice. I've heard a lot about Blackie from Sean. They're at odds a lot but seem to care about each other. Sean makes him sound totally wild sometimes." Katie said.

"He can be a handful. He has a lot of problems from the past when he was racing. Hopefully he's getting them straightened out. Basically he's a sweet guy," Meg said.

"You guys seem like you're so in love. Any wedding plans?"

"He's always telling me how much he loves me and I'm wild about him. No, he hasn't asked me to marry him yet.

"That's funny. Sean and I talk about it a lot and I think he's going to pop the question soon." Katie said.

"That's fantastic. I hope he does. Blackie would like that. He sort of assumes stuff in his head and then is surprised when other people don't know what he's thinking," they both laughed.

"I wish I could see him ride. Sean's always going on about what a great jockey he was and gets upset when he talks about this accident."

"He still rides, he just can't race anymore. You might see him ride today or tomorrow. They're going to try out the horses they want to buy."

"Oh, I'd love to see that. I guess we better find them soon and take their drinks."

They got drinks for the guys and paid. They went searching for them and found them inspecting a horse cross-tied in the aisle. Blackie was squatting down feeling the horse's legs. Sean was rubbing the horse's neck and watching Blackie. He smiled when they walked up.

"Hello ladies, did you two have a good time?" Sean said. Blackie ignored them and continued what he was doing.

"I don't know, Sean, this joint feels hot to me. See what you think." He stood up and almost bumped into Meg.

"Oh, hi sweetheart, what have you guys been up to?" he said and kissed her. She was surprised by this attention and handed him his coffee.

"Great, how did you know I needed caffeine," he said looking at the cup in surprise.

"Did you buy any horses?" She asked, smiling at him and ignored Katie who was trying to suppress a laugh.

"Well, I put holds on six horses, but we need to ride them before the auction. I like this one but I don't like the way his ankles look. I think there's a chronic problem there."

Sean stood up. "Yeah, I think you're right. Both his front fetlocks are hot."

Blackie went back and felt the joints. "Yeah, you're right. Forget him. Let's put him back."

Sean untied the horse and put him back in his stall.

"Let's see, Dad wanted two. Is four enough for us? We might see a couple at Tattersalls. Hopefully we'll get the ones we want. Did you like any of the others that we didn't put on our list?"

"Well, I liked the gray that you weren't crazy about," Sean said.

"Okay what was his number? We can go back and take another look and try him. Just because I didn't like him in the stall doesn't mean much," Blackie said.

"He was #1219, he's over near the door to the warm-bloods," Sean said.

"That's perfect, we'll look at him on the way to them. Hey, Meg, want to find horses for dressage?" Blackie asked her, putting his arm around her.

"Oh, can we? That would be great."

They walked around and found the gray that Sean liked so Blackie could take another look. Sean led the horse out and cross-tied him. Blackie walked around and peered closely at the colt, feeling his legs.

"He actually looks pretty good. Maybe it's just my aversion to grays. Let's give him a try."

Sean was pleased and wrote the number down.

"Are we going to do the riding horses now?" Sean asked.

"Yeah, let's go," Blackie said and put the colt back in his stall.

They walked around a good bit in the warm-blood area. Blackie was holding Meg's hand most of the time. She thought now that the racing stable business was over; he could relax and concentrate on the riding horses and her.

They looked at a lot of horses. She was getting discouraged when she saw a beautiful chestnut mare. She wasn't too big and had a very sweet face. Meg liked her instantly and called Blackie who was down the aisle with another horse.

"Blackie, come here and look at this mare."

He walked over and looked in the stall.

"Oh, man, she's beautiful. I like her head. Let me check her in the catalog. She's an eight year old Swedish warm-blood. Let's get her out and take a look."

Blackie ran his hands all over her. She nuzzled him when he came up to her head.

"She's sweet and in good condition. I think you should ride her later. I'll put a hold on her."

"You mean she's for me?" She asked as her hand flew to her mouth.

"Well, sure. She's only fifteen and a half hands. She's too small for me and too lightweight. She's a woman's horse."

"You mean you're going to buy *me* a horse?" She couldn't believe this.

"Honey, we're here to buy horses. Didn't you hear Keary say to look for some dressage horses?"

"For you, not for me. Keary shouldn't buy me a horse."

"Keary's not buying you a horse, I am," he said.

"I thought we had this discussion about you not buying me such expensive gifts," she said adamantly.

"Yes, we did and you lost the discussion. Hey, aren't we together, aren't we a couple?" he asked, frowning.

"Ah, well, yes, of course we're together."

"Okay, then my money is your money. Anyway, it's not a gift it's an investment in your future." He said, just as adamantly.

She gave him a big eye roll and a huff.

"That's my girl," he said laughing and hugged her.

They walked around some more. Blackie saw a big, bay gelding that he liked.

"Hey, Sean, what do you think of this guy? He's an eleven-year-old Dutch warm-blood." They stood there studying this horse and feeling his legs and back.

"He's good, but I'm not familiar with what you'd look for in a dressage horse. Why don't you ride him?"

"Yes, let's put him on the list," Blackie said.

"Are we going to eat anytime soon?" Sean asked. "I'm starving."

"We are, yes. We better do that now so we can ride these guys this afternoon. Tomorrow is the sale."

TWENTY-SIX

There was a dining room at the sales pavilion where they ate. Sean and Blackie talked about the horses they would ride in the afternoon.

"Let's do the chasers first and then go inside and ride the other two."

"Okay, do you want me to ride some or all of them?" Sean asked.

"Don't you feel confident riding them?"

"It's been a long time since I did any riding, but I'm afraid you're going to get hurt," Sean said apologetically.

"I've been riding regularly so maybe I better do it. If I feel uneasy about any of them, I'll tell you. Maybe we can find a lad to do it. There's usually a bunch of young jockeys around to help out," Blackie said.

They walked back to the stable area and went through to the outside where there was a training track with a few hurdles. Blackie found a young boy, maybe fourteen or so and gave the boy money to saddle and bring out each horse on the list. The boy ran off. Meanwhile, Blackie went into a tack room and came back with a helmet on and gave one to Sean. In about fifteen minutes, the kid came out leading the gray Sean liked.

"You want to try him?" Blackie asked him.

"Why don't you ride and let me watch."

"Okay, give me a leg up."

Sean flipped him into the saddle and he was adjusting the stirrups as he walked the horse toward the track. He trotted the gray out on the track and started a slow canter in the opposite direction of the hurdles. Halfway around the track, he turned the horse and put him into a gallop. They were standing at the rail and watched as the horse pounded toward the first hurdle. When they got close, the colt flicked his ears backward to Blackie and then forward and looked at the jump. Right at the perfect moment, he took off and flew over the hurdle. They landed steadily and galloped toward the next fence.

"Jesus, nobody rides like he does! I wouldn't have the nerve to take a horse I didn't know at that pace. I wish you could have seen him race," Sean said to Meg. She suddenly realized that a crowd had formed around them.

Someone said, "Is that Blackie O'Brien? I heard he was killed on the track. Sure and I loved watching him race."

Another man said, "That's him. I recognized him earlier but I didn't know he could still ride. I heard he was crippled. I'm going to try and get his autograph."

Blackie came back again, slower this time, standing in his stirrups. He went by them and slowed even more to cool the grey down. He came trotting back to us and pulled up by Sean.

"You're right, this guy is fantastic. He's got heart." Someone yelled to Blackie from the crowd. Blackie looked over; smiled and waved.

"Hey, Bert, how's it going?" Blackie jumped off and gave the gray to another kid to cool him off.

"Sean, I think we should definitely get him, he'll be good for your string. What do you think?"

"He looks great, but then you were riding him. I agree. I think he'll be a good addition to the stable."

Just then the men behind them came over with their catalogs and asked Blackie for an autograph. His eyes went wide and he blushed.

"Oh, sure. I mean, I don't race anymore." He said.

"I'm glad to see you're okay and still riding. I watched you win three Grand Nationals and that was a real thrill."

"Thank you. What's your name?" Blackie asked him.

"It's Jimmy." Blackie wrote something to the man and then signed the program. The man shook hands with Blackie.

"Thanks, Blackie. I think you're the greatest steeplechase rider ever. This is grand."

"Thank you," Blackie said flushing with pleasure and suddenly surrounded by people asking for autographs. Blackie graciously signed a lot of them and said to Sean as the kid brought out the chestnut gelding.

"Sean, you want to take this horse?"

"Nope. These people are after seeing *you* ride. You better do it," Sean said smiling and the crown applauded.

Blackie just looked around with his mouth open. Several men clapped him on the back.

"You've still got it. Come on!"

Sean tossed him up and everyone applauded again. He just shook his head and moved off at a trot. He did the same routine and then turned and came back at a gallop. Close to the fence, the horse pricked his ears and then put them flat back against his head. Suddenly the horse veered and went around the jump, almost unseating Blackie but he hung on. Blackie came trotting over, showing his teeth.

"Sean, give me a stick."

"You want me to get a lad to ride him?" Sean said, breaking out in a sweat.

"No, the fucker pissed me off, so now he's going *over* the jump!" Sean handed him the whip and Blackie trotted off again and went down the track. He came back at a dead run, the chestnut's ears flat back the whole time. Close to the jump, Blackie hit the horse once with the whip and yelled something at the take-off point. The gelding went flying over the hurdle and thundered on to the next one. He didn't refuse again. Sean blew out a breath of relief.

A man came up and punched Sean on the arm.

Sean turned and smiled. "Georgie, hey, how the hell are you?" Sean asked.

The man was a little shorter than Blackie, older and heavier.

"I'm good. That son-of-a-bitch always could make a horse do whatever he wanted. He could ride anything with four legs. I'm sorry, I'm George Riley. I used to race with Blackie before the accident," he explained to Katie and Meg.

"He looks good, Sean. He's heavier, but he looks in great shape. I didn't know he could still ride. The last time I saw him was in the hospital; it made me sick. I couldn't believe he was still alive."

"Hey, Georgie, this is Meg Connors, Blackie's girlfriend and Katie Frey, my girlfriend."

"A girlfriend! I see he's still as healthy as he always was." And smiled conspiratorially at Sean. "What are you boys doing here?" George asked.

"We're buying horses for the U.S. stable and for Dad. We're getting some for dressage, too. Blackie and Meg are into that." Sean explained.

"Dressage, is it now? He's got the talent. Sure and it's grand to see him up on a horse again," George said, smiling at Blackie when he rode up. The crowd applauded again.

Blackie saw us and broke into a grin when he saw Georgie.

"Hey, Georgie, you auld bastard. It's good to see you." He jumped off, gave the horse to the kid and gave Georgie a bear hug.

"Blackie, you look great. I didn't know you were riding again."

"I'm not supposed to do any racing or jumping. I'm getting into dressage though; it fascinates me."

"I'm sure you'll be great at it. I met your girlfriend, she's very pretty. It's good to see that you're settling down," George said smiling at Meg.

I am, yes. What have you been up to, Georgie?"

"I didn't have the heart for it anymore after your accident, so I retired. Now I'm doing a bit of training meself. It's not as hard on the bones."

"I'm sorry, George, but I'm happy you're enjoying yourself. Listen, let's keep in touch and Dad would love to hear from you, too. I've got to finish up with these nags. Good to see you again." Blackie gave him a punch on the arm and turned to collect the next horse. After he tried all the racehorses, he and Sean decided they wanted all six.

"Are we done? Are you happy with them, then, Sean?"

"I am, yes. I think we made some good choices. Now I hope we can out-bid everyone else."

"You mean we might not get the horses we want?" Meg asked.

"No, it's an auction. We have to bid and hope we can out-bid anyone else," Blackie said. "Let's take a break and we'll look at the others inside."

They went in and had drinks. Sean and Blackie talked about bidding strategy. Katie and Meg talked about where they'd like to go in London after they were done at New Market.

Meg didn't feel all that well. She had been feeling tired the past couple weeks but nothing she could put her finger on. She felt sort of light headed and figured it was from all the excitement. She mentioned it to Katie at lunch.

"Are you pregnant?" She asked.

"Pregnant! I couldn't be. I've been using the patch for about four months now. I haven't had a period for a couple months, but the patch does that to me. I'm not regular at all." She was shocked at the idea that she might be pregnant.

"Why don't you take a test and see. I don't know if the patch would give you a false positive or not."

"Let's go to a drugstore later. I'll tell Blackie I need something, aspirin or whatever."

"Why don't you just tell him? Last month, I was late and Sean went and got the test for me. It was negative."

"Hmm, I don't know. He gets pretty spastic about stuff. I guess I should tell him I'm not feeling well."

"Hey, if he's man enough to get you pregnant; he should be man enough to take responsibility," Katie said.

"Oh, I know he'll be responsible; I just can't see getting him upset over nothing," Meg said louder than she intended.

"I think you let him get away with too much. He's a big boy."

"I guess you're right," Meg said, narrowing her eyes at Katie.

What's she the relationship expert?

Blackie glanced over at them. "What are you two talking about?"

"Oh, we're talking about maybe shopping if we get a chance to go to London," Katie told him.

"There's a lot to see and do in London. We can go to Harrods. We have a lot to do before we get that far. Let's go see those horses. Meg, do you want to ride the mare?"

"No, I'm not feeling too hot. Do you mind riding her?" She said, suddenly feeling shaky.

He came over as they were walking out and put his arm around her.

"Are you okay, baby? What's wrong?"

"I just feel a little light headed. I'm fine. You must be tired, you've been doing everything," she said putting her head against his shoulder.

"I'm good. Tell me if you start feeling worse. Maybe we're doing too much," he said as he turned and kissed her. He looked at her and frowned.

"You're a little pale," and he felt her forehead. "You don't seem to have a fever."

"I'll be fine. I feel a little better since we ate something."

"Okay. I'm going to get these two saddled up. Why don't you and Katie sit down in the stands and I'll be out in a few minutes."

He kissed her again and trotted into the stable area. She and Katie went and sat down in the arena.

"How are you feeling? Did you tell him?" Katie bugged her.

"I feel a little better and no, I didn't tell him yet. I won't until I know for sure."

In a few minutes Blackie came trotting in on the mare and slowed to a walk. He let her walk for a few minutes and then worked her around the arena through basic gaits and movements. It wasn't too long when he rode her over to where they were sitting.

"Meg, she's wonderful; very smooth. Do you want her?"

"Yes, she's beautiful."

"Okay, she's yours," he said, smiling.

"Thank you, sweetheart, I can't believe you're actually buying me a horse. I don't know how to thank you."

"Don't worry, I'll think of something," he said laughing as he walked the mare toward the stable area.

"I just bet you will." She said smiling at him.

God, I love him. What am I going to do if I'm pregnant? What will he do? I'll be devastated if this changes our relationship. I couldn't be pregnant! We've used the patch for a while; why a problem now? Maybe the patch itself is making me feel bad. Maybe I should stop using it.

He came back out mounted on the bay gelding. He worked him around the arena and came over when he was done.

"I like this guy, too. He's not as smooth as the mare but he's very responsive. Well, I think I'm done here. I'll be out in a few minutes." He dismounted and led the horse back.

The guys came walking out together, talking and laughing. They sat down with the girls and Blackie kissed her.

"My legs are super tired. In fact, I'm cramping up a bit. I haven't done that much riding in one day in years. Let's order pizza and beer and eat in our room. I'm going to take a long, hot shower before we eat."

They went back to their rooms to get ready for dinner. Blackie took a pain pill and took a very long shower. Meg picked out her outfit for the next day and then called Katie to see how ready they were.

"We're almost ready. There's a pharmacy off the hotel lobby, so I ran in there and got you a test. I'll stick it in your purse when we come over," she whispered into the phone.

"Okay, I'm getting nervous about it. Blackie's still in the shower. He should be out soon. I'll call and order the food."

"Okay, see you in ten," Katie said and hung up.

Meg called room service and ordered two large pizzas, soda and beer. Blackie came out of the shower buck-naked, grabbed her and threw her on the bed. She got hysterical laughing at him. He was trying to be sexy, but started laughing himself.

"This isn't very seductive is it?" he laughed.

"No, especially since Sean and Katie will be here any minute." She laughed and pulled him on top of her and he kissed her deeply.

"I could *get* seductive, though," he said with a low voice.

"You better get dressed is what you better get, but hold that thought for later," she said and ran her hands down his back and patted him on the butt. He jumped up, went into the bathroom and came out dressed in jeans and t-shirt. He pulled her into him and kissed her again, deeper. Just then someone knocked on the door.

"Crap!" he said, released her and walked into the bedroom. She opened the door to Sean and Katie.

"Hey, you guys. Come on in."

Sean sat down on the sofa and turned the TV on.

"Where's the man?" Sean asked.

"He'll be right out."

Katie slipped her the pregnancy test and she stuck it into her purse.

"Thank," she said.

"Sure. How're you feeling?" Katie asked her.

"Better. Actually I think the patch might be making me feel crappy."

"Yeah, maybe. Did you order the food? I'm starving."

"Yes," Meg said and another knock came, she let room service in and paid them. Blackie came out and sat on the floor next to the table.

"Oh boy, pizza. I'm so hungry. The sale starts at eight so we'll have to get up early. I'm going to get up at six and get showered. Meg, I'll let you sleep while I'm getting ready. Then I'll get you up and order breakfast. Does that suit everyone? I mean I'm doing the bidding, so you guys don't have to be there at eight."

"I'll get up and go with you. How about you, Katie?"

"I'm game. I'm interested to see how this works," Katie said.

"Me, too." Meg said.

"Okay, I'll get everyone going; that's if I can get *my* ass up at six. Right now I'm hitting the sack."

"How are your legs feeling?" Sean asked him.

"Better. I took a long shower, so the cramping has stopped. Anything good on TV?"

"No, I think Katie and I are going to turn in. You're wearing a suit tomorrow?" Sean asked.

"I am, yes. I'd rather wear jeans but it's traditional to dress nice. I'll see you guys in the morning. Good night." Blackie closed the door, cleaned up the food trash and went in and flopped on the bed. He turned the TV on.

"Come here, sweetie," he said yawning. Meg got on the bed and snuggled up next to him. He pulled her closer and kissed her.

"This is fantastic. I love being together like this. It's fun traveling together."

"I like it too. Well, as long as I'm with you, I don't care where we are."

"Awww, thanks, honey. Damn, my legs are so tired," he said stretching.

"Do you want me to massage them? It might help a little."

"You don't have to do that. I had something else in mind for you tonight," he said nuzzling her neck.

"Just wait and I'll have your legs feeling better in a few minutes," she said getting up and unzipping his jeans.

"Whoa, I can't wait if you're going to do that."

"Oh, just control yourself for a few minutes." She said pulling his jeans down and off his feet, then started rubbing his legs.

"Oh, my darling, that feels grand," he said closing his eyes and sighing. "You have great hands, sweetheart," he mumbled.

She massaged both his legs for a few minutes and he was asleep. She got off the bed and walked around a bit, but he didn't wake up. She grabbed the test kit out of her purse, went into the bathroom and did the test. She had to wait ten minutes to read it and it was a very long ten minutes. At the end of the time, she looked at it and there it was. A pink plus sign! She was pregnant! She was stunned. She got this horrible, panicked feeling.

What am I going to do? How am I going to tell Blackie? Suppose he doesn't want a child now? I won't have an abortion no matter what he wants, damnit. Could I raise a child on my own? The answer to that is probably no. How could I work with a baby? Get a grip!

She realized she wasn't giving Blackie enough credit. She knew he was a responsible person.

Why didn't this stupid patch work? What am I going to do? God, stop it! Go to bed! We have to get up early.

She went back in the bedroom and looked at Blackie. He was still asleep; perfectly relaxed. The father of her baby. He was so beautiful. Asleep, his face looked boyish. God, she loved him! When should she tell him?

She shook her head to stop obsessing. She covered him up with a comforter and crawled under it next to him. She had to get some sleep.

TWENTY-SEVEN

The phone ringing woke her up. Blackie answered it.

"Okay, thank you," he said sleepily and hung up. His wake-up call. He dialed the phone.

"Sean, it's six o'clock. Terrible. I feel like a bleeding truck hit me. I'm going to get in the shower. I'll call you when I order breakfast. Scones okay? Later," he hung up and groaned. He sat on the edge of the bed for a couple minutes, sighed and went into the bathroom. Meg felt like death warmed over; so tired she couldn't imagine getting up. She heard the shower start and fell back to sleep. It seemed like an instant later when she felt Blackie touch her hair.

"Meg, honey, its six forty-five. How do you feel?"

"I'm so tired," she whispered.

"Do you want to sleep in? I'll come back and get you later," he said gently.

"No, no, I want to go with you. I'll get up. I'm just incredibly tired," she said and felt lightheaded when she sat up. Blackie sat next to her on the bed.

"I'm worried about you. You're not usually this tired. You're sure you're okay to get up," he asked putting an arm around her. He smelled delicious. He had on charcoal grey slacks, a white shirt, red tie and black boots.

"I'm fine, I just feel a little dizzy." She went into the bathroom and started feeling better as the hot water woke her up. She got dressed while Blackie ordered breakfast and called Sean. They came in and Katie looked at her with raised eyebrows. Meg nodded affirmatively and Katie's eyes got wide. She glanced at Blackie and mouthed, "Did you tell him", Meg shook her head and Katie's eyes got even wider.

They all sat down and ate. Blackie had ordered scones, bacon, coffee and juice. Meg felt a lot better after she got some food in her stomach.

They finished eating and piled into the SUV and drove to Kill. Blackie got them seats in the front with Katie and Meg in the second row right behind the men who studied their programs intently.

The auctioneer turned on his mike and announced. "Today ladies and gentlemen, we have a celebrity in the audience. The greatest steeplechase jockey in the history of the sport, please welcome after a long absence, Blackie O'Brien." Sean had looked up and then over at Blackie and smiled. Blackie hadn't paid any attention to the announcement until he heard his name.

"What's that? Why did he call my name?" Blackie asked, confused.

"Just stand up and wave, dummy," Sean said.

Blackie stood halfway up and waved, self-consciously and, as usual, blushed. Everyone applauded and he looked around, confused and sat down.

"What the hell was that about?" He asked Sean.

"Don't worry about it." Sean laughed and ruffled his hair. "I love you Blackie."

"Uh ... I love you too, Sean," Blackie just shook his head, going back to his program.

Blackie had a card with a number on it; his buyer number. They waited about forty-five minutes and the first horse they wanted came into the ring.

The auctioneer started the bidding high and no one bid. Finally he got down to a reasonable price and someone bid. Blackie looked to see who it was and then sat there quietly. No one else bid so the auctioneer asked for the next higher bid and Blackie held the card up. The other person bid and looked over at Blackie. Then Blackie bid higher. This went on for a while and finally, Blackie got the horse.

This went on the same way all day. The bidding on the gray that Sean liked went a little higher than they wanted, but they got him. There were several breaks for food and drinks. The guys got up to go get drinks, asking Katie and Meg if they wanted anything. They said tea and the men left.

Immediately Katie turned to Meg and asked, "What happened? When did you do the test?"

"Last night after he fell asleep. I couldn't believe it was positive. I didn't get much sleep thinking about it."

"When are you going to tell him?"

"After the sale is over. I guess tonight after dinner. I'm really nervous about it. I have no idea how he's going to react. I feel irritable and cranky today too. I'm ready to jump out of my skin. He knows something is wrong, but doesn't know what. He wanted me to stay in bed and rest but I didn't want to miss this. I'm so strangely tired."

Sean and Blackie came back in a few more minutes and gave them their tea. Sean sat down but Blackie leaned against the railing so he could talk to them.

"I'm happy with how we've done so far. What do you think, Sean?" he asked sipping his coffee. She noticed he was standing like he always did with all his weight on his left leg with the right one relaxed. She knew it was an unconscious habit because of his hip, but it bothered her.

"Yes, we got some bargains but the gray was a little pricey," Sean answered.

"That's okay. He'll probably wind up being worth it," Blackie said. "The dressage horses are next," he said smiling at her and then frowned.

"Meg, you look pale again, are you okay?"

"Yes, I'm fine. I'm just tired." He leaned forward and kissed her very gently, staring closely in her eyes.

"I don't want you getting sick. You'd tell me if anything was wrong, wouldn't you?"

"Uh ... of course, Blackie."

She shot a quick glance at Katie and he caught the look. He looked at Katie and then back at Meg, considering her for a minute but didn't ask any questions.

"I love you, Meg," he said and kissed her again.

"I love you too," she said and smiled up at him. He gave Katie another appraising look and then sat down and started talking to Sean. Katie nudged her and rolled her eyes.

They settled in to wait for the sale of the two dressage horses.

"I was thinking. Let's have all of them shipped to Dad's stable. That way we'll have more time to decide on them when we're there. Dad can keep two; just don't let him get his hands on the gray. Then we'll have the rest shipped home."

"That sounds like a grand idea. How much have we spent so far?"

"Approximately €120,000. That's kind of in the ballpark of what I thought we'd spend. These two coming up might be more expensive. Let's go out and celebrate tonight. What do you think, ladies?"

"I'm in," Katie said.

"What about you, Meg? Do you feel up to going out?" He asked her.

"Sure, honey, we deserve to celebrate after our successful horse buying day," she said, trying to sound upbeat.

"That's my girl. I'll think of someplace nice. Oh, Meg, here's your mare," he said as they led her into the ring. The auctioneer started her bidding high. Blackie whistled softly and waited to see if the auctioneer would come down. Someone else made the first bid and Blackie said, "Shit," under his breath. He started bidding and the price went up quick.

"Blackie, that's too much money."

"Shut up, Meg," he snapped at her. "That fucker better stop bidding soon."

Finally, Blackie was the successful bidder, but the mare cost him €20,000. He looked at Sean and shook his head. She thought better of saying anything more about the cost. She didn't feel up to fighting with him. He got the gelding he wanted for €15,000. He stretched and yawned.

"I have to go down and pay the man. Sean, do you want to take care of the shipping arrangements? Why don't you girls wait for us out front? I think there are some benches out there. Is that okay?"

"Yes, do you want anything more to drink?" Meg asked him.

"I need coffee. How about you, Sean?"

They went off to do their thing and Katie and Meg got drinks and went out to wait. It was a beautiful evening but she could feel a foul mood creeping into her brain.

"You know it's been a long, tedious day and I'd rather go back to the hotel and lie down. I understand why he wants to celebrate but I'm not in the mood."

"Maybe a drink and some food will help you relax. You're probably stressed thinking about telling him."

"I guess, but if he tells me to shut up again, he's going to have a fight on his hands."

"Oh boy, you are in a cranky mood!"

"Thanks, Katie; cut me some slack here. I have a feeling tonight is not going to turn out well. What do I do if he says he can't be tied down with a kid?"

"Somehow I doubt he's going to say that, Meg. Calm down. Oh, here they come. Be cool," Katie said.

"Hi, you two. Ah, caffeine!" Black said, taking the cup from Katie and sipping the hot brew.

"We're all paid and Sean made the shipping plans, so we're done here. It's five o'clock, do we want to go now and get dinner?"

"Let's go now, I'm hungry and we can take a nice long leisurely time to celebrate," Sean said.

"Is that okay with you, sweetie," Blackie said, putting his arms around her.

"Yes, that's fine," she said with as much enthusiasm as she could muster. He ran his fingers down the side of her face.

"You're worrying me. Are you okay?" he asked for the millionth time.

"Yes, jeez," she snapped at him.

He put his hands up in a defensive gesture and rolled his eyes at Sean.

"I guess that's a big yes," he said a little too sarcastically to suit her and she gave him a look. He smiled and took her hand to go to the car.

He drove to a very pricey restaurant in Dublin where they were seated at a round table and waited for service.

A gorgeous, redheaded waitress came and handed out menus. Of course she honed in on Blackie like radar.

"How are you folks this evening," she said giving him a seductive smile. He flashed a big smile which instantly pissed Meg off.

"We're just fine," he said.

"Yes, you are and what's your name, luv?" she asked in a sugary voice.

"Blackie, it's a nick name."

"Mine's Sherrie."

"Ah, like the wine," he said, like an idiot. Meg was getting ready to go over and smack that stupid smile off his face.

"Sure and *I'm* great after dinner, too." she said and he choked on his water.

"I'll be back and get drink orders in a minute," she said walking away, switching her ass. He watched her walk away.

"Did she actually just say that?" he asked Sean, still watching her butt.

"Yes, she did, sport," Sean said, frowning at him.

"Let's see what's on the menu," Blackie said, opening his.

"Yes, if you can take your eyes off her ass for a second," Meg said with more sarcasm than she had intended.

He laughed. "Honey, come on, she's just goofing around," he said innocently.

"Oh and what were *you* supposed to be doing?"

He looked at Meg a little puzzled. "I'm not doing anything." He went back to his menu.

The lovely Sherrie came bouncing back and asked Blackie what he wanted to drink, ignoring the rest of us.

"What do you have on draft?"

"Killian's, Smithwick's, Beck, Harp, Budweiser, Amstel Lite, Guinness."

"I'll have a Killian's."

She looked at Sean and he ordered the same, Katie, white wine and Meg got a Coke.

"I'll be right back, luv," and switched herself toward the bar.

Blackie burst out laughing and Sean snickered.

"What's so funny?" Meg said angrily.

"The waitress, she's funny," he said.

"I don't see anyone laughing but you. You must be enjoying it," she said getting more pissed by the minute.

"Oh, Meg, come on, that's pretty funny."

She just gave him a dirty look. He puffed out a big sigh and went back to his menu.

Sherrie brought the drinks and then said she'd take their food orders. She leaned over in front of Blackie so he could get a super look at her impressive cleavage and asked, "What would you like, Blackie?"

His eyes flickered up to her chest and he choked again. "Uh ... I'll have the steak, medium with mashed potatoes and a salad." He was biting his lip as she took their orders. When she left he started laughing.

"Jesus, Sean, do you believe her?"

"No, I don't," Sean said sternly.

"If you'd stop flirting with her, maybe she'd stop," Meg snapped.

"Meg, I'm not flirting with her, come on," he said, still smiling.

"Like hell, you're not. Did you get a good look at her tits?" Meg said, raising her voice.

"Honey, calm down, I'm not flirting; I'm making fun of her," he said, not smiling now.

She turned away and he just stared at her with a puzzled expression on his face. Neither of them said anything.

"Take it easy, this is turning into a bad situation," Sean whispered to him.

"Damnit, she knows better," Blackie said.

Meg didn't say anything. Now Sherrie came over with their food. Blackie just kept his head down.

"Blackie, do you speak Gaelic?" she asked laughing.

"I do, yes," he said warily.

Then she said something to him in Gaelic and laughed.

"Jesus!" Blackie said and threw his napkin down.

She swished her butt back into the kitchen looking back to see his reaction.

"Oh, shit," Sean said.

"What did she say to you," Meg yelled, She was livid. She was ready to scratch her eyes out.

"It doesn't matter, Meg, she's ridiculous."

"Do I always have to worry about you and other women?"

"What? When have I ever given you a reason to think I was after some other woman?" He said with narrowed eyes and gritted teeth.

"Hey, calm down you two, we're supposed to be celebrating."

"Fuck that, this is stupid. All I did was answer her," Blackie said louder.

"Oh, sure. *'like the wine'*, very cute," she said with a snort.

"Listen, little girl, you're starting to piss me off."

"I'm not a little girl," she yelled.

"You're acting like one. What in God's name would make you think I'd be interested in her? She's ludicrous; she's a slut!" he said.

"I thought that's what you liked." She said nastily and was instantly sorry. He looked like she slapped him in the face.

"Blackie, I'm sorry, I didn't mean that. I'm angry and jealous. I'm sorry," and she started to cry.

He stared at her, still angry but now confused too.

"Meg, what the hell is the matter with you? Why don't you trust me? We've been together for over six months. I thought by now you'd know I don't want anyone else. I love you," he said, frowning.

"I love you too," she said, sniffling.

"I think I know what's going on. You're uncomfortable living with me. We need to be married, and then maybe you'll trust me. I've waited too long to ask you," he said and she burst into tears.

"Mary, Mother of God! Meg, what the hell is wrong with you," he yelled at her and she yelled back.

"I'm pregnant!" and sobbed harder.

"Oh, Christ!" Sean said.

Blackie just sat there with his mouth open.

"You're what?" He said, his heart thumping in his chest.

"You heard me," she said through sobs.

"When were you going to tell me?"

"I'm telling you now."

"How long have you known?"

"Since last night," she said crying harder.

"I can't do this here. Sean, pay that stupid bitch. We're going back to the hotel. I'll call you," Blackie said, stood up, went around the table and took her hand.

"Come on, Meg," he said gently.

They walked out and grabbed a cab. Neither of them said anything. They entered their room at the hotel, closed the door and Blackie leaned against it, staring at her.

"Blackie, I didn't do this on purpose. I've been wearing the patch and using it correctly. I don't know what happened," she said rapid fire and started sobbing again. Then she couldn't breathe and started gasping for air.

Suddenly she felt his arms around her tight and his mouth against her temple.

"Meg, shhh, calm down, honey. It's okay. It's going to be okay. Shh, calm down," he crooned to her gently.

"I'm sorry," she got out between sobs.

"For what?" he said stroking her hair.

"I guess I messed up somehow with the birth control."

"Why didn't you wake me up and tell me last night?"

"I didn't want to ruin the sale for you."

"Meg, the sale isn't important. Nothing is more important to me than you."

"If you don't want to be tied down with me and a child, I'll understand," she said, crying harder again. He held her out and looked at her.

"What are you talking about? I'm so happy about this. I can't believe it. I'm kind of shocked but very happy. How would this tie *me* down? You're the one who's going to be carrying a baby around for nine months. Well, now we *really* need to get married."

"No, I don't want you to marry me because I'm pregnant. That's ridiculous."

"I don't want to marry you because you're pregnant. I want to because I love you. That's what I said at the table. I've just been enjoying our relationship so much, I wasn't thinking about you. That you might be uncomfortable living with me without being married. Forgive me. I just get so involved; I don't always see the big picture."

"I didn't know how you would react. I was worried."

"Why would you be worried, Meg? I can't tell you enough how much I love you. When I say that, I mean it with all my heart. I've never said it to another woman, ever. Do you really think I wouldn't want our baby? This is my fault for being so stupid and waiting too long to ask you to marry me. Will you marry me?"

"Yes ... I love you so much. You're so wonderful to me." She hugged him and he kissed her with so much emotion.

I must be dreaming. I can't believe he's accepting this so well. I can't believe he just asked me to marry him.

"Now we really have something to celebrate," he said smiling at her. "Let's call Sean and Katie to come over."

"Okay."

He called Sean and then turned and hugged her. "Meg, we're going to have a baby, how wonderful!"

Sean knocked and Blackie yelled, "Come in" without letting go of her. They walked in and Blackie turned to them and said,

"I guess you heard that we're having a baby. Sean, you're going to be an uncle."

"What can I say? I guess congratulations are in order. What are you guys going to do? Meg doesn't seem too happy about it." Sean said.

"I'm happy about it, I'm just in shock. I wasn't sure how he was going to react." She said, trying to compose herself. Blackie still had his arms around her.

"What about you, man? Are you ready for this? Not to bring up a sore subject but you're doing good working with Dr. Wahlman. Is this stress going to set you off? Are you going to start drinking again? I love the idea of you going down in a blaze of diapers, but *are* you stable enough for this?" Sean said seriously.

Blackie just looked at him for a few minutes then took a deep breath.

"A lot of good questions, Sean. Let's all sit down. I don't know how I'm going to handle it. But I do know that I have to take care of Meg. She's not going to do this by herself. I have to be strong for her and the baby."

"I told you, you don't have to marry me. I could do this by myself." She said sticking out her chin.

"What, you want to be an unwed mother? Not carrying my child you're not! I should have married you a long time ago."

"Why do you always think you should tell me what to do? Don't you realize I can think for myself?"

"Because I'm the man and it's my responsibility to take care of you. I'm sorry, Meg, but I'm old-fashioned. I should have known you were uncomfortable living together." Blackie said.

"I never said I was uncomfortable living with you. Where did you come up with that? I think you're the one who's uncomfortable, especially with this situation now." She said.

"Damn right I am. I didn't want us to have kids before we got married." He said, raising his voice.

"When the hell did marriage ever come up?" She asked. "You never mentioned it before now."

"Don't you want to marry me? I thought you loved me," he said, slumping his shoulders.

"Of course I love you, you know that, Blackie."

"Blackie, don't be stupid. Have you ever actually asked her to marry you? You should have taken care of business before this happened," Sean said.

"You're right Sean, it's my dumb fault. I thought I said that already. Anyway, I just asked her to marry me and she said yes, so that's it."

"Are we going to Mom and Dad's from here?" Sean asked.

"Bollocks! I forgot. I can look forward to a six hour lecture about this one," Blackie said.

"Do you have to tell them?" Katie said.

"Oh, my mother will know, believe me, the woman's psychic."

"Come on, how's she going to know? We don't have to tell anyone yet."

"Tell her, Sean. The woman always knows instantly what's going on," Blackie said.

"It's true, Meg. As soon as she sees you, she'll know. We've never been able to get away with anything. I think she's a witch," Sean said, laughing.

"We have to go there to see about the horses." Blackie said. He looked at Meg. "Do you want to get married tomorrow before we go over there?"

"Blackie, it's not a big rush. We could wait until the baby's born and then have a nice wedding," she said.

She really didn't know what she wanted to do about it. He was adamant about getting married right away, but she thought they should wait. She was content living with him even though it would be neat to be married.

"Absolutely not! We're going to be married when you have that baby." Blackie said firmly.

"You know, why don't you guys calm down? I think you both should let this sink in before you rush and do anything. Let's go to Mom and Dad's and stay a few days, then go on to London like we planned. Like Meg said, there's no real rush at this point. You can get married when we get back to the States. Talk it over with Jill and Keary," Sean said.

"I agree, Meg isn't showing yet, so you have some time. I think it's too new for you to decide anything," Katie said.

Blackie and Meg looked at each other. She smiled at him and he puffed out a big sigh and smiled back.

"I guess it's not a big rush. You're right, Sean, I'm still in shock. Do we all want to go to London and Newmarket after we leave Mom and Dad's?"

Katie, Sean and Meg all yelled, "Yes!"

Blackie laughed, "London it is then. Let's wait until tomorrow afternoon or the next day to go home. I don't know about anyone else, but I'm exhausted. Actually tomorrow we could sleep in and then do a little sightseeing. The girls have never seen Ireland and it *is* beautiful."

"That sounds perfect to me. Katie, what do you say we turn in? It has been a very long day," Sean suggested.

"Yes, let's all get up in time for lunch." Katie said.

"Good night you two," Blackie said.

Blackie locked the door and went over to Meg and kissed her.

"Let's go to bed," he said. She could tell by the low sound of his voice what he wanted and she got a rush of desire that was overpowering. She quickly changed into a silk tank and matching panties. She was turning down the bed when he came up behind her, put his hands flat on her belly and caressed it. He had his mouth on her neck, hungrily kissing her. As he rubbed her belly, he whispered, "I love that we're having a baby, Meg. I love you so much."

She moved his hands down between her legs and he moaned softly. He caressed her there until she was the one moaning. He moved his hands under her top and caressed her breasts. She could feel him behind her that he was ready. She turned around in his arms and kissed him urgently, pressing herself up against him. He moved his hands down to her butt, pulling her into him.

"I love you," she whispered as she kissed his mouth, his face, his neck. She felt so hungry for him, she might devour him. He moved her backward onto the bed, pulling her panties off as she lay down. She climaxed as soon as he entered her and she arched up to meet him. He groaned and pushed in harder and faster until he seemed to explode in her, gasped and was still. She kissed the side of his face, wrapped her arms and legs around him and held him close for a long time. He kissed her neck gently.

"Meg, I'm sorry," he whispered.

"For what? I'm starting to love this baby already because it's your baby. I have part of you inside me."

He rolled over, propping his head up on an elbow. "You're incredible. I love you."

"I love you too," she said quietly.

He finally rolled over onto his back. "You feel like going to sleep?" he asked.

"Yes. Good night, sweetie," she told him and he cuddled up close to her.

"Good night."

He went to sleep almost instantly. She lay there trying to go to sleep, but couldn't. He was making little sounds that were almost child-like and feeling his body close made her hungry for him again. She couldn't believe how her desire for him had increased lately. She knew if she waited a bit, she could get him started again, but they needed rest. She decided to let him sleep and finally drifted off herself.

TWENTY-EIGHT

Meg woke the next morning feeling relaxed and cozy but still tired. She turned over and Blackie wasn't in bed. Then she heard the shower going and he was whistling! She'd never heard him whistle before. He sounded happy. She let herself fall back to sleep and came to again when Blackie walked into the bedroom. He only had on his black underwear and looked delicious. He pulled on jeans and a t-shirt and noticed she was awake. He knelt down next to the bed, cradling her in his arms and kissed her.

"Good morning, little mommy. How are you feeling this morning?"

"I feel good, just still tired. How are you?"

"I feel great. I needed that sleep. I'm looking forward to site-seeing today. I have to call home first."

"Blackie, are you really happy about the baby?" She asked.

"I am, yes, very much. I was shocked at first, but now I'm getting used to the idea. We'll work things out about getting married. Do you want to do it back in the States with Keary and Jill? Then later we can have a big wedding at my parents' house. Meg, I love you so much and I love the idea of us having a child together," he said and kissed her. "How do you feel?"

"I'm a little scared but I love the idea too. I think I'd rather get married back home. Are your parents going to freak?"

"Probably, but we don't have to tell them now."

"Okay, let me get up and get ready," she said and padded into the bathroom.

*   *   *

They spent the whole day driving through the Irish countryside, visiting the churches, castles, county festivals.

She was falling in love with this country of Blackie's. He obviously loved it here and she could see why. It was so beautiful and the people were wonderful. She thought what it would be like to live here with him and secretly tucked that dream away in her heart.

They visited a castle that she fell in love with that was built in 1400 and had been renovated and turned into a fabulous resort. It was Dromoland Castle and it was magnificent.

They stopped in a pub in Cork and had so much fun. Several of the men recognized Blackie from racing and they bought us a round of beer. Blackie then bought the whole pub drinks. There was a small group playing traditional music and they were so good. Everyone in the pub got into the spirit of it, turning the day into a raucous, Irish party. Meg and Katie chatted with some of the women and everyone was so friendly. The whole day was wonderful.

They bought gifts and souvenirs in little shops they discovered. They bought a set of exquisite crystal wine glasses at the Waterford factory.

Meg was starting to get tired so they stopped and had dinner in a little restaurant near Waterford. After dinner they headed back to their hotel to get packed up. Blackie made her lie down and watch TV while he gathered their things.

"I can't believe you know how to pack so efficiently," she told him.

"Don't forget, I traveled all the time from the age of fifteen until the accident when I was twenty-four. That's a lot of traveling. I used to hate it but I love traveling with you. Sean used to go racing with me sometimes but most of the time I was by myself. I was very lonely most of the time."

"I'm sorry you were lonely, honey. Come here," she held her arms out to him. He slid onto the bed next to her and let her hold him. He kissed her and cuddled up against her for a while.

"This is grand but I need to get finished so we can leave."

"Okay. Thanks you for getting us packed up."

They stowed their bags in the SUV and took off for Black's parents' house near Killarney.

*   *   *

They drove up a long driveway that ended in a circle in front of the main house.

The house was gigantic. It was a beautiful, stone country house that Meg thought looked as if Queen Elizabeth might stay there for a weekend. It was surrounded by beautiful grounds, stone cottages, small, stone outbuildings and behind it were at least six old stone stables.

Blackie and Sean unloaded the bags. Meg stood there for a bit and stared at the house which was regal and elegant but still had a cozy, country farm house air about it. She went to pick her train case up and Blackie took it out of her hand.

"Hey, I don't want you lifting or carrying anything, okay," he said as he put his arm around her.

"Oh, come on, I'm fine. I'm not exactly fragile," she said.

"You have two big, strong men here to do all the lifting, so why should you. Besides you are fragile, you're carrying a baby."

"Oh God, frontier women chopped wood and stuff when they were pregnant."

He leaned over, kissing her tenderly and said, "Just let me take care of you, please." "Okay, you win. I'll let you pamper me."

"Good, thanks."

Just then the front door opened and some young men came out and took the bags in. An older couple appeared and she knew they were Blackie's parents. The man was graying, muscular, about six-two and resembled Sean a bit. The woman was the spitting image of Blackie.

Meg could never imagine him looking feminine but here was a feminine version of him right in front of her. She was beautiful! She was Meg's height and weight with coal black hair streaked with gray. She had the same beautiful blue eyes and smile as Blackie. It was odd to see how much they were alike. She could see that Jill looked more like her Dad, Kennet who was handsome in his own right. Blackie picked up his Mom, hugging her and twirled her around in a circle.

"Hi, gorgeous," he said smiling down at her.

"I've missed you, son," she said hugging him back and Meg could see the beam of love for him in her eyes.

"Now get out of the way and let me see this beautiful, young woman you've brought me," she said smacking him affectionately and turning to Meg.

"Mom, this is Meg Connors. Meg, Maeve O'Brien."

"Meg, I'm so pleased to finally meet you. I've heard so much about you. How did you ever meet this scoundrel?" she laughed.

"It's good to meet you too, Mrs. O'Brien. Thank you so much for having me at your home. I have my horses stabled at Killarney Farms, so that's how we met. Your home is beautiful." she said. Meg could already feel the sweat running down her back. Maeve was friendly but somehow Meg didn't think those blue eyes missed much. She went over and hugged Sean and met Katie. Blackie's Dad came over and shook Meg's hand and Blackie introduced them.

"So this is the girl, then. She's pretty smart looking. You better take good care of her or somebody else will," Kennet said smiling down at her.

"I try very hard to take care of her, Dad, but she's got a mind of her own."

"All the best ones do, son. She'll keep you on the straight and narrow, I think."

"She does that," Blackie said, rolling his eyes.

"Let's go in and have a bite to eat. Oh, Jimmy, let them tell you what bags go where. Sean and Blackie's rooms. I'm assuming you two girls are sleeping in with them," Maeve said with a sly smile and went inside, leaving Sean and Blackie standing there with their mouths open.

"Well, okay then," Sean said with a shrug and they all filed into the house.

The house was incredible, decorated with some of the most beautiful antiques Meg had ever seen. There was a huge foyer with a stone stairs going up to the right. An archway to the left gave way to a huge library, den. Another archway led from there to a formal dining room with a table that apparently could seat thirty people. Huge glass front cabinets held exquisite china and crystal. Off of the formal dining room were the kitchen and a more informal, cozy dining room with a fireplace. This table was laid with more functional crockery and flatware.

"Ken, do you want to fix drinks all around? I'll have a martini, dear," Maeve instructed her husband.

"Yes. Sean, Blackie, beer?"

Sean and Blackie were both drinking beer and she always had misgivings about it. He swore it didn't bother him and everyone let him drink it. To her mind, alcohol was alcohol and it couldn't help him quit drinking.

"Sure, Dad," Sean said.

"Ladies?" Ken asked Katie and Meg.

"I'll have a ginger ale, if you have it," Meg said.

"Me too," Katie added.

"And I'll have a scotch," Ken said.

While he fixed drinks, they went back to the library and sat on comfy sofas.

"Well, now tell me about your trip so far." Maeve said.

"We had a very successful trip to Goff's. We bought Dad two nice jumpers and we got four for us. I'll make arrangements for all ours to be shipped. Meg and I bought a couple of mounts for dressage," Blackie explained.

"Dressage?" Maeve said, tilting her head. "Are you riding again?"

"I am, yes. I've been working with Meg's gelding and he's good. I've won some competitions with him at Level Two. I'm having a lot of fun," Blackie told her.

"I'm glad you're enjoying it, dear, but I thought riding was out," Maeve said, concerned.

"Racing's out, Mother, not riding," Blackie said with a clenched teeth

"Mom, we saw his surgeon and he said the hip is stronger than before the accident. I saw the x-rays; they looked good," Sean said, coming to Blackie's defense.

"I don't know. You're not doing any jumping are you?" she said, frowning.

"No, I'm not jumping and dressage is all flat work. You know that. I'll be fine. I can judge for myself if I'm able to do it or not." Blackie said.

"Alright, dear, you don't have to get upset," she said.

"I'm not upset." Black said with a stubborn set to his jaw.

Terrific! What a great start to this visit.

Meg could tell that Blackie did a lot of "head-butting" with his parents; his Mom anyway.

"Dressage, did I hear that you're doing dressage? That's wonderful. Does Meg do it too?" Ken asked, walking in with the drinks.

"Yes, I'm teaching her as much as I know. Dad, I have all the paper work for your horses. I hope you like the ones we bought for you."

Blackie looked at Meg and gently pushed a strand of hair back behind her ear. He let his fingertips trail from her ear down along her jaw. He had this intense look in his eyes that she had never seen before. It was love, concern, wonder, tenderness and protectiveness all at once. She smiled at him and lowered her eyes. When she glanced up, Maeve was studying them intently.

"Are you hungry? Maybe you should eat something." Blackie said softly.

"I'm a little hungry. I'm fine, honey," she said.

Maeve got up, "Then we better go out and eat. I believe the meal is ready, anyway."

A plump woman in an apron started bringing platters and bowls out. She set a plate down and said to Sean, "How-ye, m'lord?"

"I'm good, Martha. It's good to see you."

She put a big casserole dish near Blackie.

"How-ye, Your Highness?" Blackie immediately stiffened.

"Please don't call me that, Martha. You know I don't like it," he said with an edge to his voice.

"Oh, uh, I forgot. Sorry, Your, uh, Blackie," she said looking flustered at Maeve.

"Blackie, don't pick on Martha, you know she loves you and hasn't seen you for some time. She's always called you that," Maeve said.

He sighed big and snapped at his mother, "Everyone knows I hate being called that; why can't they remember."

"Because they respect you and your title."

"For chrissake, Mom, why can't they respect how I feel about it?" Blackie complained.

"Blackie, don't talk to your mother with that tone," Ken said firmly.

"Yes, sir." Blackie said, his eyes snapping with anger.

He got up and stomped to the kitchen and said something to Martha. Meg heard her giggling. He came back in and sat down again.

"I apologized to Martha," he said.

"Thank you, dear," Maeve said with a tight set to her mouth.

"Not here an hour and you two are arguing already," Ken said shaking his head.

"I'm sorry, Mom."

"You know, son, I've been looking at you and you look better than I've ever seen you. You seem very healthy and happy. I'm sure that's thanks to Meg," Maeve said smiling at her.

"You've got that right, Mom. If it weren't for her, I'd be a total mess," he said beaming proudly at Meg.

"That's not true, honey. You've done a lot of hard work to be healthy," she told him.

"Whatever it is, I'm happy to see it. You too, Sean. I think these young women are just the ticket," she said smiling over at Katie.

Katie blushed big time and said, "Thank you, Ma'am."

"Please, call me Maeve."

Meg liked her. She liked them both. She thought his mom had the same fire in her that Blackie did. She's the first person Meg had ever seen win an argument with him. She figured he got his strong will along with his looks from her.

Blackie was absently staring at her as if she was the Mona Lisa.

"Stop staring at me," she whispered.

"Oh, I'm sorry, I didn't realize I was," he said and smiled. "I guess I was thinking how incredible everything is," he said and leaned over and kissed her tenderly on the cheek. Maeve wasn't missing any of this.

Great, we're trying to hide the fact that I'm pregnant and he's mooning at me like a lovesick calf.

"Tomorrow night we're having a dinner for a few friends, some of them already know you boys but some are here to meet you and Sean."

"Oh great! Who are these people? I don't want to meet anyone. We're here to visit you two and relax." Blackie whined.

"Good Lord, Blackie, are you always this grumpy?" Maeve said.

"I am, yes." he got up and stomped into the kitchen and came back with a cold beer, flopping back down in his chair. Maeve rolled her eyes at Meg and she smiled back.

"Are any of you going to ride in the morning?" Ken asked.

"I might," Blackie said.

"Me too," Meg piped up and Blackie frowned at her.

"What?" She asked.

"I'll talk to you about it later," he said.

She glanced over at Maeve and she was giving Blackie a quizzical stare.

"Hey, Dad, let me give you the paperwork on your horses before I forget," Blackie said. "They're in my room, I'll go get them."

"Okay, what about the horses that are being shipped to you? Don't I need their papers?" his Dad asked.

"Yes, sure, I'll get all of them and we'll see what you need." He got up and leaned over to Meg, lifting her chin up to him with his fingertips.

"Are you okay?" he said softly and she nodded and smiled. "I'll be right back," and he kissed her tenderly on the mouth. He left to get the papers and she looked over at Maeve who was smiling at her. Ken got up and followed Blackie.

Maeve started chatting with Sean and Katie. Meg was so tired she could hardly keep her eyes open and was starting to feel a little light-headed too.

Great! Just what I need, more pregnancy symptoms. Maybe I just need to lie down for a few minutes.

Blackie and Ken returned with a bunch of papers, both sitting down again. Blackie put his arm around her and then ... blackness.

Her head fell over on Blackie's shoulder and he turned and looked at her quickly.

"Did Meg just fall asleep?"

"Blackie, I think she passed out. She was very pale right before you sat down," Maeve said.

"What? Crap, did she say she felt bad?" Blackie asked as he scooped her up and carried her into the library, laying her on one of the couches. He knelt beside her, lightly patting her face.

"Meg, honey, wake up." Maeve handed him a damp cloth. "Thanks, Mom."

When Meg came to, she looked up at him.

"What happened?" she asked him.

"I think you passed out." He said, frowning. "How do you feel?"

"I still feel a little light-headed. I'm just tired. Maybe I should go up and lay down? I think that will help."

"Of course, come on," he said and started to pick her up.

"I can walk, I'm fine." She sat up, feeling dizzy but tried to hide it.

"You still don't look good," he said. She got up and walked a little drunkenly out of the room.

Blackie took her hand and led her upstairs. They went to his room and she crawled into bed.

"I'm worried, I don't like you being dizzy and passing out. Is it because of the baby?" he asked sitting next to her on the bed.

"I guess. I'm sooo tired too. You go back down and I'll be fine. I'll just lay here and rest."

"Are you sure? I don't mind staying up here with you. Everyone will understand," he pleaded.

"No, no, you go down and visit. I'll call if I need you, honey."

"Okay." He kissed her. "I love you, Meg."

"I love you too."

*   *   *

Blackie walked back down stairs and sat at the table again with a frown on his face.

"Is she okay, dear?" Maeve asked him.

"I hope so. She's going to rest."

"How far along is she, son?" his mother asked, her mouth set in a stern line.

"What?" he said, as his stomach quickly knotted.

"You heard me, Blackie. Don't lie to me."

Blackie sighed big.

"I told you she'd know," Sean said.

"Shut up, Sean," Black said, snapped.

"So you were going to hide the fact that she's pregnant?" Maeve said, her mouth in a tight line.

"No, Mom, it's just that we only found out ourselves two days ago and it's been a shock. How the hell did you know?"

"I've never seen you with a woman before, but I didn't think you treated them like they might break," Maeve said.

"Do I really treat her like that?"

"Yes," Sean and Katie said in unison.

"Oh, great," Black said laughing.

"Black, this is serious. Why weren't you using birth control? We raised you to be more responsible than this. All the condoms we bought you as a teenager; what were you thinking?"

"Mom, we were using birth control. We were using the patch. It's supposed to be ninety-nine percent effective." Blackie said.

"Well, Mr. One Percent, how'd that work?" she said and Sean and Katie burst out laughing.

"Very funny." Blackie said giving them a nasty look.

"Are you planning on getting married?"

"Of course we're getting married! This is entirely my fault. I meant to ask her months ago but I've been distracted with my problems."

"What problems?" Maeve asked.

"Mom, I've been in rehab two or three times. I still don't handle a crisis normally. When something upsets me, I want to drink. Meg has helped me a lot."

"All of this is that bastard Mickey's fault. I could kill him," Ken said, raising his voice.

"Blackie, why didn't you wait before you got her into bed?" Maeve said, scolding him.

"Hey, we knew each other for about four months before we started dating and we dated for another two months before we slept together. We really love each other, Mom."

"Are you sure she's not after your money. You're famous and you have a certain position.

"Don't say anything against her! She didn't know who I was until we started dating. She thought I was a stable hand." Blackie said, flushing. "By the time she knew who I was, she was already in love with me."

"You're sure it's your child?" Ken said.

Blackie jumped up knocking his chair over. "Watch what you say, damn it! If you knew how possessive I am, you'd know damn well it's mine."

"Ken, that wasn't a very kind thing to say," Maeve said, glaring at her husband.

"I'm sorry, son, I just want to protect you."

"Just don't make any more derogatory remarks about Meg."

"Do you love her?" Maeve asked.

"I love her more than anything in the world, Mom." Blackie said.

"Okay, then why not get married here?"

"We want to get married back in the states and after the baby comes, we'll plan a really big wedding here," Blackie said.

"Okay, if that's how you two want it," Maeve said, her shoulders slumping.

"Yes, that's the way we want it for now and don't look disappointed; you'll get your big wedding."

*   *   *

Meg woke up dazed. She lay there a few minutes until her head cleared. She could hear loud voices and had a sinking feeling Blackie was giving his parents trouble.

I better get up and see if I can run interference.

She sat up slowly and didn't feel too bad, so she got up and went downstairs. As she neared the kitchen, she could hear Blackie saying something about a wedding and he sounded angry.

Great, I guess the jig's up!

She walked into the kitchen and the conversation came to an abrupt halt. Blackie smiled at her when she sat down and kissed him.

"Hi, honey, are you feeling better?"

"Yes, thanks, I needed that nap. What were you arguing about?" She asked innocently.

There was complete silence for a couple of beats, and then Sean piped up.

"The cat's out of the bag, Meg, or should I say the baby."

"Thoughtfully subtle, as always, Sean." Blackie growled.

"Honey, it's fine. Mr. & Mrs. O'Brien, I'm sorry, we should have told you right away. We weren't trying to hide it, we're just still in shock and not sure what to do next. We just found out ourselves. We thought we had the birth control issue taken care of."

"Don't worry about it, Meg. Blackie's the one at fault. He should have been more responsible," Maeve said.

"I disagree, Mrs. O'Brien, Blackie's been more than responsible. He's also held off with marriage plans because he felt he was unstable and wanted to be well before he asked me. He's very thoughtful," she said firmly, while actually shaking in her boots that she had just talked back to Blackie's Mom.

"Do you love my son, Meg?" Maeve asked her.

"Oh, yes, very much. Sometimes it overwhelms me, how much I do love him. It's a little scary sometimes, especially when he's hurt. I don't think I could survive without him," she said, more to him than to Maeve. He gave her a strange, surprised, awe-struck look.

"What? You know how much I love you," she said.

"I know but I never heard you say it like that before."

"You know, Meg, I've never seen Blackie with a woman; well once at some party and he didn't seem very happy. I like the way he is with you; protective and sweet. He's obviously happy and that's what matters. I don't think I've ever seen him this happy. Well, maybe when he got his first pony." Everyone laughed.

"Come here, Meg," Maeve said to her. Meg got up and walked around to her, not knowing what to expect. Maeve hugged her and said, "Thank you for loving my son and making him happy. Now let's talk about this baby. How far along are you and how are you feeling?"

"I'm very tired and light-headed. I don't feel much like eating either. I guess I'm two or three months but I'm not sure!"

"It sounds like you're in the first trimester to me. Actually I shouldn't tell you this, but I was pregnant with Jill when *we* got married." Maeve said. Blackie sat there with his mouth open and then started laughing.

"Hey, way to go Dad," he said to his father who gave him a smile and thumbs up.

"Oh, Blackie, behave," Maeve said.

"Cool," Sean said and "hi-fived" Ken.

"You boys are incorrigible!" Maeve said, shaking her head. "Okay, now that you know our secret, you don't have to go spreading it around."

"Don't worry, Mom, we won't tell anyone," Blackie said still smiling.

"I don't know, exactly how much is our silence worth?" Sean asked.

Maeve threw a roll at him.

"You better keep your mouth shut, boyo."

"I don't know about you young people, but I'm tired. If I'm going to ride in the morning, I'm going to bed. Who all is going to ride tomorrow?" Ken said.

"We're going to sleep in," Sean said.

"I guess I'll ride." Blackie said.

"Me, too." Meg said, excitedly.

"Oh, no, you're not riding," Blackie said firmly.

"What, why not?" She snapped.

"Unless you've forgotten, you're pregnant." He said sarcastically.

"Don't be a smart ass, of course I haven't forgotten. Why, does that mean I can't ride?" She said.

"You passed out earlier, Meg. For chrissake what if you pass out while you're riding and fall?" Blackie said.

"I feel better now. I told you before that women have always done lots of stuff while they're pregnant. Frontier women walked all the way out West, tended gardens, and chopped wood. I'm not that damn delicate," she said.

"First of all, you're not a fucking frontier woman and you are in a delicate condition when you're passing out. You're *not* riding," Blackie said raising his voice.

"Blackie, don't yell at her," Maeve said.

"Stay out of this, Mom," Blackie snapped at her.

Meg burst into tears and yelled back at him.

"You can't tell me what to do just because I'm carrying your baby. You're always bossing me around, damn it." She said standing up and getting in his face.

"Meg, I mean it, don't fight with me about this."

"Oh, what are you going to do, big tough guy, punch me?" She sobbed. She suddenly felt very dizzy and almost fell over. Blackie caught her and cradled her in his arms while she sobbed.

"Honey, it's okay. Calm down."

"It's so beautiful here. I just wanted to ride and explore the countryside." She tearfully told him.

"I know, honey. How about if you ride in the saddle and I ride up behind you to make sure you don't fall," Blackie said.

"Oh, okay, that sounds like fun," she said, cuddling up against him.

"You want to do that?"

"Uh, huh," she murmured falling asleep in his arms.

He pulled her onto his lap and held her while she slept. He looked at Maeve and said quietly, "Where did all that come from? Mom, you know I wouldn't hit her, ever."

"I know. Get used to it. You're dealing with a lot of hormones now," she told him.

"Wow, all that was from hormones?"

"Yes, dear."

"Jesus, Mom, I really have a lot to learn."

"Don't worry, son, you'll figure it out. I can see how you're there for her when she needs you. Just look, you two just had a fight and I knew you were angry, but your anger instantly dissolved when she got dizzy. You quickly changed from angry to protective and loving. That's a good sign," Maeve told him.

"I hope so. I really feel unstable a lot of the time, so I don't know if I can handle it."

"You'll be in Virginia with Jill and Keary. They can help you. Jill hasn't had a baby yet, but they can help." Maeve said.

"Jill's trying to get pregnant now," Blackie told her.

"Oh really, that's wonderful. I'll have the priest say prayers for all of you to have healthy babies." she said.

"Why don't you pray to God yourself, why do you need a priest?" Blackie said.

"Because I believe the priest's prayers are heard before mine."

"Bullshit, that's ridiculous!"

"Blackie, watch how you talk to your mother," Ken growled at him.

"Yes, sir," Blackie said and rolled his eyes. Sean laughed at him.

"Shut up, Sean," Blackie growled back.

"Okay, all of you settle down," Maeve said.

"I think I'll take Meg up to bed. I'm tired too. Goodnight, all," Blackie said. He picked her up, carried her upstairs and tucked her in his bed.

*　　*　　*

Meg slept like a dead woman all night. The next morning she awoke to a quiet room and an empty bed. When she went into the bathroom, the mirror was steamed up so she assumed Blackie was already showered and down at the stable. She showered quickly and dressed in jeans, riding boots and a sweater. She was very excited about riding this morning but felt a little nauseated.

Oh, great, Blackie's going to have a fit if I throw up.

She walked down to the kitchen and found Maeve and Katie finishing breakfast.

"Good morning," she said cheerily.

"Good morning," they returned the salutation

"What would you like to eat, dear?" Maeve asked her.

"Oh, I'm not too hungry. Maybe tea and toast. Maybe some scrambled eggs too."

"Sit down, I'll get it for you," Maeve got up.

"Please, Maeve, don't wait on me. I can fix it myself."

"Nonsense, have a seat. All the men have eaten and are over at the barns."

"Hey, how are you feeling?" Katie asked.

"I'm a little queasy this morning. God I hope I don't throw up. Blackie will freak."

"Yeah, he's a little tense about it," Katie said. "Actually he's doing pretty well for a guy who just found out his girlfriend's pregnant. He'll figure it out."

"You think so?"

Just then Maeve came in with her food. She set the plate in front of her and Meg looked at it. She was hungry and it looked delicious, but she just couldn't put any in her mouth. Weird! She didn't want Maeve to get concerned so she sipped the tea and nibbled a bite of toast. The three of them chatted for a few minutes more and then Meg excused herself to go to the stables.

She walked over and Blackie was outside grooming a huge, gray horse, while Ken and Sean stood there chatting with him. As she walked up, Blackie turned around and saw her.

"Good morning, sweetheart; how's my little mama this morning?" Blackie asked and kissed her.

"I'm okay. I slept well. How are you?"

"I'm ready to ride. This great beast is Arrow. He's a Percheron, thoroughbred cross and very gentle. You're going to ride in the saddle and I'm going to ride up behind you."

"Oh, Blackie, I'm not going to fall. I'm not a baby. I'm a competent horsewoman," she said instantly annoyed with him. He came over close and got in her face.

"There's going to be no more discussion about this. You've passed out twice since we've been here and I'm not taking any chances of you falling. So we're riding Arrow. Is that clear?" he said with a glint in his eyes that told her he wasn't kidding.

"Okay, if you insist," she said, raising her chin.

"Good, that's my girl. It could be fun," he said with a big smile.

"Cute. Let's go, Mr. Fun."

"I'll give you a leg up and then I'll swing up behind you," he said.

"Blackie, let me give you a leg up," Sean offered.

"Oh, okay, thanks," Blackie said sticking his leg out. Sean heaved him onto Arrow's back behind Meg with a grunt.

"Christ, you're heavy," Sean complained.

"Shut up, Sean."

Blackie scooted up close behind her, putting his arms around her and picking up the reins.

"Can't I take the reins," she whined.

"Do you know where you're going?"

"No, you're right, I give up. You're in total control," she said.

"I don't want control; I want you and the baby safe."

"I know, honey. I'm happy you're being protective. I'm sorry I'm being cranky."

"I know, it's your new baby hormones." he said kissed her and rubbed his hand over her belly.

"Let's go for a ride and have some fun."

"Okay," she said, and now sort of enjoyed him cradling her with his body and arms.

"I should know by now that you're right when you get all stubborn and testy like that," she told him.

"Yeah, well, I only get stubborn and testy when I know I'm right," he laughed.

She leaned back against his chest and he kissed her hair. He put Arrow into a brisk walk and they rode along a dirt road with woods on one side and a green meadow on the other. She took a deep breath, taking in the fresh, fragrant Irish air. Grass, a hint of the sea, the moldy, mossy smells of the woods; she loved the smell of Ireland already. The road rose to the top of a hill. From there a beautiful valley lay before them so green it seemed iridescent. In the distance she could make out a glimpse of the sea.

"Oh, Blackie, this is so beautiful."

"I thought you'd like it. I love it up here." They rode through the hills and down into the valley for about an hour. Blackie told her the history of the area and showed her all the places he used to explore when he was a kid. They had so much fun. They started back for the stables and she was sorry the ride was over.

"Thank you for this. It was wonderful. I think I've fallen in love with Ireland."

"I'm glad you feel that way. This land is so much a part of me, of my soul; I want you to love it as much as I do." He kissed her neck and shoulder. She leaned back so he could kiss her mouth. He kissed her deeply and she returned the kiss.

"Let's go back now, Meg."

They got back to the stable, Blackie gave Arrow a cursory grooming and she put the tack away. He came up behind her in the tack room, circled her in his arms and caressed her belly.

"Let's go in." They went to his room and as soon as he closed the door they started taking each other's clothes off. They made love on the bed for a long time. When they were sated, they lay there talking for a time.

"We should get a shower and see what's happening." So they showered together, which was always fun with Blackie, then dressed and walked downstairs.

TWENTY-NINE

Preparations were underway for the dinner party, so Blackie and Meg hunted up Sean and Katie and hung out with them on the huge, stone patio off the kitchen. After a couple of hours they got called in to dinner. As soon as they were about to take seats, four men stood up and greeted Blackie with, "Good evening, Your Highnes."

He stopped and shook his head. "Please, don't call me that," he said with an edge to his voice.

Oh, great, this is going to be trouble.

Sean leaned over and whispered to him, "Take it easy, Blackie and ignore it."

"But that's your title, Sir. You should embrace it," one man said.

"I'm not embracing anything and my name's Blackie," he snarled.

"Son, this is Robert O'Donnell, Patrick Moore, Eamon O'Keefe and Charles Murphy. They're all ministers in the Dáil. They've come here especially to meet you," his Dad said.

"Good evening, it's nice to meet all of you," Blackie said making an effort to calm down.

"Yes, we've come to talk to you about taking your rightful place in Ireland. With your bloodlines, you're a natural born leader. *The O'Brien,* in fact." Patrick Moore said.

"My bloodlines!" Blackie scoffed. "What am I, a prized stallion? And my Dad's *Chief of the Clan,* not me".

"No, no, Your Highness, we mean you should lead your people from a government position," Eamon O'Keefe spoke up.

"I thought I said not to call me that. If you can't respect how I feel, why should I even talk to you?" Blackie said, red-faced.

"Blackie, actually they came to discuss some new proposals on social issues coming up for a vote," his Dad said.

"Okay, well then, I can just eat and don't need to participate."

"As you wish, son."

They ate in silence for awhile. Blackie kept his head down and ate. At the start of dessert, several of the men brought up referendums that were going to be presented the next week. Most of them were unintelligible to the rest of the group. Then they brought up one about child care subsidies for single parents. This suddenly got Blackie's attention.

"What's that proposal for?" He asked.

"It's a referendum to raise taxes on higher income groups to provide child care for single parents." his Dad replied.

"Of course, we're going to vote it down," Robert O'Donnell said pompously.

"What! Dad, are you serious? You're not going to pass it?" Blackie said, wide-eyed.

"Blackie, you don't understand this. It's not economically feasible to pass it," Ken said.

"I do understand. Single parents need help. How are they going to work if they can't pay for child care? That's ridiculous!" Blackie exclaimed.

"Well, the children wind up living in poverty, so they fall into the Welfare State. So they get taken care of," Eamon O'Keefe said.

"But that's worse. Don't you think the parents would rather work than be on the dole? Whose taxes pay for welfare?" Blackie asked.

"The taxes from the population across the board pay for Welfare," Ken said.

"Don't you think those of us who have the most should pay more? We should help those less fortunate," Blackie said, his faced flushed.

"Most of the higher income people are wealthy business men and landowners like us. If we pay more taxes, we won't be able to put money back into our companies. Our land and businesses are what keep the economy going." O'Donnell said.

"That's elitist bullshit. If these parents can work, there will be more people in the tax base. That's what runs the economy. You bastards just don't want to part with any of your money. You'll let the lower class get taxed to death, though." Blackie was yelling now and slammed his fist on the table.

"Blackie, please sit down. You just don't understand politics," Ken pleaded.

"For chrissake, Dad. I'm not stupid. It doesn't take a genius to see what's right. We have everything. Why shouldn't we help other people? Help them have some dignity. How would you feel if you had to watch Jill, Sean and I go hungry? It's wrong to tax people who are already struggling. Goddamnit, what's wrong with you, Dad?" Blackie yelled at his father. There was sudden applause all around the table. Blackie stood there with his mouth open.

"Very well argued, Sir. I do believe you belong in politics," Charles Murphy said smiling.

"Your father said you had the fire to run this country and I see he was right."

Blackie stood there for a second looking stunned.

"Fuck it, you people are nuts," he said stomping out of the room and onto the patio. Meg just sat there stunned herself. Blackie's parents and the others were smiling.

"You were right, Kennet, he's very dynamic and charismatic. He's got a good head on his shoulders, too. I believe he's just what this country needs," Robert O'Donnell said.

"Well, I can tell you, it's going to take an awful lot of convincing to get him into the game," Ken said shaking his head. "He can be very stubborn."

"That's just what we need, a man who will take hold and not let go." Eamon O'Keefe said.

"There's a Dáil seat for Newcastle West that's vacant. He should run for it. Your seat will be vacant when you retire, Kennet."

"Believe me, I'd retire early, if I could get him into it," Ken said his eyes dancing with excitement. "You know he's so much more the real head of the clan than me. He was born to be *The O'Brien*. Sean, Meg, Katie, you should help convince him."

"To get into politics? I don't know, Dad, I can't see him being interested," Sean said.

"You know, he's always lived by his own rules. They're pretty much what *he* considers to be right and wrong; whether they go along with conventional laws or not. He'll never give in on something he thinks is right, I can tell you that," Maeve said.

"Sean, why don't you become his advisor, you could always keep him a bit grounded," Ken suggested.

"Me, keep *him* grounded, you've got to be kidding. We fight all the time. I can't make him do anything he doesn't want to."

"I think it's a great idea, but I don't think he'll buy it." Meg said. "I'm going to go check on him." She got up and went out to the patio. He was standing there with his hands in his pockets, staring out at the night. She came up next to him.

He sighed big and said, "I know, I know, I'm an asshole for making a scene with my father's friends."

"No, I'm proud of you for standing up for what's right," she said.

"You are? You know, Meg, that scared the hell out of me. Suppose I was some prick who took off as soon as I found out you were pregnant. What if I left you with no way to take care of yourself and the baby?"

"But I have a good job and a college degree. I could save lots of money to provide for myself and the baby after it's born."

"Yes, you're educated, but suppose you worked in a pub, had no education and didn't make enough money to be able to save. Suppose you had no medical insurance. After you had your baby, you'd have to go on the dole, to even get food. Christ, that's scary. Meg, I'm glad I'm able to take care of you and the baby. Just the thought of you struggling to feed our child makes me sick."

"I'm glad you're a good guy and didn't disappear when I told you."

"There's no way I'd do something like that, you know that. I love you too much."

"I know that about you. I know you wouldn't leave me."

"Thank you," he said, kissing her tenderly.

"Do you want to go back in?" she asked.

"I don't know. Are they still there?"

"I think they're getting ready to leave. You know I've never really heard anyone call you that before. It was weird," she said.

"Oh, the 'Your Highness' thing. I know. I can't stand it. It's sick," he said in disgust.

"Well, you can be *my* prince anytime," she said provocatively.

"Mmm that sounds like fun. Yeah, I'll be the prince and you can be the serving wench. We can play *hide the scepter*." They both got hysterical laughing at that. Then he grabbed her, kissed her deeply and moved his hands down to her butt.

"Mmm, it's good to be the prince," he murmured, kissing her neck. They both started laughing again as his Dad came out onto the patio.

"What's so funny, you two?"

"Nothing, Dad, we're just being silly. Dad, I'm sorry if I offended your friends. I didn't mean to make a scene."

"On the contrary, they were very impressed with you. They think you should consider running for a seat that's vacant in Newcastle West."

"Me! In politics! That's ludicrous, Dad. I'm into horses, not politics. I wouldn't have time anyway. Also, I live in the States. How could I represent people and their problems when I don't even live here?"

"You could spend more time here. I know you want to work on dressage and training your horses, but you could do this too. *I* don't have to be there every day. The Dáil and Seanad are in session all the time. I go when there's a vote coming up."

"Dad, the dressage training is going to take up a lot of my time."

"Don't forget, I run this farm, too. I'm just as busy as you are," his father pointed out.

"Don't you forget, we have a baby on the way. I'll have to help Meg at first. I'm not really very interested in politics."

"You were interested in an Irish social problem. You had very definite ideas about it. That's what we need here, someone who will stand up for what's right and do it fiercely," Ken told him. "Will you at least think about it, son. It won't be too long until I'll retire and my seat will be vacant."

"I'll think about it, Dad, but don't get your hopes up." His Dad hugged him and Meg could see the love between them.

"We're going to leave in the morning. I want to get back and we need to get married."

"So soon? It seems like you just got here. Your mother and I miss all of you terribly. She won't be happy that you're leaving."

"I know. I have a lot of things to get working on. We'll be back soon. If not before, right after the baby's born for a real wedding. I promise."

Just then Maeve came out and asked, "What's going on?"

"Awww, wouldn't you know it; they're leaving in the morning."

"Oh, dear, you just now got here. I haven't had a minute to get to know Meg. Oh, son, I miss you so much. I wish you still lived here," Maeve said her eyes tearing up.

Blackie got agitated and stuffed his hands in his pockets and moved away from Maeve, frowning.

"Mom, I haven't been home much since I was sixteen. I'm almost twenty-seven."

"Come here, son," she said and held her arms out.

"I miss you too, Mom," he said and walked over to her. She folded him in her arms and hugged him tight. He put his head on her shoulder and Meg could see him relax in her arms and instantly realized why he liked to cuddle. He missed his mother's comforting embrace. He had been on his own from a teenager. It suddenly struck her that she had lost both of her parents at a young age. Maybe that's why they needed each other so much. She made a promise to herself to make sure he came back here more often. She thought he needed his parents love and guidance more than he would admit. He finally released his mother and they both were misty-eyed.

"We'll see you guys in the morning before we leave," he said gruffly. "Goodnight."

They went up to his room. He pulled her down on the bed, put his head on her chest and held on tight. She held him, stroking his hair for a long time. He was silent and she knew he just needed her to hold him. He was so strong physically but still very vulnerable emotionally. He fell asleep and she pulled a cover over them, letting him sleep in her arms.

Thirty

In the morning Meg awoke and Blackie was still cuddled with her. She started to get up but he tightened his arms around her. She looked into those beautiful blue eyes and they were serious.

"Don't get up yet. I want to talk to you." He paused and she wondered what was next.

"Okay, honey, what is it?"

"Will you marry me?"

"Yes, darling, of course. I said yes when you asked me two days ago. I can't wait to marry you."

"This is a lousy way to ask you. I don't even have a ring, but I'm getting one. As soon as I get one, I'll do this again, properly. I'm such a jerk."

"I said yes," she reminded him.

"I know. I love you." He put his mouth on her belly, kissing it and said, "Good morning, Baby, it's Daddy." Then he laughed, rolled her over on top of him and hugged her right. "Let's go home, honey."

*   *   *

They landed at Dulles and took a limo home. The guys started chatting on the ride home and they all seemed to perk up a little.

Sean got out a bottle of champagne and exclaimed, "I have an announcement. I've asked Katie to marry me and she said yes!"

They screamed with excitement and hugged one another.

"That's fabulous. When are you planning on doing it? I think we're going to do something small as soon as possible," Blackie said.

"We'll start planning right away and I guess do it in a couple months. Then we can all go back to Ireland," Katie said flushed with happiness.

"So you're going to get married in Ireland. Great! Mom's going to make a big deal out of it. Are you ready for that?" Blackie said.

"Yes, I know she will, but we don't want anything big. Small and elegant is what we want," Sean said putting his arm around Katie.

"Hey, where's the ring, dummy? You're as bad as me. You need to get a ring, man," Blackie scolded Sean.

"I know, I know. I thought you and I could go and look at them. What do you think?" Sean asked him.

"Okay, but shouldn't you take Katie?"

"She said she wants to be surprised, so that's what I'm doing," Sean answered.

"Katie, that's so exciting. It's going to be wonderful," Meg said.

"Hey, I can't wait to get home and see Jill and Keary's faces when we tell them our news," Sean said, happily.

*　　*　　*

They arrived at the farm, stowed their bags and walked up to the house.

Jill and Keary were in the TV room watching a movie when they trooped in. There were lots of hugs and kisses until they settled down with drinks to catch up.

"You look great. We missed you guys," Jill said.

"How was it? Are the new horses on their way? How're Maeve and Ken?" Keary asked.

"We missed you guys too. Mom and Dad are wonderful." Blackie laughed. "We had the best time. Meg is in love with Ireland and I think Katie is too. The horses should be here in a couple weeks. Wait till you see them, Keary. I think we made some good buys. We actually can't wait to go back. Oh, get this, Dad wants me to go into politics! Me!" Keary and Jill's mouths flew open.

"What?" they said.

"I'll tell you about it later, it's ridiculous, but first, we have some exciting news."

"Wait, wait, Jill and I have news and we go first, since we didn't get to go to Ireland," Keary said smiling and looked at Jill. She nodded.

"We're pregnant!" he exclaimed. There was total silence and then pandemonium broke loose with more hugs, kisses and 'high-fives'.

"We need more champagne," Sean said and went out to the fridge.

"Hey, I found some," he said juggling it and a stack of plastic glasses. He poured and everyone toasted Jill and Keary.

"All right, now what's your news?" Keary asked.

"Katie and I are getting married!" Sean yelled causing more toasting, hugging, laughing and well-wishing.

"Meg and I have news too." Blackie said quietly and everyone was silent and looked at them expectantly. He looked at her, uncertain.

"It's okay, honey," she said softly.

"Meg and I are expecting a baby."

There was complete silence and then Jill screamed, "Oh, my God. Meg, Blackie, that's wonderful. Meg, we'll be pregnant together." Keary went over and punched Blackie on the arm. "You dog, congratulations, man, that's really cool."

Again, more celebrating.

In the middle of it, Blackie raised his hands for silence. "And if anyone's wondering, Meg and I are getting married as soon as possible," he said smiling.

Keary and Sean high-fived him. They finally settled down and flopped on the sofa with their drinks. Sean poured more champagne and the party was going strong.

"When are you guys getting married?" Keary asked Sean.

"We're going to start putting it together and then do it in a few months in Ireland. So we'll all go over and party."

"I can't wait. This is going to be so much fun," Jill said excitedly. "Wedding stuff, baby stuff! I love it!"

"Oh, Jesus, here comes all the girly crap," Sean said, holding his head in jest.

"Get out! It's not *girly* stuff. I hate when you say that," Katie said, smacking him on the arm.

"See, they're already acting like a married couple," Keary said laughing. "Sean, Blackie, the best two words you guys can learn and start practicing now are 'Yes, Dear!'" Jill smacked him on the back of his head and they roared with laughter.

This reverie lasted another couple hours and by that time Meg was so tired she was feeling dizzy again.

Jill looked at Meg and said, "Are you okay, Meg, you look a little pale?"

Blackie turned to her. "Honey? Jill, she's been passing out. She did a couple times at Mom and Dad's. I'm worried about it. I think we should get her to a baby doctor. Do you like yours?"

"Yes, I do very much. I'll call in the morning and make an appointment, if that's alright with you."

"Sure, I want to get checked and make sure everything's good," Meg said.

"I'm three and half months and I was horribly tired at first. I'm starting to feel better though," Jill said.

"Maybe we should crash and get some rest. We can continue talking in the morning. If you guys want to stay, go ahead, I just need to get this little mama in bed," Blackie said. He got up and went to use the bathroom and Jill leaned over and asked her quietly,

"How's he been with this?"

"He was shocked at first. Now, however, he's getting into it and being the over-protective Daddy. He won't let me ride. He's been hammering himself though for not asking me to marry him sooner. I keep telling him it's fine, but you know how he gets."

"Oh boy, he's going to be a cute dad, but strict. I can see him being over-protective," Jill said. Just then Blackie came back in, leaned over and kissed her.

"Do you feel okay to walk down to the apartment?" he asked.

"Yes, honey, I'm fine."

"I mean we could sleep up here tonight or I could carry you," he said helping her up. She rolled her eyes at Jill who bit her lip to keep from laughing.

"Good night all, we'll see you tomorrow," Blackie said and they walked slowly to the apartment holding hands.

THIRTY-ONE

It was several weeks later, early, around six. Blackie was breathing softly next to Meg. She didn't want to disturb him but had to use the bathroom and had stomach cramps. She didn't feel good at all. She wondered what she had eaten that was disagreeing with her. She pushed the covers back and eased out of bed. She tiptoed into the bathroom and sat down.

Ahhh ... that felt good.

Suddenly she got a sharp cramp. She used the tissue and there was blood on it!

Oh God! What's wrong?

She stood up and there was blood in the toilet.

No, no! What's happening?

Instant fear clutched her heart. She looked down and blood was running down her legs. She screamed for Blackie and in two seconds he came through the bathroom door.

He stopped and stared at her, wide-eyed. "Meg, what happened?"

"I don't know," she said bursting into tears. She suddenly felt faint. He grabbed her quickly and put her back in bed. He left and came back with towels, stuffing them under her and between her legs. He picked up the phone and dialed 911.

"Hello, this is Blackie O'Brien from Killarney Farms out on Route 10. My fiancée, who is three or four months pregnant, is bleeding. She's under the care of Dr. Edward Brown. I'm going to call him next. Please hurry. Yes, thank you." Then he called Jill.

"Jill, get down here right away. Meg's bleeding. I just called 911. Call Dr. Brown and see if he can meet us at the emergency room." He hung up and got in bed next to her.

"Meg, how do you feel? What happened?"

"I got up to pee and had cramps. I thought it was something I ate. Blackie, I'm scared. What's going to happen to the baby?"

"I don't know, honey, calm down. Dr. Brown will help us. Try and lay still," Blackie said holding her. She was hysterical now, terrified that the baby was in trouble. Jill and Keary burst in.

"Here you guys sit down and let me look at her," Jill told them. Blackie and Keary went and sat at the table. Jill came over, removed the towels and checked her.

"What do you think?" Meg asked her. Just then she was gripped by a terrible cramp in her lower belly and cried out in pain. Blackie jumped up and came over.

"Meg, what happened?" He knelt beside the bed, stroking her hair.

"I had a terrible pain."

"Jill, what is it?" Blackie asked her.

"Honey, I think she's in labor," she told him, "but they can stop it with medicine."

"God, I hope so."

They heard sirens and the paramedics came into the apartment. Meg was shaking with fear Blackie sat next to her on the bed, holding her hand. They checked her vitals and how much she was bleeding. They told Blackie that they talked to Dr. Brown and they'd take her to Labor and Delivery emergency and he would meet them there. They wheeled her out and put her in the ambulance.

"Keary, can you guys drive separately so one of you can drive my car. I'll probably be at the hospital all night," Blackie asked Keary and Jill.

Then he got in with her and they took off. She had stronger pains on the way to the hospital and by that time she was beyond hysterical.

Dr. Brown was there and checked her. He told them to take her to Labor and Delivery and he and Blackie would be there in a minute. He took Blackie and got a nurse to help him change into scrubs.

Dr. Brown and Blackie came into the OR. The pains were coming close together now. Blackie sat by her head and held her hand.

"Honey, what's happening? Am I having the baby now? I can't! It's too early." She cried out in pain again. Blackie was holding her hand tight with his head up against hers. After maybe fifteen minutes, Dr. Brown asked him to go out of the room with him.

"Meg, I need to talk to the doctor. I'll be right back."

"What's happened? Don't leave me! I'm so scared, honey!" She cried. A nurse came over and took her hand.

"It's okay, sweetie. He'll be right back. You're okay. We're going to put some medicine in your IV. It'll help with the pain, honey. Just relax," she told Meg.

*   *   *

Dr. Brown took Blackie into the hall.

"Blackie, she's given birth to the fetus. It has been dead for at least a week. The hormones in the patch kept it from developing normally. It would never have survived to full term. Right now we need to put her under so we can do a D and C which will clean out her uterus. If any debris is still left in there, she'll get an infection. You can go in and talk to her before we put her under. Then you should go out and wait with your family."

"Okay, thanks, doc," Blackie said, his head down and his stomach in knots.

"I'm sorry, Blackie." Dr. Brown told him, putting a consoling hand on his shoulder. Blackie went back into the delivery room to her and kissed her. His eyes were teary.

"What happened? What's going on?" She asked him.

"Meg, sweetheart, it's going to be okay. The baby ... she didn't hear the rest, they had put her under.

*   *   *

Jill, Keary, Sean and Katie were sitting in the waiting room drinking coffee. They looked up and saw Blackie walking toward them, still in scrubs.

"Oh God, here comes Blackie, he looks terrible," Keary said.

Blackie slumped down in one of the chairs. They were all staring at him expectantly.

"Meg lost the baby," Blackie told them.

"Oh no, honey, I'm so sorry," Jill said and started crying.

"Jill, please don't do that, I can't handle it right now," Blackie told her. "They're doing a D&C, so we won't be able to see her for awhile. I guess we'll see her in the recovery room. The doc told me the baby had been dead for a week. It wouldn't have lived anyway."

"We're so sorry, buddy," Keary said, putting an arm around Blackie.

"Yeah, man, if there's anything we can do," Sean said. "This really sucks."

"I don't know if I can help her with her grief. I'm not sure what to do," Blackie said sadly. "She loved that baby and so did I."

"I think if you follow your feelings, you'll be able to help her," Jill said.

"That's just it, Jill. I'm trying to block out my feelings so I can take care of her. I'm good at burying my feelings."

"But that's not good for you. That's when you get into trouble." Keary told him.

"I know but my first priority is to take care of Meg." Just then Dr. Brown walked toward them and squatted in front of Blackie.

"Blackie, I'm sorry for your loss. You know about thirty percent of pregnancies end in miscarriage. You two are young. You have plenty of time to have children. Meg is going to be fine and she's healthy. There's no reason why she can't carry another child."

"Thanks, doc."

"Listen, no intercourse for at least three weeks or longer if she's not ready. Also, you have to wait at least six months before you can try again."

"Six months!" Blackie said looking up at him. "I can tell you she's going to want to get pregnant again right away."

"You can't let her. She's lost too much blood." Blackie's eyes welled with tears. Dr. Brown said more gently. "Blackie, if she gets pregnant right away, her body isn't strong enough to carry it. So it's going to end up the same way. You can't let that happen." Blackie nodded in agreement.

"I understand and I'll take care of it."

"Blackie, look at me. I know you're trying to be strong for Meg. But *you* have to grieve too. It was your baby too. Losing a baby now is just as hard as it would be at eight months or at birth. Don't fool yourself that this is trivial because she was only three months." He said patting Blackie on his shoulder. "Okay, she's in recovery. The nurse will come and get you when she's awake. Take care," he said and Blackie stood and shook his hand.

"Thank you, Dr. Brown." Blackie paced back and forth for a while, silent. No one else said much of anything, waiting for him to talk. He finally sat down, putting his head in his hands and sat like that for some time.

"Sean, when are you guys getting married?" Blackie asked.

"In four weeks, everything's pretty well set in Ireland. We'll stay at Mom and Dad's and fly over in the Lear, so there's not much in the way of arrangements. Are you two still getting married next Saturday?" Sean asked him.

"I don't know, maybe. I'll have to see how she feels about it. Your wedding should distract her."

"Honey, why don't you just go through with it anyway," Jill said.

"I said I don't know; don't bug me about it for chrissake," Blackie said. He got up and walked down the hall.

"I need some coffee." He said.

Jill started to go after him and Keary grabbed her arm.

"Jill, leave him alone. I don't think he can handle much of anything right now. He needs time alone and with Meg and they'll figure things out."

"I guess you're right. I just hate this happening to them," Jill said.

"Hey, maybe he'll get a fire lit under him and they'll get married in Ireland while we're there," Sean said hopefully.

"We'll see, but there's something bugging him. He needs to talk to Dr. Wahlman," Keary said.

In about twenty minutes, Blackie came back with a cup of coffee and sat down. He stared at the floor and sipped the coffee. He sighed and sat back.

"Listen, I don't want Meg punished any more for my sins; so I don't know about marriage. She'll be better off if she leaves me. Maybe *I'll* leave so she doesn't have a choice," Blackie said. Everyone started protesting at once.

"Blackie, what are you thinking? She's not being punished for anything you did," Keary said, alarmed.

"Honey, you love each other. You heard the doctor; this happens a lot. It's normal," Jill said.

"Hey, man, don't do that, it'll kill you guys to be apart. Blackie, this isn't your fault. Come on," Sean said.

"Blackie, Meg loves you too much. She won't give you up. This isn't a punishment. God wouldn't do that. He brought you two together," Katie said crying.

"I don't know. It feels like punishment," Blackie said.

"Blackie you have to move forward and forget your past. Katie's right. If God hadn't forgiven you, he wouldn't have brought you Meg," Keary said.

"You guys think so?" he asked. They all agreed. He sighed and said, "Maybe. I have to think about it some more." Just then a nurse came out and asked for Mr. O'Brien.

"Yes," Blackie said.

"Your wife is awake; you can see her in the recovery room."

"Thank you. God, I wish she was my wife," Blackie said. "I'll go in and see what's up and then I'll come get you guys."

"Okay," Keary said.

THIRTY-TWO

Meg was settled in her room, trying to think about something else when everyone filed in, hugged her and murmured words of consolation. She knew how much they cared, but she just wanted to crawl under their blanket at home with Blackie holding her. She wanted to stay that way until the pain went away. The pain in her heart.

She looked over at Blackie and he gave her a sad little smile. He looked awful. She could tell he was exhausted and totally drained emotionally. She wanted him to stay, but she knew he wouldn't sleep. She motioned for him to come to her. He walked over, leaned into the bed.

"You look so little and helpless lying there. I want to protect you from any hurt," he whispered in her ear.

"Here get in bed with me." She said.

"They're going to get pissed if I do that. They'll throw me out," he said.

"I don't care if they like it or not, I want you close to me." She said. With a very determined, stuck out chin.

"Who's she starting to sound like?" he said smiling.

"You!" everyone said. He took his shoes off and climbed over the rail, snuggling up close to her.

"There, is that better, then?"

"Yes, definitely," she sighed and put her head on his shoulder.

"I guess we should go and leave you two alone?" Keary said.

"No, you don't have to go. I just needed him near me. We can still visit."

"No, you're both tired. We need to get home and let you guys rest," Jill said. "We'll see you tomorrow, then. Just call if you need anything." She came over and kissed Meg and then Blackie.

"I love you guys. It'll be okay," Jill said tearfully.

Everyone hugged Meg and they left. She was sorry to see them go but she didn't think she could hold it together much longer. She buried her face in Blackie's chest and just let it all go. He held her tight while she sobbed and didn't say anything. She didn't need or want him to say anything; just being there was enough. The tears finally slowed and she looked in his eyes that were filled with sorrow and concern for her.

"It's okay, sweetheart, I know." She snuggled up against him and fell asleep. She woke up about ten o'clock, raised her head and he smiled at her.

"Hi, honey, did you get some rest?"

"Yes, thank you, but you need to get some too."

"I'm fine. I just want to be with you."

"No, I want you to go home and get in bed. They'll give me another shot, so I'll sleep the rest of the night."

"That's okay, I need to stay here and make sure you're okay."

"Blackie, I'm fine. I want you to go home and get a goodnight's sleep in our bed where you're comfortable," she said firmly.

"Please, Meg. I want to stay with you."

"Don't be silly, I'll be fine. Just please do what I want you to do." He stared at her for a minute and she thought he was going to get his back up over it, but he didn't.

"Okay, Meg," he said climbing out of the bed and putting his shoes on. He came over and kissed her good night.

"I love you. I'll see you tomorrow."

"I love you too, honey. Be careful driving home."

He looked back so downcast her heart lurched at the look on his face. She should have let him stay but she was in so much pain. She rang the bell for the nurse to come and give her a shot, hoping she'd get there soon.

*   *   *

It was one o'clock and Sean, Katie, Jill and Keary were watching TV. They decided that none of them could sleep, so they watched a movie.

"I heard a car pull up," Jill said getting up and looking down to the driveway.

"It's Blackie. I thought he was staying overnight?"

"I don't know. I thought so too. I'm anxious to hear how Meg is. She didn't look good earlier, really pale," Keary said.

Just then Blackie came in the kitchen door and slammed it hard behind him. Jill looked at Keary with raised eyebrows and he frowned.

"We're all back in the TV room, honey," Jill called out. No answer. They could hear him rooting in the fridge, moving bottles around almost hard enough to break.

"Isn't there any fucking goddamn food in here?" Blackie yelled.

"Uh, oh, that doesn't sound good," Sean said.

"There should be some cold chicken." Jill yelled.

"Cookies. I want some damn cookies." Blackie yelled again. More banging in the fridge. Something got thrown into the sink and broke.

"Bollocks!"

Jill went to get up but Keary stopped her.

"I want you to stay away from him."

"What do you mean? He wouldn't hurt me! What's wrong with you?" Jill said.

"Jill, you're pregnant and he sounds like he's been drinking and in a mean mood. I don't know what he'd do."

"Where the fuck are the goddamn fecking cookies?" More glass breaking.

"Sean, would you go see if he's been drinking and what's going on?" Keary asked.

"Oh, just grand," Sean said, sighed and got up. He walked out to the kitchen and Blackie was standing there, beer in hand, staring into the refrigerator. Sean came up beside him and put an arm on his shoulder.

"Hey, buddy, what's up?" Blackie just stared into the open fridge.

"Blackie?" Sean said.

"Huh?" Blackie looked at him and Sean instantly knew what was going on.

"How's Meg?"

"She's fucked up. She wouldn't let me stay with her," Blackie said staring back into the fridge.

"How long ago did you leave her?" Sean asked. He noticed Blackie's knuckles were cut up, like he'd been in a fight.

"I don't know, maybe ten o'clock. I don't remember. Hey, where are the cookies in this house?"

"I don't know but they sure aren't kept in the fridge," Sean said. "Hey, when you find your cookies bring them back to the TV room; we're watching a movie."

"Okay," Blackie said and started going through the cupboards, throwing things on the floor when they got in his way. Sean went back to the TV room.

"What's he doing now?" Keary asked.

"He's still hunting for the cookies," Sean said.

"Why didn't you help him find the damn cookies so he doesn't tear the whole kitchen apart?" Keary said, throwing his hands in the air.

"You go help him find them. I'm staying in here where it's relatively safe," Sean said, matter of factly.

"Is he drunk?" Keary asked.

"Nope."

"Then what?"Keary exclaimed.

"He's high," Sean said, "*very* high."

"What do you mean; I thought you said he wasn't drinking?"

"Keary, drugs."

Jill sucked her breath in, "Oh, no."

"What's he like when he's high?" Keary asked.

"Unpredictable," Sean said. "He's very upset about Meg."

"What do you think he took?" Keary asked.

"I'm not sure. Some kind of downer, maybe Vike and mixed with alcohol most likely."

"Vike. What's that?" Jill said alarmed.

"Vicodin or something like it. Jill, he's been in rehab before; so I thought you knew all of this," Sean said.

"I guess I did. I guess I put it out of my mind. It's too hard to think about. Isn't that a pain killer?"

"It is, yes and you know he abused them along with alcohol and coke." Sean replied.

"I don't want him bringing drugs into this house. I mean we're going to have children here soon. God, what a mess!" More slamming came from the kitchen.

"Shit!"

"Where did he get it that fast? Do you think he keeps it in his apartment?" Keary asked.

"Well, he left Meg around ten o'clock so he's been somewhere for over three hours," Sean said.

"I mean it Jill, stay away from him, please!" Keary said, tight-lipped.

"Okay," Jill said quietly.

"You, too," Sean said to Katie.

"I usually do."

Sean looked at her funny and said, Why, are you afraid of him?"

"No, I wouldn't say that. I mean he's nice and I like him a lot. He's sweet with Meg. It's just something like untamed, like there's this kinetic energy under the surface that could explode any minute. That night at the club; when he went after that guy that was bothering Meg. That scared me, big time."

"I hate that everyone thinks he's such a bad person," Jill said tearfully.

"Nobody thinks that he's a bad person, Jill, uh ..." Just then Blackie walked into the TV room with a bag of chocolate chip cookies and a beer.

"Hey, hey, hey, I found the cookies," he said in a perfect imitation of Fat Albert. He sat down between Sean and Keary, putting his beer on the coffee table and digging into the cookies. He wolfed down about six cookies and then took a long pull on the beer.

"These are awesome cookies." Blackie said.

"They go good with beer?" Keary asked.

"They go best with beer," he said and glanced at Keary. Keary was startled to see that his pupils were so dilated, his eyes looked black.

"How's Meg?" Jill asked.

"How's Meg? That's a good question," he said and stopped, a cookie halfway to his mouth and stared at the TV, as if he was in a trance. Sean touched his arm and repeated the question.

"How's Meg, Blackie?"

"Meg? She's probably all cozy in bed by herself. She's probably got her shot and is sound asleep," he said sarcastically.

"Did you guys have a fight?" Keary asked him.

"Noooo, I wasn't going to fight with her. She made me leave. She said I needed sleep. I don't want to sleep," he yelled and slammed the bottle down and beer went everywhere. "She wouldn't let me stay. I needed to stay with her; I needed to watch over her tonight. What if she woke up and she was sad. I could have been there. No, she made me leave; she said I needed to rest. I need to do something; but it's not rest. I don't know what to do. I just needed to be there tonight, but what could I do. I'm fucking useless."

"Blackie, you're not useless; you can do plenty for her. She needs you very much. She was probably worried that you were so tired." Jill said but he was staring at the TV again.

"Where'd you go after you left Meg?" Keary asked.

"I stopped at a bar and had a beer," Blackie said eating more cookies and washing them down with beer.

"Is that all you had was a beer?" Keary demanded. Jill made a face at him.

"No, that's not all. I scored some shit, too. Is there anything else you'd like to know and don't go calling Wahlman either. I won't use after this. I just needed to get through tonight and tomorrow. So leave me the fuck alone."

"What the hell were you thinking?"

"That's just it. I don't want to think or feel. Right now I have achieved a perfect state of numb and that's how I plan to stay until Meg is better."

"You can't help Meg if you're high."

"I can't help her if I'm an emotional wreck so just stop, please stop!"

Jill jumped up and went over and squeezed in between Sean and Blackie.

"Jill!" Keary yelped.

"Shut up. I know what I'm doing." She put her arm around Blackie and stroked the back of his head.

"It's okay honey. We understand. We'll help you get through this," she crooned soothingly.

"Watch this, she's going to put him to sleep," Sean whispered to Katie.

"What!"

"Shhh–just watch."

Jill rubbed Blackie's back and shoulders, talking to him in Gaelic with a low voice until he relaxed and leaned back against the sofa. Finally, he let his head drop over onto her shoulder. She continued talking to him and hugged him to her, still lightly rubbing his face. He closed his eyes and started breathing slower.

"Ohmigod, she just hypnotized him," Katie said. Everyone stared at her and then looked at Blackie.

"She's right. I've seen Mom do that to him a thousand times and never thought about it," Sean said. "He was always hyper as a kid and Mom did that to calm him down and get him to sleep."

"I never thought about it either. I've seen Jill do it the last few years that he's been here with us and it never dawned on me," Keary said.

Jill motioned for him to help her. She moved away from Blackie and let him lay down on the sofa, putting a pillow under his head. Keary put his feet up and covered him up with an afghan.

"Will he stay asleep?" Katie whispered.

"Most likely," Jill said. "I know he's exhausted. We need to get some sleep too."

"Yeah, with that crap in his system, he'll be out for days," Keary said, disgustedly. "I suppose we'll go get Meg in the morning."

"I don't know, he might surprise you," Sean said. Everyone said goodnight and they went to bed.

THIRTY-THREE

The next morning everyone had gathered in the kitchen to eat breakfast and discuss the day. It was around six-thirty, a second pot of coffee brewing, when Blackie padded down the hall. Everyone looked up in surprise and said good morning.

Blackie sort of grunted and said, "Coffee" like he was saying "help." He poured a cup and sat down at the table with the others.

"I didn't expect to see you this morning," Keary said.

"Why not?" Blackie asked gruffly, sipping his coffee.

"I thought with the drugs, you'd be out for awhile," Keary said.

"You thought wrong, Keary, it doesn't work like that," Blackie said with an edge to his voice. "Anyway, I have to pick Meg up today."

"Are you still high; your eyes are still dilated?" Keary said. "You're not going to drive like that."

"Keary, stop," Jill said giving him a look.

"Yes, I'm still high and I can drive just fine. I don't have any drugs on me, so I won't get picked up." Blackie said sarcastically.

"Yes, but you're going to have Meg in the car with you."

"So you don't care if I kill myself, you're just worried about Meg."

"Both of you stop it!" Jill yelled.

"You know better than that, Blackie, for chrissake. I'm worried about both of you. How about if we take the SUV and then you can sit in the back and take care of Meg." Keary suggested.

Blackie thought a minute and then said, "Okay, I have to go get cleaned up. I'll be back when I'm ready."

"Don't you want something to eat?" Jill asked.

"No, I'll eat later," Blackie said and left for the barn.

"Jill and I will go with him to get Meg. What are you and Katie doing today?" Keary asked Sean.

"I have horses to get ready and loaded for the track. So I'm busy all day. I don't know what Katie had in mind," Sean said.

"I was going to work on wedding stuff, but I'd like to go with you guys to get Meg. Do you think Blackie will mind?" Katie said.

"No, I don't think he'll mind," Jill told her.

"Okay, well let's get moving because he'll be back up here in about twenty minutes and will want to leave." Keary said. "If we're not ready he'll take the Porsche. I'm surprised he agreed to let us take him."

"Me, too," Jill said.

*   *   *

In twenty minutes everyone had piled into the SUV and were outside the barn waiting for Blackie. In five more minutes, he walked out wearing a black suit that was beautifully tailored to fit him of soft, silky material. The shirt was white and opened at the neck. He had on black leather boots and dark sunglasses. Keary whistled when he came out of the barn and walked toward the car.

"Wow, look at Mr. GQ. One thing I have to say for him, he cleans up grand."

"He has great taste in clothes. That suit looks like it cost a fortune," Katie said.

"It probably did." Jill said.

Blackie opened the door and got in next to Keary and said, "Let's go." They drove for about ten minutes, when Blackie said, "Oh, shit!"

"What's wrong?" Keary asked.

"I forgot my checkbook. Can we stop at the bank? It's at the next intersection."

"Sure, but do you need money?"

"I'm not sure. I didn't get an insurance card from Meg. I signed her in and they asked who was responsible and I said I was."

"Okay," Keary said and pulled into the bank. Blackie got out and walked in.

"I'm not being disloyal to Sean or anything but I've never seen a man as good looking as Blackie. He's very striking. He doesn't seem arrogant though," Katie said.

"No, he isn't. He doesn't think he's anyone special," Jill said.

"I think Sean is good looking and really hot, but Blackie's like perfect."

Just then he came out of the bank and walked toward the car. Behind him, the women who worked there came out and were watching him walk to the car. Keary and Jill started laughing.

"See, he has no idea those women are looking."

Blackie got in the car and Keary said, "Why don't you wave to your admirers?"

"What?" Blackie said and Keary nodded to the women, Blackie glanced at them and back at Keary.

"What the hell are you talking about?"

"Never mind," Keary said starting the car. "How much money did you get?"

"Uh ... five thousand." Blackie said.

"Five thousand!" Why so much?"

"I don't know! I don't know what shit costs. I know what a good horse costs, what entry fee's cost, vet fees, but nothing practical. I'm fucking useless!"

"Honey, stop saying that," Jill said.

"What's a dead baby cost? What's it cost to have your woman's insides scraped out?" he said and his voice cracked. He just looked out the window. Keary reached over and squeezed his hand. Blackie looked at him and turned back to the window, his jaw muscles working.

"What the hell would I do without you guys?" Blackie said. "You're always there for me. I'm never there for you." he said sighing.

"Of course you are, honey," Jill said

"No, I'm not. Maybe someday I will be."

"Don't worry about it; we know if we need you, you'll be there. We just haven't needed any help lately," Keary told him.

"Thanks, Keary," Blackie said. "I just hope I can take care of Meg."

"You can do this, honey," Jill said. "We'll try and stay out of it and leave you two alone. Meg will tell you what she needs and you'll be there for her. You two are going to be fine."

"I hope so," he said.

"Not to change the subject, but what's this about Ken wanting you to go into politics?" Keary asked.

"For chrissake, isn't that ridiculous? Have you ever heard of a more fucking stupid idea?" Blackie said and laughed.

"Why? I think it's a great idea," Keary said smiling at him.

"Are you out of your mind? Me! In politics; come on, Keary."

"No, he's right. You'd be great. You know how adamant you are about things when you know it's the right thing to do. Ireland certainly could use some fresh ideas." Jill said.

"I think you'd be awesome," Katie said. Blackie turned and stared at her for a moment.

"Where did you come up with that opinion?" he asked her. The intensity of his gaze made her stomach clench but she stammered a reply anyway.

"I was there when those guys were talking about the child care issue. I mean you were right about how stupid that is and you argued your point perfectly. You have a lot of intensity and charisma which I think would be good in public office."

Blackie stared at her for another minute and she felt like squirming in her seat.

"Charisma? That is funny," he said smiling.

"But she's right, Blackie. I've *never* won an argument with you. I think you have a lot of integrity that couldn't be corrupted like most of those jerks in Dublin," Keary said.

"Oh, right, look how I let myself be corrupted when I was racing," Blackie said.

"That was different. You're older and you're going to be settling down with Meg. What are they going to corrupt you with? Women? That's highly unlikely? Money wouldn't do it, you're already wealthy. Drugs and alcohol, maybe, but you're getting that under control, I hope. It's just not the same situation. You never cheated on a race, don't forget."

"Well, it's just so far out of my train of thinking. I'm trying to work on getting the dressage thing going. I don't know. I'll give it some thought," Blackie said.

*   *   *

Meg had finished breakfast and was watching TV, waiting for Blackie to come and take her home.

In a few minutes, he walked into her room. Her heart did a flip-flop like it always did when she saw him. She could never quite believe what a fairy tale she was living; that he was hers and he loved her.

He went to her and folded her in his arms.

Now she instantly felt safe and at home. She hugged him back and turning her face up, got the kiss she wanted.

"Hi, sweetheart, how are you doing?"

"I'm wonderful now that you're here. I really missed you last night. I couldn't wait until you got here," she told him, her eyes filling with tears.

He knelt down next to her, saying, "Shh, honey, it's okay. I'm here now. I missed you too last night. I had a bad night. Why didn't you let me stay?"

"Blackie, I was in terrible pain last night. I didn't want to tell you because I knew you'd get upset. I could hardly lie still until the nurse gave me a shot and then I was out like a light." Now *his* eyes filled with tears.

"God, honey, I'm sorry. I didn't realize you were hurting that much. I can't stand it when you're hurt."

"I feel pretty good today. I'm just very tired. I'm better now that you're here. You're all I need." He smiled a little sad smile and hugged her again.

Then Keary, Jill and Katie walked in and hugged her. Blackie got up and moved out of the way, still wiping his eyes.

"Hey, sweetie, how are you?" Keary asked.

"I feel a lot better today. I'm glad to see you guys."

"That's good. We were worried about you yesterday and last night. It'll be good to get you home," Jill told her.

"Meg, I'm going out to the nurses' station a minute. I'll be right back," Blackie said. "Here are your clothes. Maybe Keary can come with me and the girls can help you if you need it."

"Okay, hurry back."

*   *   *

Blackie and Keary left and she got her clothes out of the bag. He had brought jeans, a sweatshirt, socks and panties but no bra or shoes. She didn't really need either at this point.

"How was he last night?" She asked.

"He didn't do too well last night, Meg. He was up at six-thirty though, got coffee and went to get dressed." Jill said.

"You mean he slept up at the house last night?"

"He did, yes. We were talking and he fell asleep on the sofa, so I let him sleep."

"Oh, good. He looks good today. His eyes look funny though; they're all dilated or something," she said, pulling her clothes on. She was still hurting but nothing like last night. The cramps were almost gone.

"I hadn't noticed his eyes. I thought he looked hot in that suit." Jill said.

*   *   *

Blackie and Keary walked to the nurses' station. Keary noticed that all the nurses turned and gawked as they walked by. He chuckled to himself. *Charismatic* is the word, he thought. At the nurses' station the nurses stopped what they were doing and stared at Blackie.

"Can you tell me where I can pay the bill for Miss Connors?" Blackie asked.

They kept staring and finally one nurse came to her senses and said, "Uh ... you have to go to the 'Cashier's Office' on the first floor. They should have it ready for you. Are you her husband?" she asked.

"Not yet." Blackie said and went with Keary to the first floor. Keary again noticed how the nurses and aids were staring open mouthed at Blackie, smiling and giggling to one another.

Hmm, Keary thought, *superstar* is probably a better word.

They found the Cashier's Office and Blackie asked them for Meg's bill.

"Are you Miss Connor' husband?" the cashier asked.

"No, I'm her fiancée," Blackie said.

"Does she have insurance?"

"I don't know. It was an emergency when I brought her in."

"Well, you need to bring the insurance card in before we can release her," she said.

"Look, just give me the bill and I'll pay cash," Blackie said.

"But we need to bill the insurance company before any co-pay is needed, sir," the cashier said, acting like Blackie was stupid.

"Listen, I'm taking her out of here whether the bill is paid or not. So if you want any of it paid, you need to give me the bill right now!" Blackie said through his teeth.

"What is your name, sir?" The woman asked.

"Mr. O'Brien."

"Well, Mr. O'Brien, I'm going to have to call a supervisor about this. I don't know if we can release her without the bill being paid."

"Are you going to give me the fucking bill or not? I don't want to wait for your supervisor."

"Blackie, calm down," Keary said.

"I'll have to call security, sir," the lady said, her nose in the air.

"Why can't you just tell me how much it is?" Blackie said.

"The bill is $1,565.00, sir." Blackie pulled two thousand dollars out of his wallet and slapped it on the counter.

"Here, keep the change and give me a receipt," Blackie said, barely controlled.

"Very well, sir," she said and wrote him a receipt.

He took the receipt saying "Thank you," dripping with sarcasm to the cashier. He walked away toward the elevator, fuming.

"Blackie, you just gave her a big damn tip for being stupid," Keary said.

"I don't care. It's worth it to get the fuck out of here. God! Do you believe how incompetent people are?" They rode up in the elevator to the fourth floor.

"I need to walk around a few minutes to calm down before I go in and get Meg. She'll know I had an argument," Blackie said, walking the opposite way from the room.

"Oh, the nurses are going to love that," Keary said.

"Why? What's walking against hospital rules, too?" Blackie said, still irritated.

"No, the nurses will fall all over each other to get a good look at you," Keary said laughing.

"What? Don't be ridiculous. That's silly," Blackie said. Keary stopped dead and stared at Blackie.

"Don't you realize the affect you have on women?"

"No, I never thought about it. Most of them make me nervous. I only know the affect I have on them after I get them into bed." Keary looked at him with his mouth open.

"You mean all the women you had before, you think they were just attracted to you because of your fame and money?"

"Duh, yeah," Blackie said sardonically.

"Why do you think Meg was attracted to you when you first met her?"

"Okay, Meg is different. She got to know me and liked me, not my celebrity or money, just me," Blackie said emphatically.

"That's after she got to know you. What attracted her in the first place?" Keary asked.

"I don't know. What does it matter?"

"Don't you ever look in the mirror at your face, your body?"

"Yeah, sure, to comb my hair, put deodorant on. It's just me in the mirror. What the hell?" Blackie said.

"I give up! If you don't know by now, you never will. At least you're not arrogant about your looks."

"You mean the way I look is the problem?"

"I wouldn't call it a problem," Keary said.

"This is a stupid conversation. Let's go get Meg." Blackie said, turning and going back to the room.

On the way several nurses stopped and stared. Outside Meg's room was a whole gaggle of young nurses. They started giggling and whispering to each other, staring at Blackie as he and Keary approached. He stopped several rooms down.

"Is this what you mean? They're all standing around acting stupid because of the way I look?" Blackie asked Keary.

"You bet kid, give them a big smile and walk into Meg's room."

"Now I'm nervous," Blackie said.

"You're kidding me, right."

"No, I'm not! I told you they make me nervous. They didn't when I was younger but now it's different." Blackie said, starting to fidget.

"How did you manage to sleep with all those women then?"

"Mostly I was high or drunk and horny as hell. That's how. Don't forget, I *paid* most of them to sleep with me." Blackie replied.

"Why hookers, Blackie?"

"Simple, no entanglements, no responsibilities, no hassles, no complications, easy sex."

"Oh." Keary said.

"It's a moot point now, isn't it since the woman I'm in love with just lost our child?"

"Yeah, I'm sorry I …

"Okay, let's go."

"Smile," Keary said poking him in the ribs. Blackie flashed the nurses a big smile and said, "Ladies." to a lot of sighs and excited giggles. When they got inside Meg's room, Blackie shut the door.

"That's fucking crazy," he said.

"What's going on?" Jill asked.

"Nothing much. I just found out that he doesn't realize the affect he has on women," Keary said laughing.

"Shut up," Blackie punched him on the arm.

"Oh, is that what all the fuss is out there? They're waiting to get another glimpse at my prize stud, huh?" Meg said, smiling herself.

Blackie blushed red and said gruffly, "Could we please get the hell out of this nut house and go home?" He grabbed her wheelchair and pushed her toward the door.

"That wasn't funny, Meg."

"I know honey but you're fun to tease too, don't forget."

"Great, let's go," he said.

They all piled into the SUV; Meg sat next to Blackie in the back with Katie next to her and Jill and Keary in the front. She leaned her head on his shoulder and he put his arm around her.

"You're not angry with me about teasing you, are you?" She asked him.

"No, sweetie, I'm not. How are you doing?"

"I'm still sore and crampy, but the worse thing is this empty feeling I have. I miss the baby," she said.

"Let's go home and get some rest. I just want to be alone with you."

Jill looked back at them and smiled. "Do you two want something to eat when we get home?"

"Are you hungry?" Blackie asked Meg.

"No, I still feel queasy from the anesthetic. I'm just super tired."

"Jill, I think I'll get her to rest for now. We can eat later," Blackie told her.

When they got home, he helped her out of the car and up to the apartment. After he closed the door and set the alarm, he hugged her tight.

"Meg, I wish I could take away your pain and sadness somehow, but I can't. I feel really helpless."

"You're not helpless at all. You help me get through everything. What about *your* sadness? How are you dealing with it?"

He walked away from her, stuffing his hands in his pockets.

Uh, oh. Why's he being defensive?

"I'm not handling it well, Meg. Actually I'm not handling it at all. I'm pushing the thoughts and feelings away," he said, head down.

"What? What is it? You have to grieve or you can't get past it." She told him.

"You're going to get mad at me, Meg," he said, fidgeting.

"Why, honey, what happened?" She said, moving over to him but he backed away. This wasn't going to be good, she thought.

"Blackie, just tell me and we can talk about it," she said gently.

"I took drugs last night!" he blurted out and looked away. She was stunned.

"What did you take?" She asked, trying to maintain control.

"I did some pills. I didn't want to think about the baby and you going through that. I didn't want to feel the loss. I just wanted to be numb. So I did it and I'm sorry, Meg. You don't need me going off now. I just thought I could help you better if I wasn't an emotional wreck. Please forgive me?" he said, looking pitiful.

"Is that what's wrong with your eyes?"

"Yes."

"Do Keary and Jill know?"

"Everyone knows. They were watching TV when I got home last night. I got yelled at by Keary," he said still rigid and stand-offish.

"So you're still high?"

"Yes."

"Blackie, you have to stop coping with things that way. If you let yourself feel things, you can get past them. Doesn't Dr. Wahlman tell you that?"

"Yes, I know." She went over and sat on the bed.

"So when are you going to let yourself feel the death of our little baby?"

"I don't know. Maybe when you feel better."

"Honey, this is why you have all these problems with alcohol and drugs. You keep burying anything that hurts. It doesn't make it go away, it just damages you."

"I know," he said, still fidgeting.

"Come here and sit next to me." He hesitated and then finally sat down.

"Blackie, you're a very strong man. You have a lot of strength of character. Why do you think you can't ever handle emotional pain?"

"It hurts too much. I can't take it."

"I think it's become a habit. You've avoided it in the past by substance abuse, so you think that's the only way to handle pain. It isn't. You need to let yourself feel it. Blackie look at me. Did you love our baby?"

"I did, yes. I really wanted it."

"Were you starting to think about it as a child and looking forward to watching it grow up?"

"Yes," he answered, his eyes welling up with tears.

"But now the poor little thing has died and we won't see it grow up."

"I know," the tears were starting to trickle down his face.

"Please stop, Meg. I can't take it."

"Yes you can. You're strong."

"I was so happy. It was something that our love made and we'd have it forever. It was a symbol of how much we love each other. I wanted it so bad," he said and put his head in her lap and sobbed. She just held him, stroking his hair and let him get it all out. He finally stopped crying and just held on to her.

THIRTY-FOUR

The next morning, Jill and Katie cancelled the alarm and tiptoed into the apartment. They had containers they sat on the counter. Jill went over close to the bed and Blackie's eyes flew open but he relaxed when he saw it was Jill. The tension in his body awakened Meg. She stirred against him, groaned quietly and started to sit up but he put his hand on her.

"Shhh, go back to sleep, honey. It's Jill and Katie, they brought some food down."

"I have to pee," she said groggily.

"Okay. Here I'll help you get up," he said rolling to her side of the bed. "Sit up for a few minutes to make sure you're not dizzy." Her stomach muscles were still sore, so he helped her stand up.

"Do you feel okay?"

"Yes, I'm fine."

Blackie walked behind her to the bathroom "Do you have everything you need in here?"

"Yes, honey, and thanks."

He walked back to the kitchen and looked at Jill. "Hey, look at your belly. Your baby's really growing." He put his mouth on her belly and said, "Hey in there, it's Uncle Blackie. I'm going to tickle you till you puke like your Mom used to do to me." He and Jill both laughed.

"I'm very ticklish and she used to hold me down and tickle me until I threw up," he told Katie.

"I never did that," Jill said.

"Like hell you didn't."

"Anyway, that's a terrible thing to tell a baby."

"I'm just teasing. She won't remember I said it anyhow," he said, laughing and hugging Jill. "What'd you bring to eat? I'm starving."

"We brought turkey, ham, lettuce, tomatoes and bread right from the oven," Jill answered.

"Yum, I can smell it. Can I fix you a sandwich?"

"No, no. We'll go back up to the house and leave you two alone."

"Did you eat?" he asked.

"No, we'll get something when we go back."

"Stay, I'll fix everyone a sandwich."

He opened the fridge, brought out mustard, mayo, pickles and mac and cheese from the freezer. He proceeded to fix everyone a sandwich including Meg.

"Hi, sweetheart, what would you like to drink? Milk? It's healthy."

"Okay, if I must," she said, wrinkling her nose. He went back to the fridge to get milk and was rummaging around in it. She let her eyes linger on his butt and the muscles in his back. He looked scrumptious.

"Jill, I don't know if I'm going to make it for three weeks," she said dreamily.

He brought milk and a bag of cookies to the table. He poured her a glass and sat down. He looked even yummier from the front. She couldn't believe how horny she was getting just looking at him. He was happily munching on his sandwiches, mac and cheese, cola and chips.

"God, I was starving. This is so good. Thanks, guys." He looked over at her and saw she was just picking at her food.

"You better eat little girl. You need to get your strength back." She opened her mouth to protest, then thought better of it and took a bite of her sandwich.

He gave her a look and said, "Were you going to say something?"

"No, you're right," she said grudgingly.

"That's my girl." He said, leaned over and kissed her.

"Honey, would you mind putting some clothes on?"

"Oh, am I embarrassing Katie?" he said laughing over at Katie.

"You're not embarrassing me. I love looking at half naked men," Katie said laughing back at him.

"It's not Katie, it's me. You're turning me on," she said. He looked at her and laughed.

"Hey baby, this is off limits for three weeks, don't forget."

"I haven't forgotten. It would be easier on me if you got dressed and didn't look so damn good, half naked."

He stared at Meg. "You're serious?"

"Yes. I am."

"Okay," he said and got up slowly and got close to her, so her face was right at his bare belly.

"Oh, you're sooo bad! Go get some clothes on, brat!" He laughed, kissed her and walked into the bathroom. He came back out in a few minutes in jeans and a t-shirt. He went into the fridge to get another Coke.

"Oh God, Jill, that isn't much better. What's wrong with me?"

"Hormones," Jill said. Blackie sat down next to Meg and picked up his sandwich.

"Can I continue eating now that I'm decently covered?"

"Yes, you can. Just behave yourself."

"Who me, not behave, please," he said in mock indignation.

"Hmm, we'll see," she said.

"Are your wedding plans all set?" He asked Katie.

"Actually we're changing ours a little. We're getting married with you guys on Saturday," she said, biting her bottom lip.

"You are, why?" Jill asked.

"Well, we just found out that *I'm* pregnant," she said.

"Oh, that's wonderful," Jill and Blackie said. Meg was happy for them but a little jealous and sad.

"I wasn't going to say anything yet because of your loss," Katie said to Meg.

"That's okay Katie, I'm happy for you guys."

"I'm not sure we're still doing it on Saturday. I was thinking that maybe …

"What? Why aren't we getting married?"

"I was thinking we could plan a really beautiful wedding in Ireland," he said taking a long drink of his soda.

"Oh, you were. So now that I'm not pregnant, forget getting married."

He choked, the Coke came out his nose and he spit it in his plate.

"What the fuck did you just say to me?" he said, red-faced.

"Blackie!" Jill exclaimed.

"Shut up," he snarled at Jill.

"Why would you change our wedding date?" Meg asked, just as furious.

"Why the hell would you say something like that to me? You know how upset I was that you were pregnant and we weren't married," he yelled.

"I know that. I'm disappointed. I was excited about getting married Saturday," she said, glaring at him.

"And you don't think I was. I just said to Jill and Keary yesterday how I wished I had that ring on my finger."

"I'm confused now," she said, red-faced and eyes welling.

"Confused about what? About whether I love you or not? About if I wanted the baby? I can't believe you don't know me better than that," he yelled in her face.

"Blackie, take it easy on her," Jill said.

"Jill, damnit, stay out of this. It's between me and her."

"How could you hurt me like that? You really think, that now because you're no longer carrying my baby, I don't want to marry you?" he yelled and slammed his fist on the table.

"I'm sorry. I'm sorry I said something so stupid. I find it hard to believe that you want to marry me anyway. So, I was overwhelmed that it was actually going to happen. Then when you changed it," she said starting to cry.

"Oh, that's just great. Start crying! Make *me* feel guilty. That's a great weapon you women have. You know how I hate it when you cry." He was up and pacing now.

"I'm crying because I feel bad because I hurt you. I didn't mean to," she said still crying.

"Fine we'll get married on Saturday. I just wanted it to be special, not just a quick thing because you were pregnant. I wanted it to be a fairytale day for you with this gorgeous gown. You know, you're fucking spoiled. I give you every damn thing you want. You're just mean. I don't say mean shit to you like that," he said.

"God, she just lost the baby yesterday, take it easy." Jill said.

"I lost the baby yesterday, too. Just because it wasn't in my body doesn't mean I didn't love it too," he said.

"Honey, I'm sorry. Please forgive me. My emotions are messed up right now," she said sobbing.

"Fuck it! I'm out of here. I'm going to go help Sean," he said putting his boots on and slamming out the door.

"Blackie," Meg yelled after him but he was gone. She put her head down and sobbed.

"God, Jill, what's wrong with me. Why did I say that to him? I know better," she cried.

"Meg, it's the hormones, but he should have talked it over with you instead of just blurting out that the plans were changed," Jill said.

"I'm such an idiot."

"So is he. Look you've both been very stressed the last few days. Neither one of you is thinking straight right now," Jill said. We heard a lot of banging from downstairs.

"What's that?" Katie said.

"He's mad and throwing stuff around." Jill told her. "Meg, he'll calm down."

"I know but I can't believe I said something so awful to him."

Just then, Blackie came back in, slamming the door, and stomped into the kitchen. He leaned against the counter, hands in his pockets and scowled at her.

"You don't believe I'd do that, do you? You can't believe I'm capable of doing that."

"No, of course I don't. I'm a jerk. I'm sorry I said that to you." He paced back and forth a couple times, hands still in his pockets.

"Come here, honey," she said. "I really love you so much. Please forgive me."

"Don't you believe that I love *you*?"

"Yes, I know you love me."

"I asked you to marry me and I meant it. I don't say things frivolously."

"I know."

"Don't say you know because I'm not sure you know me," he said defensively.

"I just have a hard time believing it's going to happen," she said.

"Why not? I don't understand that," he said.

"I guess I'm insecure."

"Insecure about what? My love for you? What do I have to do to prove it?"

"You don't have to do anything; you've more than proven your love to me. It's me. I don't think I'm good enough, or something," she said.

"What? You don't think you're good enough? For me? That's ridiculous, Meg! I'm the one that's no damn good. I mean, look at my past. I have a hard time believing *you'd* want to marry me!" He said pacing again.

"I want to marry you more than anything. I'm just an idiot! And stop looking at me like you hate me."

"What? Meg, stop it! This isn't hate; it's anger. I'm pissed at you. How could I hate you when I love you so much? I'm always getting angry at someone around here. What about the fights I have with Sean? Just because I'm angry at him doesn't mean I don't love him anymore. That's the way families are." He said looking at her quizzically for a second. "You know. I just realized something. You've never had a family to interact with."

"I have relatives. I had a family when I was little before my folks died."

"I have lots of relatives, but I'm talking about close family. I've been surrounded by people my whole life who I knew loved me. You haven't. Maybe that's why you feel insecure. I want to marry you, pregnant or not because I love you, very much," he said looking down at her. She started to cry again and blubbered, "I love you too."

He knelt down in front of her so they were eye to eye "We can get married on Saturday if you want. As far as I'm concerned, we're already married."

"What do you mean? Because we love each other?" she asked him.

"Yes, that too, but because I'm yours, body and soul, faithful till I draw my last breath and I think you feel the same way about me. So, I think, in the eyes of God, we're already married. The ceremony is just a formality."

"Oh, Blackie, I do feel the same way. Let's put it off and plan a wedding in Ireland. I know you'd rather be married there."

"I didn't like that dress anyway. It's not my idea of a wedding dress," he said, finally smiling at her.

She took his face in her hands and said. "I'm really sorry."

"Forget it," he said and kissed her tenderly. "You know how much I wanted that baby."

"I know, just as much as me," she said and he kissed her again, hungrily.

Jill cleared her throat and they both jumped. They forgot Jill and Katie were there. The women were both crying.

"Oh, Jesus! I don't believe it. You women will cry at the drop of a hat," he said laughing.

"That was so sweet, though," Katie said, dabbing at her eyes.

"Don't you and Sean say stuff like that to each other," Blackie asked her.

"Not really, but we don't fight like you two either," she said.

"Sean doesn't have my temper."

"You know, Meg, Coke feels like shit, coming out your nose." He said, kissing her neck until she giggled.

"Okay, can I finish eating now? I'm hungry again. I need to fix another sandwich."

"You know, honey, you really should think about politics," Jill said.

"Are you guys still on that rag?" he snorted a laugh.

"But you're very good at arguing your point and when you know you're right, you get fired up about it. Why don't you talk to Dad more about it?" Jill said.

"I told Keary and Dad I'd think about it but I haven't yet. Maybe I will," he said.

"I'm getting kinda tired, I think I'll lie down again," Meg told them. "Blackie, if you want to do something else, I'll be fine."

"I might join you. I suddenly feel tired myself. Jill, we'll probably see you guys at dinner."

"Okay, you two, rest up. We'll see you later," Jill said as she and Katie got up and left.

THIRTY-FIVE

Meg fell asleep again and woke up around three in the afternoon. She opened her eyes and looked over but Blackie hadn't moved a muscle. He was really out. She hoped he was sleeping the drugs out of his system. Realizing she was famished, she threw on jeans, sneakers and a sweatshirt. When she walked into the kitchen, Jill was there by herself.

"Hi, sweetie, how are you doing?"

"I'm doing so much better; I got up and took a shower, got back in bed and just woke up. I decided I was starving, so here I am."

"What can I fix you, then?"

"I'll poke around and fix myself something. You just sit still and talk to me while I eat."

"It's a deal. What's my little brother doing?"

"Sleeping. He's out like a light. I hope he'll be back to normal soon."

"Me too. How are you feeling about him taking the drugs?"

"I'm terrified about it, frankly. I can't believe he's still handling problems that way. I told him I need to be confident that he's not going to do this anymore. He said he'd make sure I would know that I could count on him. I know that scared and hurt him. But Jill, we want to have a child together. I wonder about bringing a child into a home where the father takes drugs when something goes wrong?"

"I don't blame you, Meg. It's bad enough he's endangering his own life, but now he's drawn you into it. He has to get himself together."

"Jill, you know how much I love him. I can't live without him, but he's got to change something."

"Well, he's supposed to go to New York with Sean tomorrow and I don't know what that's about. He sees Dr. Wahlman next week so I'm hoping that will help him get things sorted out."

*　　*　　*

The next morning Meg was startled awake by Blackie sitting bolt upright in bed and calling for her.

"Meg, Meg, what day is it?

"What? Honey, ah, it's Thursday.

"What time is it?" He turned the light on and looked at the clock.

"It's six-thirty and I'm supposed to go to New York with Sean today." He dialed the number up at the house.

"Jill, is Sean there?" Pause.

"Good morning, Sean, are we still going? Okay, give me about twenty minutes and I'll be up. I've got to eat something before we leave. Is the plane ready? Okay, I'll drive my car." He hung up, rolled out of bed and jogged into the bathroom. As soon as she heard the shower going, she went back to sleep. It wasn't long and she felt him on the bed. He was on his knees, straddling her.

"Good morning, sweetie. How are you feeling?" he said nuzzling her cheek. His scent wafted over her like some erotic perfume.

"God, you smell good," she said putting her arms around his neck and pulling him down on top of her.

"I just took a shower," he said. She ran her hands over the muscles in his back and down to his butt.

"Mmm, I hate to leave you when you're all warm and soft like this," he said, kissing her neck again.

"Oh, do you have to leave right away?" she said, experiencing a huge rush of desire.

"I do, yes. Sean is waiting for me." He said, getting up and opening his closet.

She got up and went in the bathroom. When she came out he was dressed in a tan suit with a black shirt and tie. He was sitting on the bed pulling on black socks and soft, leather loafers the color of the suit. She moved in between his legs and hugged him into her.

"Meg, you're making it really hard to leave you," he said putting his arms around her and snuggling his face into her breasts.

"We're not supposed to be doing this anyway, remember."

"I know. I don't want you to leave," she said kissing his forehead.

"But I have to," he said and stood up. "I'll see you tonight. Love you, baby."

"You guys be careful in New York," she told him.

"We will, bye," and he was out the door.

She sighed and went back to bed, trying not to think about how much she wanted him.

*   *   *

Blackie finished eating, got Sean and they left in the Porsche. Almost as soon as they turned out of the driveway, Blackie said, "Sean, I'm in trouble."

"Why, what's wrong? Is Keary still on your ass about the pills?"

"No, it's Meg. I think she's having second thoughts about being with me," Blackie said sadly.

"No, man, that's impossible. She's crazy about you. I know she wants to have another baby with you, Katie told me."

"Well yesterday she kinda laid the law down. She said she needed to know she could count on me as a partner."

"What's wrong with that? Every woman needs to know her man is dependable. That doesn't mean she's breaking up with you."

"Yes, but I'm not dependable, Sean. All I've ever shown her is my instability. She hasn't seen anything yet that tells her I'm dependable. Look what I just did. She loses our baby and I go and get wasted."

"She loves you, buddy. She'll hang in there."

"I don't know. I've got to get my shit together somehow. I have to show her something good. "

"Talk to Dr. Wahlman about it," Sean said.

"I guess."

"Katie said you guys aren't getting married on Saturday. Was that her idea?"

"No, it was mine. I thought it would be neat to plan a beautiful wedding in Ireland but she got pissed. Said now that she wasn't carrying my baby, I didn't want to marry her."

"You should have gone through with it. Katie said you guys had a huge fight."

"The trouble is now I think she's glad we're not getting married on Saturday,"

"Maybe she's scared," Sean said.

"I wouldn't blame her. Sean, I can't lose her. What am I going to do?"

"Are you buying her engagement ring today?"

"I was planning on it."

"Maybe that will let her know you're serious."

"She knows I'm serious about marriage. I'm also sure she doesn't think I'm good husband material."

"How could she think that?" Sean asked.

"Would you consider marrying a guy who's an alcoholic and drug addict; a guy who is supposed to be sober but resorts to drug use as soon as the going gets tough?"

"Well, I don't know. I think you're jumping to conclusions. I don't think it's as bad as you're making it out to be."

"We'll see," Blackie said.

"Come on, buddy, cheer up. Let's make this a fun trip. I'd buy her the ring if I were you."

"I am, yes. I just hope I get to give it to her."

THIRTY-SIX

Eventually life at Killarney Farms settled into a very comfortable pattern. Blackie was winning a lot of dressage competitions with Sandman and Abba, the gelding from Ireland. Meg had won a few Level I competitions with Cloudy and her new warm-blood mare. She spent more time learning from Blackie and practicing than showing.

Blackie was getting the word out at the shows and through friends that he was trying to start a training facility. Two young guys turned up who wanted to train with Blackie. They brought their horses to the farm and Blackie was enjoying teaching and it seemed very fulfilling for him.

He rarely mentioned racing and how much he missed it anymore but never went to the track with Sean. The two guys he was teaching were a couple years younger than Blackie and very accomplished riders. They both admired his ability and hung on his every word when he was teaching. Many weekends, they'd tag along when he was showing.

Their names were Jamie and Curt and they were charming and fun. Meg had to be careful joking around with them. If they got too familiar with her, Blackie would give them a funny look, so she knew one of them had crossed a line that he didn't like. He was thinking of taking the students' horses with them soon so they could start competing. The four of them had a very easygoing, comfortable relationship. Blackie treated them as equals but they always deferred to him. The two of them had started eating up at the house when they were at the farm and were getting friendly with Sean and Katie.

Katie was a little distracted with her growing pregnancy. All of them, including Jill and Keary, joked around a lot and discussed horses and riding continuously.

Jill had a baby girl who they named Maeve and everyone doted on her. Jill was nursing and everyone was comfortable and nonchalant about it. Blackie was crazy about little Maeve and was usually holding her if Jill wasn't nursing. Sean teased him that he would soon have to grow a breast.

Keary was away a lot on farm business and when he was, Blackie became the designated babysitter in the evenings so Jill could do her manager job and rest. Many evenings they'd all trail back to the TV room to watch a movie and there was Blackie sound asleep on the sofa with little Maeve snoozing on his chest.

Meg was particularly glad to see how well Blackie had taken to a baby. He'd never been around children before and it was love at first sight with little Maeve.

Meg was anxious for them to get married and start a family too even though she worried about his drug use. But something was still holding him back. She didn't know what it was but she was sure it wasn't doubt he had about her or how much he loved her. It was something in himself that he doubted. She left him alone about it, knowing he would work it out. Meanwhile she made herself content with the status quo.

Their relationship was great. Occasionally they'd have a nasty fight about some dumb thing but the make-up sex was always fantastic. Blackie as always was very loving and sweet to her. Sometimes a little too possessive to suit her, but his passion hadn't cooled down any. Her hunger for him was almost as hot. Sean took every chance he got to tease them about how often they made love. It didn't bother her but Blackie got pretty hot about the teasing a couple of times.

He was making a name for himself on the dressage show circuit, winning practically every class he entered and was taking Level 4 by storm.

*   *   *

One evening as they were sitting around watching a movie and Sean was absently rubbing Katie's belly.

"You know Sean sings to the baby? He has a fantastic voice. Did you guys know he can sing?"

Everyone laughed but Katie and Meg.

"Yes, we know," Keary said. "Sean sang in the boys' choir at church from the time he was five until he was about eleven or twelve. In fact, Blackie was in the choir with him. They used to sing duets together because their voices blend so well."

"I didn't know you guys could sing," Meg said to Blackie.

"Oh shit, here we go with the whole 'boys choir' thing," Blackie said, groaning.

"What's the matter? You guys sounded like two angels?" Jill said.

"That's us, Blackie, a couple of angels," Sean laughed.

"You can say that again."

"Aw come on guys, you two had beautiful voices," Keary said.

"Hey, Blackie, you remember Mary Sullivan?" Sean said, smiling.

"Mary Sullivan, uh ... no, not really." Blackie said, "Who's Mary Sullivan?

"Mary Sullivan's the little girl who got you thrown out of the choir."

Blackie instantly burst out laughing.

"You got thrown out of the boys' choir!" Meg said. Blackie, Sean and Keary were laughing so hard, tears were streaming down their faces.

"Oh, shit," Blackie said, holding his side.

"You guys have to hear this story, it's so damn funny," Sean said.

"How old were you?" Meg asked him.

"Mom and Dad didn't' think it was funny and he was nine years old," Jill said, chuckling despite herself.

"Hell, Dad beat me with a switch for that. My ass was sore for a week, but it sure was worth it." Blackie said still laughing.

"Come on, what happened?" Katie said wide-eyed.

Blackie finally got control enough to talk.

"Mmm, Mary Sullivan. She was cute as a button. Red, curly hair, freckles, big green eyes. I was a very curious little boy. I knew girls were different but I wasn't sure how."

Blackie and Sean started laughing again.

"Well I got Mary behind the altar. I told her I'd give her a present if she'd take her panties off." The three men started laughing again.

"That's terrible, how old was she?" Katie asked.

"I think she was eight. Anyway, I wanted to see how girls were different but more than that, I wanted to feel it. So she whips her panties off and I got a handful. Suddenly, to my surprise, I did have a present for her." At this comment Sean and Keary laughed so hard, Meg thought they might choke.

"That poor innocent little girl," Jill said.

"Wait, wait. She wasn't all that innocent. I've got a handful of her and she grabs hold of my, uh, present and she thought it was a great present." More laughing, Blackie included. It took him a minute to get control. "So, we're happily exploring each other, when around the corner of the altar comes Father Flaherty and catches us."

More hysteria from the men and by this time all three women were laughing too.

"You know, he told *her* to put her panties back on and go home. Me, he smacked the shit out of and threw me out of the choir. I didn't think it was fair that she didn't get punished, since she was having as much fun as I was, but I guess Father Flaherty figured out it was my idea."

They all laughed some more.

"Then Dad punished me. Mom wouldn't talk to me for a week. Dad was more upset about me getting thrown out of the choir than why."

"Yeah, actually, Blackie, I think the old man was proud of you, but Mom was pissed," Sean laughed.

Blackie grabbed Meg and pulled her onto his lap.

"I was a bad little boy, honey," he said.

"Mmm, can you be bad for me tonight?" she said, seductively.

"You bet," he said, pretending to bite her neck.

"Hey, Blackie, do you still sing?" Katie asked him.

"No, I haven't in years. I probably still have a squeaky 'girls' voice."

"You couldn't, Blackie, your voice has changed. It got deeper when you went through puberty," Keary said.

"Blackie always sang an octave higher than Sean. They sounded fantastic when they sang together," Jill said.

"Haven't you guys sung together since then?" Katie asked.

"No, I pretty much quit singing after that," Blackie said.

"Why don't you sing now? I'd love to hear you two," Katie pleaded.

"Leave him alone, Katie. I just fool around singing to the baby. I wouldn't mind seeing how we sound though, Blackie."

"I have no idea if I can still sing," Blackie said.

"Come on, you had a fantastic voice when you were a kid. You should still be able to sing." Sean said. "Do you remember how to do scales?"

"Not really. Let's hear you sing. You do a scale," Blackie said.

"Okay, dude, if I do it, then you have to."

Sean proceeded to sing La La La La La in four or five different octaves. He had a wonderful voice, a light baritone. He finished and smiled at Blackie.

"Wow, you sound great. I can't do that," Black said, surprised.

"Yes, you can. You always could hit the high notes. Come on, let's hear it." Sean goaded him on.

"Come on honey, I want to hear you sing," Meg said, still sitting on his lap.

"You keep wiggling around on my lap like that, I'll be able to hit all kinds of notes," he teased. Everyone laughed.

"Okay, Christ, how do I get myself into this crap?" He sighed big and then sang a low scale. It sounded perfect to Meg.

"Ouch, that hurt my throat."

"That's too low for your voice. Start higher, around here." Sean sang a higher note. Then Blackie started the scale on that note. It sounded beautiful. He sang five or six progressively higher scales and one was better than the other. Everyone applauded when he was done and he, of course, blushed.

Meg hugged him. "That was fantastic. Come on you guys sing something together."

"All we ever sang was church crap."

"We used to sing lots of stuff. You know 'Danny Boy' don't you?"

"Yeah, yeah," Blackie said, still reluctant.

"Come sit next to me, we'll sound better together." Sean said.

Meg got off Blackie's lap and Katie moved to another chair, so Blackie could sit next to Sean.

"Ok, we'll do this in the key of G."

"Do I know what that is?"

"Yes, you do. You're stalling because you don't want to do this, so you're making it more difficult than it is," Sean hummed a note.

"That's a G which you know perfectly well."

Blackie rolled his eyes. They started the song and were in perfect harmony.

Everyone sat there transfixed. Meg had never heard anything that beautiful. After a minute, Blackie closed his eyes while his voice caressed each note. It was obvious that he loved singing and had forgotten. Both of their voices were clear and perfect. One line in the song was high and Blackie hit the note and the purity of it gave Meg goose bumps. Meg looked at Jill who had tears in her eyes.

When the song ended, Blackie opened his eyes, welled with tears and looked at Sean

"I'd forgotten how much I always loved singing with you."

Sean hugged him. "Me too, buddy,"

"Hey, Blackie, you're a perfect tenor," Keary said.

"Rats, I want to be a bass," Blackie said, making his voice really low, "It's more macho." Everyone laughed.

"You two sound incredible together," Jill said.

"Oh Jesus, now the women are going to start blubbering about it," Sean said.

"Shut up, it was beautiful."

"Let's practice. It'll be fun," Sean said, enthusiastically.

"Okay. You know racing was great for me, but it took me so far away from you guys. It's hard to get back, but I want to. It just came over me when we were singing. All the things I loved from my childhood and I've missed. I just realized how much," Blackie said seriously. "I want to come all the way back."

"Hey, sing some more. That was wonderful," Katie said.

"What else do you remember?" Sean asked Blackie.

"All the stuff from choir is mostly in Latin. Do you remember 'Tura Lura'?"

"Yes, let's try that," Sean said.

They sang 'Tura Lura'. The song was beautiful and haunting. They sang it so sweetly and tenderly; you could almost see the baby being rocked. Blackie wiped his eyes afterward with the heels of his hands.

"Shit, this is getting to me," he said, shaking his head.

"It's bringing back a lot of old memories." Jill said gently. Meg could see the muscles in his jaws working. He was trying to maintain control. He looked at Jill intensely and said, softly, "I really miss Mom."

"I know, honey, I do too. We'll go over soon and see them." Meg felt sad that he was so emotionally hurt. She hoped he could resolve a lot of whatever tormented him.

"You want to sing some more stuff?" Sean asked.

"Sure. What?"

"Sing 'Ave Maria'," Keary said. "You guys always did it so well. That and 'O Holy Night'."

"I don't know if I remember all the words," Sean said.

"I don't either. Let's try and see what we do with it," Blackie said.

They sang Ave Marie and it gave Meg chills. Sean's voice was perfect to carry the song and as a back drop for Blackie's higher notes. They sang different parts and it was incredible. O Holy Night was unbelievable. Everyone applauded and they did these little bows. Very cute!

"Okay, that's enough, my throat is sore. I'll have to work into this. I do want to practice though,"

"Yeah, me too. You sound good buddy. That was fun," Sean said punching him on the arm. Blackie threw a very fast punch to Sean's gut but pulled it at the last minute so it made Sean flinch.

"Gotcha!" Blackie said laughing.

Ah, male bonding, I love it, Meg mused.

"Is anyone doing anything about dinner? I'm starving," Black said.

"No, Gracie asked for the day off because her mother is sick. I thought you guys could get pizza. How's that sound?"

"Fantastic!" The group yelled.

THIRTY-SEVEN

One night they were sitting around talking after dinner when Keary came in. He was in DC all day on business and looked tired.

"Hey, everyone," he said kissing Jill and retrieving Maeve from Blackie.

She cried at the separation and Keary laughed. "I believe she thinks you're her dad, Blackie, I need to be around more," he said cuddling the baby to calm her. "Guess who I saw today?"

"I'm afraid to ask. Who?" Blackie said.

"Do you remember Duncan Mallory?"

"The name sounds familiar but I can't place him."

"You rode for him once about five years ago and won big. He never knew about the accident and just thought you quit riding. Anyway, he saw you at a show about a month ago in Florida and was impressed. He said he had to look at the program twice and couldn't believe it was actually you. You won a bunch of 4th Level classes and he couldn't stop raving about you."

"Okay, so?"

"He wants to know if you'll ride for him in the Washington International Horse Show in about six weeks."

"Does he have a horse?"

"Yes, he says a great one. His usual rider separated his shoulder and won't be in shape in time. He says this horse is Grand Prix level and a spectacular mover. He'll pay you $10,000 to do it."

"I'll do it for free for the exposure. Washington is a big show. I need to drum up business for the training center. If there's ever going to be one." Blackie said.

"Not so fast. There's a catch," Keary said.

"Oh, great! What?" Blackie said.

"He also wants you to ride his show jumper in the $100,000 President's Cup."

"Shit, I can't do that. Did you tell him I don't ride jumpers anymore?"

"Yes, I told him it was impossible, but he won't let you ride one without the other," Keary said, disgusted."

"What an asshole! I don't know. What do you think, Keary?"

"I think it's taking a big chance with your health. You could be crippled real fast. There are other big shows, Blackie."

"Honey, I don't want you to do it. I'm afraid you'll get hurt." Meg said.

"I know, Meg. It's taking a big chance, but I'm riding better now than I ever have, I'm just not racing. The doctor said my hip is strong," Black said, getting a gleam in his eyes.

"That sounds a lot like, 'but Keary I really want to do this', to me," Sean said.

Blackie laughed and looked at Meg.

"Are you going to tell me I can't do it because you're afraid?" He said. She looked at him for a long minute, all the fear running through her mind.

"I totally believe in your ability to ride any horse, anywhere. I'm not going to stop you because I'm afraid. I know *you're* not afraid of anything," she said.

"Thank you, sweetheart."

"You just better not get your ass hurt," she said.

"I'll try my best." He asked Keary, "Where are this guy's horses?"

"New York State. He said he could ship them down immediately so you could start working with them."

"Have these horses been entered?"

"Yes, the one is entered in the Grand Prix dressage and the jumper is in the qualifiers for the President's Cup."

"Wow, high class stuff."

"Do you think this is a good idea, Blackie? Everything's going good for you right now. I'd hate for you to be laid up again," Keary said.

"Yes, I'm worried too. What if something happens," Jill said.

"What if! What if! Christ, I could hurt myself walking down to the barn. I can't live like that. What if I win? I'd have to win local competitions for a year to get that much press. What do you guys think?" He asked Jamie and Curt.

"Oh, we shouldn't put our two cents in. This if for you and your family to decide," Curt said.

"No, I want your opinion." Blackie said.

They looked at each other. "Well, it would be totally awesome to see you kick some ass," Jamie said.

Blackie laughed at them. "Now that we've heard from my cheering section. I'm glad you guys have confidence in me."

"Blackie, we all have confidence in you, it's the damn horses that are so unpredictable," Keary said.

"I know. Okay, call him and tell him to ship the horses down and I'll decide in a week after they get here and I have a chance to ride them. If I decide *not* to do it, tell him I'll pay for the shipping down and back. Hey, what's that guy's name? Dick something?" Blackie said.

"What guy?" Keary asked.

"The jump guy. Do we have his number?"

"You mean Frank Martell?" Keary said.

"Yes, that's him. I'll call and see if he can bring some big jumps down here. We can't put them in the arena; I'll need that for the dressage training. I'll have to school the jumper outside."

"You know, Blackie it's been a long time since you've had a challenge, hasn't it?" Sean asked.

Blackie slowly smiled and said, "It has, yes."

"What do you mean, Sean," Jill asked.

"I don't think you guys ever appreciated just how competitive Blackie is," Sean said. "Right, Blackie?"

"You're right" he said still smiling. "I never thought much about it but I guess I am."

*   *   *

Blackie worked hard the next week on their horses. He pushed Jamie and Curt so he could start taking them to shows. Duncan Mallory's horses were supposed to arrive from New York the next week. Meg was having a ball riding and working with her new mare. Blackie was absolutely in his element.

He had huge jumps set up in the outside ring and was excited to start working with the New York horses. Most nights he fell into bed exhausted.

The Mallory horses arrived on Tuesday in a huge, nine-horse van with their own groom.

His name was Bobby Stahl and Blackie instantly disliked him. He was very arrogant and started off by telling Blackie who was in charge of Duncan's horses. He said no one was to touch them but him and he would get them ready for Blackie to ride. Bobby led them out of the van one by one and they were both incredibly beautiful horses, obviously well cared for.

The dressage horse was an elegant, bay, Swedish warm-blood, gelding named Torsk.

"Wow, he's beautiful. I can't wait to get on him," Blackie said. The jumper was a large, muscular chestnut gelding. Blackie wasn't sure what his breeding was at first sight.

"That's a big damn horse. He's got the ass to get over some huge jumps," Blackie said and whistled.

"What do you mean?" Meg asked him.

"Well, just look at his hind quarters. He's got a ton of muscle back there. He should be able to take me over anything."

The next day, Blackie worked with both horses and fell instantly in love with them. They were pretty much all he talked about. It became a daily gathering of the farm crew to watch him ride them.

Torsk was a wonderful mover and Blackie quickly got him in shape for the show.

The jumper, named Shangri-La, was a bit difficult. Blackie said he was a handful, but was having a lot of fun riding him. Meg was terrified whenever he was jumping him. She had a lot of faith in Blackie's riding ability but this horse was so big, strong and strong-willed, that she always worried. That was part of the reason everyone was always there to watch, because they were just as worried as she was. It was such a treat to watch him jumping a horse. She knew he used to be a champion steeplechase jockey but his control and timing were perfect.

They were excited about the upcoming show. Blackie felt that both he and the horses were as ready as they could get. Mr. Mallory had arranged for stalls for the horses and lovely hotel rooms for all of them. Bobby Stahl had a room on the same floor and Meg hoped he would stay out of their way. Blackie didn't have any use for him and tried to avoid him as much as possible.

They were staying in DC for three days. The first day Blackie just had a preliminary round for the President's Cup jumping competition. He came in third. The top ten horses went on to the final jump-off on the last night of the show. Blackie was in a very expansive mood the first evening and took everyone to dinner at an expensive DC restaurant. Keary asked Bobby to go with them, which irritated Blackie enough to keep him quiet during dinner.

"Are you okay, honey?" Meg asked him.

"I just can't stand that guy. He pisses me off. Don't worry about it, I can deal with it," he said leaning over and kissing her. When she sat back, Bobby was watching them, with an odd look on his face. It gave her the creeps. Blackie saw the look on her face.

"What's wrong?"

"Bobby was just watching you kiss me and I don't like it," she told him. He swiveled quickly and looked at Bobby who looked away.

"He better watch it," Blackie growled. "You stay away from him. I don't like the way he looks at you. If he bothers you in anyway, I want you to tell me. If he comes near you, he and I are going to get into it."

"Okay, but don't start anything. He'll be gone after the show."

"I know but until then I want you to stick close to me. I don't want you wandering around alone."

"Honey, I can take care of myself."

"Meg, I mean it. I want you to listen to me. If you're not with me, I want you with Sean or Keary, please."

"I will, I promise."

Just then, Duncan Mallory came over to say hello to Blackie who stood and shook hands then introduced Meg.

"Hey, Duncan, it's good to see you. This is my fiancée, Meg Connors." He said putting his arm around her.

"Fiancée! Well, it's good to see that you're finally settling down. How're the horses? Bobby said you could have done better in the preliminary round." Duncan said giving Blackie a questioning look.

"I don't believe in using a horse up just to get into the final round. He's jumping great. Torsk is up tomorrow night and I expect to do well with him."

"Okay, sounds good to me. I'll see you at breakfast in the morning. It's nice meeting you, Meg."

"Same here, Sir," she said politely and watched Duncan Mallory walk away to join another group of diners.

"Son of a bitch!" Blackie exclaimed. "That bastard told Duncan I didn't do well. I don't believe him. He better stay away from me."

"Calm down. He's trying to get in your head so maybe you'll mess up. Just focus on what you need to do and forget him."

"You're right. He's just an asshole. I'll get him off my mind. Mmm, you could help me with that," he said nuzzling her neck.

He made love to her that night and she told him afterwards how much she appreciated the fact that he was a great athlete. He thought that was funny.

Meg thought he'd be worn out in the morning, but she awoke early to the shower going full blast.

He came out, jumped on her, reaching under the covers to tickle her.

"Come on, sleepy head, time to get up. We have a big day." He jumped off the bed and started getting dressed. She could tell he had a big adrenalin rush going on. She knew he got excited about the shows they went to but this was different. It was bigger. It was a race! Now she realized what Sean meant about how competitive he is. The anticipation was shining brightly in his eyes. His energy was almost palpable in the room. Meg dragged herself out of bed, got a shower and dressed.

They went down to the breakfast buffet the hotel was putting out for the horse show guests. Keary and the others were at a table and waved. As the two of them walked in, Blackie had his hand on her waist guiding her through the tables in front of him. He stopped to say something to Duncan and she kept going. She knew he'd catch up to her.

She was halfway through the line when she felt his hand on her back again. He let it trail down and linger on her butt. She turned to ask him what Duncan said and was shocked to come face to face with Bobby.

"Well, good morning little lady. How are you this fine morning?" Bobby said with a leer.

Meg just looked at him and was getting ready to haul off and slap him, when Blackie moved between them and got in Bobby's face.

"Don't ever touch her again," Blackie said through his teeth. "Do you understand? She's mine and you keep your hands off."

Bobby laughed nervously and side-stepped slightly.

"I was just saying good morning. Anyway, I don't see a ring on her finger." he said, insolently. Blackie side-stepped so he was in his face again and this time, closer.

"Don't fuck with me, Bobby. Don't touch her again," he said with clenched fists.

Luckily Keary came over and grabbed Blackie's arm to break the tension. Keary pulled him away as Bobby walked off with a smirk on his face.

Meg thought how easily Blackie's adrenalin rush could have turned to violence. Even though it ruffled her feathers sometimes, right then she was glad Blackie was possessive. Bobby made her skin crawl.

"Blackie, forget him, he's an asshole. Focus on what you have to do today." Keary told him.

"Did you see him? He had his hand on her ass. I could kill him."

"You have to keep your energy focused. Don't burn it out over that jerk. Come on, get some breakfast. You two come on over to our table."

"Okay," Blackie said, picking up a plate, but she could see he was having trouble re-focusing on the food.

"Look, French toast, it looks yummy." Meg said.

He sort of snapped out of it and filled his plate, getting coffee on the way to the table.

"Hey, how're you doing?" Keary said when he sat down.

"Okay, that guy just makes me so mad. I gotta get my mind off him." Blackie took a couple deep breaths and started on his food.

"Just think about the competition. I'll help you beat the shit out of him later," Sean said clapping Blackie on the back.

He nodded agreement with a mouthful of food.

"You know there's a ton of Olympic riders here," Blackie said after a few minutes.

"Does that intimidate you at all?" Keary asked him.

"No, not really. I'm just used to the racing scene, not the show circuit."

"Does it make a difference?" Sean asked.

"No, riding's riding. I'm an outsider here, though. I don't know if the judges will be biased because of Olympic reputations or not. I have *no* reputation here."

"So you'll kick some Olympic ass," Sean said.

Blackie laughed, "I hope so." But Meg could tell it was bothering him.

"Look you had a great reputation as a winner at the track, but you still had to get your horse home first," Sean said.

"You're right. Fuck-em! All I can do is my best," Blackie said and she sensed the adrenalin starting to pump back in.

"I have to work Torsk in the training arena for awhile. What are you guys going to do?" he said.

"Can we come and watch?" Katie asked.

"Sure, there are other classes going on in the main hall if you want to watch any of those."

"I think we'd like to watch you for a bit. Are you free to watch any classes yourself?" Jill asked him.

"I am, yes, once I'm done warming him up, I'll have a couple hours to kill before I ride. I'll have to change clothes before my class." So they trailed after him to the stall area. He found Torsk's stall and the gelding was ready, no Bobby in sight. Blackie led the horse out and down a couple aisles to the training area. It was filled with other horses and riders warming up, mostly for hunter classes.

"It's a bit crowded, isn't it?" Blackie said frowning. "Dressage isn't exactly a group sport. I'll just mess around with him a little and maybe some of them will leave. You guys go up and sit in the stands," he said walking Torsk into the ring.

They found seats in the already crowded stands. There were mostly other riders in their show outfits and their trainers. There was a lot of talk about how their competitors were doing in the warm-up.

Torsk started dancing sideways as soon as he saw the other horses. Blackie got him to calm down and the two of them just moseyed around the ring for a while. Finally, Blackie started a slow very, collected trot that he was sitting to. Torsk had a very elegant, precise way of moving that was so beautiful to watch. Many of the people in the ring slowed down to watch them. Blackie moved the horse into a beautiful, collected canter.

Meg heard one of the trainers ask another man, "Who the hell is that? That's Duncan's

"I don't know. Never saw him before."

"He's good, very good," the other man said.

Meg wanted to yell, "That's my guy, Blackie O'Brien and he's fabulous!"

Jill leaned over and said, "Why are you smiling, Meg?" she asked with a grin. Meg just rolled her eyes. More people were stopping and moving out of his way. He did a half-pass across the ring at the canter and it was breath taking. He slowed to a medium trot and went by where they were sitting. Two young women in riding attire in front of them were talking and when Blackie rode by, one of them said to the other, "Who's the hunk on that bay? Is he new on the circuit? We'll have to find out and see if he's a player." Then they giggled. Meg instantly wanted to scratch their eyes out.

The first man looked at his program, "His name is Blackie O'Brien. There used to be a steeplechase jock with the same name but I heard he got killed on the track."

"I don't know. Never heard of him, but he's pretty damn good, whoever he is." The other man commented.

One of the women leaned over and asked the man, "Who did you say he was?"

"Name's Blackie O'Brien. I don't know anything about him."

"I think I need to find out," she said and Meg gave Jill a wide-eyed expression that made Jill laugh.

"Get used to it. You can't keep him hidden on the farm forever," she said still laughing.

"Is he actually in this competition? He's in jeans and a sweatshirt. Maybe that's not this O'Brien person; maybe that's the groom," the other girl said cattily.

"A groom that rides like that? I don't think so," one of the men said.

Blackie was still working Torsk in a clear arena now. Everyone had left or stopped to watch.

He was doing incredible stuff – perfect half turns on the haunches, on the forehand, shoulder-ins, half-passes at the trot and canter, serpentines down the center. He stopped in the center and did an amazing *piaffe*. He didn't even have spurs on, just his old riding boots. Then he finished with an exquisite *passage* around the ring.

Duncan Mallory plopped down next to Meg.

"How do you like our boy? This is the first time I've seen him ride Torsk. He's fantastic! The horse has never looked better."

Meg liked Duncan. He was a down-to-earth kind of guy. Very pleasant.

"Hey, Duncan, who's the new kid?" The trainer asked.

"He used to ride jump races. Now he's switched to dressage. He's riding my jumper too tomorrow night too. Isn't he great?"

The one girl turned around and said, "Hey, Duncan, is he single?" Duncan laughed, patting Meg on the arm. "Not for long. This little gal here is his bride to be."

She turned and gave Meg an appraising look and Meg gave her the sweetest "In your face, bitch!" smile she could manage.

The girl rolled her eyes and turned to the other girl and whispered something catty.

Jill nudged Meg, "Down girl," she said and Katie looked over and gave her a fist pump. Then the three women laughed.

"Jesus, I wouldn't want to be in the middle of that," Sean said to Keary.

"Poor Blackie," Keary said shaking his head.

In a few more minutes, Blackie finished the workout, walked Torsk on a loose rein and kicked his feet out of the stirrups.

Everyone applauded. Blackie looked up, startled, blushed and gave a shy little wave.

"He doesn't have a clue, does he?" Katie said.

"Nope, never did. There's not a conceited bone in his body. It's his job, he loves it and he does the best he can," Keary said.

"He wasn't arrogant even when he was winning all those Grand Nationals. Always had a problem with women though. I guess I shouldn't say that around you," Duncan said smiling at Meg.

"That's fine, I already know all about it." Meg said ruefully. She looked at Blackie and he motioned for her to go with him and she excused herself.

"I'm going to see what he wants and we'll meet you guys here or come back to the stalls."

"Okay, we'll see you later," they said.

*   *   *

When she got to him, he had dismounted and was talking to some man. When he saw her, he excused himself and walked towards her.

"Hi, honey, I have to cool him off and I wanted you to walk with me," he said putting his arm around her and kissing her. She could see Torsk was fairly lathered up, so they led him along together through the aisles and made a big circuit around the stalls.

"That was great. You were wonderful!"

"Really? He had a few rocky transitions, but all in all he went pretty smooth."

"There was a lot of buzz about who you were and how well you rode. Duncan joined us and was totally impressed."

"Oh, I didn't see him. Good, I'm glad he liked it."

A beautiful blonde leading a horse the opposite way, stopped in front of them. She looked at Blackie with a hand on her hip.

"Blackie O'Brien! As I live and breathe," she said smiling.

Blackie looked at her and frowned. "I'm sorry. Do I know you?"

"Samantha Rodgers."

"Ah ... okay. I'm sorry, I'm still not sure."

"You were riding for Tommy Marsh and I was doing the exercising. I can't believe you don't remember. It hasn't been that long, Blackie," she said with a smirk.

"Yes, I remember riding for Tom but ... ah, Samantha, huh," he said perspiration beading on his forehead.

"You used to call me *Sam I Am,* remember?"

"Oh, yes, Sam," he said recognition coming to his eyes and he instantly blushed.

"Uh ... You've grown up. How are you? It's been a long time. You look uh ... good. Oh this is my fiancée, Meg Connors," he said, looking like a caged animal.

"Fiancée? Wow! I can't believe some gal roped and hog-tied *you*," she said giving Meg an appraising smile.

"It was more like me begging and pleading for her to marry me," he said and gave Meg a *Let's get the hell out of here* look.

"Are you riding in this?" she asked.

"I am, yes. Dressage and the Presidents Cup. Anyway, I need to cool off my horse. Good seeing you," he said as they moved off.

"I'll be watching," she said suggestively.

"For chrissakes, what a pain in the ass," he said as they walked on.

"Please tell me you didn't have sex with her," Meg said.

He gave her a look. "Okay, Meg, I didn't have sex with her," he said puffing out a sigh.

"Oh my God, you did!"

"I told you never to ask me, damn it."

"Calm down, I'm not mad. I understand. How did that happen with her?"

"I went back to the barn, the night before a race to check on a horse that had a hot ankle. She was there and came in the stall with me. I turned around and she had her shirt off." He gave her a crooked smile, "It's a wonder we didn't get trampled."

"You did it right there in the stall with the horse!"

"Yeah, yeah. Look, Meg, I have to focus on what I'm doing. I can't deal with this right now and make you happy about it," he said stuffing his hands in his pockets.

"Calm down, I'm okay with it. I know what all went on. It's just a little disconcerting when I hear about the sex at the drop of a hat or shirt, as the case may be."

"Really? You're incredible, honey. That's why I love you. You actually get me."

"I know."

"You realize I had a terrible reputation as being easy. If I was a girl, I would have been called a slut," he looked at her apologetically.

"Well you're my slut now, but you weren't exactly *easy* for me at first."

"I changed all that."

"Now you're pretty easy though," she said giving him a sly smile.

"You're right. I can't resist you at all anymore." He said grabbing her and giving her a big sloppy kiss. "You know what else I love about you?"

"What, tell me?" She said.

"You let me be my old stupid, goofy self. I don't have to pretend with you."

"What! You're not stupid or goofy. Why do you say stuff like that?"

"That's the way I feel a lot of the time, I guess."

"You know what else you do that I think is cute?" Meg asked him.

"Oh, God, I don't think I want to know this," he said.

"You blush."

"What the fuck! I don't!" he stopped and looked at her in disbelief.

"You just now blushed big time when you remembered who Sam was."

"Damn it, I don't. Girls blush! Jesus, Meg,"

"Okay, okay, you don't," she lied.

"Right!" he said defensively.

"But I still think it's adorable," she said teasing him.

"Meg! Quit it!"

"Alright, come here," she said as she grabbed and kissed him.

"See, I can't resist you," he said. "We better walk this horse instead of fooling around."

So they walked Torsk until he was cool, taking him back to his stall where Bobby was waiting for him.

"I've been waiting to take care of him," Bobby said hissed.

Blackie just tossed him the reins, turned around taking Megs hand and walked away.

"Let's go get the others and watch some of the classes. I don't have to change for two or three hours yet."

They found the others and settled into seats. Everyone was having a wonderful time watching the other classes. Samantha Rodgers won the novice hunter division.

"Your friend Sam seems to have won." Meg pointedly mentioned to Blackie.

"That's great. Can we change the subject?"

"Who's Sam?" Keary asked.

"Just an old acquaintance of mine."

Keary looked at Meg with raised eyebrows and she shook her head. So Keary just let it drop. Samantha rode her horse into the ring and retrieved her ribbon, trophy and a big cardboard check. As she was leaving the arena, she looked up and blew Blackie a kiss.

"Fuck," he growled as everyone turned and looked at him. Keary smiled and opened his mouth.

"Don't say a goddamn word, Keary."

"What? Is she an old girlfriend?" Curt asked innocently. "She's hot, man and ... uh," he stopped talking when Blackie gave him a look.

"Honey, it's all good. Forget it," Meg told him. He just shook his head disgustedly.

Anyway, after he got over that whole thing, he got interested in the classes and had fun. It was a wonderful afternoon. About an hour before his Grand Prix class, Blackie turned to Meg and said he was going back to their room to change.

"Do you want me to come with you?"

"Sure, come on. Hey guys, we're going back to the room so I can change. Meg will come back here but I'll go right to the stall area."

"Okay, good luck, buddy," Keary said clapping him on the back.

Everyone wished him luck as they left and Jill kissed him.

"Blow'em away honey," she said.

"Thanks, guys. Thanks, Jill."

They walked out of the arena and went back to their room. Blackie yanked off his shirt and opened the closet, pulling out his dressage gear. Meg came up behind him; put her arms around him, caressing the muscles in his belly. He turned around in her arms.

"Mmm, that feels good," he said kissing her. "Meg, why aren't you mad at me about Samantha?"

"Because it's not your fault that she made a play for you. You didn't even remember her."

"I know but my past is always getting in the way. I hate it," he said. He started kissing her deeper, then pulled away.

"If I start this I'll miss my class, honey."

"I know but you feel so good," she said running her fingertips up his back.

"You better stop or I won't care if I miss my class," he said.

"Okay, I'll be good." She let him go and sat on the bed watching him change. He put on skintight white breeches, a white shirt that had a cravat attached at the neck and a yellow vest. He pulled on long black leather boots that came up to his knees and attached blunt silver spurs to the heels. Finally putting on a black riding coat that had tails and brass buttons, he completed the outfit with a black top hat.

"How do I look?" he asked, smiling.

"You look fantastic and ready to win."

"Thanks, baby. Let's go."

THIRTY-EIGHT

The Grand Prix dressage final was just starting. The class was filled with talented riders, many of them Olympians and beautifully trained horses. One was better than the other and Meg was starting to get nervous for Blackie.

Finally, it was his turn. He and Torsk made a very impressive entrance. Both of them were spectacular looking to begin with and Torsk came trotting into the ring like he owned it. A hush came over the audience as they moved through their program. They looked like they were in a dance together of such beauty, precision and elegance, that it was breathtaking.

When they were done and Blackie gave the final salute, there was total silence. Then the whole arena erupted in thunderous applause and cheers. Torsk and Blackie both were startled and the horse jumped sideways. They got a standing ovation as they trotted from the ring. Meg looked at Duncan and he had tears in his eyes.

"I've never seen anything that beautiful. He's a wizard with horses."

They waited for the final tally of everyone's points. It took about twenty minutes and Meg was on pins and needles. Finally, the scores were announced and Blackie won with a near perfect score. They all jumped up and down and hugged each other.

"Let's go get him," Keary yelled and they trooped from the stands to find Blackie. When they got close to the stalls, Meg saw him surrounded by a crowd and signing autographs. He looked stunned and embarrassed. He saw them and waved, breaking away from the crowd. He ran to her, picked her up and kissing her.

"I did great, didn't I, Meg?" he said, his eyes shining with happiness.

"Yes you did great. I'm so proud of you. You're incredible. You have to go back in the ring and get your trophy, don't you?"

"Oh, I guess I do. I better get Torsk."

They announced his name; he vaulted onto Torsk and trotted into the ring to get the prize. He was awarded a ribbon, trophy and a check for $20,000, all of which he handed to Duncan.

"Here, you keep the money, you earned it," Duncan said handing the check back to him.

"I don't want the money. All I wanted from this was the recognition from the dressage crowd. Really Duncan, I can't take it."

"At least take the trophy, please, I want you to have it. You did such a fantastic job, you deserve something." Duncan pushed the silver bowl toward him.

"I don't know. Isn't it supposed to stay with the horse?" Blackie said.

"I don't know about that, but I can do what I want with it and I want you to have it." Duncan said, handing it to Blackie.

"Well, thank you, Duncan. It was a pleasure riding Torsk. He's a great horse. Thank you for hiring me."

"Actually I might want you to ride him some more. Have you ever thought of trying out for the Olympic Team?"

"No I haven't. I'm more interesting in getting a business going so I can stay home and work. I've already done a huge amount of traveling in my life. I guess now I want to settle down and enjoy family life," Blackie said, putting an arm around Meg.

"I can certainly appreciate that. Especially with this beautiful girl at your side," Duncan said, beaming at her. It was her turn to blush.

"Yes, she is, isn't she?" Blackie said, looking seriously at her. "Hopefully we'll be married soon. I will consider riding for you again if you need me. Thank you for the opportunity, Duncan."

"Thank *you* and we still have the President's Cup tomorrow night. I'm looking forward to that."

"It should be exciting. I hope I can do as well for you."

"You can only do your best, Blackie, and with you, that's pretty damn good. See you tomorrow," Duncan said shaking hands with Blackie and giving Meg a little bow.

"Thank you, sir," Blackie said.

"He's really a nice man, isn't he," Meg said, as Duncan walked away.

"He is, yes. I like him a lot. I like riding for him. He doesn't tell me what to do."

"And you are wonderful. You were awesome. You had an almost perfect score."

"I did? I didn't see what it was, I just heard that I won," he said and hugged her again. He drew his head back and looked at her.

"I love you, Meg. Thanks for believing in me."

He kissed her tenderly at first and the kiss turned into a deep, hungry one that she knew only too well.

"Let's go out and celebrate tonight. Hey, guys, you want to change clothes and go out to dinner and celebrate. My treat."

"Sounds great. Let's meet in the lobby in forty-five minutes." Keary said.

They all agreed, Blackie and Meg returning to their room. As soon as he closed the door he came up behind her putting his arms around her and kissing her neck.

"What a great day. I really had fun. Did you enjoy it," he asked, working his way down her shoulder with his mouth. She always got a huge rush as soon as he touched her anyway, so this was no different.

"Yes, I had a wonderful time," she murmured as he unbuttoned her blouse and bra. She sucked in a breath as he cupped both hands around her breasts.

"Do we have time for this?" She asked, hoping they did.

"You bet! I can be very fast when I want to," he whispered in her ear. He unzipped her jeans and she turned around to face him. Kissing him passionately as she removed his jacket and shirt. He hugged her and groaned.

"I love your bare chest up against mine, you're so soft and warm," he said starting to pull her jeans down. She pushed him into a chair and lifted his foot to pull a boot off. She couldn't ignore the huge erection he had. He was watching her intently as she pulled his other boot off and went for his zipper. So quickly it made her head spin, he had her on the floor with both their clothes off. The next instant he was in her and she gasped with pleasure.

Another five minutes and they were done. He lay between her legs for another five minutes, kissing her face and neck.

"I told you I was fast," he said smiling. "Now we better shower and get dressed. We have thirty more minutes."

"You're not only fast, you're good," she said, kissing him.

"I aim to please, ma'am."

She giggled and he helped her up. They showered together, dressed and were in the lobby with five minutes to spare.

"Boy, you guys are slow," Blackie said looking at his watch. "What've you been doing, taking a nap?" he teased Sean and Keary.

"Hey, we both took showers. It takes time," Keary complained.

"I guess we're just fast," he said smiling at Meg. As they walked off, Katie whispered in her ear, "You guys didn't?" she asked, smiling.

"Oh, yes we did."

"Oh my god, that must be a land speed record," Katie laughed.

"What can I say? He's talented." Meg said with a smug smirk.

"I'm jealous but I can forget it with eight and a half months of baby in here," Katie said referring to her ever expanding belly.

"What are you two whispering about," Blackie said pulling her close.

"Just talking about our outfits, honey," she said looking innocent.

"Yeah, I bet."

They went to a posh Chinese restaurant in D.C. and had a blast. Blackie ordered champagne and had drunk several glasses before she realized he was getting a little silly. He was having fun, joking and goofing around with Sean and Katie.

She gave Keary a look and he noticed Blackie pouring himself yet another glass of champagne.

"Hey, buddy, maybe you should slow down on the champagne. You have to ride again tomorrow," Keary whispered to him. He gave Keary an irritated look and then looked at Meg. He put the bottle down and said, "You're right. I got a little carried away." Not any too soon she thought, since he was already starting to slur his words a little. He quickly switched to ginger ale. Keary ruffled his hair and patted his shoulder.

"Thanks, Keary."

Everything went smoothly after that and then they turned in for the night. Meg undressed and went in the bathroom. When she came out Blackie was flopped on the bed in only his underwear, sound asleep. She threw a comforter over him and crawled under it too, snuggling up against him.

At eight the next morning, she heard her cell phone start to vibrate on the night stand and grabbed it fast. It was Katie.

"Are you guys going to breakfast?"

"Not yet, he's still asleep. I'm going to let him sleep as long as he wants. He's got to ride tonight."

"Okay, we'll sleep in too. Call us whenever you guys get up. I'm pretty tired myself."

"Talk later, bye," she said, hanging up and cuddling up with Blackie again. He mumbled something and flopped an arm over her.

He woke up about eleven o'clock and stretched languidly. He scooped her up in his arms and kissed her.

"Good morning, sweetheart. How are you this morning?"

"I'm great. How are you? Did you get enough sleep?"

"I did, yes, but I have an awful headache. I forgot champagne does that to me. I'm glad Keary made me quit while I was ahead. I would have been no good today with a major hangover."

"What time do you have to warm up tonight?" He looked at his watch and thought a minute.

"My class is at eight; so I'll go and warm him up about seven or seven-thirty. We can eat dinner early, maybe around five. I don't want to be full of food when I ride."

"Do you want breakfast now? Katie and Sean waited for us to eat. She was tired from all the walking around yesterday.

"I guess so. She looks like she's ready to pop. How far along is she?"

"She's eight and a half months."

"Wow, I hope she doesn't drop it early. That would be too much excitement. I can't wait to see their baby. It's going to be too damn cute," he said excited at the prospect of another baby in the house.

"You really love little Maeve don't you?" She said smiling at him.

"Yes, she's adorable," he rolled over and kissed her. "I hope she's fine with Gracie watching her but they get along happily." He kissed her again and rolled out of bed, showered and dressed in his riding gear. He had clean breeches on, a different shirt with no collar that just buttoned at the neck and different, slightly shorter boots. He carried the jacket and helmet as they left for breakfast.

They had fun with Sean and Katie and then Keary, Jill and Maeve joined them for their lunch as they'd gotten up early and done some sightseeing.

Blackie and Meg went to check on Shangri-La and the others went to their seats in the stands. Everything was good with the horse, so they strolled back to the main arena. The rest of the afternoon was full of interesting classes. There were driving classes, ponies, juniors, all very colorful and exciting.

Around six forty-five Blackie was getting antsy, so she leaned against his arm and whispered, "Why don't you go start warming him up? Do you want me to come along?"

"No, I need to focus on this. It's been years since I did any real jumping. The last time was the accident, so I'm a little nervous. Do you mind?"

"No, honey. You just concentrate on what you need to do. I'll enjoy watching from up here. I love you."

"I love you too, babe. Wish me luck."

"There's no luck to it, just skill and you have tons of that. Just do your best and that'll be enough."

She was very nervous this time. She wanted him to win but he could get seriously hurt doing this. Jumping a horse had almost killed him once. She was scared and said so to Jill.

"Are you scared about him doing this?"

"Yes, my knees are shaking. I don't know if I can watch. I always loved to watch him race, but not anymore," she said and put her arm around Meg. "But you know he has an incredible gift to do this and we have to trust his judgment. I know if he thought he couldn't do this safely, he wouldn't."

"I know, I just wish it was over. How are Keary and Sean doing?

"Keary just told me his stomach was churning and Sean looks a little green over there."

Meg looked over at Sean and he rolled his eyes and said, "I'm praying hard for him, Meg."

"Thanks, Sean."

They sat anxiously through the last couple classes, sucking their breath in when they announced the $100,000 Presidents Cup. Ten horses had qualified for the final jumping competition. They had to wait a bit for the jumps to be set up. Obstacles that looked humungous to Meg and were different from the ones Blackie had at home. She hoped he hadn't misjudged what the jumps would be like.

There was a water jump, a tall picket fence with flowers around it, gigantic double oxers, three huge jumps in a row, something that looked like a Budweiser beer can, one where you had to actually jump through a hole, and hedge jumps. There were sixteen in all, set at different angles to one another. That would have confused her, as to which way to go.

Then the gate opened and the riders came out without their horses and walked through the course. Blackie was intent and focused on the course. He walked off the distance between jumps, especially the three big ones in a row. Then he stood quietly in the center of the ring, turning slowly around looking over the course one more time.

Dinner felt like a lead weight in her stomach from nerves. Each rider came in and took their turn jumping the course. Some knocked poles down, or refused to jump and four of them had clean rounds. Then Blackie rode into the ring. Shangri-La seemed nervous; he was flicking his ears back and forth and tossing his head. Blackie made a large circle around several jumps at a slow canter.

He picked up the pace slightly as he turned toward the first jump. Suddenly he and Shangri-La seemed to rocket toward the fence and they were over and landed in a split second. She thought she might pass out. Blackie was forward in the saddle, head up, looking at the next fence. They flew over that one and on and on until the last section which was those three, horrible ones in a row. He collected Shangra-Lai as they approached, then pushed him forward much faster than the other jumps. He was over the first, took two strides and over the second, then two strides and over the last one! A clean round! They jumped up and screamed and applauded. Blackie was now one of only five riders who had clean rounds. What happens next, Meg wondered.

"Sean, what do they do now, make the jump bigger?"

"They cut the number of jumps down to say nine or ten, make some higher, change the sequence and it's now timed. So whoever has the least amount of faults, in the fastest time will win."

"Oh, God, they have to go faster? This was fast enough for me. I don't think I can watch this."

"Listen, Meg, it's going to look scary but they're two things Blackie understands better than anyone in the world, timing the take-off and pace. Just remember the jumps at Aintree make these look like child's play."

"Sean that doesn't make me feel any better. I'm scared."

"He'll be fine, Meg," Keary said, patting her hand. He didn't look as confident as he sounded.

The first rider came in. She did the round in sixty-seven point five seconds with five faults.

"Sixty-seven seconds! Are they kidding? That's ridiculous?"

"Just wait. Blackie's not going to let anyone beat him on time." Sean said.

"Oh God, I hope he doesn't do anything reckless."

The next rider had eight faults and sixty-eight point two seconds. The third rider had five faults and sixty-eight point four seconds. The fourth rider had a clear round and sixty-six point seven five seconds.

Then Blackie came out on Shangri-La. The horse was tossing his head and hopping up and down, he was so excited. Meg gritted her teeth.

God, please let him keep control of that horse.

Blackie took a quick look around because the course had changed. Now there were only nine jumps but the sequence was different. She hoped he knew which way to go. He made a circle again, this time when he turned the horse toward the jump; he kicked him into gear and then ran at the first jump like a high speed train.

"Oh my god, he's going too fast," Meg yelled and sucked in her breath as he sailed over the jump and landed perfectly. Blackie turned the horse on a dime to go another direction and took that jump at breakneck speed. She couldn't believe he was racing that fast at these huge jumps. They flew over the Budweiser can at a diagonal to save ground. Every time they approached a jump, Shangri-La's ears flicked back and then forward again right before takeoff, so she knew Blackie was telling him what to do. They approached a huge double oxer at a dead run and the horse took it with feet to spare. Blackie almost stopped him to make a fast turn in the other direction and took off again, faster than ever. He flew over several more jumps and turned for home before those three jumps. She couldn't believe the speed at which Blackie drove Shangri-La forward. She was afraid to watch but was transfixed by what she was seeing. Blackie grunted as they took off over the first, landed far beyond it, immediately took off for the second without even taking a stride, another loud grunt from Blackie. Shangri-La looked like he almost landed on top of the third jump and Blackie let out this growling noise and the horse gathered himself over his haunches and leapt almost straight up in the air and sailed over the last jump. They raced to the finish line. A clear round in sixty-four point two seconds!

The crowd went crazy, jumping to their feet and cheering for the unbelievable performance they just witnessed. Blackie circled the ring at a slow canter, patting Shangri-La on the neck. He looked up into the crowd, waved and blew Meg a kiss. She and the others were crying and hugging each other with happiness and relief.

"I told you he'd do it," Sean said with tears in his eyes. In about fifteen minutes the announcer said Blackie and Shamgra-Lai's names as the winners over the loud speaker. More cheers and applause from the audience. In another fifteen minutes or so Blackie, leading Shangra Lai with a blanket on him and Duncan came walking out to the master of ceremonies in the center of the ring.

They were given a huge trophy and a check for $100,000. The crowd applauded and cheered again as they walked out.

Everyone hurried back to the stall area to congratulate him. Meg launched herself at him when she saw him. He caught her and twirled her around.

"Oh my god! You were awesome. I was so scared but you did it."

"Thanks honey." Blackie said, laughing and blushing as all of them jumped him, smothering him with hugs and praise.

"Okay you guys, that's enough."

"You were fantastic, buddy." Keary said, pumping his hand.

"Yeah, buddy, that was over-the-top cool."A teary-eyed Sean said, hugging him.

Duncan was standing around talking to people and then came over to Blackie.

"Great job, young man." He said as he shook Blackie's hand.

"Hey, Duncan, thanks for asking me to ride for you. It's been a great experience."

"I'm the one that needs to thank you. You've done such a magnificent job for me. I can't begin to thank you. Can't I pay you something?"

"No, really, I don't need the money. Listen can you and Bobby get the horses loaded without my help? I'd like to get home and my sister-in-law looks likely to deliver any minute."

"No, we'll be fine. You go ahead. Bobby can pack the horses up and bring them home next week. By the way, how did Bobby do? He's not my usual groom. That piker quit right before I shipped the horses to you."

"Uh ... he did a good job as far as grooming." Blackie said, reluctantly, trying not to show any animosity.

"I wondered but I figured since Mickey recommended him, he was okay."

"What? Who recommended him?" Blackie asked, frowning.

"Mickey Reegan, your agent. Didn't you know?"

"No. How did that happen?"

"Right after Jerry quit, Mickey called me out of the blue and said he had a friend who was an excellent groom and he'd heard I needed one. Isn't that odd? I thought you must have told him. Oh, well, as long as he did a good job. I'll be in touch, Blackie and thanks again." Duncan shook hands with Blackie again and walked away.

"Uh ... see you Duncan," Blackie said absently. "Hey, Keary, how long will it take to pack up our gear and check out?"

"I don't know maybe an hour."

*   *   *

On the way home they were animated and exhilarated, reliving every minute of the show except for Blackie. He was quiet and pensive.

"Hey, Blackie, what's the matter?" Keary asked him.

"Do you know what Duncan told me?"

"What?"

"Who do you think recommended Bobby for the groom job with Duncan?"

"I give up, who?" Keary replied.

"Mickey Reegan."

"Are you serious? Duncan told you that?" Keary said, an angry frown on his face.

"What the hell? When did this happen? Sean asked, equally disturbed.

"Blackie, what's the matter?" Meg wanted to know.

"Just a minute, Meg. Duncan told me his regular groom quit right after he hired me and Mickey called him and suggested Bobby, saying he heard Duncan needed a groom."

"Son of a bitch! That's creepy as hell. How would Mickey know that you were riding for Duncan? We need to investigate and find out how Mickey knows shit."

"Blackie, is that the agent you fired?" Meg asked. "Is he spying on you?"

Blackie stared at her. "That's a good question. What do you guys think?"

"I think we need to get the lads to look into it." Keary said, peering at Blackie in the rearview mirror. "I'll call your dad about it tonight."

"Exactly my thought."

THIRTY-NINE

A couple of days after the show, Blackie was still worn out so he and Meg just walked around and looked at the horses, talking about how their training was going. They stopped in the arena and watched Jamie and Curt schooling their horses. The boys and Blackie talked about the next few weeks of their schooling. Torsk and Shangri-La were still in their boxes, so they took a quick look at them.

"I wonder when that asshole is leaving." Blackie said, frowning.

"Jill said she thought he was packing up and taking the horses in the morning. She'll be glad when he's gone. She doesn't like him either. She said he makes her feel creepy."

"I know the feeling," Blackie said. "I wonder what that bastard, Mickey's up to?" They were still looking at some of the horses when Sean came by and asked Blackie to go and look at a horse with him in one of the racing barns.

"Ok, I'm coming. I won't be long, Meg. You run up to the house real quick, it's almost dinner time. Don't hang around by yourself. I'll be right behind you. I'm hungry," he said, kissed her quickly and went after Sean.

She went up to the apartment, washed up and turned out the lights, set the alarm and left. As she walked past the tack room she was appalled. Grooming equipment was strewn everywhere, saddles and bridles were just thrown on the floor and a can of saddle soap was left open.

"What a mess!" She said aloud. "I'm going to get after Curt and Jamie for this." She proceeded to reseal the soap, dump the grooming implements into a trunk and was hanging up the bridle when she felt Blackie come up behind her.

"Hi, sweetheart," she said as he put both arms around her and squeezed.

"It's not your sweetheart," Bobby said in a low growl.

Meg's blood turned to ice. She immediately kicked him in the shin and started to struggle.

"You bastard, you better get off me. Blackie's going to kill you," she yelled, trying to get her hands free to scratch him.

"Well, Blackie's not here is he, bitch?" He said kissing her neck and squeezing her tighter. Fear shot through her suddenly.

Oh God, Blackie's going straight up to the house, not coming back here. Shit! Maybe she could wrestle him over to the alarm. He turned her around quickly and tried to kiss her. She bit his lip and he hit her hard with his fist.

"Stupid whore! You're really going to get it now!" He said trying to kiss her again. She punched at him and tried to kick him in the balls, but he caught her leg and she went down. It knocked the wind out of her for a second but as soon as she got some air, she screamed as loud as she could for Blackie.

Oh, God, honey, please hear me.

She continued to kick and scream. Bobby jumped on top of her and hit her again harder.

"Shut up, cunt!" He ripped her blouse open and grabbed her breasts. He was hurting her, but she got a huge lungful of air and screamed again for Blackie. He hit her again and she tasted blood. Now she was pissed. She twisted her body and pulled as hard as she could to get away. He was too strong for her. He ripped her bra off and got her breast in his mouth.

"You fucking bastard, get off me," she screamed and twisted. She almost puked at the thought of him touching her. He bit her several times and she cried out in pain. She was beating him with her fists but it didn't seem to help. Meg screamed again as loud as she could and he started choking her.

"I told you to shut up you stupid bitch," he said squeezing her throat so hard she couldn't breathe.

*　　*　　*

Up at the house, Blackie and Sean walked into the kitchen. They were standing there for a few minutes joking with Keary. They started in to the dining room and as they were at the doorway, Blackie stopped dead, Keary bumping into his back.

"Blackie, what are you doing?"

"Did you hear something?" he said turning his head.

"No, I didn't hear anything," Keary said.

"I thought I heard someone call me." He moved a step and then stopped again. "There it is again. Didn't you hear that?"

"No, Blackie," Keary said.

"I didn't hear anything either," Sean said.

Blackie looked into the dining room, "Where's Meg?"

"I don't know. She hasn't come up yet. Why?" Jill said.

Blackie stood still another second and then exploded toward the door at a dead run.

"Blackie, what the hell!"

"Call the guards, now!" he shouted as he ran for the barn.

"What the hell is going on?" Keary said.

"I don't know, but you better call them," Sean said, "I'm going after him."

"Jill, call the cops, I'm going with Sean," Keary yelled as they both ran out the door after Blackie.

*　　*　　*

Meg was still struggling and kicking but fast running out of steam. She couldn't breathe. She wasn't going to give up and let this bastard rape her.

She tried twisting her body to get out from under him, but he squeezed her throat harder.

Suddenly he was gone! His weight lifted off her like magic. She rolled to her side, gasping for air and looked out into the aisle. Blackie had Bobby by the neck and was punching his face as hard as he could. Bobby tried to fight back but couldn't do much. Blackie kicked him in the nuts and Bobby went to his knees. As Blackie gave him a brutal punch to the face, Meg struggled to her feet and hit the alarm.

Bobby got to his feet and tried to run, but Blackie grabbed him by the shirt and punched him in the side. Bobby's face had blood all over it and he looked terrified. He tore away, grabbed a shovel and hit Blackie with it, who put his arm up blocking the blow. He punched Bobby in the gut. As he bent over, Blackie hit him with an uppercut and then a left. Meg knew from the sound of bone crunching, that blow broke Bobby's nose.

Keary and Sean rounded the turn into the barn and stopped. Keary grabbed Meg and asked, "What happened?"

"Bobby was trying to rape me. He cornered me in the tack room. I've been screaming my head off for Blackie."

"Well, he heard you. Are you okay?"

Just then she ran out of steam, adrenaline, anger, guts, everything and collapsed. Keary grabbed her and sat her on a hay bale as the fight continued.

"Aren't you going to stop them? Blackie will kill him," she said, so terrified she was shaking.

"Oh, we'll stop it in a minute after Blackie beats the shit out of him. We won't let him kill the guy though." Sean said. Jill came flying around the corner and stopped dead.

"Keary, stop them. Blackie will kill him."

"In a minute," Keary said.

"No, now! Do you want him to go to prison for man-slaughter?" she said punching Keary in the arm. "Come on, Meg; let's go up to the house."

"I guess you're right," Keary said reluctantly. "Come on, Sean."

Casey and Ned, Sean's assistant, showed up at the other end of the barn and stopped with their mouths open.

"Hey, we'll probably need your help," Sean yelled to them.

"Let's try and get Blackie off him, carefully. I don't feel like getting hit," Keary said.

It was obvious that Bobby was unconscious, but Blackie was holding him up with one hand and pounding on him with the other.

Keary and Sean tried to grab Blackie's shoulders. He immediately turned and went after *them*. Ned and Casey grabbed his arms from behind and held on for dear life.

"Let go of me. I'm going to kill him," he snarled breathlessly as he got away from Ned and Casey and started after Bobby again. Keary tackled him, getting both arms around him and pinning Blackie's to his sides.

"Blackie, stop, listen," Keary yelled, hardly able to hold him. "Blackie, you have to stop. You need to take care of Meg. She's hurt!" Blackie instantly stopped and looked at Keary.

"Where is she?"

"Jill helped her up to the house."

"Let go of me, damnit," Blackie said, ripping away from Keary and headed toward the house.

"Did you call 911?" Blackie yelled back at Keary as he left the barn.

Keary and Sean stood there looking at Bobby along with Ned and Casey.

"Sure and you could get yourself hurt trying to stop Blackie," Casey said. "What'd this bugger do, then?" he said nudging Bobby with his toe.

"He tried to rape Meg and Blackie caught him."

"Oh, shyte! This guy must be super stupid. We should have let Blackie keep going. Why'd we stop him?"

"Jill didn't want him in trouble for killing the bastard. If it had been me, I'd have let him go and buried the fucker in the manure pile," Keary said and they all laughed. They could hear sirens coming from a distance.

"Oh man. This is going to be dicey," Sean said.

"Yes, let's handle the guards and give him time to take care of Meg," Keary said. Several patrol cars rolled to a stop in front of the barn and four officers got out. They walked up to the guys and looked down at Bobby.

"Somebody want to tell me what happened here?" Said Officer Gruber.

"I'm Keary Connelly, the farm manager. From what I understand, Mr. O'Brien ran down to the barn here because he heard his fiancée screaming. I guess when he got here; this guy was on her trying to rape her. So he obviously beat the shit out of the bastard."

"Where is Mr. O'Brien?"

"He's up at the house taking care of her. She's hurt pretty bad," Sean said.

"Who are you guys?" the officer asked.

"I'm Sean O'Brien, Mr. O'Brien's cousin. This is Casey O'Hara, one of our jockeys and Ned Moran is a trainer."

"Oh, so you're all Irish, huh?"

"That's correct, officer." Keary replied.

This guy's an asshole, Sean thought. He better lose the "Irish" attitude before he talks to Blackie.

"Who is this bloody mess laying on the ground?"

"This is Bobby Stahl. He came down from New York as the groom for two horses that Mr. O'Brien rode in the D.C. Horse Show," Keary explained.

"So this guy's a groom? What is Mr. O'Brien's capacity around here?"

"He's the owner," Keary offered.

"Did all you guys gang up on this poor bastard?"

"No, none of us touched him. We stopped Mr. O'Brien from continuing so he could see after his fiancée."

"You mean one guy did this? Which one of you stopped the fight?"

"All of us," Sean said.

"It took all four of you to get Mr. O'Brien under control?"

"Yes, more or less," Keary said, looking at the others.

"Pretty big guy is he?" Officer Gruber and his partner looked at each other. The other two cops stood there not saying anything.

"Not particularly, he's just strong and he was a bit pissed at this guy for attacking his fiancée." Keary answered.

"So none of you actually *saw* what was transpiring between this guy and the fiancée."

"No, when we got here, the fight had already started. Meg was pretty beaten up; her throat was bruised; she told me Bobby was choking her. Her blouse and bra had been ripped off," Keary told him.

"Mr. O'Brien wants him charged with assault, attempted rape and attempted murder," Sean said.

"Oh he does, does he? Well, we'll see," Officer Gruber said sarcastically.

Oh, Christ, Sean thought, This is going to be bad.

"Hey, Tommy, call an ambulance for this guy. What about the fiancée? She should go to the hospital and they'll do a rape kit on her," Gruber said.

"I think Mr. O'Brien will prefer to take her himself," Keary said, rolling his eyes at Sean.

"I don't know that it's up to him when she goes. I'll decide that."

"Oh fuck, Keary, Blackie's going to wind up in jail if he deals with this guy," Sean said under his breath to Keary.

"I know. I can feel this turning bad already. We need to keep Blackie under control or they'll arrest him for sure."

"Do you two have something to say?" Gruber said to them, belligerently.

"No, we're good," Keary, said, with a fake smile.

"You guys can leave; I've got this under control." Gruber said to the other two cops, who gave him a disgusted look and left.

"After the ambulance leaves, is there someplace we can sit and get statements from everyone including Mr. O'Brien and the girl?"

"Yes, we can go up to the house," Keary said.

"Is that where Mr. O'Brien and the girl are?"

"Yes and her name is Meg Connors."

"Connors? What's that? Irish too?"

Just then the ambulance came blaring to a stop in front of the barn.

"That dumb fuck! We're in big trouble here, Keary. Blackie's not going to like any of this and the mood he's in, he's not going to be submissive," Sean whispered to Keary.

"Are you two whispering again?" Gruber snarled.

"What? It's against the law to talk to one another? Are we under arrest or prisoners?" Keary said getting pissed.

"I'm conducting an investigation here, so talk to me or not at all," at this statement Gruber's partner rolled his eyes at them and shook his head.

Sean made a move toward Gruber but Keary stopped him.

"Christ is that all you 'micks' ever do is fight?" Gruber said.

"There's no need to make racist remarks, officer." Keary said through his teeth.

"Yeah, right," Gruber said with a smirk on his face.

As soon as the ambulance left, Gruber wanted to go up to the house. Keary made a motion for Casey and Ned to follow and all six of them proceeded up to the house.

*   *   *

When Blackie left the barn, he ran up to the house, in the door, through the kitchen and dining room, ending up in the TV room. There was Katie sitting on one side of Meg, Jill on the other. She was wrapped in a blanket and sobbing. He stopped in the doorway and looked at her with an agonized look.

"Oh, God, honey," she sobbed, holding her arms out for him. Jill moved over so he could sit next to Meg. He grabbed her, wrapping his arms around her almost crushing her.

"Meg, I'm so sorry. I should have protected you. I never should have left you alone."

"What are you talking about? I called your name and you came and saved me. Like magic! I fought and fought as hard as I could. I was almost done for and you showed up and rescued me. Blackie, honey, you saved my life. He was choking me and I couldn't breathe," she told him, holding his face in her hands.

"Oh, God, look at your jaw. Honey, your eye is almost swollen shut. Jesus, your throat is all bruised. I'm sorry. I'm sorry," he said hugging her to him and stroking her hair.

"Meg, you better show him now," Jill said gently.

"Show me? Show me what?" he said looking at Jill, then back at her.

Meg opened the blanket so he could see the bite marks on her breasts. Three deep ones, one right next to her nipple.

Blackie squeezed his eyes shut and looked so tormented she was sorry she had shown him.

"That fucking bastard. I should have killed him when I had the chance." He pulled her onto his lap, cradling her gently as she sobbed against him.

"You're safe now, Meg," he said kissing her forehead. He held her for a long time and just let her cry.

"Jill, she needs to go to the hospital," Blackie said.

"No, no," Meg wailed. "I don't want to go. I want to stay here with you," she said pushing herself tighter against him.

"Meg, honey, I'll take you as soon as I'm done talking to the cops. I need to go anyway."

"Why do you have to go?" Katie asked.

"I'm pretty sure I broke my hand," he said holding up his right hand that was bloody, swollen and turning blue.

"Oh, God, your hand, honey, does it hurt?"

"It does, yes. But I'm worried that you have a broken jaw and we need to get those bites looked at too." He said pulling her against his chest again. He looked at Jill with tears in his eyes.

"Blackie, she's going to be fine, honey," Jill said to him and he nodded.

Keary called Jill from the dining room and she went out; coming back in a minute.

"Blackie, the police are here and want to talk to both of you," she told him.

"I'll talk to them. She's not going to give a statement until she calms down and we've been to the hospital," he said firmly and tilted her head up.

"Meg, I need to go talk to the police."

"No, don't leave me. I'm scared."

"Honey, you're safe. Jill and Katie are here. I'll be just in the other room with the guards. I won't be long," he said, unwinding himself from her grasp.

"Katie, are you okay? You don't need this upset. You're about to have your baby," Meg said.

"Just relax, Meg, I'm good."

*   *   *

As Blackie walked into the dining room, every cell in his body had attitude.

Oh shit, Sean thought, he's in no mood to put up with these two dumb-ass cops. Blackie looked at the cops a second, flicking his eyes to Keary.

"Be cool," Keary said in Gaelic.

"What did you say? What language was that?" Gruber asked belligerently.

"I just said hello in Gaelic," Keary told him.

"What, can't he speak English?" Gruber said, smirking again.

"I speak English, Officer. I'm Blackie O'Brien. I'd shake hands but my hand seems to be broken." He said standing there, looking very dangerous and intimidating.

I can't believe how big, tough and mean he can look when he wants to, Sean thought, looking at Blackie.

"You broke your hand?" Sean said and Blackie held it up.

"Oh shit, let me get some ice." Sean came back with ice for Blackie's hand.

"Here sit down and I'll put this on it." Sean told him.

Blackie sat down slowly. Sean knew this was deceptive because he knew how fast Blackie could move.

"Get ready," Keary said to Sean in Gaelic, as he moved over and stood between Blackie and the cops. Sean took a chair in the same vantage point.

"Hey, you two, no more 'mick' mumbo-jumbo!" Gruber yelled.

"What the fuck did you say?" Blackie growled.

"Forget it," Keary said. "Take it easy."

"Okay, Mr. O'Brien, can you tell me your version of what happened?" Gruber said.

Blackie stared at him for a minute before answering.

"I was here when I thought I heard someone call me. I listened and heard it again. When I found out Meg wasn't here, I realized it was her and ran down to the barn. When I got there, Bobby was on top of her strangling her. Her blouse and bra were ripped open. I grabbed him, yanking him off her and we started fighting."

"You couldn't have heard her from here," Gruber sneered.

"I have exceptional hearing," Blackie told him.

"Did she have her underwear on?" Gruber asked.

Blackie stared at him with obvious dislike. He finally answered.

"She had her jeans on and zipped up. His pants were open and he was, let's say, 'Ready to go.' That's why I kicked him in the nuts. I couldn't resist."

"Then what happened?"

"We continued fighting. I pounded him pretty good, the bastard. Then the lads pulled me off him and I came up here to see to Meg."

"Can anyone verify you're story?"

"What do you mean?" Blackie asked.

"I mean, how do I know that you didn't walk in on her fucking the guy and attacked them both ..."

Blackie was out of the chair so fast it still took Keary and Sean by surprise. They blocked him just before he reached Gruber.

"Blackie, you need to take care of Meg. You don't have time to go to jail," Keary said.

"You better shut your fucking mouth, asshole," Blackie yelled at Gruber.

"For chrissake, Gruber! You're an idiot! You're going to mess with this guy? What, are you stupid? Look at him. Do you want to wind up looking like the guy lying in the barn?" Grubrer's partner, Tommy, exclaimed.

"Shut up, you're undermining my authority," Gruber retorted.

"Authority! You don't have any authority over these people. You're supposed to be helping them. This man's girlfriend was assaulted!"

"Shut up, Tommy! "I'm not afraid of him. I'll cuff him and take him in for assaulting a cop."

"Yeah, I'd like to see you cuff him," Tommy snorted.

"Shut up Tommy! Sit down, Mr. O'Brien."

"I'll sit down when I fucking feel like it," Blackie said. Sean and Keary were barely able to contain him.

"Okay, Mr. O'Brien, let's have your girlfriend come in and give her statement," Gruber ordered Blackie.

"She's not doing any such thing. After I'm done with you, I'm taking her to the hospital," Black growled.

"I'll have a police woman take her so they can do a rape kit on her."

"She wasn't raped!" Blackie yelled.

"If you don't bring her in here, *I'll* go get her," Gruber warned.

"To get her, you'll have to go through me," Black said through clenched teeth.

"What are you stupid, Gruber?" Tommy said with a smirk.

There was a knock on the door and Casey answered it. It was Captain Leary from the Richmond Police.

"Christ, here comes the rest of the Irish," Gruber whispered to Tommy.

"Did you say something, Officer Gruber?" Captain Leary asked him.

"No, sir."

"He did, yes. He said 'Christ, here comes the rest of the Irish'," Blackie told the Captain. Gruber gave Blackie a dirty look.

"I told you I had great hearing."

"Gruber, these people are friends of mine. What's going on?"

"Mr. O'Brien here just threatened me," Gruber said giving Blackie a victorious look.

"I got a call that there was trouble out here. What happened, Blackie?" the Captain asked him.

"This guy tried to rape and murder Meg. She's all beat up. I caught the guy and cleaned his plow.

This asshole just insinuated that I caught them having sex and beat them both up."

"Are you kidding me? Is Meg okay?"

"Well, I want to take her to the hospital but this jerk is insisting she's going to give a statement."

"He's been making all kinds of racist remarks against the Irish, Sir," Casey piped up.

"Gruber, get out of my sight. You're relieved of duty. I'll talk to your Captain in the morning. Now get the hell out of here."

Gruber and Tommy got up and left.

"Blackie, Keary, I apologize for that idiot. I'll deal with him tomorrow. What can I do to help?" The Captain asked.

"I just would like to be able to take Meg in to give a statement in a couple days. She needs to go to the hospital right now. She's hurt and she's hysterical. I can't let her be put through an interrogation right now," Blackie said.

"Of course, you don't have to rush. Whenever she's ready. What are you charging this guy with?" Leary asked.

"Assault, attempted rape and attempted murder. You should see the bruises on her throat from him choking her," Blackie said.

"Do you mind if I just quickly take a look at her injuries myself?"

Blackie hesitated a minute and then said, "Let me ask her first. She knows you, so I don't think it'll be a problem. Uh ... he bit her breast too. I'd rather she didn't show you that."

"Mother of God! That bastard!"

Blackie left to go back and talk to Meg. She was curled up with Jill and Katie, shivering under a blanket.

"Honey, how are you doing? Do you remember Captain Leary?" She nodded.

"Is it okay if he comes back and looks at your bruises? He doesn't need to see the bite marks."

"Yes. He's a nice man."

"Okay, I'll bring him back," Blackie left and came back in a minute with Captain Leary.

"Meg, I'm terribly sorry this happened. I don't mean to intrude but I need to see your injuries." He knelt down in front of her and looked at her face and throat, frowning.

"Christ, how could any man do that to a woman? I don't get men like that. Thank you, Meg. I hope you feel better soon."

"You're welcome and thank you."

*　　*　　*

The Captain and Blackie walked back to the dining room.

"Blackie, I have to ask. Was she raped?"

"No, thank God. He was choking her into submission so if I hadn't shown up, he would have. She fought hard. She's little but she's feisty. She doesn't take any shit from me, that's for sure."

"Ah, a brave woman, indeed." Leary said and took his leave.

Blackie slumped down in a chair, covering his eyes with his good hand.

"Fuck!" he said slamming his fist on the table. "Ouch! Damnit!"

Keary sat down next to him, putting an arm around him.

"Come on buddy, she's going to be fine."

"I can't stand the thought of him even touching her much less beating her up and ... Shit!"

"She's a tough lady, she is. She'll be grand in no time," Casey said.

"Yeah, you got him good, Blackie," Ned added.

Blackie raised his head up. "Thanks, guys. Thanks for keeping me out of trouble. I don't need to be in jail right now." Sean handed him a beer.

"Thanks," Blackie said and drank half the bottle.

"How's your hand?" Sean asked.

"Throbbing like a son-of-a-bitch."

"You guys should probably get to the hospital, if she's up to it," Sean said. "We can drive you in the SUV or Jeremy can take the limo. Your hand isn't looking too good."

Blackie looked at his hand. It was still swollen and shades of red, black and blue.

"Shit, I guess so. Okay, let me go talk to her. She's pretty upset."

*   *   *

After getting home from being treated, they decided to spend the night at the house.

The next morning she could hardly move and he didn't say anything but she knew his hand was painful. They went down to breakfast and were greeted with wonderful news from Keary. Katie went into labor during the night and was at the hospital with Sean and Jill.

There wasn't any news yet. They were so excited they forgot about their troubles. While they were eating, Sean called with the news – he and Katie had a son, 7 lbs. 6 oz.

They named him Patrick after their little brother who died. They cried a little and laughed, then got ready and went to the hospital to see the new baby.

Little Patrick was adorable! He had blue eyes, red hair and looked like Katie. Sean was so excited, handing out cigars to all the guys. He was very funny and sweet. Blackie was happy for Sean and Meg could tell he was instantly in love with Patrick as soon as he saw him, just like little Maeve.

Meg knew she wanted to give him a child as soon as possible. He was adamant that they needed to be married first, but he still hadn't given her the ring or set a date. It made her sad.

She didn't know why he was waiting. She wanted to get on with their lives. She had no doubt that he loved her, there was just something stopping him.

Sean and Katie brought the baby home the next day. The three of them settled in their cottage and kept to themselves, enjoying their new family time together.

Meg was still shaky and spooky from the attack. Blackie tried to comfort her as much as possible. He tried to gently make love to her one night, but she couldn't relax He said they should wait and just held her.

They went to the police station and gave their statements. Bobby had filed an assault charge against Blackie, so at some point they'd have to go to court. Blackie called Duncan and explained the situation. Bobby was going to be in the hospital for a while with extensive injuries.

Duncan asked Blackie to pack the horses up and send them home in their van. He mentioned he had fired Bobby and was glad he was in the hospital.

FORTY

Meg's life with Blackie moved at a fast clip, everything falling into place. He happily worked hard every day with the horses; winning every class he entered with the new Swedish gelding, ABBA. People called to work with him and he added two new students besides Jamie and Curt who now helped with less experienced students. Blackie bought a new, humongous nine-horse van, so they could go to the shows together.

Meg wasn't doing quite as well with her new horse but enjoyed the challenge. Sometimes when Blackie was schooling her, he'd be tough and yell when she wasn't doing what he wanted. It stung her ego but she knew he was right. Late, when they were alone, he'd apologize, wiping her anger away with a kiss. He'd tell her he couldn't play favorites among the students and be easy on her just because he was in love with her.

"Well, okay, since you put it that way, riding master," she said smiling.

"I want you to be as good as I know you can be. You're a fantastic rider, you just need to work harder," he said kissing her neck.

"Hmm, you want to *show* me how good I can be," she said, trying to sound seductive.

"You bet. Hey, I keep forgetting to tell you there's a huge dinner dance at the Jockey Club in Mclean."

When is that?"

"Right at the end of the show season and it's a grand night. We'll have a wonderful time."

"Are you asking me to go?"

"Of course, I can't wait to make all the other men jealous because I'm with the most beautiful woman there."

"In that case, I'll go with you."

"Mmm, that's my girl. Come here."

*   *   *

Blackie started calling his parents a couple of times a week, talking mostly to his dad about politics. Meg thought his father was slowly sucking him into it. She didn't think he'd be happy taking time away from the training center that was finally up and running.

Blackie was adamant about quite a few issues in Ireland. One of the big ones was medical care. Compared to other countries, Ireland spent very little on health care. Blackie was almost obsessed with the idea that people had to have adequate medical coverage. He didn't like the policy Meg had and bugged her until she switched to the huge policy he carried on everyone at the farm.

Sometimes he and Ken would get in heated arguments on the phone about Irish issues. Blackie would slam the phone down and fume for the rest of the day.

Occasionally he talked quietly to his Mom and Meg wondered about these conversations because sometimes, when he was done, his eyes were wet with tears. She didn't want to ask about it since she knew his feelings were raw and close to the surface. He had a tremendous amount of guilt about his past.

Blackie and Sean continued to practice singing, mostly in the arena because the acoustics were awesome. She loved hearing him sing. He did it a lot now when he was grooming or cleaning stalls. If he wasn't singing, he was whistling the tunes.

The show season was in full swing and they kept super busy. Blackie took the new van and every person and horse that was ready, to every show he could fit in. They were winning so much that the Killarney Farms dressage team was developing a stellar reputation. Blackie took them as far as New York to be in some prestigious show. He always drove the van, paid for hotels, stables, meals, and gas for the whole gang.

Meg didn't compete every weekend and neither did Blackie. They both wanted the students to get as much experience as possible. He felt the better his students did the more credibility it gave to the training center and him as a coach.

Jamie and Curt were burning up the show circuit. Whenever Blackie rode, he drew an admiring crowd and naturally won every class. Blackie's two new students, Tommy and Matt, were winning the lower level classes consistently, sometimes coming in second, but generally putting in credible performances.

When they were on the road and at shows, they had a ball. Blackie was pretty tough on the students and stern when he was teaching, but weekends were different. He was very playful with them and encouraging. In between classes, they'd get a touch football game going and other guys would join in. She loved watching them. The students admired Blackie tremendously and always deferred to him. He was their leader, coach and mentor.

*   *   *

One day after a big show, everyone was standing by the end of the barn watching Casey work a new chaser when Jamie and Curt pulled up in Jamie's truck. They walked over carrying the trophies and ribbons from the shows.

"Hey, Blackie, what do you want us to do with this stuff? We've racked up a ton of it lately." Curt asked him.

"Hell, I don't know. Take your stuff home with you. Or you could put some up in the arena."

"Why don't you put them in your trophy room?" Keary suggested. Blackie groaned.

"What trophy room?" Meg asked.

"You mean she's never seen that room? What's the matter with you?" Sean said.

"Nothing's the matter with me, I just never thought about it." Blackie replied, giving Sean a dark look.

"Where's your trophy room?" Meg asked, puzzled.

"Shit! Sean you have a big mouth."

"Keary's the one brought it up, not me," Sean whined.

"The trophies are in the apartment, Meg, and I can't believe he never showed you." Keary said.

"Where?"

"It's a secret room. There are lots of secrets in that apartment, right, Blackie?"

"I guess," he sighed.

"Well, are you going to show us, dude?" Jamie asked.

"It's nothing, just a bunch of old junk." Blackie said, obviously being evasive.

"Blackie, that's ridiculous. It's fantastic. Just take them and show everyone the damn room." Keary said.

"Fine. Whatever." Blackie said, resigned to his fate. He walked back to the apartment, everyone following him. When they got inside, he walked into his clothes closet, clicked something and part of the wall in the foyer popped open.

"Be my guest," he said, waving a hand toward the open panel. He flipped a wall switch and lights came on in the opening.

Meg walked into this secret room and was blown away. The room extended the whole length of that huge barn and was approximately ten feet wide behind the existing wall of the apartment.

The most amazing part was what it contained. There was a glass showcase running the length of the outside wall containing hundreds and hundreds of gleaming trophies. There were silver bowls, colorful ribbons, crystal vases and huge gold and silver trophies, all neatly arranged. On a rack by the far wall was a racing saddle with jockeys silks draped over it.

Everyone gasped at the splendor.

"Omigod! Blackie is this all your stuff from racing," Meg asked, turning to look at him. He was leaning against the door with his hands stuffed in his jeans.

Uh-oh. That's not a good sign. He looks sad.

"Come on, Blackie, show them your trophies. You should be proud of them. You used to be," Keary said.

"I used to be a lot of things. This stuff isn't worth anything anymore."

"Honey, they're beautiful. Please tell us about them." Meg pleaded.

"Yeah, come on, man. This is incredible." Curt said.

"You show them, Keary." Blackie said and walked out.

She started to go after him but Sean stopped her.

"Leave him alone, Meg. This is hard for him. Keary and I will show you."

She hesitated but Keary grabbed her arm and pulled her into the room.

"Meg, he needs to get over this and move on. You will love seeing this." They walked down to the end of the room and started looking in the case. One trophy was more beautiful than the next.

"Down at this end are the ones he won when he first started racing at fifteen." Keary explained, "And it goes up to the other end in chronological order."

"This is unreal! I've never seen anything like this. How many races did he win?" Curt asked.

"I'm not sure off the top of my head but we have the records in the computer." Sean said.

"I can definitely tell you that he won more races and money than any other jockey, ever." Keary said, proudly.

"Why doesn't he like them?" Curt asked.

"It's not that, it's just since the accident, I don't think he's been in here." Keary said.

"I feel bad that we intruded and upset him." Jamie said, sadly.

"No, he needs to get over it and get on with his life. He's doing that in other areas, but he's still bogged down with regret over not being able to race anymore."

"Hey, you guys, want to see something really impressive? See those four huge silver trophies in the middle. They're from the four Grand Nationals he won." Sean said.

"Oh, God. He won four times? You mean the Grand National at Aintree, don't you?" Jamie said, wide-eyed.

"The very same." Keary said, beaming. Everyone just stood there, gawking at them in awe. Meg felt a lump in her throat. She was so proud of him. He accomplished all this and at that moment, she knew he could do anything if he could just believe in himself again.

FORTY-ONE

Meg was sitting in the kitchen watching Blackie enter show results onto a spreadsheet on his laptop. He kept detailed records for each student and horse. He was anal about everything concerning the training center. As usual, he was focused on what he was doing and ignored her, which was starting to irritate her.

Sean came in and sat across from Blackie and watched him for a couple of minutes. He rolled his eyes at Meg and smiled.

"Boyo, someone called for you Sunday when you guys were at the show." He said to Blackie and got no response. He winked at Meg.

"It was a person from the circus and they want you to train their elephants."

"Mmm, okay, thanks." Blackie mumbled.

"I got their number. You like training elephants, right?" Sean asked, barely suppressing a laugh.

"Yeah, thanks, Sean." Blackie replied without taking his eyes off the computer.

"Blackie! Jeez!" Meg said while Sean started laughing in earnest.

"What! What's wrong?" Blackie said, finally looking up.

"Could you please pay attention to what Sean is saying," she said.

He looked from her to Sean and frowned. "What is it, Sean? I'm busy."

"I said someone called looking for you when you were at the show," Sean repeated slowly.

"Well who the hell was it?" Blackie said just as slowly.

"I don't know. She hung up when I said you weren't home."

"She? Christ, now what? So you have no idea who it was?" Blackie asked Sean who flicked a quick look at Meg. Blackie caught the look.

"What, Sean?"

"Well ... she had a British accent, high brow. Very, very high brow." Sean said, pointedly. Blackie stared at Sean for a long minute.

"Vicky?" He asked with raised eyebrows.

"Maybe. Could be. Sounded kinda like her ... maybe."

"Who is Vicky?" Meg demanded a little too sharply.

Blackie sighed and rolled his eyes at Sean who laughed.

"Shut up, Sean. Uh ... Meg, Vicky is someone I used to ride for".

"Yeah, she owned the nag he was riding when the accident happened." Sean offered and Blackie scowled at him.

"Okay, so why are you giving Sean a dirty look?" Meg asked. Her eyes narrowed.

"Because her horses weren't the only thing he was riding." Sean snorted.

"Damnit, Sean! Why can't you ever keep your mouth shut?" Blackie hissed at him.

"Oh, great! Some slut from your past is calling here for you?"

"Meg, calm down. She's not a slut and we don't know if it was her anyway. Just ignore Sean, he's an idiot," he said, glaring at Sean.

"Okay, okay. Sorry. She's Lady Victoria Rupert and she's married to a distant cousin of the Queen," Sean said.

"Queen! Like the Queen of England?" Meg asked, wide-eyed.

"Yes. Why would she call me now? It's been over two years and she never bothered to call after the accident. What the hell does she want now? I don't need any shit from her." Blackie said, flushing with sweat on his forehead.

Keary and Jill walked in and could tell something was going on.

"Hey, guys. What's up?" Keary asked.

"Blackie got a call yesterday from some woman and we think it might have been Vicky." Sean piped up.

"You mean Lady Victoria?" Jill asked.

"Maybe. I don't know what she could possibly want after all this time. I never heard from her at all after the accident." Blackie said.

Meg realized there was a lot going on in his head about this woman. She decided to back off and let him have space.

"Uh ... I never told you guys this before but she showed up at the hospital when you were talking to the surgeons, before they started working on him. I didn't think you needed to deal with her at that point so I told her he was already in surgery. She got hysterical, accused me of lying, and said he must be dead. Then she ran out." Sean told them. Blackie just stared at him for a few minutes then got up and walked out. Meg sat there with her mouth open.

"Meg, honey, he'll be okay," Jill told Meg gently.

"But ... tell me who this woman is? Is he still involved with her? Were they serious?" Meg, asked, fear heavy in the pit of her stomach.

"Meg, sit down." Keary told her. He sighed, a weary look in his eyes and sat across from her.

"Meg, Vicky was married to Richard Rupert and, well, I guess she still is. Dickey is some distant cousin of the Queen and he ran around on Vicky all the time. Everyone knew about his philandering. Anyway, they own a huge racing stable and Vicky handled the training.

Several years ago, she asked Blackie to ride her horses and it wasn't long before they started having an affair, a fairly public one."

Meg groaned, "That sounds like a bit more than a one-night stand."

"Wait Meg, there's more. Dickey was always off somewhere gadding about with his latest flame. He didn't seem to care who Vicky slept with as long as he could do as he pleased." Keary hesitated when Meg looked like she might cry.

"Meg, don't get upset about this. It was a long time ago and you already know about his past. We're sorry this has come up and I know that's why he's bugged."

"I know but now I have a name for one of these women and she's calling him. What will I do if he wants to get back together with her?"

Keary laughed. "Meg, I don't think there's any chance of that happening."

"He wasn't with her when the accident happened anyway." Sean said.

"What do you mean, Sean?" Jill asked him.

"The Swedish bombshell showed up at the hospital too and asked if he was dead. I told her the same thing I told Vicky and she left." Sean replied.

"Oh, great! Now who the hell is *she*?" Meg asked, throwing her hands up.

"Sean, really! Meg doesn't need to know about all this stuff." Jill glared at him.

"I was just saying he wasn't exactly with Lady Vic at the time. I went to his hotel to get his stuff and it was obvious that a woman had been there with him. Anyway, she's a blond model that he would see occasionally, nothing serious. Dickey was in town during the Festival so I guess Blackie and Vicky were off again." Sean explained.

"You mean her husband was at the track and knew about her and Blackie?" Meg asked.

"He was probably there with some bimbo. Maybe she and Blackie had a fight but she still wanted him to ride the Gold Cup for her." Keary said.

"But what's going on now?" Meg said, close to tears.

"Not a fucking thing!" Blackie growled as he stalked back into the dining room and sat down next to Meg. "Meg, listen, there's nothing going on between Vicky and me and hasn't been for years. Not ever again either. It's old news and I'm not interested in seeing her. You have to believe me, Meg. It's you I'm in love with. Please trust me," he pleaded.

"I trust you. It's her I'm not so sure about." Meg pouted.

"That's my girl." Blackie said and kissed her.

*　　*　　*

The next day, Lady Victoria Rupert pulled into the driveway of Killarney Farms and stopped. She let her eyes sweep over the beautiful expanse of green pastures with awe. She had never been here before but had always wondered about it. Vicky was familiar with the O'Brien's operation in Ireland and visited there several times.

Not having seen Blackie for more than two years, guilt stabbed her heart. Now that she heard how well he was doing, it was time to face him. She knew she couldn't bear it if he'd been crippled or impaired in some way. Swallowing and taking a deep breath, she proceeded toward the house and barns.

She parked next to a new silver Porsche that she assumed was his. Fond memories of his old black one flooded her mind, making her smile. God, we had some fun in that car, she thought. I wonder if he's still that wild and crazy. She laughed to herself then her eyes welled up thinking of the terrible time he went through after the accident.

Oh, well, there's nothing to do for it now .Bugger it all!

Vicky got out, turned into the barn and knew it was vintage "Blackie". He always was so adamant about the cleanliness and order of the stables. No one was around, so she made her way up to the house taking a deep breath before she knocked on the side door.

After a few minutes, Jill opened the door and stared in surprise.

"Oh! Omigod! Uh ... Lady Victoria! Please come in." Jill stammered.

"Hi, Jill. I hope I'm not here at an inconvenient time." Vicky asked.

"No, of course, it's fine. Please come in. How are you? It's been a long time." Jill said, flushing.

"Thanks, Jill. I don't want to overstep any bounds, but I felt I had to see him, you see." Vicky said quickly by way of an explanation. "Please call me Vicky."

"Uh ... well okay. It has been a good while. I can't speak for him, but ... come in Vicky and we'll talk." Jill said, indicating the way to the dining room.

"Oh, dear. Maybe I shouldn't have come. I don't want to make him uncomfortable."

"I think he'll be fine. He and Sean are down at the racing barns. They should be up here soon for lunch. Come in. Keary's here and you can meet Meg, Blackie's fiancée."

"Oh, that's wonderful. I'm glad he's finally settling down." Vicky replied, her voice quavering.

"Yes, he's doing very well. Here's Keary. Keary, look who's come to visit." Jill said, looking at him with raised eyebrows.

Keary looked up from his lunch, choked and stared.

"Keary." Jill said more firmly.

Keary stood clumsily and muttered, "Lady Victoria, my goodness. What a surprise," he said, regaining his composure and moved forward to hug her.

"Keary, hello. Good to see you. Sorry for the unannounced visit. I've been up in Maryland looking at horses and thought I'd stop in. I called Sunday, but he wasn't home." Vicky said, a huge knot in her stomach as she looked at the young woman sitting at the table. The girl was delicately beautiful and didn't look happy to see her.

Uh-oh, Vicky thought. She already knows who I am and is going to be territorial. Hmm, just as I used to be about that scoundrel. Figures. Can't say that I blame her.

"Oh, Vicky. This is Meg Conners, Blackie's friend. Meg, this is Lady Victoria Rupert."

"Hello, it's nice to meet you." Vicky said.

"Hello." Meg said, quietly and sized up this woman from Blackie's past.

She's gorgeous. Of course she is, damn him. I can't believe I'm actually meeting one of them. I wonder how he felt about her. She certainly wasn't just casual sex. Keary said he had an affair with this woman. That sounds serious to me. Crap! She's got a title and everything. How can I compete with that? Dig the snooty accent too.

"Keary, maybe you should call down to the barn and tell him Vicky's here." Jill suggested with a look.

"He'll find out soon enough," Keary said, his mouth twitching to barely conceal a smile.

Jill rolled her eyes at him.

Vicky took a seat across from Meg.

"Vicky, would you care to join us for lunch. You must be hungry." Jill offered.

"Thanks but I couldn't really" Vicky said, looking sidelong at Meg who had a scowl on her face.

Great. This was a big, stupid mistake, she chastised herself. This is going to cause trouble for him with this girl but I need to tell him what happened.

Just then Sean and Blackie came stomping into the kitchen, laughing.

"Dude, that is a nasty joke," Sean said, chuckling.

"It is, yes, but don't repeat it." Blackie told him.

They washed up in the kitchen and Sean walked into the dining room and stopped.

"Mother of God!" he exclaimed and Blackie bumped into his back.

"Sean, what the hell …?" He stopped when he saw Vicky and just stared.

Sean moved sideways, glanced at Blackie and then back to Vicky.

"Uh … hey Vicky. What's up?" Sean said, stupidly and sat down.

Meg did not like the look that flashed between Blackie and this woman.

Is something still there?

Vicky was struck dumb. She had forgotten the very physical reaction she always had when she saw him. This was like a thunderbolt.

God, he looks amazing, she thought, when her mind started to work again. He looks even more incredible now and he's gained weight. Looks like all muscle.

She searched for something wonderful to say to him but came up with, "Hello, Blackie."

He just continued to look at her another minute and Vicky noticed the uneasy glance he gave Meg.

"Well, Vicky, what brings you all the way over here? England closed for the summer?" He blurted.

He just stood rooted to the spot and Vicky didn't know what to do at this point. He was starting to get that belligerent look that she remembered clearly.

"Blackie, you look wonderful. I heard you were riding again so I …

"I didn't look so hot two years ago," he said, scowling at her.

"Blackie," Keary said quietly.

"Leave him be, Keary." Jill warned.

"Blackie, I'm sorry it's been so long, but ...

"So what brings you around now? You never once called to see how I was, damnit." He said and Meg could see there was hurt in his eyes along with the anger. She was suddenly angry as well as jealous because this woman hurt him.

God, I'm just as ridiculously possessive as he is.

"I wanted to call but I was afraid." Vicky said, looking at her hands.

"Afraid of what?" He snapped.

"I was afraid you were crippled and I couldn't stand seeing you like that," she said, her eyes welling with tears.

"Christ! How do you think I felt thinking about it for more than a year? No one thought I'd ever walk again. It was a real bitch, Vicky, but I can't complain now. So why weren't you at the hospital?"

"I went to the hospital, damnit, but that blonde slut was there. You had to throw her in my face, didn't you?" Vicky yelled, getting loud.

"Oh, really. Well, good old Dickey was back in town for the Festival, wasn't he?" Blackie snarled.

"But you knew how things were. How could you bring her with you? You knew what you meant to me."

"I knew exactly what I was, revenge for Dickey's little escapades." He yelled.

"You knew how much I cared," she said, her bottom lip trembling.

Blackie shot a look at Meg and sighed. "Christ, Vicky, stop it. This is starting to sound like a lovers' quarrel and we're done. We were done a long time ago," he said, looking seriously at Meg.

"I know. I'm sorry. I didn't come here to bring up old stuff with you. Anyway, Dickey and I are back together and I'm pregnant," she said, smiling.

"Pregnant! Hey, that's great. Congratulations. Uh ... is Dickey behaving himself?"

"Yes. Actually everything is very good between us, thank you. We're very happy about the baby," Vicky said and smiled at Meg who smiled back.

Fantastic! Maybe I don't have to worry about her after all.

"Okay so why the hell did you come here?" Blackie asked.

"I need to tell you something about the accident."

"Like what?"

"I don't know if you realized it but Racketeer was dead when he fell."

Blackie looked at her, eyes wide. "Vicks, I wasn't aware of anything. Did you guys know the horse was down?" Blackie asked Sean and Keary.

"Tell you the truth; we were too concerned with you to notice the horse." Keary replied.

"God, Vicky, I'm sorry. If I could have done anything differently, I ...

"Blackie, it wasn't your fault. The horse was drugged."

"What? Are you sure? How do you know?"

"The stewards had him tested and he tested positive for amphetamines. His heart stopped over the last fence and it's a miracle that you weren't killed." Vicky said on the verge of tears. Blackie stared at her.

"Didn't they suspect you and me? How come I wasn't questioned? Why did you wait until now to tell me? Jesus, Vicky!" Blackie asked, pacing now.

"Blackie, they did a long and involved investigation. They couldn't question you since you were barely hanging on. They exonerated you because so many people came forward to testify that you would never fix a race. It took them longer to figure out it wasn't me either. My reputation wasn't as exemplary as yours."

"Why didn't you let Keary know? I was conscious after three weeks. You could have told me. I mean we have fantastic lawyers. We could have helped you."

"I know. I told you before I couldn't bear the thought of seeing you like that. That's no excuse, I realize that. There was too much guilt that it was my horse that almost killed you," she said.

"It wasn't the horse; it was who ever drugged him. Did they ever find any suspects?"

"No, they closed the investigation eventually, but I had my own suspicions," she said, her mouth an angry tight line.

"Who?" Keary asked.

Vicky looked at Keary then at Blackie.

"Lots of people told me they saw Mickey skulking around, acting strange."

Instantly furious, Blackie yelled, "Mickey! Mickey Reegan? I'll kill him if I find out that bastard did it. Do you have any proof?"

"Nothing concrete. It was rumored around that he won a fortune betting against you."

"Son of a bitch! That little rat has had it in for me since I fired him but I didn't think he'd stoop to this. Well, I take that back, I should have known he'd stoop that low. God, he tried to kill me!"

"Don't forget, Blackie, he planted Bobby to hurt you too, through Meg." Keary said.

Blackie stared at him. "Mickey's a dead man. That bastard"

"Why did you fire him?" Vicky asked.

"That's another story. One I'm too ashamed of to explain. Let's just say I caught him using me to make a lot of very dirty money." Blackie said, disgustedly.

"I'm sorry, Blackie. I saw Duncan in Lambourn and he told me how fantastic you were at the DC show and I needed to see for myself." Vicky said.

"I can never race again, but I've accepted that and found other things in my life that make me happy. Most importantly a woman that I love and who loves me," he said and smiled at Meg.

"That's wonderful. I'm so happy for you, really," she said and walked to Blackie.

"I'm happy for you too, Vicks and thanks for coming. Tell that bastard, Dickey, he had better be good to you or he'll answer to me." Blackie said and hugged her tight, kissing her on the forehead. She burst into tears and so did Jill and Meg.

"Here we go. All the women crying at the drop of a hat." Sean piped up.

"Shut up, Sean." Everyone yelled.

FORTY-TWO

It was the night of the Jockey Club dance to celebrate the end of the show season and they were dressed up for the occasion. The guys were in tuxes, the women in slinky cocktail dresses.

After dessert, the orchestra started playing and Blackie asked Meg to dance. The lights dimmed and the band played one romantic song after another. He held her close and his body felt good against hers. He kissed her neck, gazing dreamily into her eyes.

"Meg, I love you so much. I wanted to show you off tonight because I'm so happy and proud that we're together.

"I never expected things to be this perfect between us. I'm overwhelmed."

"Get used to it; things are just going to get better for us."

The music stopped and they joined the others to talk by the dance floor.

The guys left to get drinks and Katie said, "Ohmigod, this is wonderful. I'm having the best time. This is so cool to go some place fancy like this. Usually we're hanging at the barns in jeans. It was wonderful of Gracie to watch the kids for us again."

Jill said, "Yes, isn't she a dear and the children adore her. I think she spoils them with cookies, though. Oh, I'm used to these fancy events because I've been to them before but it's still fun to get dressed up and dance. Meg, you and Blackie look great together. He looks so happy."

"I know. Just seeing him this happy makes me even happier."

The men came back with drinks and they were standing around talking and laughing when someone grabbed Blackie by the arm and turned him around. Standing there was a gorgeous, buxom blonde maybe in her early forties and just dripping money. She wore an expensive looking gown that showed a lot of amazing cleavage.

The smile instantly disappeared from Blackie's face and he turned ashen.

"Blackie, darling, I haven't seen you in ages. You look fantastic."

All color drained from Blackie's face and he looked ready to pass out. She put her hand on his back, ran it down and patted his butt. He flinched. At first Keary looked puzzled, then he realized who she was and the look changed to fury.

"Blackie, sweetheart, it looks like you're back on the social scene. How wonderful. Introduce me to your friends."

Blackie looked at Keary with *help* written all over his face.

"Cat got your tongue, darling?"

Keary jumped in and said, "I'm Keary Connelly, Blackie's brother-in-law and this is my wife Jilleen, his sister." Sean introduced himself and Katie. Then Jill said, "And this is Meg Conners, Blackie's fiancée."

"I'm Dora Breslin, an old, dear friend of Blackie's," she said, giving Meg a withering look.

"Oh, yoo-hoo," Dora yelled, "Millie, look who's here."

"Fuck," Blackie said softly, and Keary grabbed him by the arm to steady him.

This skinny brunette turned and came trotting over. She was just as attractive, looked even richer and about the same age as Dora.

"Ohmigod, Blackie O'Brien, you dog. I thought you had disappeared off the earth." She put her arms around his neck and kissed him on the mouth. Meg made a move to scratch Millie's eyes out, but Keary grabbed her arm. Blackie grabbed the woman's arms from around his neck and pushed her away. He looked like he might either punch her or throw up on her.

"We should get together for old times' sake." Millie cooed.

Blackie said, "I have to get out of here," and grabbed Meg pulling her toward the door.

"Get your purse," he said as they went by their table. She retrieved it and her wrap as they headed for the parking lot. She had to run to keep up with him. They got in the Porsche and he peeled half the rubber off the tires leaving the lot. He was silent, driving fast and crazy all the way back to the farm. He screeched to a stop at the barn with the motor still running.

"Meg, I don't know what to say to you. You deserve someone better than me."

"Blackie, don't say that! Who were those women?"

"No. Don't say anything, just let me talk. I am so mortified that you saw them. I don't know how to deal with this. I had something special planned for tonight, but I'm not sure what to do now."

"Don't be hasty, let's just talk about it."

"No. I'm too stressed. I need time to think. I'm going to leave you off and go for a drive. Here's a key." He handed her a set of keys from his pocket as she got out.

"I love you, Meg," he said, as he turned the car around and spun gravel tearing down the driveway. He almost hit Keary coming in, but Keary swerved fast and avoided a sideswipe. Keary pulled up by Meg and they jumped out. By this time, she was sobbing.

"What did he say?" Keary asked.

"He said I deserved someone better than him; that he had something special planned and now he's not sure. He said he had to think and was going for a drive. What was he talking about?"

"I don't know," Keary said.

"I do," Jill said with a grim set to her mouth. "He was going to give you the ring tonight. I could kill those two stupid bitches."

"Oh no," Meg sobbed, "he was going to finally give me the ring. Now it's all ruined."

Jill hugged her. "Don't worry, Meg, he won't change his mind; he loves you too much. He's just distressed now. He'll work it out."

Keary and Sean said, "Wow, we didn't know he was going to ask her tonight."

"Who were those women?" Meg asked.

"I think those were a couple of those rich society broads that he said Mickey had set him up with. I can't believe that happened. Jesus Christ, he was getting his head straight about all this crap with Dr.Wahlman. Now this! What a couple of dumb bitches. Fuck!" Keary yelled and punched the barn wall.

He put his arm around Meg. "Don't worry, he's going to be all right and you two are going to be together. Hey, Jill did you see her go after Millie? I had to pull her back. Good girl."

"What did he say when he left?" Sean asked.

"He said he was leaving me here and going for a drive; that he had to think"

"Okay, let's go in and get settled, wait till he comes back and we can talk to him then," Keary suggested.

They went in the house, changed clothes and decided to watch a movie to get the incident off their minds. It was one o'clock when the movie was over and they decided to go to bed. Jill said she'd wake Meg, who stayed up at the house, when she heard Blackie return.

Meg startled awake the next morning, threw a robe on and ran downstairs. Keary, Sean, and Jill were having coffee and looked glum.

"Is he home?"

"No," Keary said, looking up at her. "We haven't seen him or heard anything."

"God, suppose he had an accident. He was driving wild on the way home." She started to cry; she felt so helpless.

Jill jumped up and put an arm around her.

"If he'd had an accident, we would have heard from the police. Come sit down and have some tea."

"I want to see him and tell him that none of that matters and how much I love him." Jill sat her down and brought tea.

They didn't hear anything all day. Sean and Keary went down to the barns and Jill, Katie and Meg just puttered around and watched TV. They couldn't concentrate enough to do much of anything. Everyone was quiet during dinner.

Meg finally said, "I can't stand just sitting here. I'm so afraid something happened."

"He'll come home soon." Keary said.

Just then, the phone rang and Sean snatched it up.

"Hello." He put his hand over the phone and said, "It's Mom."

"Shit," Keary said. "She's going to want to talk to Blackie. Put her on speaker."

"Hello, Maeve," Keary said.

"What in God's name is going on over there? Blackie's here and he's falling down drunk!"

"He's there?" Keary said, wiping his hands over his face.

"Yes. What happened? When he got here, he pounded on the door so hard we thought he'd break it down. Dad let him in and he was so drunk he could hardly walk. We got him to sit down and tried to get some coffee into him, but he grabbed the scotch and drank it. I thought you told me he wasn't drinking? What's going on over there?"

"Why didn't Dad stop him?"

"Have you ever tried to stop him when he's like this? You can get hurt. He has this huge diamond ring with him, was crying and saying something about Meg. I thought he asked her and she had the ring. What happened? Did she change her mind?"

"No. He didn't get a chance to give it to her last night. What happened then?"

"Then Ken tried to get him to talk but he went into a rage, yelling about 'fucking whores' and he destroyed half the dining room. Chairs, windows, it's a mess."

Where is he now?"

"He finally passed out in the den. Dad put him on the sofa and has three of the lads watching him, but if he gets violent again, I don't know if they can control him."

"Do you have any tranquilizers?"

"Keary, I'm afraid to give him anything. I don't know if he's just been drinking or if he took any drugs."

"Maeve, he hasn't been drinking for some time, so if he's consumed that much alcohol, you might want to call the paramedics."

"Oh, dear God! I'll do that right now. Please hurry and get here as soon as you can."

"We're on our way." Keary hung up and made some other calls.

"All right, the Lear just got back. They're going to change pilots and get it ready to go. Let's throw some clothes in a bag and be ready to leave in thirty minutes. We have to get to Dulles ASAP."

* * *

They finally settled in the plane and took off.

"Why don't you try and take a nap while we're flying; it's not going to be fun when we get there," Jill told Meg.

She tried to sleep but was too nervous and worried. Jill came over and offered her a mild sedative to settle her nerves, which worked because she woke up when they were landing in Dublin. They got in a rented SUV and took off with Keary driving. When they pulled into the driveway, they were shocked to see it empty.

They scrambled out of the car and Sean banged on the front door. Martha, red-eyed and sniffling, opened it and burst into tears when she saw Jill.

"Oh, m'lady, tis awful, just awful!" Martha exclaimed and fell into Jill's arms.

"Martha, what happened? Where is everyone?" Jill asked, her voice shaky.

"They took Master Blackie to hospital. He was bad off, m'lady," Martha said and started crying harder.

"For God's sake, what happened?" Keary shouted.

"Keary, don't yell at her, she's upset enough. Martha, dear, do you remember what hospital they took him to?

"Oh goodness, let me think, m'lady. It was all so upsetting … .I believe it was Bon Secours over in Tralee."

"Thanks you, Martha. Are you here by yourself? Are you fine, then?" Jill asked.

"Aye, m'lady, Eamon's coming up as soon as the horses are put right for the night. I'll fix us a bit of supper. It'll give me something to do. I'll pray for Master Blackie, m'lady, I will."

"Thank you, Martha. We'll let you know what's happening. I assume my parents went to the hospital as well?"

"They did, yes. Himself and Her Ladyship were dire upset, they were. Oh, poor, dear boy," Martha said, and started crying again.

"We'll be back later," Keary told Martha.

"Yes, Sir."

"Come on, Jill, let's get going." Keary said, pulling Jill to the car.

Sean and Katie were quiet through the whole scene with Martha. Keary looked in the rear view mirror as he sped off for Tralee.

"You okay, Sean?"

"No, how could I be, Keary? He must be bad if they had to take him to the hospital, "I can't …

Sean put his head in his hands and Katie put an arm around him.

"He's tough, Sean. Don't think the worst, damnit!" Keary said, driving as fast as the small roads allowed.

When they got near Tralee, Keary got confused. "Where the hell is the damn hospital? Shit!"

"Keary, calm down. Take the next left and after a few squares, turn right." Jill said.

They squealed into the hospital lot, parked and hurried to the ER.

"We're here for Blackie O'Brien. Can you tell us where he is, please?" Jill asked the nun at the desk.

"He's in Intensive Care. Are you a relation, then?"

"I'm his sister. Which way is it?"

"Go up to the next floor and to the end of the hall. Only one family member for five minutes at a time. I believe his parents are with him now."

"Thank you, Sister," Jill said and they headed for the elevator.

When they got to the ICU, Kennet was sitting in the small waiting room, looking into a coffee cup.

"Dad," Jill exclaimed. He looked up then rose and hugged her.

"Dear Lord, I'm glad you're all here." Ken said, eyes red and puffy.

"Is he all right? What happened?"

"Christ, Jill, you don't want to know. He's so sick. They've got him hooked up to IVs and machines doing God knows what. Your mother's been in there for a bit. We're taking turns. I can't believe this happened. I thought he was doing so well," Ken said and choked up.

"Take it easy, Dad. He's going to be fine," Keary said putting his arm around his father-in-law.

Meg dropped into a chair and started to cry. Katie sat next to her and took her hand.

"Meg, he's here where he's safe. They're going to do their best to get him well. He'll be fine, sweetie." Meg just nodded, tears running down her face.

"Dear girl, take heart. He's very strong. They'll have him right in no time." Ken slumped into a chair.

"Christ Jesus, I feel so helpless. I don't know what to do," Ken said, tears in his eyes.

Maeve came through the door to the ICU and sagged when she saw them.

"Thanks to God, you're here. I can't handle this," she said as Keary helped her to a seat.

"What's happening, Mom?" Sean asked.

"The doctor said he'd be out shortly to talk to us," Maeve said as she turned on her husband.

"You see what your *wild warrior spirit* has done. It's going to wind up killing my son," she yelled at her husband.

"He's my son too and that wild spirit might just pull him through, woman. I'll not hear another word!" Ken snarled and stomped out of the room.

"Oh, dear, we're both so stressed."

"We know, Mom," Jill said and sat down to console her mother.

A tall man in scrubs came through the ICU door.

"Are you the O'Brien family?"

"We are, yes. How is he?" Keary asked.

"I'm Dr. Malone, Mr. O'Brien's vitals are slightly better than when he came in but not much. He's seriously dehydrated and his heart rate is very high because his heart is trying to get the alcohol out of his system. We're giving him fluids, IV, with some medications in it to keep him from metabolizing the alcohol. We got the tox report back and luckily the only thing in his system is alcohol, no drugs. I have to tell you that the alcohol in him is at the lethal level, so he's not out of the woods yet. We're doing everything we can to help him."

"Thank you Dr. Malone," Ken said.

"Another couple of hours and we'll see. I'll keep you informed."

"Meg, would you like to go in and see him. I'll go with you," Keary asked.

Meg nodded and got up.

"Keary, only one of us at a time," Sean said.

"I don't give a shit. She needs someone with her."

"You're right. We'll wait out here."

"Meg, come on, honey, let's go see him," Keary said, gently and they walked into the patient area.

When she saw him, she almost fainted. He was so pale and sick looking. All the machines he was hooked to were blinking and beeping.

"Holy Mother!" Keary said.

Meg walked up beside the bed. She bent and kissed his forehead.

"Blackie, I love you. Please get well," she said, tears falling from her eyes. She was terrified that he wouldn't make it. "Keary, what if he doesn't ... she murmured through sobs.

"Don't even think that. He's tough. He's been through worse than this. He's a fighter. I know he's fighting this and I've never seen him give up. Just pray and don't give up hope."

"I won't be able to live if something happens to him," she whispered.

*　　*　　*

The waiting room was quiet and gloomy. No one was saying much. Kennet returned. He and Maeve were locked in a stony silence. Keary came back in alone.

"Is Meg with him," Jill asked.

"Yes, I thought she needed some time alone with him. She's beside herself, poor girl."

"Keary, does all this have anything to do with that bastard, Mickey Reegan?" Maeve asked him.

Keary hesitated and then said, "Well, indirectly. Why do you ask?"

"We heard through some horse people about some of the nasty things that Mickey got Blackie into, the drugs and other problems," Kennet said.

"Ken saw Mickey in a pub in Dublin and beat the daylights out of him. I think he's behind all of the unhappiness that Blackie's been through," Maeve said.

"You're right. I'd like a crack at Mickey myself," Keary said. "Meg knows about it all and Blackie's been seeing a shrink for the last few months and doing better. Friday we went to a Jockey Club dinner dance and two society bimbos that were in Blackie's past, thanks to Mickey, pounced on him and made asses of themselves. He was horrified and couldn't take it. He took Meg back to the farm and then took off. We didn't even know where he was."

"Oh, my God." I'll kill that Mickey myself."

Meg walked into the waiting room, sobbing. Jill hugged her and settled her in a seat and handed her a cup of tea.

"I want to see him. Katie's going in with me," Sean said with a grim set to his mouth.

"Okay, call us if he comes around," Ken said.

Sean and Katie walked through the doors hand in hand to Blackie's room.

"Oh, God!" Sean gasped and Katie hugged him.

"He's going to be okay, honey. Don't worry."

Blackie groaned and started thrashing around a bit. A nurse came in and injected something in his IV and he quieted down.

"Come on, buddy. You can do this, I know you can. You're tough. Remember when we were kids? You were fearless. You always jumped off the cliff into the water first, man. Come on and fight …

Blackie's eyes fluttered open but looked unfocused.

"Blackie, can you hear me? It's Sean, buddy."

"Meg … he said just above a whisper.

"She's hear, man. I'll get her." Sean said and rushed out to get her.

"Hey, he's awake. He said Meg's name. Come on all of you," Sean motioned for them to follow him. They surrounded the bed with hopeful faces.

"Blackie, honey, can you hear me?" Meg murmured to him. Blackie's eyes opened but he just moaned and closed them again. His heart rate monitor was still beeping fast.

"Blackie, come on, wake up. We're here for you, buddy," Keary said.

Blackie's eyes fluttered open again.

"Keary … what happened? Where am I?"

'You're in the hospital. We're all here, buddy."

Blackie closed his eyes and seemed agitated. The nurse came in again and checked a couple of the machines.

"Would you all mind going out for a bit? He needs to rest. I'll ask Dr. Malone to come and talk to you."

"Okay, thank you, Sister," Maeve said, not too happy with that order. They waited for awhile and finally the doctor came in to see them.

"Well, he is doing better. It's going to take some time to get all the alcohol out of him but the medications are working. I'm going to keep him here for at least another day. You folks might want to go home and get some rest. He's going to be out for a time. We'll call you when he's fully awake and coherent.

'Thank you, Dr. Malone," Kennet said.

"I don't want to leave. I want to stay here with him," Meg said with a stubborn set to her chin.

"Meg, dear, he's going to be asleep most of the time. I don't like leaving either but since he's no longer in any danger, we should go home, get something to eat and rest."

"Okay, I guess," Meg said, with little enthusiasm. "Can I go in and say goodbye before we leave?"

"Yes, we'll wait for you in the car," Jill said.

Meg walked back to his room and stood there and looked at him.

God, I love him so much and I thought we were going to have a happy future together.

Have children. Jesus, what a mess. I can't deal with this. What if we have a family and he kills himself like this? I can't even think about that, it's too hard. He was doing so well coming to grips with his past. I have to think long and hard about our relationship.

Meg stood next to the bed and took his hand. His was sweaty and he didn't respond to her touch. She leaned in and kissed him gently on the mouth.

"I love you, Blackie. I love you more than anything, more than my own life," she whispered to him but he didn't move. She turned sadly, and walked out to the parking lot.

*   *   *

Back at the O'Brien's house, everyone was trying to relax in the den with drinks or coffee.

"Meg, he's too sick right now to be with you. I know you're devastated," Jill said.

"I think I want to go home but I want to make sure he knows that I'm not leaving him. I just need some space and time to think. Keary will you tell him that and tell him I love him," she said.

"Yes, Meg, I'll make sure he knows. Don't worry about him. He's going to be good. I'll call and tell you what's happening. " Keary said, gently, "As soon as we get home, he's going to the hospital. In fact, he's going right from the airport. I've already arranged it with Dr. Wahlman. Try not to worry. I think you should stay at the farm with us so you're not alone."

"I feel like I'm abandoning him." She started to cry again.

"Meg, he has to do this by himself. You can't get it out of his head for him," Jill said.

"Okay. Are you staying here?" Meg asked her.

"No, I'm coming with you. The guys will take care of Blackie. They'll let us know how things are. I don't want you to be there by yourself. We can leave for the airport when you're ready," she said.

Meg nodded. She hated to leave but she couldn't stand being there any longer.

*   *   *

The next day Keary went to the hospital to bring Blackie back to his parents' house.

He was still groggy and in and out of hangover induced sleep. Dr. Malone told Keary that Blackie was able to go home but should be watched for signs of seizures or black-outs. Keary was in the room waiting for the release papers as Blackie was not very successfully trying to get dressed.

"Was I in an accident? What happened?" he started to get up and couldn't.

"Blackie, listen. You got drunk and flew over here and your Mom called the paramedics," Keary told him.

"What the hell? We're in Ireland? I feel like shit. Why'd Mom call the EMTs?"

"Blackie, don't get upset but you were so drunk, you were out of control and then you passed out at the house."

"Fuck," he said putting his hands over his face, "why, what happened?"

"Uh ... well, the Jockey Club dance and ..."

Blackie looked at Keary and frowned then suddenly remembered.

"Oh God, oh fuck. I can't believe that happened. No, no, I can't take it." He tried to get up, staggered and sat quickly back on the bed.

"Blackie, calm down, it's okay. Come on, you have to get control." Keary said.

"Keary, Meg saw those idiot women, she knows what happened with them. I can't face her. I want to die," Blackie said.

"Well you almost did and they're not worth your life. What would Meg do then if you killed yourself, you idiot?" Keary told him.

"What are you talking about?" Blackie said. Keary got and in Blackie's face.

"You asshole, your alcohol level was up in the lethal range. If your Mom hadn't called them, you'd be dead. What a wonderful way to go out. You have to face this shit like a man," Keary said. "Hey, dumb ass, I had to hold that little girl back. She was going to take Millie out."

"Shit! I'm so ashamed Meg saw them."

"Oh, quit feeling sorry for yourself. Those women embarrassed themselves, not you. They're the assholes. You have to quit doing this. We can't lose you."

"I need to get up," he said.

Keary came over and helped him to his feet. He wobbled. Keary grabbed him and sat him on a chair. He looked spacey, like he might pass out any second.

"Here, put your head between your knees," Keary said as he took his head and bent him over. "Is that better?" Blackie nodded and sat up.

"Come on, kid, let's go home."

*   *   *   *

Blackie slept for two more days. The third morning everyone was in the kitchen at breakfast when Blackie came in and sat down. He had showered and shaved but looked very shaky.

"Good morning," he said quietly.

"Good morning," they all responded.

"How are you, sweetheart?" Maeve asked.

"I don't know yet, Mom," he said.

"You want some coffee?" Keary asked.

"Yes."

Keary got him coffee and put the cup in front of him. He tried to pick it up but his hand was shaking so that he spilled some.

"Sorry," he said and put it on the table, bent down and sipped out of it. Keary patted him on the shoulder. Blackie just sat there sipping the coffee without saying anything. He just frowned into the coffee cup.

Finally, he said, "I want to tell everyone how sorry I am about this." No one said anything at first and then Ken spoke up,

"Son, we're sorry that so much unhappiness has come into your life. We pray to God that things will change for the better."

Blackie nodded and said, "Thanks, Dad, I hope so too." Blackie was quiet for a long time and then said quietly to Keary, "Where's Meg?"

"She went home with Jill."

Blackie flinched as if Keary hit him.

"Yeah, I guess so."

"Blackie, she wanted me to tell you that she's not leaving you, she just needed to think. She said she loves you," Keary told him. Blackie just nodded, looking into his coffee.

"I guess I'm going back into rehab, huh?" he said.

"Yes, I've already made arrangements. Dr. Wahlman wants you in his hospital, so he can take over your treatment. We're going right from the airport," Keary said.

Blackie nodded. He looked around and noticed the mess in the dining room.

"What happened in the dining room?"

No one said anything. He frowned and said again, "What happened in the dining room?"

Finally, Ken said, "You happened."

"What?" Blackie went in and looked at the mess. He stood there with his hands in his pockets, wide-eyed. Maeve came up and stood next to him.

"Mom, I can't believe I did this. I'm so sorry."

"It took a lot of anger to do this. You have to get rid of that anger or it will kill you," she said.

"All your priceless antiques," he said shaking his head.

"Blackie, you and our family are the only things in my life that are priceless."

He looked at her and hugged her tight. They both went back and sat down.

"Keary, I hate to ask you but can you get a crew to come in here and clean that up and fix whatever can be fixed? I'll pay for it."

"Sure. Are you about ready to get going?"

"We have to leave now? How long am I going to be in there?"

"Yes, we're meeting Dr. Wahlman at the airport and you'll be in there as long as it takes, buddy," Keary said putting his arm around Blackie.

"It's going to be hard being away from Meg but I guess I need to get used to it."

"Hey, stop it. She's not leaving you. Just concentrate on getting well. You can't do this anymore. This time was too close," Keary said.

"I know. I'm scared, Keary. What if I can't do it? I thought I had it under control. Oh, where's the ring?" he asked.

"Maeve put it in the safe. You want me to take it with us and put it in the safe at home?" Keary said.

"Yes, please. Okay, let's do this."

Blackie hugged his parents, then he, Sean and Keary left for the airport.

FORTY-THREE

Blackie was already in the hospital for a month. Keary said he was doing okay but not great. Meg missed him so bad she could barely stand it, so she threw herself into work and riding. She worked hard at keeping busy but it didn't help much. If she was able to talk to him or visit, it might have been better but that was against the rules. At first, she stayed up at the house with Jill and Keary, but soon moved into his apartment. Somehow, she felt closer. It smelled like him and his clothes were there.

One afternoon, after finishing her riding, she walked up to the house to visit with Jill. They were so close now. It helped listening to Jill talk about Blackie and their childhood.

"Meg, what a welcome visit. I was just thinking about you. Have a seat and I'll get you tea," Jill said with a smile.

"Hi, yourself," Meg said as she sat down and took the tea from Jill. "I hope I'm not bugging you too much, always hanging around."

"Of course not, it actually helps me a lot because I miss Blackie so much."

"I was just thinking the same thing about you," Meg laughed. "Any news?"

"Yes, actually, we can go visit. Keary and Sean are there now and we can go tomorrow if you want," she said.

"Oh, tomorrow, wow, that would be great. Does he want visitors?"

"Let's wait and see what Keary and Sean have to say."

They talked and she helped Jill put out the dinner buffet. In a few minutes, Keary and Sean walked in. Keary kissed Jill and said hello to Meg. They got food and sat down.

"How's Blackie?" Jill asked.

Keary sighed big. "I think he's doing well. Dr. Wahlman wasn't there so we didn't get to talk to him. Blackie's lost weight, so you'll be shocked when you see him. He seems nervous. He wouldn't sit with us at first; just paced. Finally, he started to relax and sat down. He said to tell Jill hello and then asked if you were still around, Meg. I told him you were here but I don't think he believed it. He thought his treatment was going well, but didn't want to talk about it. He seemed sad and easily spooked."

"What do you mean spooked?" Meg asked.

"When you're talking to him, he looks like he's going to jump up and leave any minute. He did get up a couple times. I don't know if they're giving him meds, but he looks like it. Are you guys going tomorrow?" Keary asked.

"You sure he'll want to see us?" Meg asked suddenly apprehensive about seeing him.

"He might act nervous but I'm sure he'll love seeing you," Keary said.

*   *   *

Jill and Meg got to the hospital around ten in the morning. They sat in the visitor's area at a small table. Meg kept fidgeting, so Jill took her hand and held it.

"Don't worry, honey, it'll be okay. He's still the same person you fell in love with.

Just then, Blackie walked into the room. Meg gasped because he looked bad. He had lost weight and his face was gaunt. He had on a pajama top, jeans and socks. When he saw them, he stopped and jammed his hands into his jeans. He turned around a couple times, as if he might leave, then stood and stared at them again.

Jill and Meg both smiled and waved. He gave a half-hearted little wave and finally walked over and sat down.

"Hi," he said quietly.

"Hi, honey." Jill said.

"Hi, Blackie, it's good to see you. I've missed you," Meg said trying to keep her voice from shaking.

"Me, too," he said quietly, not looking at her.

To keep the conversation going, the women chattered away about the horses and the farm. He didn't say anything. He seemed to relax and put his hands on the table. Meg wanted to touch him so bad, she reached over quickly and put her hands over his but he pulled away and stuffed them back in his pockets.

Damn, why did I do that, she thought, it was too soon.

Anyway, in a minute he put his hands back on the table and moved them a little closer. Slowly she moved a hand over and put it on his. He didn't move them this time. Gently he put one hand on hers and traced it with his fingertips. It was all she could do to keep from crying. Jill had tears in her eyes. They sat there for a long time holding hands.

"I love you, Blackie," she said quietly.

"I love you too," he said barely above a whisper, then got up suddenly and walked out. Jill and Meg burst into tears.

*   *   *

Nine weeks later, Keary and Sean were visiting Blackie again. They were sitting there when he walked in now looking wonderful. He shook hands with a big smile.

"Hey, man, you look great." Sean told him. "How's it going?"

"Good, I'm happy with how I'm feeling. Dr. Wahlman said I can go home in a couple weeks."

"Great, that's fantastic. The girls are going to be so happy," Keary told him.

"Uh ... what's Meg doing?" Blackie asked tentatively.

"Hey, man, the woman's moved into your apartment. She's got girlie crap everywhere," Sean laughed.

"She did?" Blackie said, wide-eyed.

"I hope you don't mind," Keary said.

"No, that's great, I love it," Blackie said smiling. "What made her do that?"

"At first she was staying in the house and then she started staying in your apartment. Then last week she sold her condo, furniture and just moved her clothes and stuff in." Keary told him.

"That's great. I can't wait to get home and start back working with the horses. I need to patch things up with Meg. She must still have a lot of doubts about me and how stable I am."

"Well, we're all a little worried about that. If something upsets you, can you handle it now?" Keary asked him.

"I feel confident that I can. Dr. Wahlman, at some point will talk to all of you and he wants to see Meg and I together weekly to help me stay on track," Blackie said.

*   *   *

Meg, Jill and Katie were so excited when they heard he was coming home, they jumped up, screamed and hugged each other.

"Oh God, I hope he's not upset that I moved in. I should have asked him first. I mean it is his place."

"He was happy to hear that you did it. Wait till you see him, he looks fabulous and seems confident and self-assured," Keary told them. "Sean and I will get him next week. He says he feels great."

The day Keary and Sean brought Blackie home, the girls were so nervous they couldn't sit still. They got up early, cleaned his apartment from top to bottom and then started in on the house. In the middle of the afternoon, they stopped, showered and changed. Meg wanted to look good the first time he saw her.

They were in the kitchen when Keary's SUV pulled up. They quickly got drinks and sat down in the dining room.

When Blackie walked in, he took her breath away. He looked wonderful. He smiled big, kissed and hugged Jill, Katie and then walked over to Meg. He stood in front of her just staring, then smiled really big and said, "Hi, Meg," and folded her in his arms and held tight. She just melted into him – he felt like home.

"I love you, Meg. I missed you so much." He said and kissed her like she loved to be kissed.

"I can't believe you're home," she said and kissed him back. He picked her up and twirled her around.

"Hey guys, I want to visit with all of you so much but right now, I need to spend a few days alone with Meg. I have a lot of things to talk over with her and things to decide about our future, if she still wants one with me."

"Honey, of course ..." she started to protest.

"Wait until you hear what I have to say," he said. "I had Jeremy stock food in, so you guys won't see us for a bit."

As they started to leave Blackie turned and said, "I can't thank you all enough for always being there for me."

Then taking Meg's hand, the two of them walked down to the barn, their arms around each other. As soon as they walked into the apartment, Blackie stopped, looked around and smiled.

"Hey, I like what you've done with the place,"

"Is it okay that I moved in? I'm sorry I didn't even ask you."

"Of course, it's fine. This place is as much yours as it is mine. I kind of like it better with your things around. It needed a woman's touch. I'm glad you sold that condo. He reached out and pulled her into his arms with a serious expression on his face.

"I love you, Meg, but the first thing you have to decide is if you still want to take a chance and be with me. I know none of this has been easy for you and I'm sure you have a lot of doubts about me. I can't give you any guarantees, but I will pledge that I'm going work on my issues with a minimum of drama. Dr.Wahlman is still going to work with me and with both of us. I know I scared you to death and I'll never do that again. I have too much to lose. I just know I want to spend the rest of my life with you, if you'll still have me?"

"Blackie, I've had time to do a lot of thinking. I was terrified that you were going to die and I didn't know if I could live with that possibility always in the back of my mind. I'm still a little unsure of how you will handle another incident like the one at the dance. I believe in you and I believe you will do great things if you give yourself the chance. I'm willing to stick by you and help you accept your past and move forward. The things that I'm totally sure of are my love for you and the knowledge that I can't live without you."

"You don't know how happy you just made me. I can't believe you're willing to take a chance on me. Thank you, sweetheart. Will you still marry me?"

"I can't wait to be your wife!"

"God, I love you." He said and kissed her long and deep. They made love with such passion and urgency, the emotion overwhelmed her. They spent the next three days getting to know each other again. They talked for hours on end and made love until they could hardly move. They talked about their future together, the demons of his past, the things they each wanted to accomplish in life, starting a family. They laughed, played like kids, cooked when they were hungry and watched old romantic movies. Meg knew she would always cherish that time they spent alone, just happy to be together.

FORTY-FOUR

It was now four days since Blackie had come home from the hospital. Meg loved being alone with him but actually she was getting a little stir crazy, cooped up in the apartment all the time. She woke and knew she was still up against him from the night before. She turned over slowly and looked at him. God, he was beautiful! She never got tired of looking at him. She turned a little more, cuddling into his arms. He stirred, curling an arm tighter around her.

"Mmm, good morning, gorgeous," he mumbled.

"Good morning yourself. Did you sleep well?"

"I always sleep perfectly when you've made love to me the night before," he said, stretching and pulling her on top of him. He kissed her hungrily and moved his hands down to caress her butt.

"Mmm, you want me for breakfast?" he asked, kissing her again, harder.

"Sounds yummy, sweetie, but maybe we should show our faces up at the house this morning for a change," she said, kissing him back.

"I actually think we'd have more fun here," he said, rolling on top of her and kissing her neck. If he kept that up, they wouldn't be going anywhere, she thought.

"Honey, you've been in the hospital for three months, they're excited to see you and find out how you are."

He rolled over onto his back and sighed. "You're right. I want to see them too. I missed them a lot. I just like having you all to myself for a change," he said growling and tickling her neck with his beard stubble.

"Stop, brat! Come on and get in the shower, it's getting late."

"We could save time if we showered together," he said, kissing her breast.

"Cute! Yeah, right. I have a feeling it would turn into a very long shower."

"Where's your sense of adventure," he said laughing and moved off the bed toward the shower room. She watched him go, enjoying the view of his naked, gorgeous butt. On second thought, maybe breakfast could wait. No, she knew he had to get back on some kind of healthy schedule.

She rolled out of bed and got clean clothes, waiting her turn. When he came strolling out of the bathroom wearing just a towel and a smile, she ran past him quickly, to resist looking.

He laughed when he popped her on the butt with the towel he'd been wearing.

After they dressed, they left the apartment, walking hand in hand up to the house. It was a gorgeous day! A light breeze and the sun shining. She suddenly felt a little sad, leaving the apartment after such a special time together. He looked at her and then pulled her to him.

"I know. I feel it too. I'll never forget the last three days. I can't tell you how much it has meant to me to be alone with you, listening to me spill my guts and telling you my hopes and dreams. I've never told anyone before. I love you so much," he said, kissing her tenderly. She couldn't tell him she felt the same because of the lump in her throat. A couple tears escaped, trickling down her cheeks and he brushed them away with his thumbs.

"Come on, let's get breakfast, I'm starved."

Jill was standing at the dining room window, drinking her tea and enjoying the beautiful day.

"Wow, the love birds have finally left their nest and are headed this way." Keary stood behind her and looked.

"I thought we'd never see them again. Shit, he looks rough. He's lost even more weight. I thought they had Jeremy stock the place," he said.

"He did and they have plenty of food. I just think Blackie's been expending a lot of physical energy, if you know what I mean," she told him with raised eyebrows.

"Good Lord. I should have known"

"Well, what did you expect? They haven't seen each other for months, Keary. Cut him some slack and don't tease him, please," Jill said, firmly.

"Aw, come on Jill. It's always so much fun to tease him," Sean said, laughing.

"Right, dummy, that's why he's broken your nose four or five times," Katie said, sarcastically.

"Oh, yeah, I forgot about that," Sean said. "Hey, who wants to bet he knocked her up since he's been home?"

"Oh, for God's sake, Sean!" Jill said.

"I'll take that bet," Keary said, smiling.

"You two are awful," Katie said, disgustedly. Sean and Keary just laughed.

"Okay, let's go jump him when he comes in," Keary said, getting up.

Blackie and Meg walked into the kitchen, everyone smothered him with hugs.

"God, I missed you guys. It's so good to see you all."

"Let's go sit down and hear all about it. You two must be hungry too," Jill said.

"Yes, I'm starving." Blackie said.

"Me, too."

They went into the dining room, Blackie and Meg stopped at the buffet to get breakfast and coffee. They sat down at the table with the others, Blackie digging right into his food. She watched him eating. He was almost gaunt; he had lost so much weight. He looked tired, too. She hadn't noticed how bad he looked since the light was always dim in the apartment.

"Do you feel okay, honey?"

"I do, why?" he said looking at her.

"You just look tired and I didn't realize how much weight you've lost."

"I didn't think I looked that bad. I didn't feel much like eating for the first couple weeks I was in the hospital."

"Aw, honey, why didn't you eat?" Jill asked.

Blackie sighed and looked at her. "Jill, I was so agitated when I went in. The thought of being away from you guys and Meg made me crazy. You know being away from home was torture; I couldn't deal with it. It's funny all the years I was alone, racing, I thought I was having a good time. I couldn't do that now if I wanted to."

"Oh, honey, we're so sorry you had to go through that," Jill said, crying.

"Jill, stop crying. I feel so good now. I'm strong, emotionally. I can actually feel the difference. So let's not mourn the past. I want to move forward with my life and celebrate the future. That's what Meg and I have been doing the past three days. We've been talking about the future." Blackie said.

"I have a lot of stuff to get off my chest and new ideas to discuss with all of you. Let me know when it's a good time; it's going to take awhile."

"No time like the present. I didn't really have anything planned for today. How about you, Sean?" Keary said.

"I was going to watch Casey work some of the chasers before next week's races, but Ned can do it. This is more important," Sean said.

"Thanks, guys. I don't know quite where to start. I guess the most important topic is Meg and I. After all the shit I've put her through, I can't believe she still wants to marry me. So I've talked to Mom and Dad and the wedding is going to be April 15th at Dromoland Castle. Mom's taking care of the food and you girls need to work on the dresses, tuxes and whatever. I'll take care of the accommodations." Blackie said, beaming.

"That's wonderful, congratulations, you two," Jill said.

Sean punching Blackie on the arm. "Way to go, dummy, you're finally getting this gig moving."

"I know. It's about time, isn't it? What a dumbass, I've been," Blackie said shaking his head.

"Stop it, it's okay. A lot has been going on to distract you," Meg said.

"The next thing is the farm. I want to change ownership and change things with the racing stable too."

"What are you talking about?" Keary asked, frowning.

"I want to change the ownership from me and divide it up equally amongst all of us and ...

"No, that's ridiculous! Mom and Dad gave the farm to you." Keary protested.

"Let me finish, Keary! It's not ridiculous. You all have worked harder than I have to take care of this farm and me. You deserve to share in it."

"Come on, Blackie, we never thought you'd throw us out on the street or anything, but the farm is yours."

"Not anymore. I don't want it all. Shit, just listen to me. I've already talked to the lawyers and they're drawing up the papers. The three of us kids and our spouses will share the farm in thirds. Jill and Keary, Sean and Katie and Meg and I will each have a third ownership. If one person in a couple dies, their third automatically belongs to the surviving spouse. There is one main stipulation. If any spouse of us three children divorces us, they forfeit their share of the farm." Blackie said, seriously.

"What in God's name are you thinking?" Jill gasped.

"I'm just protecting the blood ownership. I'm not making any insinuations about anyone.

Listen there's more. The racing stable is already incorporated and I'm taking my name off it completely."

"What the hell! You're riding put the stable on the map. You should have it more than anyone," Sean exclaimed.

"It's mine, so I can do what I want with it, damnit! Would you guys stop arguing with me and listen?" Blackie said, getting frustrated with them.

"Okay, shut up you two and let him talk," Jill scolded.

"Thank you. I have my own business now. I want to incorporate it and put mine and Meg's name is on it. I think it will be easier for tax purposes if things are separate. The racing stable will just have Keary and Jill and Sean and Katie as owners. I'm also changing my will. Since I'm taking care of the property issues, what's left are my personal assets which will be divided with cash settlements to you guys with the remainder going to Meg and any children we have. I don't think I need to leave any money to Mom and Dad, do you?"

Everyone was quiet for a few minutes, looking at the floor.

"What's wrong guys?" Blackie asked.

"We don't want to think about something happening to you. We don't want any of your money either," Keary said, looking sad.

"Oh, come on. I don't want to think about anything happening to me either. However, I'm stronger now and I need to be responsible for people I love. I want to know that all this business stuff is taken care of. It makes sense to do it ahead of time. I know you guys don't need any money; this is just something I want to do because I love you."

"Whatever you want to do, we'll go along with it." Jill said

"Okay, new subject. I want us to spend Christmas in Ireland. All of us, including Casey, Jeremy and Ned. I know Mom and Dad would love to see the kids for the holidays. What do you say? We can manage the stable with us gone can't we? Jamie and Curt can take care of our horses and I'll just close down the school until I'm back. Come on, what do you think? Give me some input here." Blackie asked, hopefully.

"I can ask some of the neighbors if they have any extra people that could come over and feed, maybe turn them out in the morning. Could Jamie and Curt keep an eye on the whole place?" Sean asked.

"What about Jessie and Billie? They drive over from Middleburg sometimes to help when we have a lot going on." Keary added.

"Then you think we can manage being away for a week and a half, say, at the most?" Blackie asked them. Sean and Keary looked at each other for a few minutes, thinking and then nodded.

"Yes, I think we can do it," Sean said.

"Great! Let's get on it, making arrangements with people. I'll make flight plans. You girls happy with doing this?" Blackie asked them.

"Yes, that sounds fantastic. What a wonderful idea. I can't wait. I loved it the last time we went," Katie said, happily.

"Meg and Katie, you have not had Christmas until you've had it in Ireland. Mom goes nuts with the food, decorations, music. It's incredible," Blackie said, his eyes shining with excitement.

"Okay, buddy, I'll go on one condition," Sean said.

"Oh Jesus, what?"

"You have to promise that you'll sing with me for Mom and Dad," Sean said, smiling.

"Are you kidding me? You're serious?"

"Of course, I'm serious. They'll love it. They haven't heard us sing since we were kids.

Come on, it'll be fun," Sean pleaded.

"But let's practice before we go because I sound like shit," Blackie said.

"No you don't! You both sound great. Come on, they'll love it and so will everyone else," Jill coaxed.

"You girls can organize Christmas in Ireland. Oh, I want to take Meg to New York to shop before we go. New York is neat at Christmas. Does anyone else want to go with us?"

"Yes!" Everyone yelled at once.

"I guess that's one of my better ideas. So, let's see. Next Thursday is Thanksgiving. Do you want to go the week after that? Does that make sense? I don't want to wait until too close to when we're leaving for Ireland."

"I think the week after Thanksgiving sounds about right. What do you think, Katie?" Jill asked.

"That will be perfect. That way we'll have time to wrap the gifts and get everything ready for the trip," Katie said.

"We can take the Lear up and I'll rent a car or maybe hire a limo so we won't have to bother with parking. Hey, what's happening for Thanksgiving, Jill?" Blackie asked.

"We're having a big feast here for us and the whole crew. Gracie is making preparations and Meg, Katie and I are helping. We have a lot to be thankful for this year," Jill ended on a solemn note. Blackie looked at her and looked sad too.

"Okay, you guys. Enough of this maudlin shit. I'm ready to party. I have so much to be happy about; I refuse to think about the past and the dumb crap I did to everyone. So let's move on to the next subject- houses!"

"What are you talking about now?" Sean said, playfully punching him on the arm.

"Well, as soon as Meg and I start having kids, we want to build a house up on the ridge.

The view up there is spectacular. The apartment is going to get too small fast even with one baby. Sean, you know you and Katie should build one next to us. Your cottage has to be getting too small now with Patrick."

"Oh, Seanie, could we?" Katie said, pulling on his arm.

"Yes, I don't see why not. That would be cool. I hadn't really thought about it. You

"Yes, that's what would be neat about it. It would be like a family compound. Our houses won't be far from this house. What do you and Keary think?" Blackie asked Jill.

"We'd miss seeing you guys all the time for meals," Jill said.

"Are you kidding? We won't get rid of them that easy. The way these two eat, they'll still be underfoot all the time." Keary said.

"Ah ... another thing about houses is that Meg and I will need to rent or buy a house in Ireland soon, maybe."

"Why on earth would you need to do that? Can't you just stay at Mom and Dad's?" Keary asked.

"We can, yes, temporarily, but the thing is, I'm going to run for the seat in the Dáil that Dad has been bugging me about. Their house is not in the same district, so I can't use their address for long. Of course it may not matter because I probably won't win," Blackie said, gently and this statement met with stunned silence.

"No comments from anyone?" he asked.

"We're just blown away, buddy. That's the last thing we thought you'd ever consider doing? We thought you hated politics. What happened?" Keary asked, looking confused.

"I've been talking to Dad for quite some time about this. Over this last year, on and off we've talked and argued a lot. I don't know if this is a good thing for me to do. I'm interested in some of the social issues at home and I'd like to do something about it." Blackie said, hesitantly.

"Do you think you'll like it? What motivated you to talk to Dad about it?" Sean asked.

"Since the accident, I've questioned why I'm still alive."

"Honey, why would you even think that? We love you and you're here for us and Meg. You're here to live a happy life," Jill said, getting upset.

"Jill, you don't understand. I should have died in that accident. There's no way anyone could have lived through that. I believe, for some unknown reason, God saved my life and I need to know for what purpose. I have to find something meaningful to do with my life besides riding horses."

"Maybe God loves you enough that he just wanted you to stay here and be happy," Sean said.

"I *have* found a lot of meaning in my life with Meg and you guys. I just get the feeling I'm supposed to do something good to make up for the bad stuff I've done. Anyway, I'm going to try this and see what happens. I might hate it after I get into it. I'm sure a lot of people become cynical in public service. I need to go home the first part of next week and register as a candidate. So there it is." Blackie said, shrugging.

"You know whatever you want to do, we're always behind you. We'll help you any way we can. But why the hell do you think you wouldn't win?" Keary said.

"Well it's a local election and nobody knows me over there," Blackie said.

"What the hell! Everybody knows who you are in Ireland. You're famous, for God's sake! The greatest steeplechase rider ever, come on!" Sean exclaimed.

"Eh, I don't think so. People forget and I wasn't *that* famous," Blackie said.

"I think you'll be surprised. I think people know you. Besides, most people know that you're going to be *The O'Brien*." Keary said.

"Oh, how could I forget that? Jesus! Anyway, thanks, guys. I appreciate that and I know you're always there for me."

"What's going to happen to the Dressage Center while you're in Ireland doing that?" Sean asked.

"Good question. I think it's going to be tricky. I'm going to have to do a lot of flying back and forth. I don't want to give the center up. I think Parliament is in session all the time, so I'll have to figure out what to do with the students during show season. Jamie can school the lower level students and I'm hiring him to do just that. The upper level people will be a problem. Maybe I can take some of them to Ireland with me and school them at Dad's. I have to work that out yet." Blackie said.

"Okay, what else is going on with you? You might as well tell us everything now." Keary said. Blackie sighed and looked at Meg for confirmation.

"Go ahead. You might as well get it all out while you feel like talking and have time." She told him reaching for his hand. He took it and squeezed it, looking nervous.

"When I was in the hospital, Dr. Wahlman hypnotized me pretty much every morning and then in the afternoon we'd talk about whatever surfaced. He got me to remember a lot, but I'm not ready to talk about it. Most of it is awful. I still have work to do with him." Blackie stopped and looked at Meg again, then looked at the floor for a long time.

"Honey, it doesn't hurt me for you to talk about it. I know it's painful for you but *I'm* good with it," she said, gently.

"I know. Dr. Wahlman had mentioned this woman I knew named Yvette. I hadn't remembered anything about her but he said the whole thing surfaced during hypnosis and then I remembered it consciously. I don't know where to start." He hesitated for a few minutes and then sighed.

"I lived with Yvette in Paris for about a year and a half. Her name was Yvette Benoit. She was a prostitute and she was the mistress of a very powerful Frenchman. I rode for him at the Hippodrome for about six months. One day he introduced me to Yvette at the track, saying she wanted to go to some Gala thing in Monte Carlo and he couldn't go because of business. Looking back, I think he introduced us on purpose. We were supposed to be there for two days but we ended up staying for a week. I slept with her the first night we were there." He said, frowning at Meg.

"It's okay, Blackie."

"After we got back, I figured that was the end of my employment with him, but it wasn't."

He called me and said he was happy that Yvette had such a good time and had a couple horses he wanted me to start riding for him. I was a little confused by this but thought what the hell."

"Yvette and I started seeing each other regularly and I would stay at her apartment whenever I was in Paris. One day he called me in his office and told me he didn't want the complication of Yvette anymore; that he was getting too old. Apparently she wanted a child and he couldn't afford a scandal since he was married and had four grown children. He wanted out of the situation. He said he knew I'd be good to her.

So I took over her expenses, the apartment and her clothes. She still saw clients but not when I was in the country. After about six months, she started talking to me about wanting a child. She wanted to quit the business, move back to her parents' estate and raise this child by herself. She didn't want a husband, just a baby. She was eleven years older than me. I was twenty-one and she was thirty-two. At the time, I didn't want to be tied down with a wife and child anyway, since I was traveling a lot."

"Well she kept after me and I finally said okay. She got pregnant after two months but she miscarried that baby. Three months later, she got pregnant again. She was incredibly happy. She told her parents that she would move home right before the baby was due." Blackie stopped talking and stared at the table in front of him.

"Honey, why didn't you tell us?" Jill said.

"No, if I had told you guys, you would have told Mom and Dad. Mom would have freaked if she knew her first grandchild's mother was a French whore. She would have wanted to see the baby too."

"Did *you* want to see it?" Jill asked him.

"No. I was afraid if I saw it, *I'd* want it," he said, frowning.

"Blackie, what happened to her?" Keary asked, quietly.

"She's dead and so is the baby."

"Oh dear God! What happened, honey?" Jill asked.

"She was three months pregnant and I didn't have any races for five days, so we drove to the Riviera and stayed in a villa on the beach. She was so happy. I couldn't believe how happy I made her." He stopped talking again and seemed off somewhere, remembering. No one said anything for a few minutes. Jill and Katie were close to tears and Meg hoped they didn't say too much to upset him. She knew this was very hard for him to talk about. She trailed a finger along his cheek and he gave her a sad little smile.

"What happened, buddy?" Keary said.

"We drove back Sunday morning because I had a race on Monday. I was driving her Ferrari. This woman was totally drunk and crossed the median and hit us on the passenger side. The car spun around several times. When the car came to a stop, I immediately looked over at Yvette to see if she was okay." He stopped talking and his eyes filled with tears. He waited until he got his voice under control before he spoke.

"As soon as I saw her, I knew she was dead. I just sat there for a few minutes, looking at her in disbelief." He drifted off again into his memories.

"The car caught fire, so I jumped out and went around to pull her out. I knew I couldn't do anything to help her, I just didn't want her to burn." he said, choking back tears.

"I went back later to look at the wreck and I have no idea how I got her out of that car. It was absolutely crushed on her side."

"I called her parents and the older man who had introduced us. I took care of the arrangements. I took her to her parent's home and they had a service there at the family burial grounds. I told them about the baby and I think it made it easier for them somehow. That was my only consolation, that at least she died happy. I never went back to the apartment. I just had them close it up and I still pay the expenses. I was going to go with Meg and clean it out but I don't think I want anything that's there."

"Maybe there are some pictures you might want," Jill said.

"No. I don't want Meg seeing pictures of us together and I don't need a picture to remember what she looked like."

"What did she look like, buddy," Sean asked.

"She was tall, almost as tall as me. Maybe five nine. She was thin with long blond hair and big blue eyes. I'd have to say she was the most beautiful woman I've ever seen." He paused again, deep in thought.

"Did you love her, buddy?" Keary asked him very gently.

Blackie looked up at him for a long time and finally said, simply,

"Yes." And Keary nodded.

"Her death started me on a terrible downward spiral of drugs and alcohol. I stayed drunk or high so I didn't have to think about it and gradually I repressed the memory. During that time I was till racing but not as much. I did a lot of partying and that's when Mickey started sending me to those weekends in the Hamptons. Dr. Wahlman is convinced that something bad happened during one of those weekends, but I still don't remember."

"I started to straighten out a little and got back in better shape and then I had the accident. You know I wonder about Wahlman's philosophy of getting me to remember this awful stuff. I mean the memories are still painful, so why remember them? He seems to think, if I remember incidents and can now deal with those memories without turning to drugs and alcohol, I'll be able to handle anything. It doesn't feel so good, though."

Meg hugged him; he grabbed her and held her very tight for a long time. He finally looked up at her and said, "God, I love you so much. You're so good for me."

"You know, I've been talking all damn day. Why didn't someone stop me? I don't know about anyone else but I'm famished. Let's go out someplace and have dinner. We need to celebrate my return to semi-normalcy," he said laughing.

"You call yourself semi-normal? Boy, I'd hate to see how crazy abnormal is!"

"You're a good example, asshole," Blackie said, punching Sean playfully on the arm.

"Prick," Sean called him, punching him back.

"Hey, you just looked at that watch. Who gave it to you and what does it say on the back?" Keary asked him. Blackie looked at it for a minute then took it off and turned it over. He read it and his jaw muscles clenched.

"Is 'Y' Yvette? Jill asked him. He nodded and read the inscription in perfect French.

"It means, 'My body and soul are yours forever, Yvette'." He said softly and tears spilled onto the watch. Jill hugged him and said,

"She must have loved you very much." Blackie just nodded again, sadly.

FORTY-FIVE

The rest of the week, Blackie worked with all of his students, getting them up to speed. He also started working with Katie, using Cloudy to teach her to ride. She couldn't stop talking about how much fun she was having, learning to ride from Blackie. Sean loved it and teased her about listening to Blackie or he would yell at her. Blackie thought the teasing was very funny since he wouldn't yell at Katie no matter what she did.

Meg spent the time before they went to Ireland on Sunday, riding her mare and getting clothes ready for the trip. She and Jill had been talking to Blackie's mom on the phone almost every day about plans for Christmas and the wedding. The idea of actually being married to him, being able to be with him always, having children with him, was making her head spin. She was getting nervous, too, thinking about the wedding itself. They were going to be extremely busy soon and thinking of all there was to do was making her nauseous.

As soon as they got back from Ireland, it would be Thanksgiving, then they were going to New York to shop for Christmas, his campaign would start and then back to Ireland for the holidays and finally the election.

Sunday they flew to Ireland. Meg was wasted after the long flight and just wanted to go to bed and sleep. They had dinner with Maeve and Ken, however and that was a lot of fun, giving her a second wind, so she stayed up all hours talking to Maeve about the wedding. Meg became so fond of this woman who was so sweet yet had a very strong personality like her son. Sometimes it was a little freaky because she looks so much like him, or he looks like her. They could be twins.

Blackie got up early to go to the election board with his dad. Meg elected to stay in bed, luxuriating in being lazy. She was awfully tired and couldn't bring herself to crawl into the shower. She had fallen back to sleep when Blackie got home, snuggling up next to her.

"Hey, sleepy-head," he whispered, "how come you're still in bed? Of course I like you here, warm and soft," he said, running a hand under the covers and along her hip. She could tell he was interested in getting back in bed but she felt too tired for love-making.

Hmm, that's not like me. Usually I'm ready to go whenever he even looks a little frisky.

"Hi, sweetheart. How'd it go at the election place?" She asked, hoping to distract him.

"Great! I'm all registered. The whole thing is a little scary, now that the election is looming in the near future," he said, rolling on his side and propping an arm under his head.

"Come on, don't be nervous. You're going to be great. You're going to set this country on it's ear. They'll love you for your integrity and all you want to do to help your people," she told him, caressing his face.

"I'm glad *you* think so. I'm not so sure anymore." He said, sighing.

"Why do you suddenly doubt yourself?"

"I'm a little bit confident. It's just so different, something I've never tackled before. If it had to do with horses, I wouldn't think twice. Anyway, forget that, I'm more interested in you this morning," he said, rolling onto her and kissing her hungrily.

"Mmm, you taste good, but I'm still so tired. I think I have 'jet lag' or something," she said stretching and closing her eyes.

"You're not getting sick are you? Have you had 'jet lag' before when we've flown over? I usually don't notice it but I'm more used to the trip back and forth than you are. Want me to let you sleep awhile?" he asked, looking concerned.

"Do you mind, honey? Just a bit longer and then I'll get up. Hold that thought you just had for later, though. Okay?"

"You bet, sweetheart. I won't forget what I was just thinking," he said, playfully biting her neck.

"Thanks, I'll be up soon."

"Ok, I'm going down and talk to Mom and Dad." She instantly fell back to sleep.

The next day they flew back to Virginia and now Meg was totally wasted. Blackie didn't seem tired at all. He had more energy than ever since getting home from the hospital. She groaned, realizing that the next day she was helping Jill with Thanksgiving preparations.

*   *   *

The guys were making pests of themselves while the women worked on the food. Meg was cutting up apples for a pie, trying to keep ahead of Blackie who was eating slices as fast as she cut them. She started slapping his hands when he reached in the bowl but he was too fast and made off with three more pieces, laughing and high-fiving Sean who was dipping a spoon in the pumpkin pie mix that Katie was stirring.

"Don't you two have something to do in the barns?" Jill asked.

"Hell no! This is way more fun and we can't wait until tomorrow," Blackie said, laughing at her.

"Keary, can't you find something for these two to do?" Jill asked.

"All right, guys, let's go chop some wood so we can have a nice roaring fire tomorrow," he said, getting up and shoving Sean and Blackie toward the door.

"I thought we had plenty of wood already chopped," Sean whined.

"Well, you can chop some more, just in case," Keary told him.

"This sucks. We need to be where the action is," Blackie said.

"Well the women will get done faster if we're out of their hair, so shut up and chop."

Katie, Jill and Meg laughed as Keary pushed them out the door.

"Poor guys, they were having fun," Katie said.

"I know but they get like two puppies when something like this is going on and we'll never get finished with them in it. Let's make an extra pie for tonight just to make them feel better," Jill said, smiling.

They finished the preparations late, Jill putting the huge turkey in to bake around midnight. While it was cooking, they snuggled in front of the TV with drinks to watch a movie. Blackie pulled her on his lap and she cuddled against his chest, feeling exhausted but happy. It wasn't long before he started kissing her neck, running a hand down her thigh. She knew where this was headed. She couldn't resist though, turned her face up to him and got rewarded with a hungry kiss.

Hmm, maybe I'm not too tired after all.

Thanksgiving was the most fun she thought she'd ever had. Everyone was in a festive mood; the guys goofed around and got really silly. They ate so much they couldn't move and still had dessert. Later they fell asleep in front of the TV, watching yet another football game.

*　　*　　*

The next couple weeks flew by what with wedding details, Christmas shopping and decorating, planning the shopping trip to New York and the trip to Ireland for the holiday.

Meg continued to feel exhausted all the time and Blackie continued to bug her about being sick. She tried to perk up around him so he wouldn't bring it up.

They were all so busy with everything. Blackie was working non-stop with the horses and the students so they would be able to continue their schooling without him for a few weeks Sean, Casey, Keary and Ned had been at the tracks almost daily to get as much racing in as possible.

One afternoon when Blackie was teaching, Meg was deciding about clothes to take to Ireland. She got out her 'daytimer' to go over dates for the trips. Looking at notes she had made, she saw that she should have gotten her period last week. She looked again and wondered if she had the date wrong.

"Let's see, today is Friday, December 12th and ... oh, God!"

She was due on December 5th; over a week ago. She was late! Oh, crap! Blackie was going to have a fit, she thought. He wanted them to be married before she got pregnant again.

She suddenly felt light headed and sat down. A baby! She felt exhilarated and scared at the same time.

Suppose I lose this one? I can't go through that again, neither can Blackie.

She just had to hope and pray everything was okay. She needed to talk to Jill and called up to the house. Jill answered.

"Jill, I need to talk to you. Are any of the guys up there?"

"No, sweetie, Keary's in Mclean and Sean's at the track. I thought Blackie was still teaching. Are you ok?" Jill said, concerned.

"I'm fine. I'll be right up," she said and raced up to the house. She burst into the kitchen and Jill looked up.

"I'm late!" Meg said, panting.

"As, in you had an appointment today?" Jill asked, confused.

"No, I'm *late,* late!"

"Are you serious?" Jill said her eyes wide.

"Yes, very serious!"

"What happened? How do you know?"

"I was just looking at my calendar, figuring out the timing for our trips and I was supposed to get it December 5th!"

"You're a week late already! How do you feel?" Jill asked.

"I've been incredibly tired lately and haven't said much about it because Blackie gets spastic if he thinks I'm sick."

"You were so tired before. Does he have any idea?" Jill asked.

"No, not at all. I'm just blown away. He's going to have a fit that I'm pregnant and the wedding isn't until April. What am I going to do, Jill?"

"Listen, calm down. He's not going to have a fit. He's going to be so excited and happy. You know how much he wants a baby." "I know but he wants us to be married first. He was upset before because we weren't married." Meg said.

"Hey, has he been using birth control?"

"No, not at all"

"Then it's his fault, so he can't complain and he won't, Meg. You just wait and see," Jill said, smiling.

"When should I tell him? We're supposed to go shopping in New York the end of the week and then it'll be Christmas."

"You could just ...

Just then Blackie came through the door and they both jumped. He had a bloody rag wrapped around his left hand. He went right to the sink, removed the rag and stuck his hand under the faucet.

"Honey, what happened?"

"I was cleaning some old hay from under Abba's feed bin and I slashed my hand on a nail. It was down close to the floor sticking out about four inches.

The wound was long, deep and bleeding profusely. He washed it with soap and water then dried his hand with a paper towel.

"Where's the alcohol? Jill, do you know if my tetanus shots are current?" he asked, pressing tightly on his hand. Jill ran to the bathroom and came back with the alcohol. Blackie poured some on his hand and swore, clamping the towel back on it.

"I'll check the records and see about your shots, honey. Do you think you need stitches?"

"Nah, it'll be fine. I'll just press on it for a minute. I need some coffee," he said, walking into the dining room. "Pour me some, Meg, would you, please?"

"Sure," Meg said, helping him. He took a sip and she saw the towel was soaked with blood. Jill came back after looking up his records.

"You had a tetanus shot when you had the accident, so you should be fine. Here let me look at that," she said, taking his hand and removing the towel. Meg could see that it was still bleeding.

"Honey, this looks too deep and the bleeding hasn't stopped. I think you need stitches."

Blackie made a funny noise and his knees buckled. He grabbed for the table, missing it and they grabbed for him but he went down in a heap, flopping onto his back. They both screamed in panic.

"Oh, God, Blackie, Blackie! Honey," Meg said, down on the floor with him. He was out cold. Jill had let go of his hand and it was bleeding all over the place.

"Oh God, I didn't think it was bothering him. I shouldn't have mentioned the stitches. Crap! Let me get a cold cloth." Jill said, running into the kitchen and bumping into Keary as he came in.

"What's the matter with you? You look upset," he asked.

"Blackie passed out, come and help us!"

"Passed out! What the hell happened?" Keary said, went into the dining room and saw Blackie on the floor.

"Oh shit! Blackie, come on buddy, wake up! What happened to his hand?" he asked, kneeling next to Blackie as Jill gave him the damp cloth. "Somebody put some pressure on that to stop the bleeding. Christ, he really cut it!"

"He cut it on a nail in the barn, came up here, washed it off, put alcohol on it and when I looked at it and said he needed stitches, he hit the floor," Jill said.

"Keary, this is bad, look at it," Meg said, taking the towel off to show him.

"Damn, he does need stitches. Keep pressure on it. Let me see if I can get him to come to. Blackie, Blackie wake up," Keary said, shaking him gently. Blackie sort of moaned, moved his head and then looked at Keary, confused.

"Keary, what happened?" he said, softly.

"You passed out, buddy. What've you been doing to yourself?" Keary said, smiling at him.

"I don't know. What do you mean?" Blackie said, frowning.

"You cut the shit out of your hand,"

"Huh?"

"Just lay there a minute while I put some kind of dressing on it." Keary said, getting up and going to the bathroom. Blackie raised his hand up and looked at it.

"Fuck! How the hell did I do that?"

"Nail in the barn. Does it hurt, honey?' Meg asked, putting his head in her lap.

"Yeah. You mean I cut it in the barn and came all the way up here to pass out. what a wuss," he said, looking up at her. She kissed him on the forehead.

Keary came back with gauze and tape. He knelt down next to them and started bandaging Blackie's hand. Blackie tried to get up, but Keary put a hand on his chest

"Just be still a minute while I do this. I don't want you passing out again. I'm taking you to the emergency room, buddy. You need stitches."

"Oh, hell no! I don't!"

"Don't argue with me, you're going and that's it," Keary said, fussing at him.

"Shit!"

"Okay, that'll hold you until we get to the hospital. Here, get up slowly and just sit still a minute," Keary said. Blackie sat up and looked a little groggy.

"Here's your big strong man, Meg. Fainting over a little scratch. Christ, what a baby!" Blackie whined.

"Shut up! It could happen to anybody," Keary said, shaking his head. "How do you feel? Think you can stand up?"

"Yes, damnit, I can stand up." Blackie said, getting to his feel. He still looked a little wobbly.

"Oh, boy," Keary said. "Ok, let's get going.

They both left for the hospital. Jill and Meg dropped into chairs and stared at each other.

"Good Lord! What else will happen today?" Jill said, looking exasperated.

"Actually, that was enough for me," Meg said, puffing out a sigh. "Is he accident prone, or what?"

"No, he's not. It's just a dangerous place to work. Hey, we need to get you a pregnancy test and see what's going on. I think I still have some up in my bathroom," Jill said.

"Oh, I don't know. Do we have to do it now?" Meg whined.

"Don't you want to know? The sooner the better."

"Yeah, I guess you're right. Let's do it."

"Good girl. I'll be right back," Jill said, running up the steps. She was back in a minute, waving a test kit. "Here you go, use the bathroom down here. Hurry up,"

Meg took the kit and went into the bathroom and used it. In no time, there it was - PINK! She was pregnant! Jeez!

"It's positive, Jill," she said, smiling as she came out of the bathroom.

"Ohmigod! Congratulations, sweetie. I'm so happy," Jill said, hugging her. They both burst into tears, hugging and jumping around.

"When should I tell him? I'm so happy but I'm nervous about telling him."

"Honey, why? Believe me, he'll be sooooo happy, he won't be able to stand it. He wants this, you know that," Jill said.

"I know. I'm so happy, I can't stand it."

"Hey, what if you wait until Christmas to tell him. What a wonderful surprise for him and everyone else. In Ireland, in front of Mom and Dad and everyone," Jill said, excitedly.

"What a fantastic idea, but can we keep it from him until then?"

"I don't know, but I bet it will be fun trying. Let's try and keep it from the others too," Jill said.

"You're on. You know it's hard to keep secrets from him,"

"More of a challenge. Let's get rid of this evidence and wash our faces before they get back."

FORTY-SIX

They arrived at Dublin airport Christmas Eve morning, in happy holiday spirits. Keary, Jill and little Maeve; Sean, Katie and baby Patrick; Ned, Casey, Jeremy and of course, Blackie and Meg. They were festive, excited and noisy, everyone talking at once.

Meg still didn't have an engagement ring on her finger.

It'd be great if I got the damn ring for Christmas but I'm not holding my breath. I bet he comes up with it after I tell him my news.

They piled into a stretch limo at the airport that took them to Blackie's home. Everyone sang Christmas songs, Sean and Blackie doing some of the ones they were going to sing for Ken and Maeve. Blackie and Meg snuggled like bunnies in the limo, kissing aggressively.

"Happy Christmas Eve, sweetheart! I'm so happy we're here I can hardly stand it. I love you so much, Meg."

*   *   *

The limo halted in front of Blackie's house and they scrambled out still laughing. Maeve and Ken threw coats on and hustled out greeting them with happy smiles. Everyone hugged and kissed, the folks surprised and pleased to see Ned, Casey and Jeremy again. Blackie hugged his mom again for a long time, then she kissed Sean and Jill, flustered with emotion.

"Good Lord, let's get in out of the cold. We can have a drink and get toasty by the fire. Maeve, you can kiss your babies some more in the house." Kennet said herding them inside. "Just leave your luggage in the hall and we'll sort it out later."

Ken ushered everyone into the huge living room that was breathtaking with candles, decorations and a welcoming fire roaring in the huge stone fireplace. Meg stared open-mouthed at the beautiful tree that must have been twelve feet tall standing in one corner. It was so sparkling, bright and ethereal; it looked like a "fairy" tree. There were gingerbread men hung from their heads with velvet ribbon, spun glass spheres reflected every candle, crystal crosses and icicles hung by red satin ribbons, green and blue plaid ribbon encircled the tree; spun gold fibers adorned every bough, real lighted candles perched on limbs and at the top was the most beautiful crystal angel. She inhaled its pungent evergreen fragrance.

"That's the most beautiful thing I've ever seen," Meg whispered in Blackie's ear.

"Isn't it? You're beginning to get an idea why I love Christmas here. Mom goes nuts with it and everything is just magical. I have such fond memories of Christmas at home; I wanted you to be here with me."

"Thank you, sweetheart. I'm so happy to be part of your life."

"I wouldn't *have* a life without you, Meg."

Just then, Maeve came up behind them, hugging the two of them. Blackie put his arm around her and kissed her cheek.

"Mom, this is wonderful. I couldn't wait for Meg to experience Christmas here."

"You don't know how wonderful it is to have all of you home and the babies are too adorable. It's good to see the boys. Are they staying for tomorrow?"

"No, they're here for dinner and later they're going to their parents' for tomorrow. They'll be back later in the week." Blackie told her.

"Good! Right now I want to borrow this beautiful girl for just a few minutes and I'll bring her right back, dear."

"Okay, I'll go help Dad with drinks. What do you two want?"

"I'll have a hot wassail," Maeve said.

"I'll have ginger ale, honey," Meg said.

"A wassail and ginger, coming up."

"Meg, dear," Maeve said putting her arm around Meg's waist. "I can't thank you enough for making my son so happy."

"Oh, Maeve, believe me the pleasure's all mine. He's so wonderful."

"I'm pretty sure he feels the same way about you and please call me 'Mom'."

"Okay, thank you, Mom" she said and Maeve hugged her.

"So how are the wedding plans coming along? Are we still good for the April date?"

"Well, we might want to move it up earlier," Meg said tentatively. Maeve searched her face for a minute.

"You're pregnant!" Maeve gasped.

"Shhhhh! He doesn't know yet. I just found out last week and Jill and I thought it would be special to tell him tomorrow when we're all together."

"Wouldn't you rather tell him privately, dear?" Maeve asked.

"I thought about it, but we're so involved in each other's lives and they love him so much. He's gotten so much closer to you guys lately with the phone calls. I just thought it would be a wonderful thing for everyone to see his reaction when I tell him. Sean's already making book that he'll cry."

"He's probably right. Blackie's always been very emotional, which I'm sure you already know."

"Oh boy, do I!

"Sure and I can't wait until tomorrow, but tonight let's get wasted!"

"Mom! What are you thinking?"

"I'm thinking we have a lot to celebrate and here's the man of the hour with our drinks," she said, turning as Blackie came up.

"Ladies, your drinks," he said, handing them theirs and keeping one for him, taking a sip.

"Blackie, I thought you weren't drinking anymore," Maeve said, frowning.

"I'm not, Mom, this is ginger-ale."

"Okay, my beautiful son, let's party!"

"You've got it." he said and they took a big slug of their drinks.

"This is so wonderful, Mom. I'm so happy to be here." Meg said.

"We're just as happy to have you, dear. I'm going to go look for those grand babies. I'll see you later."

"Okay, Mom." Blackie said.

"Blackie, thank you for suggesting this. This is just totally special for me. I haven't had many Christmases with my family," Meg said, sadly.

"I know. That's one reason I wanted to do this. You're part of my family now and I wanted this for both of us. Hey, when did you start calling my mother, 'Mom'?"

"A few minutes ago when she asked me to."

"Cool."

"You don't mind do you?"

"Of course not. I love it. She's going to be your mother-in-law after all."

"I thought it was pretty neat myself. You know I like your parents so much. I like them best because they made you," she said, snuggling up against him.

"Thank you. Have I told you in the last hour how much I love you?" he said running a hand down her back.

"No and I'm feeling pretty neglected," she said, pretending to pout.

"Oh, shame on me. Well I love you more than I can express in words. How's that?"

"Nice. I want you to prove it later."

"Mmm, I think I can manage that," he said, kissing her. When he released her, she noticed Maeve carrying Patrick and holding little Maeve by the hand.

"Honey, look at your Mom with her grandbabies."

"Oh great. If we stay too long, she'll have them spoiled rotten," he said, with a grin.

"I thought that's what grandparents were for," she said thinking of the news she had to tell him. She couldn't wait to see his face. She had a hard time believing it was finally going to happen for them.

"I guess you're right. I can't wait to have one that she can spoil."

Ken bellowed dinner was served in the dining room. The crowd circled the huge table laid with Christmas china, greens, and centerpieces of fruit with plaid bows, candles flickered, their glow reflected in crystal goblets and gleaming silver cutlery.

Dinner was fabulous! Seafood bisque was served first, its delicate flavor tantalizing Meg's taste buds and warming her. Then next course of roast beef with grilled vegetables and tiny potatoes made her mouth water just smelling it and it was as delicious as it smelled. The next course was fresh fish that tasted like it just jumped out of the sea along with sautéed squash and mushrooms. A salad of fresh greens, apples, currants and cheese with a wonderful maple dressing. Topping it all off for Meg was the news that dessert was coming. She groaned with pleasure.

"Are you okay?" Blackie whispered.

"Do they always eat like this? The food is incredible!"

"They do, yes, but not this fancy. All this was raised right here on the farm, the beef, vegetables right out of the garden and the fish was caught this morning from the Irish Sea. I love it. This is the food I grew up on, everything fresh. Mom made the bread this morning. Bread's her thing. The butter was churned here too."

"It's wonderful. No wonder you're so healthy, eating food like this. The wine is good; does your dad make that too?"

"No, he buys it at the liquor store in Dublin," Blackie said, laughing at her.

The dessert arrived and it was a beautiful Irish Christmas Cake with marzipan icing; made with dried fruit and whiskey in it. It was so good, she wanted more but felt in danger of popping.

"This is the best cake I've ever tasted. I need the recipe so I can make it for you sometime."

"When we're old and the grandchildren come to visit?"

"Hopefully before then but that does sound wonderful," she said looking at him wistfully.

"I'm looking forward to growing old with you," he said.

"Hey, are you and Sean going to sing tonight or tomorrow?"

"I hadn't thought about when. Tonight's as good a time as any. I'll ask Sean what he wants to do."

"Your parents don't have a clue, do they?"

"They don't, no, and that's why it's going to be fun. They haven't heard us sing since we were, maybe eight or nine. Right before I got thrown out of the choir," he chuckled.

After everyone finished eating and relaxed talking and reminiscing about Christmas' past, Blackie went to Sean and said something in his ear. Sean looked at Blackie and shrugged, nodding, and smiled over at her. He whispered to Katie and she looked at Meg and did a little silent, excited applause.

Eventually everyone meandered back into the living room, giving after dinner drink orders to Ken. Blackie and Meg snuggled together in a huge chair close to the fire. She was so content after that wonderful meal, gathered with his family and leaning back against him. He nuzzled her ear and whispered.

"I love you. I can't tell you how happy I am that you're here with me."

"I know how happy you are because I feel the same way. This is wonderful," she told him, snuggling closer and putting her head on his chest. They were just getting comfortable when Sean jumped up and stood in front of the tree, motioning for Blackie to join him.

"Okay, here we go. Wish me luck that I don't totally screw this up. Sean will have my head."

"Are you kidding me? You're going to be great. Just relax."

He stood next to Sean, instantly shoving his hands in his pockets, so she knew he was nervous.

"Okay everyone. Mom and Dad, Blackie and I have a little surprise for you. We've been working on this for only a few months, so cut us some slack. This is something you haven't heard for quite awhile and we hope you enjoy it."

Sean took a deep breath and looked at Blackie who just nodded and they stood closer together and started singing "Danny Boy". They sounded fantastic! Perfect harmony and pitch. Meg looked at Maeve and Ken whose mouths had dropped open. They were transfixed. Blackie hit the high notes, his voice clear as a bell. Halfway through the song, Maeve started to cry and Ken looked like he wasn't far behind her.

The guys went on to sing Christmas songs, their voices filling the huge room and bouncing off the high ceiling, so it sounded like they were in an amphitheater. Everyone was entranced. Even though the rest of us had heard them sing, this was a special performance. Blackie's voice was incredible. He hit some high notes that Meg didn't know existed. Sean sounded incredible as their voices blended perfectly. They sang some traditional Irish songs in Gaelic that Meg hadn't heard them do before.

She couldn't get over the two of them doing this together, making their love for one another very obvious. They usually joked around or fought, so she hadn't realized how close they were. They sang a beautiful song called, *Green the Whole year Round* that she had heard Blackie whistling but hadn't heard the words. It was so lovely; the words just warmed her heart. Sean spoke at last.

"This last song has a lot of meaning for both of us, but I think Blackie needs to sing it by himself," Sean said looking at Blackie.

"What! Why? We practiced everything together," he said pulling on Sean who was trying to go and sit down.

"Just shut up and do it!" Sean said patting him on the shoulder. Everyone applauded and cheered as Sean started to leave, so he got back beside Blackie and they both did this funny little bow that was obviously from their Boys Choir days. Everyone hooted and cheered even more.

Sean finally broke away and sat down, leaving Blackie standing nervously by himself, deep in thought. He took a deep breath and walked over, kneeling in front of Maeve and took her hand. She immediately started crying and it was obviously making it harder for Blackie to continue. He started singing a beautiful Irish song about what it meant to be far away from Ireland call *The Isle of Innisfree*. He sang it first in Gaelic and then in English and the tears rolled down his face the whole time.

At the end, he kissed her hand and she grabbed him, hugging him tight and there wasn't a dry eye in the house. Then everyone exploded in applause and cheering, Blackie grabbing Sean and pulling him up to the tree again. They sang *O Holy Night* so beautifully, they sounded like angels. When they were done, Maeve and Ken got up and hugged both of them and made everyone quiet down so they could say something.

"This is the most wonderful gift I could imagine, to hear both my boys singing together again. I can't tell you how much this means to Dad and I. You two sound wonderful. It does my heart good to know that you love being here in this country of your birth. You've both been physically gone too long and I know Blackie has been gone from this place spiritually for some time." Maeve said. Blackie looked at the floor, his jaw muscles working.

"But I feel his spirit has been renewed and has brought his heart back home to Ireland where it belongs," Maeve said, hugging him.

Blackie came over to Meg, flopping down and pulling her on his lap. He wrapped his arms around her, burying his face in her neck. She could tell he was still emotional. She held him close for awhile and said, "Are you okay, sweetie?"

"Yeah, it's just a little rough being back home. It brings up a lot of old feelings. The fact that I've been alienated from them because of my old lifestyle doesn't help. I've been trying; talking to them on the phone and making decisions for my life that are more in line with their morals. It still can't erase the way I've hurt them in the past."

"Honey, they love you and they're happy that you're getting your life turned around and settling down. They've been so worried about you and want you to be happy. Relax about it. We're here to have fun and tell them your ideas for the future."

"You're so good for me. In the past, I've always ended up drinking when I was home and things got crazy. It never turned out well. Now that I'm with you, I feel so much better about everything and I can handle it."

"Maybe that's due to the work you've done with Dr.Wahlman, not just being with me."

"Well that's a big part of it but no matter how I think I can handle things when I'm talking to him, it feels different when I'm actually in the situation."

Just then a small combo that had come into the back of the living room started playing some soft jazz.

"Ok, we're here to have fun, so let's dance," he said, taking her hand, pulling her onto the floor in front of the tree. He took her in his arms and they danced for a long time. It was very relaxing being in his arms, close to his body, swaying slowly to the soft music.

He drew her tighter against him, kissing her warmly.

"You taste delicious, honey, I'm getting turned on dancing with you. I like the way your body feeling moving with mine."

"I was just thinking the same thing. Do you want to turn in soon?" She said dreamily.

"Mmm, that sounds wonderful," he said, stopped dancing, and they made their way over to his parents to say goodnight. They went to their room and as soon as they got in the door, he put his arms around her and kissed her deeply. His kisses always took her breath away and made her light-headed. He gently carried her to the bed.

"It's after midnight, sweetie. Happy Christmas," he said and made slow, sweet love to her.

*   *   *

The next morning Meg awoke to church bells ringing in the distance and Blackie bouncing out of the shower with just a towel on. He straddled her on the bed, drowning her with kisses.

"Hey, wake up sleepy head, it's Christmas morning! I bet Saint Nick has been here. Come on, I'm hungry and I can't wait until you see what I got you. Come on, honey, get up." He said, excitedly and rolled off the bed to finish getting dressed. He pulled on jeans and a sweater. She quickly jumped in the shower, washed her hair and dressed in jeans and a cozy fleece top, finishing off with fluffy slippers to try and get her feet warm.

They went down to breakfast which was another huge buffet of goodies. Eggs, bacon, ham, scones, trout, sausage, more Christmas cake and cookies. Blackie was filling his plate to overflowing, as usual.

"I'm going to get fat if I keep eating like this," she complained.

"Not a chance, sweetheart. This stuff is good for you. You can't eat too much of it. Especially the cake. Yumm!" he said pouring himself a big glass of orange juice. She took a small amount of almost everything, got a cup of coffee and went and sat next to him.

"Merry Christmas everyone," they said and got the same response from all those already eating.

"Blackie, would you and Sean like to do the honors this year, dear?" Maeve asked him.

"Sure Mom, I'll be glad to," he answered.

"What's that mean," Meg asked.

"It means that Sean and I get to give out all the gifts from under the tree. It's fun. We goof around a lot while we.re doing it. You'll see."

"That does sound like fun. When does that happen?"

"As soon as we're done eating," he said smiling. In about twenty minutes, Blackie got up and yelled to Sean.

"Hey, Sean let's get this show on the road."

"Okay, buddy, I'll be right there."

Sean and Blackie went up to the tree, sat on the floor and started going through the huge pile of gifts. The first ones they picked out were for the kids. They called to the kids and helped them open the gifts. Little Maeve got an adorable little doll dressed in pink and Patrick got a huge dump truck. They both paid attention to the two children until they were happily playing. Blackie grabbed a present that was for Keary, yelled to get his attention and heaved it to him like a football. Maeve had a fit!

"Blackie, this isn't a rough-house game! Take it easy."

"I'm just messing around, Mom. It'll be good." He said, laughing.

He and Sean got up and handed all the gifts out, piling the kid's gifts near them, and sat down again.

"Okay, everyone, dig in," Sean yelled and everyone started opening their gifts. It was bedlam. Everyone exclaiming over the goodies. Blackie and Meg had given Jill and Katie beautiful earrings in each ones birthstone surrounded by diamonds. They gave Sean and Keary Rolex watches. Blackie had picked out this incredible diamond necklace for his Mom and bought a Land Rover for his Dad. Meg's head was spinning with the ridiculously expensive stuff they gave each other. Ken was overwhelmed by the new truck.

"Blackie, this is really too much. You shouldn't have done this," he said.

"Dad, I got tired of you rattling around in that ancient thing you drive," Blackie said.

Maeve and Ken gave them an antique dining room set; the wood had a rich, deep patina. Meg got gorgeous lingerie, earrings and cashmere sweaters. It was all too much. Blackie got new dress dressage boots that were so soft they felt like butter, a new saddle that was apparently handmade, also cashmere sweaters. Meg had pictures of the two of them made to give to everyone but she went a little overboard. Everyone loved them; they each got a large collage of six pictures that were her favorite ones of them.

Then Blackie and Meg exchanged gifts. She was very excited because she was hoping to get the long awaited engagement ring. She had butterflies in her stomach. She gave him a black leather, hand-crafted bomber jacket that looked amazing on him. He loved it. He handed her a fairly large blue velvet box. She opened it and inside was the most exquisite necklace she had ever seen. The whole chain was encrusted with tiny, round diamonds. The pendant a diamond Celtic cross. It took her breath away.

"I want you to wear that on our wedding day. Do you like it, honey?" he asked her. She looked up and everyone was watching them. She loved it. She couldn't imagine wearing something so beautiful, but she wished it had been the ring.

"Honey, of course I like it. I love it. I've never seen anything like it. Thank you, sweetheart," she said hugging him. "Here, help me put it on." He took it and put it around her neck and fastened it.

"It looks even more beautiful on you, Meg. I'm glad you like it."

Everyone applauded and she got up and went around so everyone could see it up close. It took a lot of effort for her to hold back her tears of disappointment. She didn't want to hurt Blackie's feelings, but she was confused about why he had never given her the ring,

He kept looking at her and she didn't know what else to say to him. Everyone else was staring at them too.

"You're disappointed, aren't you?" he asked.

"Honey, of course not! What are you thinking? How could I be disappointed? This necklace is so beautiful. Don't be silly." She told him, feeling bad that he was upset.

"Here, maybe this will make you feel better," he said, tossing her another, smaller box in red velvet.

"Blackie!" Everyone yelled at him.

"For chrissake, do it right, dummy," Keary said, laughing.

"Okay, okay. I was just kidding around," he said laughing. He took the box from her and turning serious, he got down on his knees. Her heart did a huge flip-flop and she thought she was going to pass out.

"Meg, I know this has been a long time coming and I know I've put you through more than any woman should have to handle. I love you more than my own life. Will you do me the incredible honor of becoming my wife?" Meg jumped him, both of them tumbling to the floor, kissing each other passionately amid woops and cheers from the others. When they finally came up for air, Blackie asked the crowd, "Hey, did she say yes?" To lots of laughter.

"Yes! Yes! Yes!" She yelled at him.

"Did you look at the ring yet? Funny girl."

"Oh, no. Sorry, honey," she said, opened the box and was stunned. In it was an exquisite heart shaped diamond ring that sparkled like the stars.

"Oh, my God. Blackie this is unreal. It's so … she couldn't speak, just started crying and hugged him. He took it out of the box and put it on her finger.

"I love you, Meg," he said looking deeply into her eyes.

"I love you too, Blackie."

Everyone was cheering, jumping up and surrounded them with hugs and congratulations.

"Thank God, he finally did it," Sean said and raised his glass in a toast. "To Blackie and Meg!" Everyone toasted them and cheered again.

"I don't think I could get any happier than I am at this moment," Blackie said to everyone, smiling.

"I bet I could make you happier," she said. He looked shocked for a second and then said, "Honey, I know you can make me happier, but we can't do that in front of my parents and the kids."

"Blackie, behave." Maeve scolded him.

"Okay, I give up, how are you going to make me happier?" He said as everyone suddenly became silent and expectant.

"You're going to be a daddy," she told him. The smile suddenly vanished from his face. He looked at her, his eyes like saucers. "What?"

"You're going to be a daddy," she said louder.

"You're pregnant?"

"Yes." She said and he dissolved into her arms, his face buried in her neck and she knew he was crying. He pulled back and looked at her again.

"You're sure?"

"Yes, yes."

"Oh, God, this is wonderful. You did make me happier. Happier than I've ever been." He said, grabbing her and kissing her exuberantly. Everyone was congratulating them again. All the men were clapping him on the back. All the women were kissing and hugging her and then him. Blackie kept wiping his eyes with the heel of his hand. They were both laughing and crying at the same time.

"When did you find out?" he asked her.

"I was late three weeks ago and then waited another week to do the test and it was positive. I told Jill and we both thought it would be really special to tell you today with all your family here. Do you mind that I waited to tell you?"

"No, that's okay. It is a special day. Thank you, sweetheart," he said, kissing her tenderly. "I can't believe it! We're going to have a baby," he pulled her onto his lap and just held her.

"Wow, what a surprise. I wasn't really expecting this." He said looking at her seriously

"It just takes the right time and circumstances. Those wonderful days we spent together, it was almost inevitable.

"You think that's what it was? Those three days holed up in the apartment alone together were amazing."

"I loved that. Just the two of us alone, for three days, talking about the future, about us, making love. I felt closer to you those three days than I ever have. It was wonderful, honey."

"Yeah, it was, wasn't it? We should do that more often. Hey, are you feeling ok? You're not dizzy and light-headed like you were before, are you?" He asked, suddenly remembering.

"No. So far I feel fine. I'm tired a lot but that's normal in the first trimester."

"Good. You let me know if you don't feel well. Promise me."

"I will. Don't start worrying about me right away. I'm fine," she said, tilting her head up to be kissed and was rewarded with a very sweet, gentle kiss.

"What about the wedding?" he said

"What about it?"

"Well, if we keep it in April, you'll be five months pregnant. Will your dress still fit?"

"No, it won't. I didn't think about that."

"Hey, Mom! Is there any chance we can move the wedding up to say the middle of January?" he called to Maeve and she came over and stood by their chair.

"I don't see why not. I'll call the wedding person at Dromoland and see. I'll call tomorrow. Meg, do you feel embarrassed about being that far along at the wedding?"

"No, not really. I don't care what anyone thinks about it. Blackie just pointed out that my dress won't fit and I love that dress."

"Okay, dear. I'll see about it. You two don't worry about a thing. You just take care of each other." Maeve smiled at them, happily. "I'm going to be a grandmother again."

THE END

Or maybe it's just the beginning?

AUTHOR'S BIO

I've had a passion for horses my whole life. I started riding at age eight and rode until well into my thirties. I was lucky to have my own horse and a pony for ten years. I rode in a lot of horse shows and eventually learned dressage and became fascinated with it.

I'm retired from Johns Hopkins University where I did Electron Microscopy for the Neurology Department.

Warrior Spirit and Blackie O'Brien have been a story developed in my head for maybe twenty years. Blackie has the same passion for horses as me.

I'm a member of the *Romance Writers of America, Maryland Romance Writers, Maryland Writers Association, Harford Writers Group and Mid-Atlantic Independent Book Publishers Association (as an author).*

READERS' PAGE

Dear Readers-

I hope you enjoyed reading Warrior Spirit as much as I enjoyed sharing it with you. Warrior Spirit and the whole *The King of Ireland* series have been a work of love for me for almost twenty years.

I hope you'll visit the links below, to my website and Jean Carroll on Facebook. I'd love for you to subscribe to my mailing list on my website. You'll be able to keep up with the rest of the series and find out what Blackie, Meg and the gang (including the villainous Mickey) are up to.

The mailing list news will let you know about book releases, excerpts from books, extra scenes (that didn't make it into a book), contests and giveaways.

Link to Jean Carroll's website: *www.jeancarroll45.com*

Link to Jean Carroll on Facebook: *www.facebook.com/kingofireland1*

Any comments or questions, please email me: *jean.carroll45@gmail.com*

Thanks again for reading Warrior spirit and I hope to see you again in Ever After- Book 2

Writers need feedback from readers to find out how they're doing and what readers like and would like to see changed. If you would like to, please give this book a review on the ebook seller you purchased it from.

Thank you so much, Jean Carroll

www.ingramcontent.com/pod-product-compliance
Lightning Source LLC
Chambersburg PA
CBHW030618250626
47154CB00006B/1840